Incident at North Point

INCIDENT AT NORTH·POINT

MARC MILNER

Vanwell Publishing Limited

St. Catharines, Ontario

*We acknowledge the financial support of the Government of Canada through the
Book Publishing Industry Development Program for our publishing activities.*

Vanwell Publishing Limited
1 Northrup Crescent
P.O. Box 2131
St. Catharines, Ontario L2R 7S2

Printed in Canada

02   01   00   99   98   5   4   3   2   1

Canadian Cataloguing in Publication Data

Milner, Marc
    Incident at North Point

ISBN 1-55125-011-X

I. Title.

PS8576.I5743165I52 1998   C813'.54   C98-930505-8
PR9199.3.M54152 1998

For Matthew and William

Now entertain conjecture of a time
When creeping murmur and the poring dark
Fills the wide vessel of the universe.

                              Shakespeare, *Henry V*

Chapter 1

"Where the hell are we now, Andy?"

Lieutenant Bill Dickson had just stepped from the open bridge of *Q246* into the tiny wheelhouse, where the Fairmile's only other officer, Lieutenant Andrew Noiles, laboured over the navigational plot. Noiles had worked without a fix since the previous morning, when they made landfall off New Waterford, on Cape Breton Island. Then they had patrolled across to the Newfoundland side of the strait on dead reckoning and turned in the early hours of the morning, without sighting land. Now they were battling their way against wind and seas back across the Cabot Strait on a heading of 215 degrees.

The seas had risen during the night into a long ocean swell eight or ten feet high, driven northwest through the strait and into the Gulf by a steady twenty-five-knot breeze. The passage southward during the hours of darkness was an endless rollercoaster ride. Dickson tried to adjust their course so they met the seas head-on, but the motor launch pitched and wallowed badly. The cold and the spray made it almost unbearable on deck, but few found comfort below, where the hull echoed with each pounding sea.

It was early in the season to be at sea in a Fairmile, especially under such marginal conditions. By rights they should have been ordered back to Sydney yesterday. But no-one ashore seemed to notice the deteriorating weather, so the five launches of the 8th Flotilla, in line abreast several cables apart, carried on with their patrol.

That morning the weather had finally closed in. Just after sunrise the low overcast and approaching front brought a heavy, driving rain and dreadful visibility, as warm moist air poured over the cold sea. Dickson had been on the bridge almost constantly. He was wet through from the spray and rain, driven down the folds and seams of his slicker by the force of the wind. He was dead tired and chilled to the bone. But he could not abandon the bridge. Somewhere, off to starboard in the murk, was the rest of his flotilla: Jackson, Thoreau and Aubrey. Minnifie hung on, just visible to port.

Dickson's anxiety about *Q246*'s present position grew throughout the morning. The Cabot Current, a two- or three-knot stream of Gulf water, ran close along the northeastern coast of Cape Breton on its way to the Atlantic. If they were on course, and on time, they would be in the current soon. If they were too far west of their estimated course they might pile up on the craggy, surf-beaten shore near Cape Smokey. And if Andy's reckoning was way off, and the current had set them far to the east, they might miss Cape Breton entirely, especially in this weather. If that happened the next landfall was Sable Island – or Brazil.

The tell-tale sign of the current would be a steepening of the seas and shortening of the wave interval where the outbound current pushed against the southeasterly wind. Dickson thought he had detected a change and had come below to confirm its cause. He stood now with his feet braced, one hand on a deckhead handle and the other on the edge of the plotting table, trying to see without drenching the chart.

"I put us about here, Skipper," Noiles said, his pencil stopping at a spot still well out in the Strait. The estimate confirmed Dickson's other suspicion; the worsening of the sea was due more to increasing wind than a collision of wind and current.

"Shit!" Dickson muttered. "I'll get Saunders to confirm that with Minnifie."

Dickson eased away from the table, put his back against the bulkhead with his feet splayed well forward, pulled his sou-wester back on his head, tied it tight and then clambered the three short steps back to the bridge. As he shot through the door the crashing sea and the sharp howl of the wind in the mast and signal halyards echoed through the wheelhouse.

Three other figures huddled on the motor launch's tiny, sodden bridge. The port and starboard lookouts stood wedged against the motion of the ship, in opposite corners. Saunders, the yeoman of signals, his face beaten red by the wind, stood amidships, one hand on the forward bridge bulkhead the other jammed into his slicker pocket, riding *Q246* through the waves like she was a mustang at the Calgary Stampede.

Dickson immediately noticed that the portside lookout was facing aft. He was about to say something when his eye caught two figures, well astern, working on the lashings of the depth charges. It was Babineau, the chief petty officer, and the quarterdeck lookout. *Q246* was taking the sea just under her port bow, corkscrewing her way forward. Occasional breaking waves swept the after portion of the boat, pushing against the depth charges in their cradles along the deck. There was little likelihood that Babineau and the rating would be swept away, as both were well secured to the lifelines rigged the night before. The lookout was simply acting prudently. A brief eye contact and a nod sufficed to confirm that all was well.

Dickson gazed off to port, straining through sheets of rain as *Q246* reached the crest of a wave to see if he could pick out Minnifie's boat, *Q287*. Yes, there she was, a low, grey shape on a parallel course about two cables away. If she was any farther off she'd be lost entirely. He watched her for several minutes. When they were both in troughs Dickson lost sight of the other ship except for her mast, but the wave pattern was not uniform and some part of *Q287* could always be seen. Once that was determined Dickson nudged his signalman.

"Saunders!" Dickson shouted through the rain and pounding seas, "ask Minnifie to send us his estimated position."

"Aye, Sir," came the prompt reply. Steadying himself against the portside of the bridge and lining up *Q287* as best he could in the sight, Saunders began to send. The aldis lamp was small, but it was enough at this range despite the rain.

In a few moments Saunders' parade-ground voice boomed through the pelting rain. "Acknowledged, Sir. Won't be more than a few minutes now."

Again a nodding of heads sufficed. While he waited Dickson absent-mindedly followed the motion of *Q246*'s bow trying to guess the height of fall. It all reminded him of how much he hated motor launches.

This was Dickson's second year in Fairmiles and his continued presence in the small ships was entirely his own fault. He was simply very good at his job. One year at Queen's University studying engineering had been enough to grant him officer status in the Volunteer Reserve when he joined the Royal Canadian Navy in 1941. His training was rudimentary, but a head for mathematics made his navigation course, given by old Ben Siverts, a snap. Dickson hoped that a reputation as a skilled navigator would save him from the dreary jobs that befell many of his class and get him to sea – and into action. Why else, he kept asking himself, would anyone join the Navy?

But timing is everything. Although the Navy scrambled in 1941 to find enough men for its burgeoning fleet of corvettes, Dickson went to the war signal station in Saint John and his faith in naval administration had never recovered. During those four dreary months Dickson also developed a genuine hatred for the weather along the Fundy coast: cold and damp in the summer, and – so he was told – colder and damper in the winter. Not a southern Ontario boy's idea of happiness.

Dickson was saved from his dreary purgatory in late summer when he joined the old armed yacht HMCS *Raccoon*. She spent 1941 tramping around inshore waters, doing nothing special, but at least he was at sea and Dickson made some deep and lasting friendships. He accepted it as a useful start, got his watch-keeping certificate and looked forward to bigger and better things. When he asked to transfer to a new ship in early 1942 they posted him to motor launches, of all things! The only consolation was the chance for rapid promotion, since there were usually only two officers in each launch.

When Dickson's skipper fell ill in July he got temporary and later permanent command. The summer was filled with action in the Gulf of St. Lawrence, especially in July and September, when U-boats heavily attacked convoys. Dickson watched much of it happen from the bridge of *Q246*. The experience crushed the exhilaration of action, leaving Dickson with a feeling of utter frustration.

Battling U-boats inshore was like trying to wrestle fog. They struck at will and then quickly disappeared into the night or down into the complex and impenetrable waters of the St. Lawrence. All the escorts could do was fill the night sky with the luminescent fireballs of tracer ammunition, or boil the ocean with depth charges, killing whales and fish. They were always too late to intercept or prevent an attack, and too poorly equipped to find and kill the attacker.

Dickson's final illusions of war as a great adventure were shattered in September when *Raccoon* was blown apart by torpedoes while escorting a convoy in the river. Nobody even saw her go: just two muffled thumps that obliterated the ship, her crew and Dickson's only real friends on the east coast. All they ever found were bits and pieces of wreckage along the north shore of the Gulf weeks later. Dickson was left with a grim determination to live just long enough to avenge his friends and the humiliation of the inshore campaign. That, and a recurring dream filled with helpless men constantly drifting just out of reach in oily debris-ladden water.

Command of a motor launch flotilla was perhaps not the best way to obtain his revenge; but in February 1943 it looked as if the only way out was up so Dickson had accepted the assignment. Besides, command of a flotilla in Canada might earn him command of a motor torpedo boat or even a motor gun boat overseas, the real high-speed, daring-do stuff.

But now as he stared out over the tumbling sea Dickson had to admit that he had made a serious error in judgement: the only thing these motor launches were likely to kill were the people in them.

Dickson was lost in thought as Noiles slipped through the wheelhouse door and joined him on the bridge. For awhile the two officers stood silently, faces fixed against the wind and rain. The motion of the launch was easy as she rode over each wave, but as her bow slammed into the next everyone's weight was thrown forward. It was an easy rhythm provided you were braced for the lurch: up, roll to starboard, pitch forward, roll to port, bang – into the next wave: up, roll to starboard, pitch forward, roll to port, bang. And all the while sheets of rain, driven beneath clouds so low the sea and sky were one, swept over the boat.

"You know, Dick," Noiles used the nickname given to Dickson aboard *Raccoon*, "the ancient Greeks counted sailors among the dead – now I know why."

"You asked for it, you stunned bastard," he replied, his drenched, red face expressionless. "If you had any sense you'd have stayed on the west coast!"

"Naw, not a chance. I didn't join the Navy to be bored to death!"

"It's a fair bet, Andy, they didn't make you an officer because of your superior judgement," Dickson snarled through the noise and the rain. "You traded a cushy billet in Esquimalt for this! Jesus Noiles, the boredom of this fucking business will kill you soon enough if you don't drown first."

"Can't be all that boring, Dick. This boat saw lots of action last year – "

Dickson's cold stare stopped Noiles in midsentence. "Rescue work. Picking up the survivors and burying the dead. You could call that action. Naw, Andy, you've traded a good job for 112 feet of spruce packed with enough gasoline and high explosives to blow it all to rat-shit!"

"It's true, then?"

"What?"

"That one of these blew up last year?"

"Yup. Gasoline. Ripped the middle right out of her and killed the stokers below deck. Which is why these newer ones are fitted with Admiralty diesels. A little more speed and a whole lot safer."

Saunders' voice brought them sharply back to the present.

"Here you are, Sir" the yeoman said, handing him a soggy sheet from a signal pad. It read '46.27.16 N, 59.22.01 W' in very tidy writing. Dickson nodded thanks and approval, and passed the paper to Noiles.

"Here, Andy, just about where we expected."

Noiles glanced at the figures. "Well, at least we have sea room, and with the wind in this quarter there's no danger of the Gulf ice drifting down on us. It would be hard to pick it out in this weather."

"No kidding."

"How much ice can she take, Dick?"

"None. She's got two overlapping layers of planks on her hull and some paint. ... Look, take her for a bit, Andy, I'm going aft to put on something dry."

Noiles nodded and Dickson picked his way aft to the officers' quarters that he and Noiles seldom used at sea. The cot in the wheelhouse was usually enough, since one of them was always on watch. But the wardroom was uninhabitable at sea in any event. Instead of venting the exhaust gases of the engines aft at the waterline as any sensible designer would do, some bonehead at the British Admiralty decided to give Fairmiles a proper midships funnel for a nicely balanced appearance. Any forward movement drove the engine exhaust directly down onto the quarterdeck and into the officers' quarters.

The smell of diesel fumes permeated the room as Dickson shed his slicker, wet duffle coat and sweater. The stench and the motion of the boat brought on a wave of nausea that discouraged lingering. Once into dry clothing Dickson pulled his slicker on and scampered back on deck, grateful for the fresh air that slashed through the funnel smoke.

When Dickson arrived back on the bridge Noiles handed him a steaming cup of cocoa. "Here, thought you might need this." Dickson nodded. "Everything all right back there?" Noiles enquired, anxious about the depth charges in their cradles and the other equipment that was frequently struck by breaking seas.

"Uh huh," Dickson muttered between gulps of cocoa. Leaving Noiles to the dubious delight of guiding the boat through the on-coming seas Dickson shifted to the starboard corner of the bridge. There, sheltered from the wind and much of the rain, he took a sip from his mug. Stunned bugger, he thought to himself, hasn't learned to lace it with rum yet. He was almost finished when Saunders' bearded and sea-drenched face appeared. "Beg yer pardon, Sir, but there's a schooner fine on the port bow."

"Right. Let's have a look."

As Dickson squinted Saunders pointed through the rain and mist. She was not easy to see. No billowing cloud of canvas set her apart from the seamless grey backdrop. Her black hull, not much bigger than a motor launch, lay low in the water and on this tack Dickson was looking at the leech of what little sail she carried. Just by the way she moved Dickson knew she was heavy laden. Her bow cut deeply into each successive wave, shouldering the sea out of her way. Her weight and the press of her sails gave the schooner a much more comfortable motion than a motor launch, and all who watched her from *Q246* did so with some trace of envy.

Dickson lifted the voicepipe cover and passed slight variations in heading to the helmsman until finally, through the salt-splattered windows, the cox'n could see her easily.

"Cox'n?" Dickson bellowed down the voicepipe.

"Aye, Sir."

"Put me just under her starboard quarter within hailing distance – and mind your helm in this sea."

The cox'n didn't need reminding, but he was not resentful. The schooner was much heavier, and as long as they stayed downwind of her – but not directly under her lee – the lighter launch would be driven to leeward faster than the schooner. It was a simple matter of holding relative position.

The little knot of men standing in the pilotage – Dickson, Saunders, Noiles and the two lookouts – had been joined by Babineau, the chief petty officer. Each sized up the schooner as the distance closed. There was no doubt she was a Grand Banker, but she had seen better days. Neither the foremast nor the main carried a topmast, just enough of a stump to lift the gaff of the courses. No chance of her setting topsails or topmast staysails. The sails, what could be seen of them from this angle, looked threadbare. As the view improved it was clear that her double-reefed fore and main courses were badly stained and heavily patched. Only the storm jib, perhaps because it was seldom used, seemed sound.

Babineau observed with a wry grin, "Jesus, what I wouldn't give to have da salvage from dat ship!"

Only Noiles turned to Babineau with a look of bewilderment and muttered "Fish?"

Knowing grins broke out but no-one interrupted.

"No, Sir," said Babineau, "not fish, Sir, definitely not fish. You seen her rig, dere. No topmasts and all, jis a couple of mainsails and a small jib – she don't carry much crew, eh ...? But, you needs a big crew to fish from a Banker, Sir. Somebody gots ta pull all dem dories and lines and shit. So, you gots a big crew you kin carry a big suits of sails. Not like dis ol' girl here."

Noiles pointed at the ship. "She's got dories stacked on her deck."

"Oh, yes Sir, but dem's firewood, Sir! Jis firewood. I bet dey bin in dose chocks longer dan you been in pants – beg yer pardon, Sir – and dere's only a couple each side, anyway ... See? Meby da ones on top get used fer a tender, eh? but mose of dem I suspec' are painted in, won't come free until she hit bottom, real hard like."

Babineau was on a roll and Noiles was getting an introduction into the peculiarities of east coast shipping. "And do you see dem sails, Sir, da courses I mean – da big ones, da main ones – how old dey look? No Sir, dis here is a cheap run ship wit a small crew, probly doin' short voyages."

"Wouldn't she be coming from the Grand Banks?"

"Not likely. Not dis far wes. Da mose direct course is a hundred miles er more furdder out."

"So what's she doing?"

"Coming from St-Pierre and Miquelon, mose likely, and I bet she ain't carryin' French bread!" Babineau laughed at his own little joke. Noiles' look of bewilderment merely deepened.

"Trading with the enemy, if you ask me Sir," Saunders growled, throwing a cold stare at Babineau, "that's what it is, trading with the enemy – booze er not."

Noiles looked more perplexed than ever. It was a remarkable comment from Saunders, whose red face was only partly the result of wind and weather. Catching Saunders' glance Noiles offered a tentative, "No longer the enemy, Saunders, those islands are 'Free' French now, have been for over a year."

"That may be, Sir, officially. But I don't trust them bastards." Saunders drew the cuff of his slicker across his face, wiping away the rain that pooled in his moustache and beard. "Before the French navy invaded them islands in December 1941 every signalman on this coast knew they was reporting our shipping movements to the Nazis. They got a high-frequency radio on St-Pierre," Saunders said, "and they was jabbering away to France and Martinique and wherever all through 1941. Some of us heard it."

"Was it shipping intelligence?" Noiles asked.

"Can't rightly say, Sir. I don't speak French." Saunders was a little defensive now that his conspiracy theory was no longer watertight.

"Besides, they had their goelettes – them little coastal schooners – all over the Grand Banks, in among our convoys – "

Babineau couldn't resist interrupting, with a sly grin on his weatherbeaten face, "Very clever of dose Frenchies to have da convoys routed right trew da fish, eh!"

"Don't change the facts!" Saunders shot back.

"You know, Mr. Noiles," Babineau continued, "we almose invaded dose islands ourselves in 1941 – it's for sure! One of my sons, dere, who's in de army said dey had a whole battalion waitin' at Debert, Nova Scotia, for half a year ready to land ..."

Saunders cast a doubtful glance Babineau's way, which brought forth a quick "It's true, it's true!"

"Anyway, dose French ships what done dat – da corvettes and da big sub, dere, da *Surcouf* – I was abord dem in 'alifax when dey was in jis before de invasion."

"Did you know it was going to happen?" Noiles asked.

"Naw, but we all suspec'. Dere was a whole bunch of us French Canadien dere, I tink I was de only Acadien. We was dere because we could all speak French, eh? But dose French guys, dey couldn't understand me!" Babineau chuckled. "Dey said my French was too old. We 'ad dis officer named Audette, some lawyer from Montreal, eh. He spoke good French so he did mose of da talking. Suit me fine.

"I was dere, on da *Surcouf*, when Captain Miles came to visit; da formal visit you know. Dey had bands, and da French Admiral was all decked out, like, and de Captain arrived in a staff car, dressed in he's long coat – you know da one wit tails – and a old hat, pointy at both ends, gold braids, swords and all da shit.

"He was drunk! Oh my Gawd, he was in some bad shape. Aw, aw, aw! And when dey piped him aboard da tide was low, eh, and so was da sub, and he slip and fell straight down da ladder onto da deck! My Jesus it was some funny. All of dem French sailors got him to he's feet and poured him below. We nearly died laughing – almose got on charge fer dat one, me."

"And they were all Free French?"

"Yeh, I guess. Anyway dey lef 'alifax and went and invaded St-Pierre and Miquelon about Christmas time."

"And the signal traffic stopped?" Noiles asked, looking at Saunders.

"No, not so's you'd notice," Saunders growled. "But the bastards got theirs in the end anyway."

"*Surcouf*, you mean?"

"Yeh. Heard they got sunk in the Caribbean last year – all hands lost," Saunders added sullenly.

"Da British," Babineau interjected.

"The British what?" Noiles asked.

"Da British done it. Dey sunk *Surcouf*. She called into Bermuda, eh, to da British dockyard dere, and the Brits put a mine on her hull. A few days later," Babineau explained with a wide grin on his face and his hands raised, "when she was well out to sea, boom! No trace, no survivors."

"Why would they do that?" Noiles asked incredulously. "She was Free French, on our side ..."

"Beg yer pardon Sir," Saunders intruded, "she was French and she was on their side. *Surcouf* was a rogue sub and the Brits did the right thing. You can't trust any of them." This last was directed at Babineau.

Caught between these two inveterate rumour-mongers Noiles ended the chatter by putting up his glasses and trying to focus through the rain on the schooner.

As *Q246* closed to hailing distance they were able to read the name in faded paint across the stern. "She's the *Cecilie Zwicker*!" Noiles reported.

"A Lunenberger," Dickson grunted: he and everyone but Noiles could figure that one out from the name alone.

In a calmer sea Dickson might have boarded the *Cecilie Zwicker*, but no-one was going to try that today. The schooner's captain knew that, too. He was easily distinguishable on the schooner's quarterdeck as the dark figure with the megaphone. Perhaps since the schooner lay upwind and his voice carried more easily, her captain was the first to hail.

"Hello Naivy!" The deep voice rang across the intervening waves. "Cap'n Lohnes here, how may I be of assistance?"

Assistance, indeed! Babineau smiled at Saunders, whose face was fixed in a permanent scowl. A good offence is the best defence.

Dickson raised his megaphone, drawing the deep breath he needed to battle the wind, and then replied, "Good afternoon to you, Cap'n. A bit nasty today?"

"Oh, I donno so much. It's fair blauw, good fer driving along!"

This much was obvious. Dickson now tried to get Captain Lohnes to talk about his course, cargo and destination. But the good Lunenberger would not be drawn.

"It's a foine wind fer a run down the cowst, and old *Cecilie's* foinest point of saylin'."

"Have you seen anything unusual or spoken to any other ships?" Dickson shouted over the crashing seas and heavy rain.

"Nauw, we ain't seen nuthin' since leavin' Fortune two days ago. Jist a lot of fog, like, and the same weathah."

They then exchanged estimated positions, for which Lohnes thanked him and suggested Dickson was a little further east than that. Was there anything he needed?

"Nauw, thank yee Mr. Dickson. I expect the weathah will cleah a bit this evenin' when the cauld front comes through, and if the wind don't back to sou-west too much we'll be home in a day or so. An' if it comes a blauw, well there's plenty a' places to luff-up at along this showa."

Dickson bent briefly to order the cox'n to back away, passed along his last regards to the *Cecilie Zwicker*, stowed the megaphone and watched as the two ships slowly parted.

"Should we have boarded her, Dick ?" Noiles asked later as they sat in the wheelhouse. "I mean, Babineau says she was probably carrying illegal booze from the French Islands to Nova Scotia!"

Dickson idly swilled the cocoa in the bottom of his mug. "Well, sure as hell she wasn't carrying fish. But no. We're not the RCMP, and there's no point in risking anyone in a boarding. We'll report speaking to her, and her position, and leave the suspicions to the police. If we stopped every fucking schooner and small coaster we suspected of illicit trade we'd have no time left to look for Germans."

With that Dickson jammed his empty mug into a tight spot in the wheelhouse bulkhead and clambered back on deck.

It was shortly after speaking with the *Cecilie Zwicker*, with the glass still falling and the warm front fully upon them, that the starboard lookout – a new lad, from Saskatoon – reported a submarine. A low, grey shape, he said, with a deckhouse amidships, fair on *Q246*'s starboard beam, running with the wind and the sea. "I seen it movin' northwestward, on an almost opposite course to ours." He'd had a fleeting glimpse of what looked like a conning tower, obscured by sheets of rain and spray.

"Are you sure?" Dickson demanded. The young lad had been uncertain that it was anything at all, and had been slow to alert the port lookout. It all happened so quickly, he explained, and with the object moving away, there was nothing for anyone else to see.

Still the earnestness and sincerity of the lad's report convinced Dickson that he had seen *something*. Without radar there was no chance of seeing through the rain and mist. The only possibility was a listening watch on the asdic, the underwater acoustical detection system carried by all escorts. Normally Dickson would have had his asdic operator search actively for the sub, sending out a series of high pitched pulses and waiting for a return echo. But if the sub was on the surface it was better to use the transducer to simply listen for the sub's engines, and even that would be a long shot.

"Right!" Dickson said. "It's time we broke radio silence anyway. Saunders, get the flotilla on the radio-telephone, give them our estimated position and order them to come around to 320 when I give the word. We'll try to shake out in a search line, a cable apart, waves astern and conduct a listening search downwind. Got that?"

"Aye, Sir."

"Do you think it will work, Dick ?" Noiles enquired.

"No. But once we get the sea astern of us it's at least worth a try. We won't get a quieter course." A brief pause followed, "Nor a worse one! In the meantime, close up a crew on the forward gun once we've come around, just in case, and get Findley on the asdic."

Noiles disappeared into the seamen's mess to rouse the men while Saunders passed orders on the radio telephone. Within minutes two crewmen were standing by the 20mm oerlikon gun mounted on the foc'sle. *Q246*'s other two gun mountings – a twin .5" machinegun and another 20mm gun – along the centre line aft of the funnel, stood unattended. Dickson figured there was no sense in getting everyone wet and cold.

"Asdic's closed up, Dick. Findley said he'd wait until we settled on the new course before trying anything," Noiles reported.

Dickson grunted a simple "Okay".

The flotilla acknowledged the orders and Dickson brought the motor launches around to the northwest. It was a cruel heading. *Q246* wallowed badly as the sea rolled under her stern, along her length and then away downwind, leaving the boat to slide backwards off the wave and twist sideways. The cox'n wrestled with the helm to hold her steady, but the pitching of the previous course was traded for yawing and rolling. Dickson waited a few minutes, hoping that she would steady, and then scrambled into the wheelhouse to speak to Findley.

The 112-foot Fairmile motor launches carried a rudimentary asdic (what the Americans called sonar), a small, fixed transducer protruding from the keel just back from the bow. Findley could not swing it from side to side, like those in the larger ships, nor could he change the horizontal angle. But in this case it did not matter. Dickson wanted to listen for engine noises – diesel engines from a sub running on the surface.

"What've ya got, Findley?"

"Nuthin'. It's no use, Skipper. It's like listening to waves crash on a beach. Here." Findley passed his headset to Dickson, who put one speaker to his ear. Through the other ear he heard Findley explain. "The set's quenching too much. All I can hear is the splash of water over the transducer. Every time we pitch or roll it drowns out all other sound. There's no chance we'll detect engine noises in this sea."

"And if we went faster?"

"Worse. Just one continous roar."

"Stay at it," Dickson ordered, handing the headset back to Findley.

Minnifie soon reported the same problem and, when Thoreau's boat cleared the mist on the port side he, too, complained that the asdic set was useless.

"Tell them to keep at it, Saunders, 'til I say to stop, understood?"

All that was left was to plot the estimated track of the contact and to establish a search pattern that, Dickson hoped, would intercept it some miles ahead. The new course reduced the problem of the wind, but also eliminated what little shelter the bridge provided. The driven rain now poured in from behind. Saunders took refuge in the lee of the funnel. Dickson didn't consider pulling rank and taking the spot for himself. A motor launch was too small for that kind of bullshit. He needed Saunders and the signalman had earned the perk. Dickson assured himself that Saunders would not escape his share of misery in this life.

Q246's two officers watched the dreary proceedings for some time before Noiles broke the silence.

"Dick, were you on this coast when the business of the French Islands blew up?"

"Yup."

"So what was it all about? If you believe Saunders those islands were nothing more than an enemy base."

"Yup, they were."

"So how come we didn't invade them? How come we let them go on doing that?"

"Politics, Andy. The Vichy French – the ones that made peace with the Germans in 1940 – they were officially neutral and all that shit. Right?"

"But their country was occupied?"

"The south and the French overseas empire stayed out of German hands."

"But Vichy was pro-German right?"

"Yup."

"Babineau says his son was in the army and that they were ready to invade St-Pierre and Miquelon ..."

"Yup."

"So? Why the hell didn't we? I mean, Jesus, that means Saunders was right! Pro-fascist islands smack in the middle of our shipping lanes."

"Americans, Andy, Americans."

"What do they have to do with it?"

"Everything. They're bigger than we are, and they like Vichy France. They told us to lay off, so we did."

"So the Free French did it?"

"Yup. Steamed out of Halifax and right into St-Pierre, just like that."

"Did we help?"

"The Americans thought we did. I guess they kind of went ape-shit when it happened, blamed our government. Maybe we did help, turned a blind eye. Navy might have helped, but from what I hear our politicians were too scared to act."

"So Saunders was right."

"Oh, I wouldn't put too much stock in what Saunders says. He's a good signalman, but as narrow and as dense as a two-by-four." This last comment brought a rare, thin grin from Dickson. "And you thought you'd come east to fight the Germans, eh? As a Cape Bretoner would say, 'She's some fucked-up, boys!' and Andy you don't know the half of it!"

In the afternoon the warm front passed through and the weather cleared a little, the wind eased and the sea fell slightly. Visibility improved and the flotilla gradually reassembled. But if there ever was a U-boat it was nowhere to be seen. In mid-afternoon the flotilla received the recall order from Sydney. Dickson did not protest. The U-boat sighting was dubious at best, useful as a training exercise maybe, but few in *Q246* believed that the lad from the prairies had seen anything more than a low, scudding cloud. By 2135 all of the 8th flotilla lay snugly alongside at Sydney.

Chapter 2

The Naval Board usually met in a dismal, windowless room well suited to both the simple tastes of naval officers and the tedious work of the Board. Its seven members dealt with the humdrum aspects of naval administration: pay and allowances, leaves, promotions, engineering, property, food, buildings, and the like. On those occasions when the Naval Minister chaired the meetings however, the Board met in his spacious office in the East Block on Parliament Hill. For the Board's work was also the stuff of money, of politics, and of patronage, and thus the Minister, Angus L. Macdonald, took a proprietary interest in its workings.

And so it was today. Macdonald preferred the tall, heavily draped windows, bulging bookcases and overstuffed chairs of his own office to the narrow rectangle they used at Naval Service Headquarters. After all, beneficence and largesse ought to be administered with some style...

As he watched the Board members file in his mood was as dark and sombre as their uniforms. Since his appointment in 1940 Macdonald, a dour, long-faced Nova Scotian and former premier of the province, had carried these men's ambitions for naval expansion to Cabinet in Ottawa with unbridled enthusiasm. They had always wanted a big navy, and Macdonald had delivered.

In truth, he had done more than that. He and his cabinet colleagues in Ottawa had pushed additional ships on the Navy, more corvettes and minesweepers, than they had asked for – simply because Canada was able to build them.

Macdonald also pushed (against the Navy's better judgement) to build destroyers in Halifax, ships the Royal Canadian Navy desperately wanted but the country lacked the expertise to build. Thanks to him that expertise would soon be in place, in Nova Scotia. The Navy would get its destroyers, if the war lasted long enough, and Nova Scotia would have a leg up in any bidding on postwar ship construction.

On the other hand Macdonald seldom intruded into the operational side of the Navy. Once it had its ships the RCN organized and fought its own war. So far it had been a useful division of territory. But now, in the spring of 1943, a tide of unrest in the country was seeping in around this ambitious naval policy, sucking the sand out from under Macdonald with each passing day. In fact, he reflected moodily, his credibility in Cabinet was in free-fall.

Even Connolly, his executive assistant, was whining that they had built the wrong kind of fleet. "We should have built destroyers from the start," Connolly had been saying for weeks. With destroyers the Navy could hit back, take the war to the enemy like the British were doing in the Atlantic. A far more popular tactic with the Canadian people than just escorting convoys.

But hell, even Macdonald's attempt to do that had blown up in his face. The new destroyers ordered in Halifax were way behind schedule, and a push was on to complete them. It was an open secret that Stephenson, the Chief Engineer, was complaining to his Board colleagues about the destroyer project which had swallowed up the skilled workers desperately needed to modernize the existing fleet.

Everything was turning to shit in his hands, he thought bitterly. It was time for the Navy to repay the debt.

It was all Macdonald could do to sit quietly, watching wearily as the Board members took their seats and fussed with their papers. Vice Admiral Percy Nelles, Chief of Naval Staff, sat to Macdonald's right at the desk, the Deputy Minister to his left. The other Board members; the Chief Engineer, Chief of Naval Personnel, Chief of Naval Equipment, the Vice Chief of the Naval Staff and the Board secretary, sat at a long table running out from the desk. A National Geographic map of Western Europe taped to the wall between the two windows was the only visible concession to the war in the room.

The Naval Board could never keep itself from descending into the minutiae of naval administration and so the meeting went on much longer than it should. Macdonald did his part, moving the meeting through its agenda, but his mind was clearly elsewhere. By late morning the desk and table were littered with coffee and tea cups, full ashtrays, and jumbled files. The spring sun slanted in the windows, pouring shafts of bright light through the cigarette smoke and gloom of the office. The effect seemed to remind the Board members that it was nearly noon. It was also Friday, and so when no-one answered the call for new business Macdonald, his patience eroded, ended the meeting.

He crushed his dying cigarette in the ashtray, closed the file in front of him with a snap and reached for his teacup. Others in the room rose stiffly from their chairs, stretched aching backs and legs, and stuffed folders and notes into briefcases. The simple act of moving soon stirred their blood and, being busy men, they were not long in shuffling towards the door.

Through the murmur of plans being made to follow up on problems, or for lunch, Macdonald turned toward Nelles. "A word with you, if you please Admiral," Macdonald said softly, his hands wrapped around the teacup, and his mind wrestling for a way to open the conversation.

"Of course, Sir," Nelles replied.

Although it was quietly done, the implied request for privacy was heard by the others, who quickened their pace.

Macdonald stared absently at his teacup, lifting his gaze only to share a knowing glance with Jones, the Vice Chief of Naval Staff. Rear Admiral Jones had arrived in Ottawa at the end of 1942 after two years in command at Halifax. Convinced that most of the Navy's problems started at the top, Jones was eager to remake Naval Service Headquarters in his own image. He had already started a whispering campaign behind Nelles' back and was working to undermine Macdonald's trust in his Chief of Naval Staff. Jones silently collected his files and followed the others out the door, his departure punctuated by the firm click of the latch. Nelles dropped his case and some folders on a chair and moved to the window, putting both hands onto the small of his back and stretching as he gazed down on the scurrying figures below.

For a moment he imagined himself a prisoner looking out on the world: it seemed so long since he had done anything *normal*. The frenetic pace of naval expansion over the last three-and-a-half years had consumed all his waking hours, and there seemed no end in sight. When he was finished here a staff car would whisk him down Elgin Street to an office where paperwork simply piled up in his absence. There weren't enough days in the week to get ahead of it. And then there was the war at sea to think about. They'd done all right so far but things could be better. "Time," Nelles muttered under his breath as he looked down on the lawn, "I just need more time on all fronts..."

Macdonald sat motionless and the silence grew. Finally Nelles, still half lost in the imagery of his imprisonment offered, "That went well, I think. It was good of you to sit in. We have a lot on our plate at the moment."

It took a few long seconds for Macdonald's distracted reply. "Yes." In the uneasy silence he finished off the dregs in his cup, choosing his words with care. Then he leaned back and finally began to speak.

"Aircraft carriers for the fleet are a good idea, don't you think? Could be the solution to our problems in the mid-ocean if we can get them in service before the end of the year. We could start killing U-boats."

"Perhaps," Nelles replied, still staring out the window. He barely restrained an impatient sigh. So that's what he wants to talk about. "But we can't do it without British support, and you know they think we're overstretched."

"And what do you think?"

"I agree with the Admiralty. We're up to our necks in worn-out corvettes, a shortage of repair yards, too few fully trained and experienced officers and, frankly, too many operational commitments. We can build a fleet air arm after the war."

Macdonald pushed his teacup to the back of his desk, just beyond his finger tips, folded his hands and weighed his thoughts. "You are aware, Admiral," he finally said, "that I think aircraft carriers would be a good thing ..."

"Yes Sir." This much was evident from the Naval Board discussions.

"The Prime Minister also thinks that aircraft carriers would be a good thing," Macdonald continued. "He agrees that we built the wrong fleet for this war. We built too many little ships, too many ships with no real offensive power."

Nelles had heard mutterings like this before from Macdonald's staff, but never directly from the Minister.

"We built what we could, Mr. Minister, and we have secured the Atlantic against the U-boats. It is those little escort ships which have kept the Allied war effort going, and they have given us a high profile in the war at sea." Nelles had turned his back to the window and spoke in careful, measured tones. "Without them we would not be in charge of all ocean convoys between New York and the Grand Banks, we could not provide over a third of the escorts between the Grand Banks and Britain, and we would not now have our own theatre of operations in the northwest Atlantic. I – "

Macdonald rose abruptly, cutting him off. Why couldn't Nelles see this as clearly as he did?

"Admiral, do you have any idea – any idea at all – what's going on in the War Cabinet? The whole country is seething with unrest. The electorate is ugly, the press is against us, my God even that new polling business, whatever it's called..." Macdonald gestured wildly.

"Gallup."

"Yes, Gallup, even they claim that the country would throw us out like that," he snapped his fingers, "if we went to the polls today."

Nelles remained rooted to his spot while Macdonald paced, fumbling with a fresh cigarette in increasing agitation.

"I quite understand, Sir," Nelles said stiffly.

"No, I don't think you do, Admiral." Macdonald stopped pacing and looked directly at Nelles. "Frankly, Nelles, when it comes to politics I don't think you'd know shit if you stepped in it! So let me explain." He was pacing once more. "English Canada, and the national press, hate us for doing too little in this war. Hard to blame them. Everyone else is fighting: the Australians, the New Zealanders, South Africans, Indians, Brits, Russians – Christ, even the Americans now. But our Prime Minister is so afraid of casualties our army is sitting on its ass!"

Nelles knew that Macdonald always pushed for greater involvement in the actual fighting, without any success.

"The army fought gallantly and with honour at Dieppe and Hong Kong," he countered.

Macdonald smirked contemptuously. "Yes, yes, two heroic disasters. But no government can build public support around hopeless causes. We don't need more Canadians dead, Nelles. We need to kill Germans."

"I see," Nelles said craftily. So this was not about aircraft carriers after all. "So that's why the First Division is going to Italy?"

Macdonald stopped. "How did you know?"

"There's little that goes on in Ottawa that we don't get through the rumour mill eventually. I think this is a bad idea. The golden rule of the Great War was that Canadians fight together, under Canadian command and in Canadian formations. By breaking the army into pieces all over Europe we not only lose control, we lose the prestige Canada should achieve from fielding the First Canadian Army. It's a dreadful error, Mr. Macdonald, and all for short-term political purposes."

Nelles lit a cigarette before continuing.

"Isn't it ironic that just as Cabinet capitulates to public clamouring for soldiers' blood the Navy has won full control over its own forces, and operational control over vast areas well outside of Canada's territorial waters? Murray's new command in Halifax is the first Allied theatre of war to be commanded by a Canadian."

"Don't lecture me, Admiral!" Macdonald snapped. "The decision to send the First Division to Italy is sound: they will come back to Britain for the invasion of France. As for the Navy," Macdonald said, his voice rising as he turned away from the window, "you are in no position to gloat! The government has given you everything you've asked for since 1939 ... the dream of any service commander. The Prime Minister has made the Navy one of his top priorities, higher than even the army, has he not?" Macdonald did not look for a reply. "And I have personally carried your estimates and requests to the War Cabinet. I," he emphasised, tapping his chest and leaning towards Nelles, "I have assured my Cabinet colleagues that the Navy was one of the best investments Canada could make."

Macdonald's insinuation touched a nerve and Nelles rose to the defence of his service. "And so it is. The Navy has achieved what no other Canadian service has ever done: it is on the verge of commanding its own theatre of war in the northwest Atlantic. We have the second largest fleet in the North Atlantic – bigger than the Americans, and – "

Macdonald carried on as if Nelles hadn't spoken.

"And despite building a huge navy, and a bloated air force, this country is in a foul mood. There appears to be nothing – nothing! – that the largest fleet in Canadian history can do about it. Not a friggin' thing. Our navy can neither deliver the government from its current crisis, nor even defend our own coast!" Macdonald leaned forward with both hands on the table, looked Nelles in the eye, and said coldly, "Just what can our Navy do, Admiral?"

Nelles' first thought was of Admiral Sir Dudley Pound's comment that it is only politicians who imagine that a navy is not earning its keep unless it is charging madly about the ocean.

"We have been around this before, Mr. Macdonald," Nelles said finally. "Our Navy earns its keep well enough making sure the Atlantic is safe for shipping. Convoying ships is absolutely vital. You know as well as I, Mr. Minister, that everything that happens in Europe depends on what we do. Every bomb, every bullet, every man, every kernel of grain, every piece of ore, my God even ninety percent of the aircraft get to the front because we do our job. If we did not make the Atlantic safe there would be no-one left in Europe to fight the Germans."

"Maybe so, Admiral," Macdonald replied dismissively. "But who the hell looks after *our* shipping, eh? While Canadian corvettes defend Allied shipping in the Caribbean, Allied shipping off the US east coast, Allied shipping in the Mediterranean and Christ knows where else, *our* shipping gets clobbered in the Gulf of St. Lawrence! Twenty-two ships in the Gulf alone last year. Sufferin' Jesus, Nelles! People along the coast watched the ships explode! The shoreline was littered with wreckage and bodies. For God's sake Nelles," Macdonald was nearly shouting now, "where do you think Bloc Populaire support in Quebec comes from? Huh? Who do you think supports those bastards? Not only are we damned in French Canada for fighting 'Britain's war', we can't even keep the St. Lawrence River open! So we closed the Gulf to shipping last September – and thousands were thrown out of work. Thousands, and most of them friggin' Quebeckers."

Nelles was unsure whether he should attack this latest outrage or let the Minister vent his spleen. In the end he settled for a grim "I know, Sir."

"You don't know *shit*, Admiral. The Navy took a beating in the Gulf last summer, but it was the government who got the shit kicked out of it! Twenty-two ships sunk, people scared half to death, thousands out of work, Quebec politicians pounding on my door – my door! – harassing me in Parliament. And I took the heat in Cabinet. I was the one who placated Louis St. Laurent. *And* I won Chubby Power's support. *And* I promised the Prime Minister that it would be only a one-time thing. And now look: we're at it again!"

Nelles' equanimity was nearly shattered, and his voice was sharp. "The decision to close the Gulf for the 1943 shipping season was not only the right thing to do, it was a bold and courageous thing to do! It was your duty as a Minister of the Crown – "

"Don't tell me what my duty is!" Macdonald shot back. "Your duty, Admiral, is to remember that you are the professional head of the Canadian Navy, not some squadron of the British fleet."

This was a new tack from the Minister. Macdonald was an anglophile and had never failed to support aid to the British inside and outside of cabinet – until now. Nelles sensed a sea change in the Minister's attitude and knew where it came from. Jones.

"It's a global war, Mr. Minister."

"It sure the hell is, and it's being fought right here on our doorstep, too! If we hadn't loaned those twenty corvettes to the British late last summer for the North African landings – "

"Seventeen, and one of them British."

" – and if we'd had that new radar and heavier guns the British miraculously found for those ships – after we handed them over – it would never have been necessary to close the Gulf in the first place."

"Had it not been for the British destroyers operating out of Halifax last year we could not have run convoys in the Gulf as long as we did. Ask Admiral Jones, he'll tell you as much! And as for the corvettes, those ships would never have received that new equipment if we had kept them in the Gulf – "

"Exactly, Nelles! Those bastards in Whitehall find the equipment when it suits them."

Nelles himself was shouting now. "It's not the same bloody thing. Good God! Protecting troop transports packed with thousands of men requires the best possible equipment, it was sensible for – "

Macdonald finished the thought his way. "It was sensible for the British to look after their own interests and leave us to shift for ourselves."

Nelles was nearly apoplectic. "Cabinet approved the transfer!"

"Based on your advice. And what about those ships from the North Atlantic run we loaned them this past winter, eh? The cream of our escort fleet in the mid-Atlantic transferred to the British at the stroke of a pen!"

"That transfer was only temporary, you and the Cabinet know that. Besides, we had no grounds to resist the temporary removal of our ships from the mid-ocean. The losses from trans-Atlantic convoys under our escort were simply too high ..."

"Too high! Too high!" Macdonald threw his arms up with each exasperated repetition.

"Yes, Sir. When a third of the escort force accounts for eighty percent of the losses that's too high."

"Really, Nelles – and how much of that was our fault, eh? The British determine who escorts what, right? So they got all the fast convoys and we got saddled with the slow ones."

"It's not that simple."

"It's dirt simple to me. We escort the old tramps that belch smoke and give away the convoy's position, get blown all over the damned ocean in any kind of wind, and aren't fast enough to outrun someone's grandmother. We have to defend them with inadequate and poorly equipped forces, and the British blame us for the high loss rate! It's bad enough to get roasted over the balls-up inshore last year, thank God Parliament hasn't found out about the mid-ocean."

"Yes," Nelles sighed. He too was glad that the collapse of the naval effort in the mid-ocean in 1942 had gone unnoticed at home. Then he added sullenly, "But we have benefited from the transfer."

Macdonald stared at him, mystified. "Apart from international embarrassment, what the hell did it get us?"

"It got us modern equipment and access to training for our best ships and men. As I told you last January when we brought this before Cabinet, the best place to get modern British equipment is in Britain. In the last few weeks those escorts have rejoined the battle in the mid-ocean. Why, just east of the Grand Banks there are so many U-boats it's impossible to route all the convoys clear of them. Canadian escorts are back in action, Mr. Minister, and will soon be sinking U-boats."

"And they will be sunk hundreds, thousands of miles from our coast."

The contempt in Macdonald's voice was more than Nelles could stand. How could he make the Minister understand the global nature of the naval war? "For the love of God, this is a global war! It will not be won or lost in the Gulf of St. Lawrence!"

Nelles regretted the outburst as soon as it was out of his mouth. It was true, but it was not what the beleaguered politician needed to hear.

Macdonald gave him both barrels. "No! But our war will, damn you, you must see that!"

"With all due respect, Mr. Minister, we can manage very well without routing ocean shipping through the Gulf ..."

Nelles was about to elaborate but Macdonald held up his hand. "No, I know the argument well enough. Keeping ocean shipping out of the St. Lawrence is a major saving in tonnage for the Allies. I've made this case to Cabinet often enough. But my God Nelles, look at this from my perspective. Closing Montreal and shifting the work to Halifax or Saint John or Sydney is a Maritimer's dream. But how long do you think I can win that argument in Cabinet, eh? And how long do you think I can keep the Quebec ministers, and the Prime Minister himself, at bay – not to mention the Bloc Populaire. No, it's your turn. Time for you to deliver, not just to me but to the government and the country!"

"We're doing all we can ..."

"I don't think so, Admiral! Why the hell do you suppose we're breaking up the First Canadian Army and sending troops to Italy, eh? War isn't about standing guard, Nelles, it's about politics: it's about mobilizing national morale and effort, it's about keeping people busy in the factories and content with the way their government is handling things."

"Surely getting the army into the fray will take the heat off the government?"

"The Italian operation is not scheduled until later in the summer, perhaps the fall. The government needs good news now – news it can bring to Parliament and publish in the press. Not about how Canada is profiting from the war, and quietly soldiering along. But news about how we are taking the war to the enemy, that we are killing Nazis. It's blood the people want." Macdonald thumped his hand on the table. "Blood! Not damn convoys safely escorted!"

He crushed his cigarette in the nearest ashtray and lit another, giving Nelles an opening.

"But we've given you that! We sank subs in 1942 and the Prime Minister announced to Parliament this past February the sinking of a U-boat in the Mediterranean by *Ville de Quebec*. And there will be more!"

Macdonald's face curled in a cynical grin. "You seem to have missed the point, Admiral! Canadians – especially French Canadians – aren't interested in subs sunk in the Mediterranean or any other Godforsaken corner of the world! They want something here, on our front doorstep ..."

"Which is why I say that your, the government's, announcement in March that the Gulf of St. Lawrence will remain closed for the 1943 shipping season was a courageous one."

"Courageous my ass! It's an act of political suicide!"

It was Nelles' turn to pound the table, "We have consolidated our forces and taken operational control on the east coast, just what we need to sink subs. Surely you can see that, Mr. Minister?"

Macdonald's response was cold. "I'll tell you what I see, Admiral, and what my Cabinet colleagues see: a huge fleet built at enormous expense that cannot save the government from an angry electorate!"

"The Navy is a national institution, not some creature of the Liberal Party ..."

"I shouldn't have to remind *you*, Admiral, of all people," Macdonald roared, jabbing his cigarette at Nelles, "that the Navy was founded by a Liberal government, that the first ships built expressly for it in the 1920s were ordered by a Liberal government, that Mr. King oversaw the expansion of the fleet in the late thirties, and that this government – this government! – has built the Navy into what it is today! For Christ's sake, Nelles, the Navy owes everything to the Liberal Party – everything!"

The outburst finally sapped Macdonald of much of his fury. Nelles stood dumbfounded by Macdonald's sudden burst of emotion. When the Minister spoke again his voice was icy calm.

"Admiral, you know that if Bracken and his Tory crowd ever gain power they will drive this country to ruin. They have no standing in French Canada: none. They would force conscription on the country and it would be just like 1917 all over again: the Ontario militia in the streets of Quebec armed with baseball bats and machine guns. Then where would we be? Eh? Think about it for a moment. We wouldn't be sending aid to the British. No! We'd be fighting our own little war right here!" Having made his case to the only man who could salvage his position in Cabinet, Macdonald dropped sullenly into a chair.

Nelles was flushed with anger and frustration. Cleary Macdonald would accept neither explanation or placation. He gathered his things, closed his briefcase and stuffed a stack of files under his arm. His instinct was to bolt, but duty and years of training kept him in place. Finally he said, "If you have no further need of me ..."

Macdonald did not look up, simply waved his hand in dismissal. As Nelles' hand touched the doorknob the Minister called out a warning. "Admiral!" Nelles turned slowly. "Your plan for the Gulf better work. If you don't kill a U-boat there soon one of us will be looking for a new job, and it won't be me."

Nelles said nothing, and left the door open on his way out. Storming through Macdonald's outer office he noticed Jones, the new Vice Chief of the Naval Staff, sitting calmly, wreathed in cigarette smoke, a newspaper folded neatly on his lap.

Chapter 3

The pungent smell of a freshly lit cigar was evidence that the captain was in. With some trepidation Lieutenant Commander Clive Belanger rapped on the glass and pushed his face through the open door. Without shifting his gaze from the gun wharf across the Narrows the captain shot out a gruff "Yes!", just as Belanger's shoulder cleared the edge of the door.

"Here are the training reports you asked for, Sir."

"Ah! Belanger. Thank you!" the captain replied, with something approaching warmth. Chummy Prentice was normally gruff around his subordinates – hence his ironic nickname – although not from any want of kindness. As Captain of Destroyers at Halifax he was responsible for the operational efficiency of local escort vessels. A Canadian who retired to British Columbia after a career in the Royal Navy, Prentice was recalled to active service in 1939. Since that day he had been driven by a professional desire to get the best from his men and ships. Now he had the core of the fleet under his thumb and it was time to whip them into trim.

The men of the lower deck had little to fear from Chummy Prentice. Theirs were the willing hands and backs that made the ships function, and he treated them with equanimity. It was the officers who feared his wrath. Prentice would accept failure that was the result of genuine initiative and a desire for greater efficiency in killing U-boats. But woe betide any officer who did not work as hard as Prentice himself, or lacked zeal, or abused his power or was personally ambitious. That was why Belanger approached the lion's den with caution. It spoke well for Belanger that the lion warmed to his presence.

As Belanger turned to leave Prentice barked a curt "Hang on a minute" and pointed to a chair. Belanger sat. Prentice parked his cigar in the ashtray, sat behind the desk and opened the file. In the same motion he reached for the rimless monocle housed in the inner pocket of his tunic.

Belanger had believed, before becoming Acting Training Commander in Halifax, that Prentice's famous monocle was purely an affectation, a prop to make a point with greater drama, or scowl with greater effect. It spoke volumes for the captain's relationship with the lower deck that he tolerated their good natured kidding about his eyepiece. On one occasion a division of Prentice's ship's company had all worn monocles on parade. Prentice inspected the ranks utterly unmoved. Back in front of the parade he threw back his head, flipped the monocle into the air, and caught it squarely between the right cheek and eyebrow. "When you can do that", he said, "you can all wear monocles." The lower deck swore by the story.

Belanger assumed it was apocryphal, part of Prentice's well cultivated mystique, but it had never occurred to him that anyone would actually use such a glass for reading.

Nonetheless, when Prentice jammed the monocle into his craggy features there was no gainsaying it would stay. The most distinguishing feature of his bulldog-like face was the virtually continuous bushy brow that held the top of the slender glass. The fierceness of the captain's pugnacious countenance was emphasized by his hair, well slicked and combed straight back. Combined with his typical bluntness, professional competence and singleness of purpose – killing the enemy – Prentice was formidable and intimidating.

He said nothing as he flipped through the two dozen single-page reports. Each report was organized under headings: asdic, gunnery, navigation, communications, and depth charges, followed by a general summary on the efficiency of the ship. Each entry noted the state of these skills and commented on the personnel involved. Belanger had written the reports himself, a task he did not enjoy.

"Pretty average lot," the captain observed in an off-hand fashion as the final report slipped from his hands. Belanger could only mutter a quiet "Yes Sir," resigned to the interrogation to follow, report by report, ship by ship, function by function, officer by officer.

"What do you make of *Castlegar*?"

"She did well in her anti-submarine practices," Belanger responded cautiously. "She had no trouble finding the sub in good conditions. Anderson has a good plotting team and they were never fooled by false contacts. Mind you, asdic conditions were good and *P553* was limited in her evasive action."

"In other words, good at finding a clockwork mouse?"

"Well, as good as time on a training sub will allow."

"Better than average?" Prentice shot back, then answered his own question, "I see your reports on the other corvettes – *Tracadie, Botsford, Watson Lake* and the rest – are all much the same."

"True," Belanger replied somewhat defensively. "The fleet has good asdic ability now. The asdic ratings are experienced, especially the Higher Submarine Detection ratings, and the anti-submarine officers have all had at least a year of seatime. Most have had some training in the UK."

Prentice knew all of this and more, and Belanger knew that he did. The captain also knew most of the officers, having served with them in the mid-Atlantic during 1941 and 1942. Indeed, Prentice had trained many of the corvette captains.

"And what do you make of *Tracadie*?"

Belanger weighed his words carefully. "Probably better than average ... overall."

"No doubt, Belanger," Prentice retorted without looking up from the desk, "but what about Wagner, what kind of ship does he run?"

"Candidly?"

"Candidly."

"Wagner's a bloody fool, a Tartar to his men, and a drunk into the bargain. His ship is a mutiny waiting to happen, and I wouldn't blame his men if they shot him and dumped the body in the sea."

"I've often wondered why his crew haven't reported him washed overboard! Still, I think you're too kind, Belanger. Wagner is a bully and a pompous fool, but with a modicum of ability. That's a very dangerous combination. If it weren't for his fool's luck he'd be driving some patrol boat on the west coast by now – he may yet."

Another pull on his stumpy cigar brought forth billows of smoke from Prentice's mouth and nose – along with a final question about the corvettes. "So, *Lakeville*'s the best of the bunch, eh?"

This was a deliberately impish and awkward question. *Lakeville* was Belanger's corvette, newly assigned. "Maybe so, Sir," he answered cautiously. "Her real strength lies in Fergus, the anti-submarine officer, and Kozlowski, his Higher Submarine Detection man. Fergus is a great guy. Kozlowski's a bit wayward, but both have an ear for a sub, and a sixth sense for what it will do. *Lakeville*'s depth charge and gunnery crews are good – well, average, they know their job and do it well enough. I think, if I may say so Sir, she is also a happy ship." Belanger knew it was inconceivable to Prentice that a ship could be efficient if it was unhappy.

The discussion ran briefly to finding another anti-submarine officer for *Beauceville*, and then onto the enduring problem of ever finding any submarine in inshore waters.

"You know, Belanger," Prentice sighed, "I'm not sure that training ships in St. Margaret's Bay is such a good idea. It's unaffected by large freshwater runoff, and its water temperature is almost always uniform top to bottom. Sound runs straight and true, no problem with the bottom: if you can get a ping on the sub you've got 'im. Christ! I could find a sub in St. Margaret's Bay with a glass-bottomed bucket and a rowboat!"

Belanger smiled slightly. "Indeed, Sir, I'm sure you could." It was an honest sentiment.

"That's the problem, Belanger," Prentice said, leaning over the desk and pointing his cigar firmly in Belanger's direction. "The areas where our men have to deal with U-boats are complex, with tide rips, different temperature layers, fresh water, boulders on the bottom and all that crap. It doesn't matter how good your asdic team is, *Lakeville* needs a good measure of luck to find and sink a sub in Canadian waters."

"I couldn't agree more, Sir, but the new radars will help enormously. With the 10cm set we'll be able to find them on the surface and destroy the wretched things before they can get under."

Prentice nodded agreement, but sat silently puffing on the last of his cigar. Belanger could almost hear the wheels turning in his head.

Prentice shifted his attention to motor launches. No-one believed that Fairmiles constituted a threat to a well handled U-boat, but they had some value. No submariner could risk a hole in his pressure hull several thousand miles from home in waters dominated by enemy surface and air forces. But the launches were frail, poorly equipped craft. Prentice nonetheless worked through their reports with the same ruthless enthusiasm he applied to the corvette files. After all, anything that could carry a gun might kill a U-boat.

Here, too, the reports were mixed: *Q287* was good all round; *Q269* was average with a poor set of officers in charge; *Q273* Belanger confided, and Prentice concurred, was probably more a danger to those around her than to the enemy. She would have to be sent back for personnel changes.

The 8th Flotilla of five launches now based at Sydney, was the best of the bunch. Prentice took special care to fully review their status.

The Navy's equipment was generally second rate, and the ships were being asked to perform tasks for which they were neither designed nor equipped. Getting the best out of these vessels required good people, so any discussion of efficiency naturally turned to which captains and officers could be expected to get the most out of what they had to work with.

"Dickson?" Prentice asked.

"A hard case, personality wise, and given to profanity, but a driver and considerate of his men," Belanger answered. "If anyone can get the best out of a Fairmile it will be Dickson. His own, *Q246*, scored very well in the anti-submarine practices, and he handles the group well. All of his captains, Minnifie, Jackson, Thoreau and ... " Belanger searched his brain for the missing name.

"Aubrey."

"Yes, Aubrey," Belanger continued, "They are all competent. Moreover, most of them know Dickson from last summer, when they served in the Gulf together. He has basically assumed his predecessor's approach to command. The 8th also has a good signalling staff, which means the group functions with a minimum of fuss."

"And what about their surface action exercises: how did they go?"

"Oh, very well indeed," Belanger replied, shifting in his chair, "very well indeed. We did the usual 'officer of the watch' manoeuvers and spent some time on surface gunnery actions both as a whole flotilla and in two divisions. Dickson and his captains have thoroughly discussed what is expected of divisional tactics against a surface contact, and the 8th performed these with little need for detailed signalling."

"The new 20mm oerlikons add a bit of punch," Prentice offered offhandedly, "now at least if they have to hit something they can. Have all the 8th been re-equipped?"

"Yes."

"Good. Anything else Belanger?"

"Ah ... no, Sir, I think that's about it."

Prentice passed the file across the desk.

"Will that be all, Sir?"

Prentice responded by passing the cigar box, a signal that the formal proceedings were over. Once the cigars were lit and drawing, the captain allowed himself an uncharacteristically reflective mood.

"You know, Clive," he said, slipping idly into the familiar, "today we finally took charge of our own fate."

Belanger understood the allusion. "Yes, Sir. Very fine parade, a fitting start to Admiral Murray's command."

Up to now, Rear Admiral Leonard Murray had been the Commanding Officer for the Atlantic Coast, responsible for little more than Canada's puny territorial waters within twelve miles of the coast. As the new Commander in Chief for the Canadian Northwest Atlantic, all anti-submarine and convoy operations between the Gulf of Maine and Baffin Island, and east to the edge of the continental shelf, were now in Murray's hands.

"So," Prentice continued, "now that we finally have the Americans off our backs, we can get on with the war. Did you know, Clive, that a hundred and ten ships – one hundred and ten ships!" he repeated, jabbing nicotine stained fingers again in Belanger's direction, "were sunk in the Canadian zone last year while you and I were skylarking in the mid-ocean?"

"Good God! I knew of the twenty-odd ships lost in the Gulf, but a hundred and ten ships? A bit astonishing."

Prentice paused to take another pull on his cigar. "Now, many of those hundred and ten ships were steaming independently early in the year, before the convoy system was fully established. Some were from trans-Atlantic convoy battles, the ones that you and I fought, that spilled over into the fog of the Grand Banks. Chased a few U-boats there myself last year, without luck – as I suspect you did."

Belanger nodded.

"Still, we were shut out. The enemy scored all the points and we got zip. Jones and the band of incompetents here in Halifax didn't sink a single sub – not one! Most of those useless bastards who ran that inshore campaign are in Ottawa now, running the whole friggin' Navy! God save us all!"

"God save the Navy! Do you honestly think this new command arrangement will work? Murray and Jones have hated each other for years."

"Decades," Prentice interjected. "It goes well back, to their naval college days. Don't know the details of that, but I do know that when Murray and I were trying to get the Newfoundland Escort Force up to speed in 1941 Jones sabotaged us at every turn. Murray had the most important operational command, Jones was supposed to get the ships into shape and feed them to us. It was like running in sand. Not much better last year."

"And now?"

"And now Jones is Vice Chief and will doubtless bully old Percy Nelles off the throne, while Murray commands the fleet. A house divided."

"So, do you think Jones made a hash of it last year?"

"Absolutely. The Navy got roasted in Parliament over those losses, especially in the Gulf." Prentice muttered something inaudible under his breath. "The decision to close the St. Lawrence to ocean shipping was a gutless capitulation. You could follow that caterwauling way out in Newfoundland – at least I got a regular dose of it from Murray's office. It was our first major naval defeat, Belanger. At least that's the way the nation saw it, and it's hard to blame them."

"So, what would you have done, Captain?"

"Training! Training and leadership. The bunch who ran the inshore war here last year never understood the importance of training – they still don't. Hell, they don't even know what training is. As for leadership, well shit. Clive, the only effective countermeasure we had in 1942 was aircraft. The bloody air force, of all people. None of the naval escorts could cope – Christ! When Jones had this command none of them were trained properly!"

"So, do you think the Germans saw it as a victory for them?" Belanger asked, rather cautiously.

"Damn right! Absolutely! The Hun might be many things that we anglo-saxons are not, and thank God for that, but they're not dumb. No, hell. All they have to do is basic operational research in their logs and reports of proceedings; it's all there."

The whole fleet knew of the personal and professional animosity between Admirals Murray and Jones, but Belanger had never gotten to the bottom of it, and he wasn't sure now if he wanted to.

"... And that bloody fool Jones never stood up to the US navy admiral in Argentia, let him meddle in everything we tried to do. D'you remember last summer when I took my training group to sea in support of Canadian convoys under attack on the Grand Banks? We helped a couple dozen convoys or so. I think you went on one of those cruises, did you not?"

"Yes."

"Well, that bastard in Argentia had the gall to protest to Murray about my 'freelance operations' – freelance! Jesus H. Christ! Canadian warships help other Canadian warships battle a wolf pack, and some foreign admiral, who doesn't have enough ships to form a single escort group, objects because we never asked his permission! And you know what?"

Belanger shook his head from side to side.

"Within weeks of my training scheme collapsing the US and the Brits had set up that collection of clapped-out destroyers called Western Support Force to do the very job that I had been doing! Well, at least we tried – Jones never had the guts, too worried about offending someone. Small wonder things were such a disaster last year."

Prentice seemed spent after this flurry of passion and paused to take another puff on his cigar. Then he offered his final assessment. "You know what the real problem was in 1942, Clive? Huh? Do you? Too many God damned admirals in charge, and too many bloody politicians watching!

"All ships are safe from a dead U-Boat, Clive ... So we have to kill the buggers when they enter our waters this year; it's that simple." Clouds of smoke now spiralled around the Captain as he worked up to full speed. "Everything else is secondary – convoys, patrols, the works – even the Naval Staff agree on that! They have closed the Gulf to ocean shipping again this year, but not because we're on the run. We're laying a trap! Any German submariner foolish enough to enter Canadian waters this summer will have the hounds of hell down on him, mark my words! We won't have to coddle shipping, we can go straight to the bastard and sink him.

"That's our part, Clive," Prentice eased back a few revolutions. "The government has taken an enormous political risk in closing the Gulf to ocean shipping before any attack develops. Nelles, too, has taken a tremendous personal and professional risk in pushing for the closure. We've got his support, at least, in Ottawa. So, we must destroy – kill! – anything that enters."

Belanger had shared in the preparation of plans to meet the U-boat onslaught of 1943, and he enjoyed these moments of reflection on the course of the war with someone in a position to influence it.

"Do you think the plan will work, Sir? I mean, you've operated inshore and some in the Gulf – you know what the conditions are like. Do we have a snowball's chance in hell of sinking a sub inshore?"

Prentice stabbed the desk blotter with the fingers that held his cigar. Ash scattered as each successive point was hammered home.

"This time we are ready," Prentice drummed. "And we have a good mix of well-trained and well-equipped ships, as you bloody well know. We have no ocean convoys in the Gulf to get in the way. The biggest problem is localizing the enemy, getting him into a small space where our weapons and sensors can pin him down. Coastal shipping," he added with a wave of his hand, "can help us: they're the honey and the bees will come to them. Every time the Germans slam a torpedo into a ship it resolves the location problem."

Belanger found the idea of localizing a U-boat by its attack unsettling, but he had to admit that the flaming datum was the only effective way of determining a U-boat's presence.

"Bit hard on the merchant seamen, Captain."

"We're at war Clive. It's a fair trade. Hell, the British will trade two large ocean-going ships for every U-boat they kill. The cost to us of a few small coastal vessels will be little indeed. No submariner wants to return home emptyhanded, and when they betray their presence by attacking, so much the better."

Prentice rose from his chair and moved to the window overlooking the harbour. "The changes we've made to the tactical doctrine of those ships down there – replacing 'safe and timely arrival' of the convoy with counterattacks on any sub that approaches – should have been made last year. If Jones and his gang of bungling incompetents hadn't been too cowardly to go after subs inshore last year, we would not be in the soup now.

"Christ, Belanger," he added more quietly, "the offensive against the U-boat has already started in the mid-Atlantic. You've seen the plot lately?"

"No."

"Go by and take a look. The northwest Atlantic is so full of U-boats you could walk on them from St. John's to Iceland. It's just a matter of time. The Brits have new support groups in action now, and the US will soon follow. We've anticipated those changes in the Canadian zone."

"The Gulf forces?"

"Partly. We've earmarked six corvettes with the latest 10cm radar for the Quebec force. They'll have to deal with U-boats on the surface in the River and off Anticosti."

"Sensible, since asdic conditions in the river are so dreadful."

"Quite. But they're better in the Gulf, and that's where the two groups of Bangors will operate."

"Two?"

"The long-range group will conduct regular patrols and respond to sightings. The short-range Bangor minesweepers of Gulf Support Force will be ready to assist as needed. We'll operate those out of

Gaspé, if possible."

"It's a good mix, Captain; the best radar in the corvettes where the asdic conditions are poor, and the best asdics on the minesweepers in the central Gulf."

"I think so. My new escort orders for all Halifax-based groups put the onus of the underwater search on the Bangors. Their type 127 asdics and gyro compasses make all the difference."

"I quite agree," Belanger said with a chuckle. "In 1941, in my first corvette, just dropping a few depth charges threw the magnetic compass out 140 degrees! 140 degrees! I didn't see the sun or a star for two days – didn't know where the hell I was."

"That was not an isolated incident, Clive, believe me, and the corvettes are little better off now. So the Bangors are my principal anti-submarine ships."

"And the motor launches?"

"We'll flood the Gulf with four flotillas. I've labelled them Gulf Strike Force," Prentice said with a wry grin. "It's mainly to ginger-up the crews, Clive. We have to do something with them and they do give us a greater presence."

"So, you really have a scheme for the Gulf, and the ships to carry through?"

"Yes, and thanks to you and your predecessor we have them trained and just about ready to go. The Bangors will be up to speed in about ten days. All we need now are the U-boats!"

"But if a U-boat submerges in the Gulf we aren't going to find it even with the Bangors. I mean, they can do what they did last year, put one sub off Father Point and another off, say, Gaspé and just wait for the targets to roll by them. When things heat up, they just dive into the river or the Gulf and we can't find them."

"You're right, Clive, finding them underwater is well nigh impossible. But the buggers still have to surface to breathe and to recharge their batteries. This year we have modern radar that can find them easily on the surface. We have enough ships to saturate a search area so the sub cannot surface easily. He can't stay down there forever! And that's where my other scheme comes in."

Prentice smiled impishly again. "We're going to try these new 'hunts to exhaustion,' as the Brits call them. Subs can only stay down twenty-five or thirty hours, thirty-six at most. We'll put a ship on the spot where he submerged and place others – especially the radar-equipped ones – at intervals from that datum."

"Based on the average submerged speed of a sub."

"Right, about two or three knots. That's why we need so many ships, to flood the area. And why we can't be tied down to escort duty. If we cover the probability area properly – either visually or with radar – we'll detect him when he comes up for air."

"And if he spots the ships and pops down again?"

"Gammon! He's now down on dead batteries. We'll just flood the new search area and start working out again. But with his cells exhausted he won't be able to go far or stay down long. When the U-boat's crew begin to drop from carbon-monoxide poisoning he'll surface. We'll just wait 'em out, and kill 'em when they're choking on their own breath."

"So closing the Gulf to shipping then makes total sense."

"Total sense. We don't have to coddle shipping and we get the flexibility to make the expanding searches work."

"But what if the subs don't come back?"

"The Germans will come back ... they have to. They do their homework," Prentice argued. "They know where they scored well last year with minimum risk. How could they resist the temptation to repeat their victory of 1942? Huh, tell me that? They closed the greatest artery of North America with absolutely no loss to themselves." He paused, then spoke more softly. "We've got to sink subs this year, Clive, and we will, you mark my words."

Belanger was still doubtful, sure that the Germans would soon sense that the Gulf was barren of ocean shipping. Then they would concentrate on the main trans-Atlantic convoys running between New York and the Grand Banks.

"And if they attack offshore, off Nova Scotia or in the Gulf of Maine?"

"Gammon again. The Halifax-based escort groups are already in good shape, I've been working on them since December. Shifted their tactical doctrine from simple escort duty to primarily U-boat killers already. Jones should have done that last year. Escorts off Nova Scotia never have to deal with more than one sub at a time – airpower keeps the Wolf Packs well out to sea. So those escort groups have been taught to attack any contact vigorously, for as long as it takes."

"Makes sense when you put it that way, Captain. And the asdic conditions are better."

"Much, particularly on Georges Bank and around Sable Island. The Bangors ought to be able get anything that submerges there."

"Gammon."

"Gammon!" Prentice repeated with a smile.

Belanger had to admit the Old Guy had worked out the technical problems. Deeper water without the mixing of a heavy flow of fresh water created favourable asdic conditions for hunting offshore, at least in summer.

Prentice watched Belanger's face as the younger man mulled over the pros and cons of the plan – and he could see the doubt written there.

"It is imperative, Clive, that we kill a U-boat inshore this summer. One kill in the Gulf is worth a half dozen off Sable Island!" It was only a slight exaggeration.

The two men had nearly finished their cigars when the Captain's secretary stuck his nose through the door.

"Yes Boothby, what is it?"

"Beg pardon, Cap'n. You have an appointment with Admiral Murray at 1100, and you might first wish to review the reports of proceedings from escort groups W.4 and W.10 – communications problems with the RCAF. Also your comments on the report from recent BX-XB convoys are ready and are in your basket for signature."

While Boothby spoke, Prentice crushed out the last of his cigar, signalling the end of the discussion. Belanger was on his feet.

"Right, thank you, Boothby. I shall want to talk more about assignments to the various Gulf Forces in the next few days, Clive, you might give that some thought."

"Certainly, Sir. Will that be all?"

"For now, yes ... Oh, there is one other thing. We shall lose our grip on the motor launches when Joe Heenan becomes Captain of Motor Launches later this month. Do what you can to get them in the best shape possible. Heenan's all right, I suppose, but he's likely to accept whining and complaining from his officers. We mustn't let the MLs lose their edge!"

The last point was delivered with a trace of a grin on Prentice's face. His opinion of Heenan was already well known to Belanger, but of greater concern was losing control of any portion of the fleet. Prentice was loath to have anyone else tinker with it – especially now that he was getting it into the condition he wanted. Belanger's assignment to whip the motor launches into shape was simply the final shot in a long, and ultimately unsuccessful, rearguard action against the establishment of a separate Captain of Motor Launches.

So it was with a smirk of collusion on his own face that Belanger departed with a simple, "As you wish, Sir."

By the time Belanger emerged onto the front steps of the headquarters the last traces of the parade had long vanished. The cool damp of the sea hung heavy over the dockyard, pushed down by the low, scudding cloud. At least the wind had eased and backed around to the southwest. Belanger fixed his collar against the cool air, and set off for jetty five.

Chapter 4

HMCS *Lakeville* lay amid a cluster of small vessels at jetty five, the corvette wharf. From the jetty the overall effect was a collage of earth tones: grimy whites, blue and green vertical surfaces smeared by rust, weathered canvas dodgers, greying rope and shoring timbers, soot stains, prematurely aged wooden coca-cola cases piled under the after gun tubs, and worn smoke-blackened ensigns shifting fitfully in the rising breeze. It was a bewildering muddle – clobber and baggage, clutter and chaos. Unless one counted masts or funnels it was not easy to tell just how many of these little warriors lay stacked alongside.

Yet order and system prevailed at jetty five. The corvettes farthest out belonged to the local Halifax-based Western Escort Force. They were numerous today because a convergence in the convoy cycle left few escorts at sea. Those closer to the wharf were undergoing training or en route to much needed refits. *Lakeville*, second from the wharf, had been refitted over the winter at Liverpool, Nova Scotia, where Belanger joined her in late March. She was now ready for sea but not yet assigned.

The primary objective of *Lakeville*'s crew was to get as far away from "Slackers" as possible. The city was crowded, expensive, and inhospitable to anyone in uniform. It was also home to the professional navy. The "Pusser Navy," with its penchant for British mannerisms and accents, big-ship ambitions, parade ground bullshit, and strict attention to naval hierarchy was a constant irritant to wartime volunteers – "hostilities only" men who joined up to beat the Nazis and then get on with life. This "Sheep Dog Navy", their status marked by wavy or braided rank stripes on their cuffs or "H.M.C.S." on their cap tally, wanted adventure. And that meant serving "over there", where the action was.

At the very least the crew of *Lakeville* hoped for assignment to Mid-Ocean Escort Force, based at St John's, Newfoundland. Those guys sailed the North Atlantic run, battling the Wolf Packs at sea and Allied sailors ashore in Britain. Better still, many thought, would be getting assigned to a British or Mediterranean-based escort force, farther from the RCN and closer still to the action. Anywhere but here, and the sooner the better. They all knew that *Lakeville* was hardly the cutting edge of the anti-submarine fleet and new ships were on the way. If they did not get away from Halifax soon they might be trapped there for the rest of the war.

Few of *Lakeville*'s crew lingered on deck in the cool morning air following the parade, but it wasn't the weather that drove them below. The broken, puffy clouds promised a glorious day. Nor would the threat of an occasional shower disrupt their lolly-gagging on deck. *Lakeville*'s chief boatswain's mate Petty Officer Howard Ryan, however, would. Ryan was the only man on the ship who was in the regular Navy, and had been for nearly twenty years.

Nothing hurt Ryan's sense of propriety more than idle seamen cluttering the deck. As "The Buffer" he was responsible for upper-deck maintenance and there was always work to be done. No one wished to try his patience. The safest course was to stay out of sight, even though there were ample men under punishment to form the working parties. After all, *Lakeville* had been in Halifax for five days. But it was also Saturday, and the afternoon routine of Make and Mend, a holdover from the days when sailors made their own clothes, meant free time and a run ashore – not the time to run afoul of Ryan.

Despite the risk, a small knot of seamen clustered on the port side of the welldeck, leaning or sitting on the foc'sle ladder, the bollard and the port bulwark. The welldeck trapped the warmth of the sun and provided shelter from a still fitful but rising breeze, well away from those painting *Lakeville*'s starboard side under Ryan's supervision. The men would, of course, have preferred to be where their idle commentary on the fate of those who got caught could have greatest effect. But it was tempting fate just to be on deck, so they were best off well away from those engaged in meaningful employment.

It was less than a half hour to Up Spirits, when the daily half-gill of black navy rum, "The Black Death," was issued, followed an hour later by Hands to Dinner. At 1315, the port watch was at liberty to go ashore. The short-term objective of those with leave passes was to ensure that nothing during the next couple of hours prejudiced that liberty. Their longer-term problem was what to do once they got ashore.

It required initiative and imagination to do more than take a quiet stroll or swill a bottle of bootleg booze behind a bush in the Public Gardens. Anything else usually involved standing in endless lines, being grossly overcharged, or ending up on charge. Somewhere between bored to death and dead drunk was a nice balance. But how to find it?

Such was the task that now confronted this wayward detachment of *Lakeville*'s port watch. Leading Seaman Stan Kozlowski was a farm lad from southern Alberta. Tall, fit and handsome, Kozlowski would have looked like Errol Flynn if the Navy allowed moustaches. "Full beards er nuthin'!" his petty officer had barked during basic training, "Shave that crap off yer face." Kozlowski was also a natural athlete, and like many thus gifted he thought rather well of himself. Those who knew him accepted the bullshit along with the brains and ability, even if deep down they didn't like his self-centred scheming.

"I say we crash the dance at the Knights o' Columbus Hall, most of you don't got no money anyway!" Koslowski was proposing. "'Sides, the food's good and the babes are, too ..." Kozlowski paused to draw on his cigarette and then continued, smoke streaming. "What else er we gonna do? Ever since that fire in St. John's last winter they don't let many into the dances, even here. So, we gotta crash it – in the back door. I dun it before."

Kozlowski's challenge was taken up by Sylvain Deschamps, the torpedoman, which on a corvette meant he handled depth charges. The only bonafide Quebecker on the ship, Deschamps was quickly dubbed Alphonse, and the nickname was just as quickly shortened to 'Phonse.

He was not as tall as Kozlowski, softer spoken and, if the truth be known, a much more successful lady's man than his Prairie shipmate.

"So, who's da band enaway?" 'Phonse asked idly. Kozlowski hesitated, reluctant to answer.

"Swirling Eddy and the Waves," he offered finally.

"Aw shit, Kos!" someone burst out, voicing the group's opinion of the band.

"I know, I know!" Kozlowski said defensively. "So anybody got a better idea, huh?"

"So, hows about we go to da Marcus Show den?"

"Jesus, 'Phonse! You crazy? We'd spend the whole Gawdamned day standing in line and probly still not get in." The others nodded, agreeing reluctantly with Kozlowski. The Marcus was the only strip show in town, but getting in required so much time and money that only the land sharks – of which there were plenty in Halifax – had any chance.

Terry Macpherson, another torpedoman, picked up the subject. "That rules out the Orpheus, too. The lines are so long for the flics we'd have to have survivor's leave to take in a show."

"That could be arranged!" Kozlowski flicked the butt of his cigarette past Macpherson's ear and over the side.

Speculation now turned to seamier prospects and descended into good-natured kidding over who had scored where with whom. Kozlowski was notorious for his luck with women, but no-one would suggest that his success derived from grace and good manners. What he didn't win by a direct assault he took by dogged siege work. Nothing fancy, nothing criminal, just determination to get laid. It helped that Kozlowski was always ready to alter the objective if the current siege looked like going into overtime or his leave was running short. Kozlowski's instincts ashore were ruled not by good taste but by "maintenance of the objective," a sound military maxim. As the night wore on, booze, dim light and growing abandon provided increasingly varied options.

Kozlowski's messmates could understand *his* success with women but 'Phonse mystified them. What Kozlowski won by main force and persistence typically fell into Deschamps' hands with little effort, for he too was seldom shut out in a run ashore. Somehow, 'Phonse seemed to let himself be 'coerced' into an act of kindness. Many of *Lakeville*'s crew simply put it down to his quiet French, but that didn't cut it in many east coast ports where Quebeckers and Acadians were a dime a dozen. Others ascribed it to 'Phonse's boyish good looks, like a waif that needed mothering. Those who had seen him in the shower knew that 'Phonse was not in the same league as Kozlowski, and speculation had it that not size but dexterity must be crucial. Indeed, the relative merits of size and dexterity was the subject of an ongoing debate in number one mess, a debate sustained by boredom and the strikingly attractive nude that graced the large calendar on the forward bulkhead.

Just as they concluded that Halifax offered no more to sailors on leave in May 1943 than it had earlier in the war, Kozlowski played his trump card.

"What about the Ajax Club?"

"The what?"

"The Ajax Club, that club for British and Allied seamen – you know, cheap booze, good food, nice place, nice girls, no lines. What more could we want?"

"You seem to be fergetting sumpthing, Kos," Macpherson shot back. "We ain't friggin' British nor 'Allied'. Canadians ain't allowed in and we're never gonna get in."

"Sure we will. Our uniforms is all the same as the Brits, right? You kin all fake some kind of Limey accent." And then he did so himself to everyone's embarrassment. "'Phonse kin keep his trap shut, at least until we're in and then he kin pretend he's Scottish!"

"Scottish!"

"Yeah, ain't you never heard of Old Admiral Scotty Brodeur, the Franco-pusser guy whose accent was so thick the Brits thought he must be from Scotland? It's true! No shit. I heard it from Ryan. 'Phonse kin just thicken it up a bit and Bingo! instead of being from Outrement he's from Orkney!"

'Phonse liked a scam as well as the rest, and was already beginning to work on his "Ach aye's", but he was not going to let Kozlowski win that easily. "I tink yer full of shit, Kos, ders nobudy whats gunna bleave I came from h'Orkney nor any udder place like dat, even if I jiss keeps my mout shut."

Macpherson pointed to the front of his cap. "What about this?" In peacetime or for those posted to larger warships, the ship's name was embroidered on the front of the cap ribbon, or tally. With so many small ships and the fleet expanding so quickly, most Canadian tallies bore the simple "H.M.C.S." of hostilities-only personnel. The cap tally – and the wearer's accent – was the only thing to distinguish a Canadian sailor from any other in the British Commonwealth.

"What're we gonna do?" Macpherson commented with a note of contempt in his voice, "stuff our caps up our sleeves!"

"Jeeze yer stupid Macpherson," Kozlowski snapped. "Once we get ashore, we'll change tallies to RN ones – like this." And he pulled an H.M.S. cap tally from his pocket. "Don't you guys have one?" Looks of bewilderment passed between them.

"Shit! How do you guys manage anyway? 'Phonse? Mac? Naw, you're too dumb anyway! Art? ... Suffering Jessus, how we gonna beat the Nazis if none of you can take the initiative?"

"So much fer de h'Ajax Club," 'Phonse commented dryly, and turned towards the mess. Kozlowski grabbed him by the arm.

"Naw, we ain't beat yet," said Kos. "Mac, you still got them nylons tucked away?" Macpherson simply looked absently at the deck. "Don't play dumb, the whole night depends now on yer answer. Do you got them nylons er not?"

"Yes! Yes I do!" Mac was a scrounger, that was his chief contribution to the small cabal, but he was reluctant to part with anything.

"Good," replied Kozlowski, "cause there's a coupla stokers in that old Brit four-stacker *Montgomery*," he pointed down to the clutch of destroyers in the lower dockyard, "who will trade anything fer nylons. They're good as gold in Ole Blighty ..."

At that moment the pipe for Up Spirits brought the whole debate to a crashing halt. Macpherson was to get the trade goods together, and the clandestine assault was to commence promptly when leave was piped at 1315.

As the group moved off to the seamen's mess Macpherson got some small revenge. "Don't forget Kos, you owe me Gulpers on today's tot ..."

Arch Maynard, *Lakeville*'s junior signalman, was usually part of the crowd that was planning the infiltration of the Ajax Club. He had recently been switched to the starboard watch and, worse still, had drawn duty as gangway sentry. Armed with an old Enfield and bayonet, Maynard patrolled the main deck near the galley where a few beaten fenders kept the corvettes separated, and where the open welldecks, lined up from wharf to outermost ship, formed an easy, continuous thoroughfare. Maynard, his back to the jetty, was absorbed by the animated discussion from Kozlowski and his gang when *Lakeville*'s executive officer, Lieutenant Campbell Fergus landed on the deck beside him.

"Maynard! How the hell are we gonna beat the Germans with the likes of you?" Fergus, a full head and shoulders taller, howled above the shaking sentry. "Do you have any idea what the charge is for neglect of such an important duty as gangway sentry?"

Maynard whirled around, gasping in fright. "Yes Sir!" he stammered, pulling himself upright. "Stoppage of grog, Sir."

"Bullshit Maynard!" Fergus retorted, shoving his face in so close that Maynard stopped breathing. "I could have you sent to cells! Get yourself sorted out!"

Fergus had no intention of doing more than issuing a reprimand on the spot, but Maynard was too frightened to notice the mock severity in Fergus' voice. In any event, the dressing-down was delivered largely for the benefit of the second figure who dropped to the deck.

"This is Ordinary Seaman Harkness, our new radar operator." Fergus jabbed a thumb over his right shoulder. "Take him to the quartermaster so he can get a place to stow his gear and sling his mick 'til we fit him into the watchbill." With that Fergus disappeared into the deckhouse.

"Well," Maynard offered rather sheepishly to Harkness, "welcome aboard *Lakeville*."

Harkness looked no older than himself, perhaps nineteen, and anxious. Maynard recalled that feeling. "Yer first ship?"

"Yup. I did training at sea, a few days at a time ... but nothing permanent. Is Lieutenant Fergus always like that?" he asked cautiously.

"Oh, Mr Fergus is okay," Maynard said quickly. "He was right, anyhow."

"What's she like, *Lakeville* I mean?"

"Fine I guess. The usual collection of oddballs and misfits. The CO's okay as long as you carry your weight. He's an older guy, thirty-two about. The petty officers are typical, not bad. And the messdeck, well, you'll get used to it. We all do."

Harkness, not much reassured by this, murmured, "I s'pose."

Maynard was about to abandon his post and lead Harkness forward into the seamen's mess when Petty Officer Ryan came along. "Hello Maynard, what have we here? Another strong back and idle mind committed to freeing the world from fascism?"

"OD Harkness, Chief, the new radar operator," Maynard muttered.

"Well, welcome aboard Harkness," Ryan said, extending his hand. Harkness, unsure of what to make of this gesture of humanity, pumped Ryan's arm with nervous enthusiasm. "Your first corvette, Harkness?" Ryan asked with genuine interest.

"Yes Chief, my first ship, actually."

"You'll love it. Finest seaboats in the world. They'll ride through anything Poseidon can throw their way! And, Harkness," said Ryan with a twinkle in his eye, "She'll roll on wet grass, so I hope you have a strong stomach! Grab your kit and follow me, we'll find the Killick of the seamen's mess."

Ryan crossed the welldeck, shot in under the foc'sle overhang, and disappeared through the watertight door leading to the seamen's mess. Harkness nodded to Maynard, grabbed his kitbag and hammock, and followed.

Being the lowest form of naval life and encumbered by kit Harkness had to force his way through the men queuing up for grog. As he did so Ryan arrived with Kozlowski in tow. "The Killick's ashore, Kozlowski will show you where to stow yer kit for now. And Kozlowski, this young lad has never been on a corvette before. Give him a quick tour – now!"

Kozlowski answered with mock enthusiasm, "Aye, Chief," as Ryan disappeared out the messdeck door.

"Well, Harkness, this is home." Kozlowski sighed as he swept one arm toward the crowded mess. "Designed for twenty men. Fifty live here now. Throw yer kit on top of the locker and we'll take the five cent tour ... No! Not there, that's Aldridge's space. If he finds yer kit there you'll have to dive for it. Over there ... good, let's go on deck."

The two men stepped through the door and into the sun of the welldeck. "This here," Kozlowski began, "is what's called a Flower Class corvette 'cause all the Royal Navy ones got flower names, like Sweetpea er whatever. *Lakeville*'s about a thousand ton, two hundred feet long, and based – so they claim – on a whaler. I guess they figured if a ship could catch whales it could catch subs. This one hasn't but she's seen a lot of action."

Kozlowski pulled out a package of cigarettes and offered one to Harkness, who declined.

"You'll git yer belly full of the sea in this barge. She rolls her guts out even on the calmest day. I seen solid waves come down into this well from over the foc'sle there," Kozlowski pointed up and forward, where the main gun was mounted, a gleam of mischief in his eye. "Yes, I believe Harkness, you will have ample opportunity to spew yer guts out on *Lakeville*!

"But, she can go like stink, too. And when she does the seamen's mess there rises and falls as much as fifty feet! Jis like bein' on a elevator, only faster. Let's take a walk." Kozlowski set off down the starboard side of the ship.

They both paused to look up the mast, then Harkness muttered "I trained on that radar up there, the SW2C and learned how to repair it."

"Well, if you know how to repair it you've got a full time job here. That crap's always on the blink, and useless anyway."

"Not always," Harkness offered in defence of the old set.

Kozlowski really did not want a lecture on the merits of the one-and-half-metre-wavelength set. From his perspective it was fickle and a waste of effort.

Immediately aft of the main deckhouse a short ladder led up to a door a few feet above the main deck. Kozlowski mounted the ladder and motioned for Harkness to follow. "The most important part of the ship," he announced with ceremony. "The galley! Perched up here just above number one boiler." Kozlowski opened the door and the warm smell of fresh bread and boiling vegetables assaulted them. So did the cook. "Get out Kozlowski, you thieving bastard! Get out! You'll get your share when dinner's piped!" Kozlowski snapped the door shut. "The cook's our greatest danger, at sea or alongside. Rumour has it he's a Nazi."

"This here space," Kozlowski continued as they sauntered down the deck, "from here down to the end is all machinery. Wide open from the keel to the engineroom skylight. We get fished in there and the cold sea rushes in, boilers blow up and we sink like a friggin' stone.

"And these," Kozlowski paused to slap a hand on a depth charge resting on one of its throwers, "these here is *Lakeville*'s main weapon, 350 pounds of torpex and we carry a hundred of 'em – enough explosive on this ship to re-arrange most of the dockyard. There's two throwers on either side and," he walked aft to the quarterdeck, "there's two rails here that run to chutes in the stern.

"There's two kinds of men on this ship with missin' or crushed fingers." He held up one hand with two fingers bent back imitating a maimed hand. "Greasers, 'cause they gotta stick their hands into the engine to check fer hot bearings, and depth charge crews, 'cause they get 'em crushed by the charges. When you meet Macpherson you'll see what I mean. If you get yer finger caught in them rails aft, the charge'll take yer finger right off. I seen it done."

Kozlowski nudged Harkness with his elbow and led the way up a ladder to the top of the engineroom casing. "This here's the after gun tub," he grunted, "and the ship's twenty-inch searchlight there just behind it."

"Those are just machine guns," Harkness said in surprise. "I thought corvettes were supposed to have something bigger back here."

Kozlowski laughed. "Some corvettes got oerlikons, some a two-pounder. The Canadian Navy makes do with two twin fifties back here. Lots of lead flying!"

"That's good, isn't it?"

"Good fer nothin'! Oh, you can kill people with them, if you can get close enough; but these bullets just bounce off a submarine. No, apart from depth charges – which is the real weapons of this ship – the only gun worth mentionin's on the foc'sle. C'mon I'll show ya." With that Kozlowski set off along the engineroom casing, past the funnel and the tuba-like ventilators, and up onto the bridge.

"This here's the place for you, Harkness – the new radar hut. See!" He pointed to a little box-like structure on the after end of the bridge with what looked like a lighthouse lantern on the top.

"Yes, the type 271, 10cm radar set. Looks new."

"Yup, jis built this past refit. Go ahead take a look."

Harkness turned the dog on the door and peeked inside.

"Just like the one I trained on."

"Ain't that grand. This here's all the signalman's shit, halyards, flag locker, stock box for signal lamps, and they got signal lamps on either bridge wing."

Kozlowski shot around the corner of the charthouse, past the machine gun mounting on the starboard side to the forward railing. From there they could see the foc'sle deck.

"There it is, my son, the weapon that has the whole damn U-boat fleet quaking in its boots – the four-inch Mark Nine breech-loading gun."

"I guess this, too, is pretty useless?" Harkness asked tentatively, catching the mood of his tour guide.

"Absolutely," Kozlowski replied with confidence. "This here weapon was designed before the Great War and discarded from some old battleship 'cause it couldn't hit shit. According to the gunner's mate – never a reliable source, Harkness, remember that, all gunners is just bullshit and gaiters – this gun'll throw a thirty-two-pound shot 12,000 yards if the wind's right and the sea's calm. Near as we can figure, the Canadian Navy uses it to scare U-boats into diving so we asdic operators can nail 'em with depth charges."

Kozlowski pointed down. "The welldeck you already know. Seamen's mess is just forward, under the overhang. In any kind of a sea this welldeck is awash. Almost anything that's shipped onto the foc'sle deck there runs aft and pours down in there like Niagara Bloody Falls. In rough weather it's impossible to get yer food forward from the galley without gettin' half the Atlantic in it! Fuckin' stupid."

"So where does everyone else mess?"

"Mostly forward. There's two messes on the lower deck, under the welldeck, plus the wardroom for the officers. Gotta use companionways to get down to 'em all. If you ask me, all them lower messdecks is death-traps. If her bow goes under and water pours in, ain't no way anybody's ever gonna get out."

"Aren't the lower messdecks connected?" Harkness asked with some trepidation.

Kozlowski looked at Harkness with mock severity, "Great sufferin' Jesus boy! Not on yer life! You don't expect the Navy wants officers and POs hobnobbing with ratings? No siree. Each of them lower deck messes is sealed from the other. Let's get outta here."

As they walked along the side of the charthouse Harkness could not resist a long look inside. Kozlowski stopped to explain. "That's the asdic equipment over there on the port side, and a plotting table here in the corner. Them voicepipes, like the ones along the forward railing, lead down to the wheelhouse, wireless room, captain's cabin and all that. We'll have a look in the wheelhouse on the way down, and then hustle forward. Cook will soon be serving grub."

After turning Harkness over to the startled Maynard, Lieutenant Fergus stomped through the deckhouse lobby to the companionway. He took the top three steps on the ladder with his feet, slid one hand under the coaming to find the handgrip, then swung himself down lightly to the wardroom lobby. His furious muttering was audible long before he appeared below.

"Never in all my fucking days have I been so deeply pissed off with some fucking son of a bitch ... If he thinks for a fucking minute that he's done with me he's suffering from the deepest possible fucking delusions ... Where, in the name of Jesus, does that stunned bastard think he can fucking get off with ...."

This was ignored by Lieutenant Bert Samuels, the duty officer, who was quietly pouring a cup of tea in the wardroom. Samuels knew Fergus well enough to take avoiding action when the XO entered the room with all guns blazing. Fergus always blew off steam that way, and he was still at it when he landed heavily on his back on the wardroom settee.

"Tea?" Samuels offered softly.

Fergus broke his cursing just long enough to bark, "Two sugars" then carried on, although the stream of oaths soon resolved itself into mumbling.

Samuels handed the cup to his executive officer. "Bad day at the office, dear?"

"Shove off, Sam. Don't you have rounds to do or something? Thanks for the tea."

"I just had a go 'round. Ryan's PO of the watch. He handles things far better than I do. Besides, he knows where to find me. I take it the meeting with our fearless and intrepid asdic training staff did not go all that well?"

"What a bunch of stuffed shirts. If those bastards were any good at killing krauts they'd be at sea. We got our target every time during our ASPs, that sub was dead over and over again, and all that son of a bitch running the asdic simulator could say was, 'Fergus, you still do not have the measure of your enemy' – the measure of our enemy! – Jesus, what the fuck does he know? If that turd was such a crackerjack U-boat killer he'd be doing it, not pissing around on the beach."

"So, have we killed a sub lately?" Samuels chided.

"Go ta hell!"

Samuels was a very good listener, but he'd heard it all before. Fergus was a first class anti-submarine officer, and he knew it. He and Kozlowski could get more out of a type 123A asdic set than anyone Samuels knew. They could even find submarines with it. Fergus and Kozlowski were something of a matched pair. Both acted as much on instinct as on formal training. Most of the problems Fergus had with training staffs had to do with form – he seldom followed the manual, but he got results. He had joined the Navy to fight Germans. Procedures were usually slow and cumbersome, and mastering the technical niceties of anti-submarine warfare, if they did not promise immediate results, simply got in the way. Fergus knew instinctively what his target was going to do, and much of his success – and that of Kozlowski – lay in anticipation and on intelligent guesswork based on scanty information. It worked. When training commanders chastised him for not following proper procedure Fergus could not see their point.

Samuels had only to act as a willing ear until the storm blew over, which it did, in short order.

"Is there anything to eat?" Fergus asked after a short pause. He ate continuously, as befit his age.

"Cook left some of this cornmeal bread," Samuels offered, pointing to the pan sitting on the sideboard, "But I guess that's it until dinner."

Fergus declined. "Where's Uncle?" It had taken only hours for Belanger, at least ten years older than his officers and at thirty-two an old man by their standards, to be dubbed Uncle. Belanger accepted it as a term of endearment, but not in front of the men.

"He's off to see Captain (D). Didn't say why, but I suspect he's trying to get us assigned to the North Atlantic run. We're about due for allocation to some operational role."

"If we don't get to sea somewhere, soon, we'll have the whole Godforsaken ship on charge. D'you see that gang Ryan has working topside?"

"Yup. Ryan says if the weather holds he'll have the starboard side finished by 1500. Apart from fuel, a few stores and some ammunition, we're about ready to go. When do we go to four hours' notice for steam?"

Fergus threw back the last of his tea, wiped his mouth with the back of his hand and slowly sat fully upright. A long sigh ended with "Ah ... day after tomorrow," which he repeated more softly. "Day after tomorrow."

Samuels asked the only question that mattered. "Where?"

"I dunno, Old Man. I really dunno."

"Nothing on the grapevine?"

"Nothing – not a sausage."

"Shit," Samuels muttered quietly, "I hope we get outta here."

Fergus rose and headed for the door, placing his hand gently on Samuels' shoulder as he passed. "Me too!"

Chapter 5

Captain Horace Arbuthnot Beechum-Walney, RN, DSO, DSC and Bar, paused to allow traffic to pass, and then smartly crossed Elgin Street thinking how all-Canadian Ottawa looked. The heavily wooded Gatineau hills crowded the city from the north; a plume of sulphurous smoke billowed from the paper plant across the river from the Parliament buildings; and now this – the newly completed Naval Service Headquarters.

The new Pentagon in Washington was steel and poured concrete, a symbol of the American imperium. The Royal Canadian Navy's new building was quintessentially Canadian: war-built, wood-framed, with white clapboard siding and a distinctly temporary flavour.

Although he missed the cherry blossoms it was delightful to be out of Washington. The weather in Ottawa was cool and fresh. The northwest wind was ripping great holes in the heavy overcast and the air had a just-washed feeling. It all conspired to put a bounce into Beechum-Walney's gait.

At the main entrance he exchanged salutes with the sentry who glanced at his military ID and introduced his escort. Then he began the circuitout passage through the warren that led to the chief of naval staff's office. Even Walney's soft tread echoed through wooden corridors bright with sunlight from offices on either side. The building smelled of freshly laid linoleum and curing paint. People brushed by him with an air of quiet efficiency.

At the CNS's outer office the captain was passed from the care of his escort to that of the Chief's personal secretary. "The Admiral won't be a moment, Sir. Would you care for some tea?"

"Thank you, no." Before Walney could settle on the settee the inner door opened and an officer in shirtsleeves, heavily laden with files, hurried out. Hot on his heels – sleeves rolled up, glasses on the end of his nose and a sheaf of paper in his hands – came Vice Admiral Nelles.

Like all permanent RCN officers Percy Nelles had done virtually all his training, and most of his seatime, in the Royal Navy. It was while serving time in British ships that Nelles and Beechum-Walney came to know each other. In 1930, as commanders, they had served together in the cruiser *Dragon* during its tour of South America. When *Dragon*'s captain suddenly took ill Nelles was promoted to acting captain and assumed command for the remainder of the three-month cruise.

Thinking of those days Beechum-Walney reflected on the old naval toast, "A bloody war and a sickly season," the two ways to early promotion on a foreign station. Then he would add, "Or join one of the colonial navies!" where promotion came faster, and with less hassle. Nelles made full captain in 1933 and a year later was confirmed as the new Chief of the Naval Staff of the RCN. While Beechum-Walney laboured on as a senior commander, Nelles shot up the seniority list. By the late 1930s Percy Walker Nelles, all five-feet-six, one hundred fifty pounds of him, was the youngest Rear Admiral in the Empire. Beechum-Walney could only wonder at Nelles' good fortune.

The man Walney saw now looked worn and haggard. Nelles had always had the long, tired-looking bespectacled face of a senior clerk. Indeed, Walney always imagined Nelles cast as Bob Cratchit, an apt image since dealing with the Admiralty was much like dealing with Scrooge. The only thing about Nelles that betrayed his profession was the anchor tattooed on his left forearm.

Four long years of war had taken its toll on Nelles. The stress, word had it, had led to a collapse of health in mid-1942 and hospitalization. Hypertension and a spastic colon was the diagnosis, caused by the strain of managing the Navy's war effort. Flying frequently did not help, as Nelles had a nervous stomach and loathed airplanes. The four days in hospital in September 1942 had worked wonders and Nelles now took time to relax, eased up on the cigarettes, and abandoned his three shots of whisky every night, at 1800, 2100 and 2300.

But there was no cure for the crushing burden of building a navy in wartime. Beechum-Walney could see the sheaf of paper shake as Nelles passed it to the secretary. According to the gossip the trembling in Nelles' hands had returned this past spring. Both of Nelles' parents had died at sixty-two, and few would have given the fifty-one-year-old Percy that long.

"Beech! How wonderful to see you, it's been far too long! Do come in."

The two men were a study in contrast. Beechum-Walney was a tall, gaunt figure, with chiselled features, hawk nose and deeply sunken eyes. His emaciated look derived both from genetics and a habit of eating sparingly. Rather bookish and more widely read than was customary for a naval officer, Beechum-Walney claimed Norman Beauchamps ancestry, a claim well supported by his gallic nose, but the Walneys had been impoverished rural gentry for generations – the austere lifestyle came naturally.

Beechum-Walney had also been broken by hard years of war service, virtually all in the Mediterranean, first as captain of a destroyer, and then as captain of his own flotilla: Crete, Matapan, Gulf of Sirte, Malta convoys, Syrian campaign. By 1942 he was on the Admiral's staff at Alexandria, and then in early 1943 he was posted to the British Admiralty Delegation in Washington. Now prone to drinking before noon, he retained a ready smile and a quiet, elegant charm that masked a sharp-tempered, hard-driving destroyer captain, consummate sailor, and superb tactician.

"Thank you for seeing me at such short notice, Admiral. I very much appreciate it," Beechum-Walney said as he settled into a chair.

"Not at all, I am delighted – and please, Percy will be fine," Nelles said. "Haven't seen you since *Dragon*, I believe. Ten years at least – too long."

"Almost thirteen years! Thank you ... Percy. It is grand to renew an old friendship."

Old friends yes, but after long and active careers Beechum-Walney and Nelles had little in common.

"I must say," Beechum-Walney offered as a way to break the ice, "you have done awfully well since last we met. Not just you, but your navy. It is a remarkable accomplishment. Remember the kidding about the "Two Ocean Navy", eh what? Two destroyers on the Atlantic, and two on the Pacific coast! My Lord, but you have done a splendid job."

"It's very kind of you to say so, Beech. We now have 60,000 personnel and nearly 200 warships, from the Aleutians to the Mediterranean, and from the Arctic to the Caribbean. We presently contribute fifty percent of the escorts on the main trans-Atlantic routes ...."

"Yes," Beechum-Walney interjected, "I am well briefed by my American colleagues, and I must say they are very impressed. Your new Canadian Northwest Atlantic has made a bit of a splash in Washington." With a large and impish grin, he added, "They seem to think you feel the United States Navy is the enemy, rather than the Germans!"

"A slight exaggeration – but just," said Nelles, offering a cigarette to Beechum-Walney, who declined. Nelles tapped the end of his cigarette automatically on the desk, lit it and then went on.

"By last year there were nine separate commands on our east coast – nine – all tripping over one another. Something had to be done. Since virtually all of the US navy had either gone south or to the Pacific, it was logical that we should command whatever came out of the rationalization. Besides," he said, blowing a cloud of smoke to his right, away from his guest, "it was silly having a foreign admiral command almost the entire Canadian navy within sight of our own coast. They had to be pushed out, Beech."

All agreed that the command arrangements in the northwest Atlantic in 1942 had been a shambles, but in 1943 London and Washington were asking whether it would be any better under the Canadians. Beechum-Walney's next question therefore was natural. "Murray has things in hand, does he?"

Nelles was a bit annoyed, not least because he had heard it asked so often. His answer, given amid a cloud of smoke exhaled from mouth and nose was a sour, "Where do you think the Americans learned the job?"

Beechum-Walney was taken aback by Nelles' tone. "Quite right, Percy," he said hastily, "It's true that you carried the US navy through its introduction to war for the first half year or so. Quite right."

"But things are going well at present, are they not?" Beechum-Walney continued. "I understand that RCN ships have sunk a few U-boats of late. Surely that's good news to add to the establishment of the new Canadian zone?"

"Yes, one could say we are on the mend, after a rough year in '42. Murray's new command is a start. We've brought most of the fleet home from North Africa and the Caribbean, so there's some fat available to modernize the fleet this year. It is all a painfully slow business, and a couple of submarines sunk in the Mediterranean do not cut much ice here in Ottawa. We need success closer to home, especially after last summer."

"The closure of the Gulf again this summer was reported in the Washington papers. But, if I may come to the purpose of my visit, I think I can help."

Nelles had assumed that Beechum-Walney was there on technical business – fittings for British frigates under construction in Canada, radar issues, and the like – and was taken aback by the offer of help with the inshore U-boat problem. For a moment he did not know what to say, while his guest waited, uneasily shifting in his chair.

"Please tell me if you have a solution for us!"

"Admiral ... Percy, I have been asked by the Admiralty to convey to you some classified information which, if acted upon with skill and daring, will almost certainly lead to the destruction of a submarine in the Gulf of St. Lawrence this spring."

"I see," Nelles said cautiously. What the hell was he getting at?

Beechum-Walney said guardedly, "Please forgive my formality, but I must begin by reminding you that the information I have to convey is of a most confidential nature, secured at great risk by operatives. Should knowledge of it fall into the wrong hands, those who obtained it will be in mortal danger."

"Beech, you can be assured that whatever you say to me will be held in the strictest confidence, and that goes as well for my director of naval intelligence. I am sure we can fashion a cover both for the nature of the information and the sources."

"Quite," Beechum-Walney replied. "I assure you that was never in doubt. There are any number of ways to fudge a submarine sighting. However, you will understand my anxiety over this intelligence when you have the full picture."

There was a brief pause – a ceremonial drawing of breath – during which Beechum-Walney placed his cap and gloves on the corner of Nelles' desk.

"Are you familiar with a French group known as the Cagoule?"

Nelles drew pensively on his cigarette before muttering softly, "French ultra-right group, pro-fascist, anti-semitic, anti-democratic. They attempted a coup d'etat in France before the war ..."

"Yes, two coup attempts actually, 1934 and 1937."

"Right, I'd forgotten the earlier one. As I recall this Cagoule was just a bunch of thugs, really, a large para-military organization, sworn to secrecy on pain of death. Cloak and dagger, death or glory kind of business. All told, a rather nasty crowd."

"Thoroughly nasty," Beechum-Walney grunted, "but more than just thugs I am afraid."

"What happened to them after 1937?"

"Most went into exile in pro-fascist states – Spain, Italy, Germany – and to parts of the French Empire, especially north Africa and Syria. Some, I understand," he said after a short pause, "came to Canada as well."

"Wouldn't surprise me," Nelles observed. "We have certainly had our own problems with pro-fascist movements."

"Since the German victory of 1940 the Cagoulards have slipped back into France and heavily infiltrated the Vichy government."

"They were active in Pétain's régime?"

"Intensely. We believe, also, that they have been very active in Canada as well since 1940."

Beechum-Walney looked for a reaction but Nelles' face remained unmoved. Did he know? he wondered.

"Please go on, Beech."

"Yes. Canada's large French population is a very conservative one. As you know they have never enjoyed warm relations with the French left – or any left for that matter. One need only read some of L'Abbe

Groulx's work to know that."

Beechum-Walney hoped that Nelles would not press this last point, as he knew little or nothing of the politics of French Canada apart from what the Secret Operations Executive rep in Washington had told him.

"And, of course, those elements in French Canada share the Nazis' and fascists' intense disdain for the Jews ..."

Nelles interrupted. "Anti-semitism is not confined to French Canada. We in English Canada turned our backs on Jewish refugees before the war – sent them packing."

"Quite right, Percy. I suggest only that the pro-fascist element in French Canada is particularly strong. Moreover, it has been fuelled by the actions of your own government, in maintaining diplomatic relations with Vichy-France until that régime collapsed last November."

"No doubt."

"And as part of that arrangement the Canadian government allowed agents of an avowedly pro-Nazi state to move freely in your country and to distribute pro-fascist and anti-war propaganda. Am I not right?"

"What's your point, Beech?"

"Simply this: it's a fair bet that Cagoule operatives are now present here. At the very least pro-Vichy propaganda has circulated widely in Canada. And even though you have jailed the mayor of Montreal ..."

"Yes, Camille Houde."

"Even though you have jailed Houde and others like Arcand, there is little doubt that strong pro-fascist elements remain at large. And that, as a result, French Canada remains decidedly against the war effort."

"'Decidedly' is a bit strong," Nelles offered. "But there has been considerable unrest in Quebec over the war effort. Last year's referendum on conscription for overseas service revealed the fundamental differences in attitudes. Seventy-five percent of English Canada voted to absolve Mr. King of his 1939 pledge not to introduce conscription. Seventy-five percent of Quebecers voted against. English Canada wants to do more in the war, French Canada is content with less. It is a cruel dilemma."

None of this was news to Beechum-Walney, but he sought to draw Nelles. "The U-boat attacks in the Gulf of St. Lawrence last summer heightened those tensions?"

"That's putting it mildly," Nelles responded. "All hell broke loose in the Commons. We were over-committed and could do nothing to stop the attacks. Full marks to the government though, they accepted our recommendation to close the River and Gulf and took the heat for it."

"So the decision to do it again this year is very bold and, I dare say, politically dangerous."

"Dynamite. With the war now going well for the Allies it's not clear how long the government can withstand the impatience of English Canada to get in the fight – or Quebec howls over the closure."

"And the trick for Canada is how to fight the Germans without increasing the risk of battles in its own streets, am I right?"

"In a nutshell, yes. It's not as bad as 1917, but the government is soft-pedaling the issues and pushing for more active involvement ... The notion that enemy operatives may well be undoing our war effort is, however, alarming." Nelles looked Beechum-Walney straight in the eye. "Are you suggesting that a fifth column of pro-fascists is actually operating here? Do you have information that Canadiens have been assisting U-boats in the Gulf?"

"Goodness no, nothing like that!" Beechum-Walney answered with discernible haste. "However, we do believe that the Cagoule, your current domestic political problems, and submarines are connected. You see, we believe that Vichy France – actually an organization called the Service d'Ordre Legionnaire ..."

"The Foreign Legion?"

"No, no! The SOL is a Vichy equivalent of the Nazis SS – same purulent ideals of racial purity, master race, and all that nonsense. No," Beechum-Walney continued, "the SOL and the Cagoule have been busy since the collapse of the Vichy regime last fall in laying the groundwork for even closer collaboration between the French right and the Nazis. For the SOL, the Cagoule and other French fascists the war has entered a desperate phase.

"You see," Beechum-Walney went on, "the French right have invested heavily in a German victory. They have built, retooled and committed existing French industry to the German war machine: trucks, airframe parts, even portions of submarines. As well, of course, coal, steel and other essentials pour from France into Nazi hands. Those industries stand to lose a fortune if the Allies win."

Nelles rose from his chair and stood, gazing absent-mindedly out his office window. His mind was racing. Beechum-Walney was right, but he knew much more than a technical liaison officer ought to. Just where was he going with all this, and how did subs come into the picture? "So where does Canada fit into all this?"

"Well, we believe that French fascists have conspired to infiltrate an *agent provocateur* into Canada by submarine, someone who will take up where the Vichy diplomats left off. Someone who will continue to fuel anti-democratic and anti-war sentiment in French Canada. Apart from fostering instability and disrupting the Canadian and perhaps American war efforts their specific purpose is rather unclear. Most likely they simply want to work quietly within the pro-fascist elements to unsettle Canada's war effort. It is also possible that they intend to foment civil war."

This last was the spectre that had walked the corridors of power in Ottawa since 1917. Borden's Union government had attempted to introduce universal conscription for war service. There had been rioting in Quebec and the militia from Ontario was sent in. The rioters were put down by cavalry charges. Quebec city was in a virtual state of siege, with barricaded and sandbagged public buildings, machine guns on rooftops, armed guards with fixed bayonets. Such images were on the minds of every member of Mr. King's government, as they worked to get maximum war effort without Canada ripping itself apart.

The scene raced through Nelles' thoughts as he stared blankly out the window, forgetting for a moment that someone else was in the room.

"You must admit, Percy," Beechum-Walney continued after an uneasy pause, "that the fabric of your nation is under considerable strain. The Bloc Populaire is yapping at the government over its handling of the war. If the pro-fascist or anti-war movement gains further momentum it will be hard for Mr. King's government to sustain its war effort, let alone assure domestic peace."

He let that sink in and then added, "You may recall that the Germans took Russia out of the Great War by putting Lenin on a train to St. Petersburg – something of a lethal injection. If a Cagoulard or

SOL operative can mobilize anti-war sentiment here, it may well have the same result."

Nelles was silent, assessing the problem. It was obvious that Beechum-Walney and his counterparts wanted him to intercept this infiltrator, perhaps kill him. But why? Why didn't they simply act on the information themselves?

Beechum-Walney, unable to read Nelles' silence, nevertheless risked his next step.

"You know, Percy, it is also possible that the agent is being sent here to do something quite dramatic. One single, destructive act to sabotage Canada's war effort."

"What on earth could that be," Nelles wondered out loud, a look of total bewilderment on his face. "There is no single target – no factory, no bridge, no laboratory, no rail line – so vital that one man, or even a group of desperate men, could destroy to bring the war effort to a stop."

"I was not thinking of an attack on a target," Beechum-Walney said quietly. "No, I was thinking of a person, the lynch-pin of your government's frail national consensus – the deputy Prime Minister, Mr. Louis St. Laurent."

The idea of a foreign agent assassinating a senior politician had never occurred to Nelles. Indeed, it was preposterous. Yet, an attack on St. Laurent, Mr. King's Quebec lieutenant, would critically weaken the government's position in French Canada. Coupled with other developments, it might prove catastrophic. Certainly, the assasination of Mr. St. Laurent would be a far greater consequence than that of Mr. King.

"Are you certain of this?" Nelles demanded.

"No, of course not! Look, Percy, we have no knowledge whatsoever of the intent of this mission. I was merely offering a number of possibilities. Please don't misunderstand. We simply do not know."

"Mr. King has already lost one Quebec lieutenant, in 1941." Nelles said almost absent-mindedly as he began to pace. "Lapointe held the Quebec caucus of the Liberal party in the government – did so for two decades. King was fortunate to lure St. Laurent in as his replacement, you know," he said, shooting a glance at his British visitor. "St. Laurent holds Lapointe's old riding of Quebec East, and his portfolio as justice minister. More important, Beech, St. Laurent is deeply respected and trusted within Quebec – he's the only Quebecker of any stature in King's government."

"So I am given to understand. But Percy, I must remind you, we do not know what the purpose of this clandestine mission is.

"However, we are reasonably certain of who the infiltrator is, a certain Monsieur Lemaige-Bonnier."

"And what do we know of Monsieur Bonnier?"

"Quite a bit, as it turns out." Beechum-Walney relaxed slightly. He had achieved his purpose, he felt. Nelles was suitably alarmed. He reached for the cigarette case on Nelles' desk. "D'you mind?"

"Not at all, help yourself," Nelles said. Surely this was all preposterous. Would the Vichy French go to such lengths to secure Canada's downfall? He half listened as Beechum-Walney droned on.

"Bonnier was a small businessman and local politician in Provence, before moving to Paris in the late 'twenties. We don't know when he joined the Cagoule. However, we do know that he participated in the 1937 coup attempt, perhaps the one in 1934 as well. In any event, he fled to Syria in early 1938. In 1940, after Reynaud's government resigned and Pétain capitulated to the Germans, Bonnier helped to found the local SOL in Damascus, fought against us when we invaded Syria in 1941."

Beechum-Walney held back many critical details, including the knowledge that Bonnier was implicated – very deeply indeed – in the alleged murder of Australian prisoners by the SOL following the brief Vichy French counterattack along the Litany River in late June 1941.

"Bonnier managed to get out of Syria and ended up in Algeria. We suspect he was involved in the murder of Admiral Darlan last December, just as he was about to deliver French North Africa into the Allied camp. His whereabouts since last December are not precisely known."

Nelles lit yet another cigarette. This was heady stuff. If Beechum-Walney was right, the threat to Canada was real and the returns for so small an act were potentially great. After all, had the Naval Minister, Mr. Macdonald, not repeated ad nauseam that Canada held the fate of the western world in its hands? Nelles didn't believe him for a moment – the Americans played that role – but underlying Macdonald's assertion was the bitter national debate over Canada's role in the war.

While the politics of the moment raced through his brain, a more immediate concern gradually surfaced. If the fate of the nation, even without the elimination of Mr. St. Laurent, remained in doubt, the same could not be said of his own. Macdonald had made that perfectly clear. Maybe politicians could never accept that the unsuccessful campaign in the Gulf in 1942 just had to be endured. Nor would they accept that Canada, and the RCN, had done the right things strategically. Yes, ships were sunk in the St. Lawrence River, and men had died as Canadians watched from the shore. But there was a war on! The Navy had kept the main convoys moving, and the tide had turned against the Axis in the Pacific, in North Africa, and in the Atlantic, too, because of that sacrifice.

Nelles had never doubted the wisdom of the Navy's actions until his tiff with the Minister last week. Now, try as he might he couldn't concentrate on the up-side of 1942. Maybe the Navy had been too committed offshore. Maybe it ought to have done more in the Gulf. But what? Why couldn't politicians understand that once the subs submerged in the River and Gulf they simply could not be found. Until the fleet got new asdic equipment U-boats would always be safe in the St. Lawrence when they submerged. God! Even if they had had good asdic in 1942 the fleet's radar was too primitive to detect U-boats on the surface.

And even geography conspired against them. All the convoys had to run along predictable – and easily intercepted – routes. Until the fleet was consolidated, refitted and re-equipped it could neither defend shipping in the Gulf nor sink U-boats. How many times did he have to tell Macdonald that? Now, here was the chance to redeem the disaster of 1942. If this sub could be found, it and its dangerous passenger destroyed ...

"This is really astonishing news, Beech. I am deeply grateful. I presume you have some more precise information on the U-boat's itinerary. What can you tell me of the actual plans to land the agent?"

"We know quite a lot, actually – but I daren't say how we came by the information. Suffice it to say we believe it to be extremely reliable. I would not be here otherwise ..."

Nelles, his suspicions aroused by these comments, could not resist interrupting. "So why not intercept the U-boat yourself?"

"Quite ...." The abruptness of the question took Beechum-Walney by surprise. "Good question. You understand, of course, that finding a single sub in the vastness of the North Atlantic is virtually impossible." Nelles nodded. "Frankly, I also suspect that the Admiralty is loath to divert warships from the new offensive against the Wolf Packs in mid-ocean. In any event, as you know, the chances of finding the sub are best at the point where it will come to land the agent, and that we do know. So your lads are the ones for the job."

"Where?"

"On the Gaspé coast, probably between Chandler and Percé. It's the most accessible part of the Quebec coast apart from the river. It's well connected to the rest of the country by rail and the like. My Special Operations Executive friends," he added with a wry grin, "tell me you've already nabbed one of these buggers along that coast."

"You're into more than technical liaison, Beech!"

"So it seems, Percy, so it seems."

"I suppose you know all about our German friend then – you don't need to hear it from me."

"I know you nobbled him pretty smartly once he was ashore, and have turned him around."

Nelles gazed idly at the cigarette between his fingers. "Well, if the truth be told, Janowski wanted to be caught. It's very quiet along the Gaspé coast, and few people check into the New Carlisle Hotel at 9:00 am on a November Monday morning. Fewer still speak with heavy German accents and smell of forty-four days at sea! The Belgian matchboxes and outdated Canadian money didn't help either. No. It didn't take Sherlock Holmes to nab Janowski – the hotelkeeper's son figured him out in quick time."

"And he's now transmitting for you!"

"Yes. We got him, his radio and his code books."

"And the sub got away."

"Apparently Janowski had been hiding along the shoreline for three days, claimed to have landed on the sixth of November. We didn't collar him until the ninth so the trail was cold by the time our ships arrived."

"That won't be the case this time."

"So, when and where?"

"The exact location depends on local conditions. But we are certain it will happen somewhere between Chandler and Percé, a little north of where Herr Janowski came ashore."

"What evidence do you have?"

"I'd rather not say, except that it is based on intelligence from an SOE operative."

"Fair enough. When?"

"Sometime next week, probably the night of May fifth or sixth. You will have to check local tides and moon phases to sharpen up the time. I am not at liberty to say much more."

"And this intelligence is reliable?"

"In our experience, absolutely."

"So." Nelles' training was already at work. "Allowing for a seven to eight knot surface cruising speed the U-boat should be entering the Cabot Strait on Monday or Tuesday?"

"Yes ... hard to say, though. She may want to reconnoitre the landing area the night before – I would – which means the submarine may be entering the Gulf now or at the very latest tomorrow."

A look of sudden consternation came over Nelles' face. Beechum-Walney caught the expression and looked rather sheepishly at the floor by his shoes.

"My God! You've left it rather late, Beech, don't you think! Why the hell didn't you bring this to my attention sooner?"

The delay was deliberate, but Beechum-Walney could not say that. All Beechum-Walney understood was that his bosses wanted the RCN to act quickly and decisively. More warning would have produced elaborate interception schemes, more complications, more likelihood of the secret being revealed, and no greater certainty of success. A few days' notice would be enough. Moreover, the scheme certainly could not have been hatched while the Americans had operational control in the Gulf. The warning had been finely tuned to Murray's – and the RCN's – first day of command.

"Look, I am sorry, Percy. I came up from Washington to brief you the moment I knew. I am afraid you shall have to make the best of it."

"And so we shall," Nelles answered, stepping out from behind the desk, "And so we shall. The obvious thing is to call in the chief of naval intelligence, Commander deMarbois, and you can repeat the details to him. We can then trump up some intelligence estimate, send it down to Halifax and have them proceed as if this was a routine DF intercept or sighting. Sound okay?"

"Splendid."

Nelles flicked the intercom on his desk. "Harding, send for Commander deMarbois, tell him it's urgent." Then looking at the ash-laden stump of the captain's cigarette he said, "Can I offer you something to drink?"

"Well, now that our business is largely done ... I believe it is the senior officer's privilege to declare that the sun is over the yardarm. Do you have a restorative on board?"

"I do indeed," Nelles answered, taking the few steps to a filing cabinet. "The spirit locker is down below on this vessel, too," he said with a smile, drew out the bottom drawer and removed a quart of Canadian Club.

"Will this do?"

"Marvellous!"

Nelles poured a generous tot into two water glasses. "No ice I'm afraid. Would you like some water?" Beechum-Walney shook his head and took the tumbler. He looked at it briefly, swilled the neat rye gently in the glass, raised it slowly and said, "To the hunt!"

"To the hunt!"

And sucked the contents down in one gulp.

Chapter 6

"Sir? Sir? ... are you awake, Sir?"

Belanger heard the plea, but it seemed distant, meant for someone else. It was also too gentle to draw him from his deep sleep. Even the rocking of his body failed to disturb his slumber, accustomed as he was to sleeping in a pitching corvette. Only when the voice called, "Lieutenant Commander Belanger, Sir!" was the deep fog of sleep parted.

"What! ... What!" Belanger mumbled and then shot out a petulant "What is it Samuels!"

"Commander Waite from the Admiral's office is here, Sir, with an urgent message."

"Very well. Show him in!"

Like all sailors, Belanger had learned to get by on a few hours of sleep taken at odd times of day. He went out like a light and, at sea at least, switched on with the same sharpness. But the recent work-ups had been trying, and there had been much to do during the past week alongside at Halifax. Moreover, harbour routine induced a relaxed vigilance and the expectation of uninterrupted sleep. On this Saturday night, while half of his crew drank themselves into a stupor ashore, Belanger had joined the other half who were taking advantage of a quiet night to catch up on desperately needed sleep. Samuels did well to wake him so easily.

Belanger swung his feet to the floor and still had his face buried in his hands when a light footfall announced Commander Waite. Without looking up Belanger offered a weary, "Hello Gary. What is it now?"

"A little something from Admiral Murray, Clive," Waite replied, placing a sealed envelope in Belanger's hand.

Even without his glasses Belanger could see that it was addressed to him personally with instructions that it be hand delivered by an officer. "What is it?" Belanger asked, although he knew that Waite could not – would not – tell him what it was about. Waite said nothing.

In the end the envelope contained nothing more than instructions to bring his ship to immediate notice for steam, and to report to the Admiral's office at 2245.

"For the love of God, Gary! Why all this cloak and dagger stuff?"

"You'll find out soon enough. I can't hang around, I have a few more of these to deliver. See ya shortly." With that Waite disappeared down the darkened passageway, leaving Belanger to gather his wits and bring his ship to life.

"Samuels! Samuels!" No reply. Belanger muttered darkly to himself "... where the hell is he ..." before trying one final blast, "SAMUELS!"

"Yes, Sir? Sorry, Sir, I was waiting on deck."

"Right. It appears we are going to war ... or somewhere. Roust Chief Edwards from his mick and tell him we need steam on both boilers ASAP. Make sure Mr. Fergus knows as well – we are to go to immediate notice for steam." Belanger glanced at his watch, "What time are the men on leave due to return?"

"Midnight, Sir."

"Good. We won't be able to move much before dawn in any event ..."

"And we still have to refuel and re-ammunition, Sir, before we can sail."

"Yes, Samuels, you are quite right. If this is a major flap they'll lay on the fuel barge tonight and have extra hands at the gunwharf tomorrow morning. In the meantime, get the ship on the go, will you, while I see what the Admiral has in store."

It wasn't just tonight's interrupted sleep that made Belanger groggy. Nearly four years of disturbed sleep, plus being a decade older than his fellow officers had worn him thin. But he enjoyed the company of youth and the challenges of command at sea. And it beat the hell out of his civilian career, managing the Montreal branch of the family wholesale business. In fact Belanger, the son of a successful Québecois businessman and a Westmount anglo mother, could easily have sat out the war, piling up a fortune in war work. But there were enough older brothers to do that, and it never occurred to him. "When your country is at war, you go," Belanger had told the recruiting officer. "It's as simple as that."

Most of his Montreal peers were officers in the Black Watch, now in Britain as part of the Fifth Brigade of the Second Canadian Division. The army was the choice Belanger's father preferred. Not only did it suit the Quebec militia tradition of which his forebears were intensely proud, but also much of Montreal society was represented in the Black Watch. However, Belanger plotted his own course. For nearly four years now he had fought seasickness, the cold, the wet – and the Germans – living on cocoa and cold sandwiches, involved in the action. So far the Black Watch had not fired a shot in anger. All his pre-war friends dined off china in snug messes and let the NCOs run the battalion. Sometimes Belanger envied them. For the most part, though, he loathed their idleness and cavalier attitudes. Their time would come, he couldn't help but think, and he would be much better off in a bucking corvette.

Apart from the order to report to Admiral Murray's office, inducement enough for Belanger to dress and get ashore, mounting curiosity also drove him. Such an order, so late in the evening and delivered by an officer – Belanger had never known it to happen. "They could have just sent a signal," he muttered quietly as he dressed.

The summons to the Admiral's office was so unusual that his mind filled with visions of do-or-die raids on the German coast – all led by Lieutenant Commander Clive Belanger in blackened face with tin hat, and pistol in hand, followed by a small, desperate band of darkly clad, heavily armed and rather sinister-looking matelots. But who, or what, were they after? Assassination? Recovery? Capture of something of vital importance to the war effort? Or – more likely – was it just another bloody exercise?

Probably just another of Prentice's stunts, just another night of disturbed sleep, to no purpose. Most likely designed to see just how well *Lakeville* responded to an entirely improbable situation. That thought prompted a barely audible "Damn!" as he pushed the tails of his shirt down inside his trousers. If Prentice was up to something it was unclear how to respond. If *Lakeville* was good enough at this exercise, they might get away to the North Atlantic run again. On the other hand, if they were too good Prentice might try to keep them around as part of his 1943 offensive against U-boats in Canadian waters. Simply performing badly was not an option. Prentice would never let them go until they were ready.

More than anything else, Belanger, like the rest of *Lakeville*'s crew, wanted to get into the mid-ocean battles against the Wolf Packs. He had spent much of his war there, watching the U-boats attack almost unhindered, and the merchant ships go down, one after another. It was bad enough in the fall of 1941, when Belanger operated out of St. John's as a junior watchkeeper on the old four-stacker destroyer *St. Jacques*: no radar, no radio-telephones, no training – and no leadership to speak of. The U-boats had clobbered RCN-escorted convoys. British officers chided the Canadians for being useless for anything other than rescue work. 'Lots of opportunity for that in your convoys, eh what!' "Bloody Englishmen!" Belanger muttered.

Then, the problems had been insurmountable. Even communication was a major task. Their wireless sets were often tuned wrong, and they lacked signal lamps for communications at night. Most of the corvettes didn't even have binoculars, much less a telescope with which to read flag signals. Once part of that unprepared fleet, *Lakeville* had come a long way since 1941 – she now had good radar, radio-telephones, better guns, proper signal lamps, a telescope, and enough duffle coats for the whole crew. The single, swinging magnetic compass remained, as did the same primitive asdic, but the new additions to the ship would have given her a fighting chance in 1941.

Belanger understood why the Germans had scored so well against Canadian-escorted convoys in 1941, but the bitterness remained. And in the fall of 1942 when the Wolf Packs again hit them in the mid-Atlantic, the escorts were better equipped and more experienced. But there were also many more U-boats, and they swamped the defences of the slow convoys escorted by Canadians. Belanger had watched it all from the bridge of the corvette *Castlegar* as her executive officer. Try as they might, the RCN mid-ocean groups were always forced to react – usually too late – to an initiative by the enemy.

Again the Royal Navy – equipped with the latest kit, their destroyers fitted with direction finders to locate the shadowing U-boats as they sent off reports – sneered. *And* they escorted the fast convoys to boot, which were hard to find and hard to catch.

Belanger grabbed his cap and made his way ashore. He was not sure who pissed him off more, the Germans who ripped into his convoys with impunity, or the British, who blamed the heavy losses to RCN convoys on bungling incompetence. *Castlegar* had left the mid-ocean in December 1942, just before the British had temporarily forced the RCN out of the North Atlantic run to rectify their shortcomings in training and equipment. "Sorry, old boy," one Royal Navy colleague had told him in January when the best of the RCN was being pulled from the mid-ocean. "Your chaps simply cannot cut it. Time for the first eleven!" Pompous bastard! Belanger had thought, what the hell did he know about pushing a slow convoy through the mid-ocean?

Belanger had kept those thoughts to himself and, in the interests of imperial solidarity, his fist, too, despite an overwhelming urge to smash it into the officer's face. Now, many months later, Belanger derived no satisfaction from knowing that when the British took over the slow convoys they too got clobbered. In his darker moments Belanger felt it served them right.

So maybe the RCN wasn't so bad after all. Maybe, given half a chance and some good equipment, they could sink U-boats and get a little of their own back. Belanger had heard that the Navy's mid-ocean groups, re-fitting and re-equipping under British command in the eastern Atlantic since January, were about to go back onto the North Atlantic run. That's where he wanted to be, where he had a few scores to settle.

The trace of light snow earlier in the evening had dissipated but the air was sharp and cool. An instinctive glance skyward – looking for stars or the moon – revealed solid cloud, yet the air had definitely changed. The cold front had passed, Belanger concluded, and the weather would clear tomorrow. That was good. It would be easier to go to war on a sunny day.

More people were crammed into Admiral Murray's office than Belanger had expected, and a curious bunch, too. The Admiral sat behind his desk, a solid, barrel-chested bear, with a round face and hands like catcher's mitts. His ruddy complexion bespoke his Pictou County Nova Scotia heritage, as did his love of rugged sports. Indeed, his nose still sported scars from last winter's encounter with the chiefs and petty officers' hockey team. Only when he spoke, with a slightly cultivated mid-Atlantic accent, did Murray's years of naval service become apparent.

By all accounts Murray was an excellent seaman and ship handler. Beyond that Belanger did not expect much. Like the handful of other 'straight stripers' who ran the fleet, Murray had grown up in the tiny prewar navy. And like his regular-force contemporaries, Murray had been propelled into high command more by war than by ability. Belanger did not resent Murray; "The greatest guy in all the world," he would say, if asked. Only if pressed would he add, "but not the brightest." Apart from forthrightness, honesty, and integrity Murray's strength as the new Commander in Chief, Canadian Northwest Atlantic, was that he surrounded himself with good and able men.

When Belanger entered the office Murray was chatting idly with his intelligence officer, Mitchell, whom Belanger did not know. Three other corvette captains immediately caught his eye: Anderson of *Castlegar*, Lindhurst of *Watson Lake*, and Wagner of *Tracadie*. Anderson had taken over *Castlegar* during her recent refit. Belanger knew him and Lindhurst only through the working-up exercises just finished. Good fellow, he thought as Anderson nodded recognition. Wagner he knew only too well, as an ambitious and pompous fool. Belanger sat as far away from him as the room would allow.

Wagner's presence disturbed Belanger; he did not relish having anything to do with him. First among the corvette captains present in age and seniority, Wagner had a reputation for aggressive action in the face of the enemy, often leaving his convoys utterly unguarded to pursue the most tenuous of U-boat contacts. Many felt this was the kind of pluck the Navy needed, but for the most part Wagner charged madly about the ocean to little purpose. Belanger regarded him as reckless and unprincipled. Wagner's U-boat kill, which had earned him a DSO, had been blind luck. He had made the most of it in his report: blazing gun battle, high speed turns, shadows of death lurking in the fog. A little creative writing skill goes a long way. Scuttlebutt around the ward-rooms of the fleet had it otherwise: anyone could have rammed a sub lying motionless in a fog. Moreover, Wagner was obsequious to his betters and a bully to those under him, qualities that Belanger loathed.

The tension in the room was broken by the arrival of Captain Prentice, and the staff officer of operations. "Ah, Chummy! Welcome," Murray said warmly. "I think you know everyone here ..." Handshakes all around punctuated the shuffling of chairs as they all squeezed into the Admiral's office, with an eye to rank and seniority.

"Well, gentlemen, thank you for coming along promptly. I am pleased that we were able to find you all, especially on a Saturday night!" The nervous laughter eased some of the tension, and Murray went on. "I regret that the captain of *Innisfail* could not be found on such short notice so his Number One, Lieutenant Perkins here, is stand-ing in."

"Now to the business at hand. We have received some extraordi-nary information – Gawd knows how – about a U-boat in Canadian waters, one we hope to kill! I think the best way to proceed is to let Captain Prentice give us the gen, as the air force types say, and then we'll hear from Ops on what they propose. Chummy, over to you."

"Thank you Admiral, and once again good evening gentlemen," Prentice intoned in his best classroom voice. "I shall get straight to the point. We have excellent intelligence – wholly reliable intelligence – which indicates that a U-boat will attempt to land an agent along the Gaspé coast, somewhere between Chandler and Percé late next week. Indeed, we think it likely the attempt will be made on Wednesday or Thursday night. It all depends on the U-boat's rate of advance and con-ditions of moon and tide. We understand that the U-boat left Rochfort, France, early last month and allowing for a cautious passage, it ought to pass the Cabot Strait in the next few days. We have no intelligence on which U-boat it is, what type, who is in command or, apart from the intent to land someone, what the mission is about.

"Now, some of you will know that an agent was landed on the Gaspé coast last year in November, near New Carlisle. That gentleman had instructions to contact the Canadian Fascist Party, and especially Adrien Arcand, among other things. Obviously German intelligence were unaware that Arcand and his henchmen had been in the pokey since 1940. That does not mean, however, that there is not a lot of mischief an agent could achieve.

"The director of naval intelligence in Ottawa tells me that there are many pro-fascists still active in Quebec province. Two of these groups are," at this point Prentice consulted his notes, "something called L'Action Nationale and the Jeune Canada movement. Apparently they are under surveillance but cannot all be arrested.

"Quite apart from attempts to de-stabilize the political scene in Canada," he continued, "there are, of course, any number of things an agent might accomplish. Intelligence on shipping movements is perhaps the most timely and useful to the Germans.

"Perhaps more important for us in the Navy – as well as for the government – is the desperate requirement to *sink* a U-boat in Canadian waters. If we cannot do that, the Germans may well return in strength; and the government most certainly will be down on the Navy like a ton of bricks. This may be the best chance we have to trap and sink a sub." With that he nodded to the Admiral and sat down.

"Thank you, Captain. So you see, gentlemen, we have a unique opportunity here, but one in which the nature of the information must remain guarded. We will provide disguised information while you are at sea – aircraft sighting reports and the like – should we obtain further intelligence that will sharpen your hunt. Be alive to those instances and, above all, follow your orders implicitly, even if they do not square with your estimation on the spot. Mitchell here, my intelligence officer," the Admiral said, pointing to the small, ruddy faced man, "will keep you informed. Do you have anything to add, Commander?"

"Just a small point, Sir," Mitchell responded, rising and nodding anxiously in Prentice's direction as if asking permission to speak. "At present we have no indications of U-boat activity in the Gulf. None. Ice remains in the Cabot Strait off Cape St. Lawrence and no local traffic has yet commenced. As you know, Sir ... ah, gentlemen ... ocean traffic has been suspended in the Gulf for the season, so there seems little in the way of substantial targets for U-boats in the area. We expect they will conduct a number of probing patrols later this spring to determine that.

"At the moment – despite some rather spurious 'sighting' reports from nervous coast watchers and high-flying aircraft – we believe that there is no U-boat in the Gulf or River. So, if this special intelligence is correct, you have only one U-boat to deal with, and no shipping to worry about. I might add, there are no Allied submarines in transit in the area either. If you see a sub, it's the enemy. That's all. Thank you, Sir."

"Thank you, Commander Mitchell. Now here's how we hope to sink this bugger." Murray leaned his bulk out over the desk and fiddled with a pen as he spoke. "Captain Prentice, the Ops people and I have worked out what we believe is a sound plan involving your ships and a few others. The force is the right mix of ship types and capabilities to deal with any eventuality over the next week to ten days. First, the Cabot Strait is patrolled to the east of the ice by the British trawlers *Ayrshire, Cape Mariato* and *Paynter*. They are already on station, and represent our first barrier. These patrols can be reinforced immediately only with the 8th Motor Launch Flotilla, presently lying at Sydney.

"As for the Gulf itself, I propose a retiring barrier – really two such barriers – starting in the central Gulf just west of the present ice pack, and shifting westward to the sub's supposed landing site by late Wednesday afternoon. One barrier can be provided by the 143rd Motor Launch Flotilla, lying here at Halifax; it's about ready to go. The main hunting force will comprise a mix of larger vessels: the corvettes *Castlegar, Watson Lake, Tracadie, Lakeville* and the Bangors *Innisfail* and *Mabou. Mabou*, by the way, will be joining from Sydney as soon as she can get away."

The main force of six ships was scarcely enough to cover the central gulf, and the Admiral caught Belanger's eye.

"Forgive me, Sir, but is *Beauceville* not available also? She had perhaps the best records during her work-ups ..."

"No, unfortunately, she continues to have serious engine defects and won't be ready for a week or more. I agree, gentlemen, that the main force is small, but rest assured we have plans to expand it.

"The main force is, I believe, a good mix. All the ships are at present unassigned, have just completed their work-ups, and are ready for sea. *Castlegar* and the Bangor 'sweeper *Innisfail* have good type 127DV asdics – about the best we have so far. Moreover, the operators have had time in the last week on a tame submarine, so they will be up to speed on real echoes. The corvettes all have type 271P radar and ought to be able to find anything on the surface at night or in fog. And of course, they have all recently completed work-ups.

"The general plan is for the main force to take station in the central Gulf as soon as possible and maintain a barrier patrol there for several days. If nothing happens by Tuesday, we shall draw the motor launches of the Cabot barrier force into the Gulf to bolster the main force. Then the whole group will retire inwards, towards the Gaspé coast, in expectation that the enemy has arrived undetected. The question that needs to be resolved is how we deal with the U-boat itself near the landing site."

"Assuming it gets that far!" Prentice snorted.

"Beg your pardon, Admiral, may I speak?"

"Yes Commander Belanger, please do."

"I share your concern about what we should do off Gaspé itself. If we lay a trap it will be evident, perhaps too evident, that we knew of the U-boat's presence and mission. That might compromise the intelligence source. We must somehow ensure that the patrols and hunting forces appear to be routine, drawn to the area by normal means – accident, or incident, air reports, anything. We must assume that the enemy is monitoring our radio traffic and can tell the difference between routine traffic and special operations. Incidents needed to draw forces into the central Gulf can be worked out, but we must be extremely cautious."

"I couldn't agree more," Captain Prentice chimed in. "That's why it would be best if we could find and sink her in deep water. Once she's inshore we risk betraying our prior knowledge, and if she submerges she'll be damned hard to find – maybe impossible. That being said, we ought to be able to anticipate the times and places available for landing an agent. I don't think our friend who landed the agent at New Carlisle was typical. That rather gutsy gentleman chose a gently shoaling beach.

I think, however, that the average submariner wants as much water under him as possible, to ensure a quick and safe retreat. He needs to – and therefore we need to – find an area where the bottom drops off quickly, where the coast is secluded and where the influence of tide, current and wind is minimal. Prominent headlands, lights and the like, which will make such a clandestine operation safer need also to be considered – "

Prentice was interrupted by Admiral Murray. "How do we know he will put the agent ashore himself? Surely a rendezvous at sea with a local fishing boat or goelette would be less hazardous for the U-boat?"

"But also much harder to manage, and might force the submarine to stay in the area too long," Prentice replied. "No, Sir, I think he will come in, put the chap ashore as expeditiously as possible, and get the hell out. That way he can control the timing."

A pause followed, and the admiral looked around the room. The three escort commanders said nothing. "Very well then," Murray concluded, "we seem to be in agreement about our U-boat captain's likely course of action. Although, Chummy," he added as a personal aside, "it seems unlikely that we will be dealing with an 'average' submariner, and it is entirely possible that he will choose a shoaling beach for this landing. In that case, however, we would have to watch every beach from Grand Manan to Cape Chidley!"

Murray then turned his attention back to the larger group. "We have a good idea where he will land, gentlemen, and that will help us figure out how to deal with him. Chummy?"

"With your permission, Sir?" Prentice said, unrolling a chart on the admiral's desk. The chart covered the Gaspé coast from Cap des Rosiers to Chandler.

"It is a fair bet, gentlemen," Prentice said with a sweep of his hand over the chart, "that he will stay well clear of Gaspé Bay – too much likelihood of naval traffic there. No, he needs an area much as I have already described, and there are two along this coast – one immediately south of Cap Blanc here, just below Percé," and he jabbed the chart with his finger, "and the other here just under Cap d'Espoir. I can't imagine he'll try his luck twice in a row farther up the Baie des Chaleurs, so these are the only two likely spots."

Belanger caught the admiral's eye.

"Yes, Commander?"

"With all due respect to Captain Prentice, there are two other options for landing an agent. Both the Magdalens and the area around North Point on Prince Edward Island have French-Canadian inhabitants. Are these not possibilities too?"

Prentice jumped in. "We've considered these, I assure you. The Magdalens are simply too remote, and it would be difficult for any stranger to move through them without undue attention. Northern PEI is little better in that respect. Small, rural population, tightly knit community, and it's still an island. No, our man will want to move quickly into a large population. He can do that easily from the Gaspé."

The officers crowded around the chart and considerable discussion followed on the probable influence of moon, tide and the coastline in sheltering and abetting a landing. The consensus was that Captain Prentice was right, and Murray brought the proceedings to order once again.

"It remains now to settle the final details of the phases of the operation. Captain Prentice!"

"Right. The Cabot barrier is already partially in place, with the three RN trawlers. We will bolster it immediately by sending out the 8th Flotilla tomorrow morning. The main force will sail from here tomorrow morning as well, under –" he nearly choked on his words, "Lieutenant Commander Wagner in *Tracadie*. They will take passage via the Canso Strait and establish a patrol line in the central Gulf, in deep water north of the Magdalens as soon as possible. The actual disposition of forces will be co-ordinated between Commander Wagner and our plot here. These forces will retire, starting on Tuesday evening, towards the Gaspé coast with the intention of arriving off the landing site at dusk on Wednesday.

"Any sub making a transit of the Gulf will stick to deep water, and that's where our patrols ought to stay. If we must send forces south of the Magdalens we will send the motor launches, and that decision will be taken here, in Halifax.

"Once they have fallen back to the Gaspé coast the main force will spring the trap while the motor launches form an outer perimeter around the area. Ships may be detached to the Gaspé base at *Fort Ramsay* for fuel and stores as required. Should we learn that the U-boat has already landed its agent or is otherwise in retreat towards the Cabot Strait, we shall conduct a retiring search plan eastwards, reversing the pattern as outlined. The usual wireless and R/T procedures apply, and I have arranged a briefing for radio personnel for tomorrow morning at 0600."

"Thank you, Captain," Murray said. "Gentlemen, are there any questions? Yes, Anderson."

"Forgive me, Sir, for stating the obvious, but this is – with all due respect – a pretty feeble response, is it not?" All eyes now turned to the new corvette commander, and Belanger was particularly taken by both the directness and the point of Anderson's comment. "I mean, shouldn't some of your best equipped ships, especially the destroyers in Western Local Escort, be sent on this one, if it's so hot?"

"A good point, Anderson," the admiral replied, and was about to tackle the question when agitation and a look of consternation caught his eye, "Ah, yes? Captain Prentice?"

"Thank you, and forgive my interruption, but I really must speak to that. Gentlemen, I cannot emphasize enough the imperative that any kill made in Canadian waters in 1943 *must* be made by a Canadian ship of war. We all share the humiliation of 1942, whether we served inshore or in the mid-ocean. We've finally gotten the Americans off our backs and are in a position to command our own operations. We are now at liberty to deal with the threat in our waters in *our* way with *our own* ships. It is bad enough that three British trawlers happen to lie, at this very moment, in the best position to kill this U-boat. We needn't increase the chances of the British sinking a U-boat in the Gulf by filling it with RN ships – or Norwegians or Americans, for that matter. No, we have skilled and experienced personnel and we have adequate ships and equipment of our own for the task. No-one said it would be easy, but we are unlikely to have such an opportunity again. This U-boat must be killed, and it must be killed by a Canadian warship in Canadian waters. This is our chance to ensure that another year like 1942 does not happen."

"I couldn't agree more – nor could I have put it better," Murray said. "This is one for the RCN."

"What role has the RCAF been assigned then?" Belanger asked.

"None, specifically," Murray admitted, looking nervously at Prentice. "We shall employ air patrols as we see fit, and use them to our advantage, but the air force knows nothing of this operation itself for the moment. Leave Eastern Air Command to me. Any other questions?"

"Yes, Sir!" It was Wagner. "How much latitude do I have as main force commander?"

"Once on station you may deploy your ships as you see fit within the general guidelines provided by Captain Prentice. Unless and until contact has been made on the U-boat you will, of course, maintain wireless silence, although you may use radio-telephones sparingly. We will maintain a plot and move you about. There is no question that you, as the man on the spot, have ultimate authority over the movement of your ships and the conduct of operations. However, I would caution you to conduct yourself in accordance with my intentions. Assume that our intelligence people have the latest information, and trust what we order you to do. I know we have stressed the need for individual initiative under my command, but in this case we must keep you all on a short lead.

"In other words, Wagner," said the admiral with an impish grin, "you are at liberty to succeed, but if you screw up be sure you have spread the burden widely!"

"Understood, Sir ... perfectly."

"Other questions?"

"Yes Sir." It was Belanger. "I have already given orders to raise steam for immediate departure, Sir, but I must refuel and complete stores before I can do so. If I wait until daylight it could well be noon before I sail. If you could arrange for a fuel barge to come alongside sometime tonight and for extra hands at the gunwharf tomorrow morning I could sail at 0800."

"Quite so, Belanger. What about the others? Anderson? Wagner?" They were already fuelled and stored, and would be ready to steam at 0730. *Innisfail* was in a similar situation to *Lakeville*, and so the fuel barge was laid on for 0330. It was also agreed that the main force would sail in two divisions; *Tracadie*, *Watson Lake* and *Castlegar* at 0800 hours, and the other two together as soon as possible thereafter. They would rendezvous at Port Hawkesbury before passing through the Canso Strait. *Mabou* was to join the main force in the central Gulf.

"Right. Anything else?" the admiral queried.

"Yes, one final thing, Sir," Belanger said. "Actually two things, if you would. The first is that this is still a puny force. Surely the prospect of sinking a submarine in the Gulf warrants a major effort! Flood the Gulf with escorts, for God's sake! Strip the Western Escort Force groups and pour ships into the area!"

"Can't be done, I'm afraid, for two very good reasons. There is an enormous concentration of U-boats edging westwards in pursuit of Convoy ONS 5. They're just south of Cape Farewell now. If they spill over into the Grand Banks fog the escort groups operating north of Halifax will need reinforcing. The second reason is that we cannot risk compromising the intelligence by anything so overt as a major reallocation of forces. And your second point, Commander?"

"Speed, Admiral, speed! If the U-boat runs on the surface, the main force'll never catch it. A surfaced U-boat always has a knot or two on corvettes and Bangors. With all due respect, Sir, the main force is inadequate without destroyers."

"Very true, Belanger, very true indeed. Captain Prentice?"

"Since this is a wholly Canadian operation we cannot send *Chelsea, Montgomery* or any of the other Brit destroyers based in Halifax. However, we will pull the first available RCN four-stacker from a Western Escort Force group, and send it immediately into the Gulf to join the main force. If we can spring a second, we will. As the Bangors assigned to the Gulf forces become available over the next few days we'll slip them in as well. Consider yourselves merely the lead element, gentlemen. We will build the main force up as quickly and effectively as resources and circumspection allow. My hope is that this bastard will be on the bottom before that first destroyer arrives."

Wagner slumped noticeably. A destroyer captain would outrank him. Belanger, among others, breathed easier knowing it, and Murray offered his regrets. "I'm afraid, Commander Wagner, that when this destroyer arrives he'll take over command of the main force. Until then however, it's your show.

"Anything else? ... Nothing? Thank you, gentlemen, and good hunting."

The meeting adjourned and the officers filed quietly out of the room, each lost in the details of the discussion, the problems to be sorted out prior to sailing and the week ahead. Wagner, not surprisingly, lingered. Chatting up the admiral no doubt, Belanger thought, although as the designated senior officer of the main force he had every right to do so.

No sooner had Belanger cleared the outer office and altered course for the nearest exit than he felt someone grab his elbow. He turned to see the grizzled face of Captain Prentice.

"Clive, I want to speak to you for a moment."

Prentice led him down the corridor, out of sight and sound of the admiral's office.

"I want you to work with Wagner on this one ..." Prentice offered tentatively.

"That's asking a lot," Belanger retorted sharply. "But surely you did not expect otherwise?"

"No, of course not – but Wagner does."

"And he bloody well should, too. He's a charlatan, Chummy, and an obsequious drunkard. Probably a pederast as well. For the love of God, what is Murray thinking?"

"I can't say for sure," Prentice answered in honest frustration. "I suspect he thinks this is just some exercise concocted by the intelligence people to keep us sharp."

"And what do you think?"

"I'm inclined to agree. It makes sense. We've only just taken over from the Americans, so how quickly can we get ships into the Gulf, eh?"

"Sounds like something you'd try!"

"Yes. I admit it's a bit out of character for Jones and his lot."

"And Wagner?"

"He's the most senior escort commander available. He has to be senior officer of the main force. I don't like it any more than you do."

"Yes, and when Wagner makes a cock of it, he'll blame everyone around him!"

Prentice could only nod agreement.

"Well then," Belanger observed dryly, "tell the Admiral to appoint someone else to command the main force – you, for instance – and leave Wagner home."

"Can't do it, old boy. Wagner has seniority – and the ear of the Admiral."

"Then Murray's more of a fool than I thought."

Wagner talked a good line, dressed in pusser fashion – handkerchief up the sleeve and all – and affected a mid-Atlantic pseudo-pommy accent. He was also a very good navigator. But an incompetent leader, and quite likely to exceed his authority.

"You know that Murray would not countenance any suggestion that Wagner is incompetent," Prentice continued with barely controlled anger. "I'll hustle a destroyer out to you as soon as I can. In the meantime Wagner must be cajoled into doing what's right. You'll have to baby him, Clive."

Prentice placed his hand on Belanger's shoulder, and Belanger glumly took his leave, his echoing footsteps blending with Prentice's softly spoken and earnest "Good luck, Clive!"

Lakeville was going off to war, finally, but in the wrong direction, to the wrong place, and under the wrong senior officer, to chase a U-boat that some lunatic from Ottawa claimed – on God knows what evidence – was going to land a spy.

Chapter 7

"Off caps!" The command echoed loudly through *Lakeville*'s tiny wardroom, adding measurably to the whole disagreeable business.

"Read the charges, if you would, Chief," Belanger said solemnly to Ryan, the chief petty officer.

"Leading Seaman, Kozlowski, W.P., B37542!"

"Sir!" Kozlowski answered.

"Charged with riotous conduct, conduct prejudicial to good order and wilfully destroying or injuring the clothes and effects of others in that he did, on the evening of 1 May 1943, precipitate a brawl at the Ajax Club for British seamen, which resulted in extensive damage to the club's furniture, necessitated the intervention of the Shore Patrol, and sent several ratings to hospital."

Kozlowski's bruised face and swollen upper lip remained unmoved while the charge was read. Macpherson, whose face looked little better, winced slightly when the same charges were repeated after his name.

"Thank you, Chief," Belanger said. "Mr. Fergus?" It was the divisional officer's duty to speak in defence of his men.

"There is no question that Kozlowski and Macpherson here were engaged in a fight at the Ajax Club, Sir and, if the truth be known, gave better than they got ..."

"That's hardly the point, Mr. Fergus," Belanger interrupted wearily.

"Right. Sorry, Sir. But it is clear, Sir, that their behaviour was largely an act of self defence and that the burden for starting the fight lies with the two British ratings from *Chelsea*, who are, unfortunately, in hospital. I should think, Sir, that a simple charge of fighting would be more appropriate in this instance."

Belanger shot a quick glance at Fergus, who was careful not to make eye contact. With the emphasis on the word 'simple' Fergus was throwing Kozlwoski and Macpherson to the tender mercies of their captain. The punishment for fighting might be anything from stoppage of grog to two weeks in solitary confinement, much milder than that of the charges just read.

"What do you men have to say for yourself?" Belanger demanded. "Kozlowski?"

"Beg yer pardon, Sir, but the charges seem a bit severe. We was not involved in a riot, Sir, it was simply an act of self defence ..."

Belanger cut him off. "You don't deny participation in the fight, being drunk and unruly, having to be restrained by the Shore Patrol and ... and," Belanger fumbled for the report, "'beating two RN ratings so severely that they had to be hospitalized'" he continued, reading from the report of the Shore Patrol, "'and contributing to the extensive damage sustained by the Ajax Club'?"

Kozlowski stiffened. "Permission to speak freely, Sir?"

"Granted."

"That's nothing but a pack of lies, Sir. It was men – seamen gunners – from a British merchant ship that beat the living shit out of those two RN types. Broke chairs over 'em, as I recall, Sir. I won't deny that we was fightin'." Given the condition of his face he could hardly deny the obvious, "but we done it with our fists, Sir, like real men. If we had not been backed into a corner by the rest of them we would never have stayed on for the brawl, we would'a bin outta there. Them charges, Sir, is just bullshit! ... Begging yer pardon, Sir."

"Then, Leading Seaman Kozlowski, you would have me reduce the charges?"

"Well, yes Sir. We was provoked, you see. I mean, we didn't go to the Ajax Club to start a fight, only to pass a quiet evening, Sir. It was them bastards – I mean, seamen – from *Chelsea*, Sir, what started it ..."

"I see." Belanger scanned the charge sheet and then looked up again at Kozlowski's beaten face. "One might suppose that the two of you contributed to the altercation by your presence in a club reserved for British seamen. How did you get in, in the first place?"

Silence.

Kozlowski was not about to talk and Macpherson as usual would act on his mate's lead. In the awkward silence Ryan handed Belanger a battered seaman's cap. "This here may explain it, Sir. If ya would care to look inside as well ..."

Belanger took the crumpled cap, with its "H.M.S." tally around the outside, turned it over and there, in bold letters on the cap liner was "Macpherson, Edgar B. H.M.C.S." and a service number. The jig was up.

"Able Seaman Macpherson, would you care to explain this?" Belanger said, holding the cap so his name could be plainly seen.

Macpherson's first inclination was to simply blame Kozlowski: after all, it had been his idea. But he relied instead on an offensive strategy designed by Kozlowski to appeal to Belanger's sense of fair play and his sympathy for ratings on leave in Halifax. It was a moment of inspiration.

"A *rouse da la guerre*, Sir!" Macpherson answered firmly, eyes straight ahead, staring fixedly at the scuttle behind Belanger's head.

"I see," mused Belanger. "So you were on a 'cutting out' operation?" He paused. "Then this was, Macpherson, a premeditated act of infiltration and you – both of you – were spoiling for a fight ..."

"No Sir!" Kozlowski barked instinctively, then regained his senses, "Beg yer pardon, Sir." Interrupting the Captain was never a safe bet, but Macpherson's opening shot had lightened the tone of the proceedings. Kozlowski now aimed to push the new mood as far and as quickly as possible. "We was there on a mission, so to speak, but only to have a good time, a few drinks and chat up the girls, Sir –"

"And when the British sailors found out who you were and what you were up to you were asked to leave, and you resisted?"

"Well, yes, Sir – but politely."

Macpherson echoed Kozlowski, "Yes, Sir, very politely like."

"So," Belanger muttered, "you had no intention of leaving even when asked?"

Kozlowski took up the challenge. "It was well on in the evening, Sir and – if you'll forgive me, Sir – the evening was going well. We wasn't making no trouble, nor would there bin any but for those guys from *Chelsea.*"

Having let the two seamen make their case Belanger now saw an opportunity to trip them up.

"Your argument that the use of H.M.S. cap tallies was a legitimate *ruse de guerre* is insupportable," Belanger said smugly. He intended to hoist these two Sea Lawyers on their own petard. "Do you two know that it is against international law to engage the 'enemy' while flying false colours?"

Macpherson didn't know what the hell the captain was talking about, and the thought had not occurred to Kozlowski. They had entered the Club under H.M.S. tallies and had in fact contravened the laws of war. Belanger paused to allow the point to sink in, amused by the discomfort on their faces.

"Beg your pardon, Sir, but I believe that under international law the false colours must be struck before the first shots are fired."

"Yes, Fergus, that is correct. What's your point?"

"Well, Sir, Macpherson and Kozlowski had to doff their hats when they entered the club, right? So they were not wearing them when the fight broke out and the first blows were exchanged. Therefore, it cannot be argued that Kozlowski and Macpherson contravened international law."

Broad grins broke out on the ratings' battered faces.

Belanger was dumbfounded. The seriousness of the whole affair, sidetracked as it was by Macpherson and his own playing along, was now completely undone by Fergus' idle intrusion. The two bruised and battered seamen, abetted by Fergus, had turned the whole thing into a farce. Belanger went straight back to the charges at hand.

"The charges of riotous conduct and conduct prejudicial to good order are too severe in this case – though God knows, Kozlowski, your service record indicates a consistent pattern of misbehaviour prejudicial to good order. A charge of fighting and wilful destruction of effects is more appropriate in this case. Since the fighting could not be termed a "violent assault" under the Naval Discipline Act, I will not have you two sent to cells. Nor will I, in this instance, disrate you, Kozlowski, although let this serve as a warning.

"Thirty days' stoppage of leave and thirty days' stoppage of grog will suffice, I think, but both of you are reminded that I will not be so lenient the next time around. Dismissed."

As Ryan marched the two ratings out Belanger turned to Fergus and the business of the day. "Right, Number One, let's get t'hell out of here. Two more days in this bloody city and half the God damned crew will be in hospital and the other half in the brig."

Belanger instinctively tugged at the collar of his duffle coat, pulling it tighter around his neck as he walked to the forward edge of the bridge. At least the snow had stopped. It hadn't amounted to much, but it had made refuelling during the night a bitter task. The previous evening the wind had backed around to the northwest, following the passage of the cold front, drawing arctic winds down behind it. The morning had a bite, although the wind direction and the low, fast-driven cloud promised better weather later in the day. It would be cool but fresh, and brilliant with spring sun.

Belanger drank in the whole day's weather in one quick sniff and a glance. Not a bad day to be at sea. If he kept *Lakeville* close to the Nova Scotia eastern shore on his way to Canso there would be little opportunity for the present wind to pile up much of a sea, and visibility would be excellent. Tugs were already pulling apart the rafts of corvettes alongside jetty five, as a local escort group sailed with a convoy to Boston. Only one corvette remained outboard of Lakeville, and tugs already had lines aboard her. Belanger determined he would not submit to such an unseamanlike departure.

"As soon as that ship has cleared," he said to Fergus, "cast off one and four, save the springs and we'll get away from here ourselves."

Fergus already knew that Belanger would have *Lakeville* jostle her way out of the pack. A combination of rudder and propeller would open a space just large enough between the inboard and outboard ships to allow her to slip out forward. But the tugs had ruined that option, and the only demonstration of seamanship left was to get away before the tugs could barge in.

As soon as the outboard corvette slipped her last line Fergus was off to *Lakeville*'s port side, megaphone in hand. By the time Belanger arrived on the port bridge wing all lines except the two springs, bow and stern, were being coiled on deck.

"Right," he said to Fergus, "hold number two and we'll kick her stern out." Leaving Fergus to supervise the lines, Belanger stepped over to the wheelhouse voicepipe. "Wheelhouse, Cap'n here: slow ahead, port fifteen." The order was repeated below by the cox'n, the engine-room telegraph set to slow ahead and the ship's wheel put over to port fifteen degrees. The combination of helm and engine settings, along with tension on the spring would force *Lakeville*'s stern away from the inboard ship.

Soon the vibrations of the propeller could be felt and the gentle sound of the wash caused by the turning screw rose between the two ships. Fergus and Belanger watched intently, their concentration broken only by a reminder to the foc'sle party to reset their fenders slightly to prevent the two ships from grinding together.

Gradually, *Lakeville*'s stern came away, the space between the two ships opening like a clamshell. Then Belanger nodded to Fergus to slacken the aft spring and prepare to cast it off while keeping tension on the fore spring.

"Stop engine. Slow astern." *Lakeville*'s bow pulled away, opening a gap of about ten feet between the two ships. This stage had to be precise, lest it drag *Lakeville* back onto the inboard ship. Once the bow began to swing Belanger ordered "Stop main engines, rudder amid-ships" and instructed Fergus to cast off the two remaining lines. Once certain that the lines were aboard he ordered "half ahead".

The whole manoeuvre went off perfectly. *Lakeville* steamed out of her berth with ease and swung over to the other side of the narrows, where she lay alongside an ammunition lighter for little more than thirty minutes to complete her stores. By 0855 she was heading down the harbour.

Lakeville's crew manned the side as they passed the dockyard, but the departure of one more little ship for the Atlantic war passed virtually unnoticed. Only the personnel who operated the boom across the entrance to the harbour and those at the port war signal station at Camperdown Head were obliged to record *Lakeville*'s passage to sea. Her consort, the Bangor-class minesweeper *Innisfail* trailing a half-mile astern drew perhaps even less attention.

The other division of the main force, *Castlegar, Tracadie* and *Watson Lake*, had sailed at 0800 and were now beyond the horizon. Belanger was in no hurry to join up. They planned to rendezvous at Port Hawkesbury, and he was better off on his own for the day.

As *Lakeville* rounded Chebucto Head, Belanger ordered the helmsman to steer 145 degrees, almost due southwest, a course he would have to hold for over an hour until *Lakeville* cleared the long, swept channel that formed the wartime approaches to Halifax harbour. Only then could *Lakeville* shape a course for the Strait of Canso. The course reduced the following breeze to nearly nothing and the corvette glided along steadily and easily, her funnel smoke drifting lazily overhead and her wake rolling smoothly away to either side. Fergus had already left the bridge to get on with his morning duties, leaving Samuels in charge of the forenoon watch.

"I think a bit of breakfast and a cup of tea would be in order, don't you Samuels?"

"Aye, Sir, I do indeed," the officer of the watch replied, and with that Belanger went below.

"You'll find this quite a change from the SW2C," George Smythe, *Lakeville*'s radar officer, explained as Harkness took his place at the console for the first time.

"Yes Sir. I had a look at one briefly during training."

The tiny radar hut still reeked of fresh paint. It was barely big enough for Harkness to sit in front of the set with Smythe standing behind him. Atop the hut, in what looked like a lighthouse, was the antenna. Because no-one had yet developed a nitrogen-filled cable long enough, the antenna and the operating console had to be only a few feet apart. As a result the operator's position was high in the ship and the antenna was much lower than ideal. But it was a workable compromise, the set was excellent, and there could be easy communications with the bridge.

"I understand that this one sweeps automatically?"

"Yes," Smythe replied. "It takes about two minutes to go a full 360 degrees, and gives an excellent picture of what's around you. But you've got to watch something doesn't creep up on you from ahead while the antenna's sweeping around. Its good – very good – out to about 7,000 yards. The really big improvement, apart from the greater sensitivity of this 10cm set, is this new Plan Position Indicator." Smythe pointed to the cathode ray tube in the centre of the receiver. "Here, trade places with me and I'll show you how it works."

Smythe leaned over the voicepipe that connected him with the SW2C operator two decks below, told him to shut down his set for its periodic rest, and then commenced start-up of the type 271.

"You've got to be very precise in your start-up or you'll blow circuits," Smythe cautioned. "Flicking the switches in the wrong order could mean a day's worth of repair work."

Soon the radar hut was filled with the hot smell of glowing vacuum tubes and circuits. A bright glow appeared in the centre of the screen, followed by a single line, a trace, that radiated from it to the two o'clock position and swept slowly in a clockwise direction like a second hand on a watch.

"That's us, in the middle," Smythe said, "and the trace represents the direction of the radar transmission.

"Every time you start up the set needs to be tuned, just like the old SWIC," Smythe instructed. "Set the gain to minimum, turn off the anti-clutter switch – this one here – and then set the range scale. We'll try to pick up *Innisfail*. She's about three thousand yards behind us, so we'll set it to medium."

"Now," he continued, "adjust the brilliance until the trace is visible ... there. Then sharpen the focus and reset the brilliance so the trace just disappears. Once you've done that, readjust the gain so that a speckled background is just visible. Again don't set the thing too bright. It's a pretty flat sea today, so you can sharpen the anti-clutter control right down ... there, like that. When it's rough you have to leave the anti-clutter setting pretty coarse, and that can eliminate small targets at longer ranges – like a U-boat.

"Then you can do some final, fine adjustments on the focus, gain and range scale to clear up the picture and voila!, the world is laid out before you."

Harkness watched as the radar made one complete revolution.

"That's *Innisfail*," said Smythe. "She'll turn up pretty steady in position. The view astern is sometimes confused by the funnel on low-lying, close targets, but she's far enough away to detect easily."

Amidships on the port side the radar etched a jagged series of headlands and islands about three miles distant. Harkness was amazed at the clear picture before him.

"That's Cape Canso, actually it's probably Andrew Island." Smythe went on to name the various headlands that formed the southern approaches to Chedabucto Bay.

Harkness had trained on the SW2C, the 1.5 metre wavelength radar that *Lakeville* carried at her masthead. It could detect objects and display their range on an 'A' scan screen. The size and nature of the target had to be guestimated from the size of the spike. But the true nature of a SWOOK contact could be determined only by seeing it. This new radar, however, was a world apart.

"If you want to concentrate on a particular sector," Smythe instructed, "you switch off the automatic rotation and use this handwheel on the deckhead to your right. You can then sweep a given area repeatedly. Take this section of coastline here. It'll come up better if we adjust the range scale to long ... there. In a flat calm and heavy fog, you should be able to see anything that moves – or doesn't – near you. You can see the shoreline like a map and ships stand out clearly."

Harkness sat for some time, fiddling with the controls, adjusting the range, focus and gain to see what produced the best picture, as the islands and headlands edged their way towards the bottom and off the screen.

Soon a perceptible change in the ship's movement confirmed the radar evidence that they had cleared Cape Canso, which gave the northwest wind a much longer fetch. It drove a fairly sharp sea across Chedabucto Bay, piling it up over the Canso Ledges. *Lakeville* pitched and rolled as the waves struck her port bow and she shouldered her way through them. It was, Harkness concluded, bloody marvellous. How the hell had they managed before with the awful SWOOK?

"Signal from *Tracadie*, Sir."

"Thanks, Maynard." Belanger held the thin sheet of signal paper tightly in both hands, so he could read it in the eddying breeze. "It's from Wagner," he said to Fergus. "He intends to lie at the government wharf at Venus Cove, in Mulgrave, instead of off Port Hawkesbury. Makes sense. Port Hawkesbury is too exposed and Venus Cove is a good anchorage in this northwest wind. I expect it's fairly whistling down the strait. This wind'll back by morning and if we lay up overnight we'll have a following breeze for the narrowest and most difficult portion of the strait tomorrow."

The Strait of Canso between Nova Scotia and the island of Cape Breton is the southernmost entrance into the Gulf of St. Lawrence, and for ships approaching the Gulf from the south it saves about seventy-five miles. However, the time saved can often be lost if wind and tide are set against a northerly transit. In those conditions ship-handling is especially tricky, and a rocky bottom and swift tides along the fourteen-and-a-half-mile strait make anchoring an unreliable business. Steady steaming around the eastern side of Cape Breton might lead more comfortably into the Gulf, but in early spring there is a risk of contact with the last of winter's ice. Canso was the sensible route for the main force.

Belanger stepped into the charthouse, and passed along word of the new rendezvous. "Okay," Samuels replied. "We should be alongside at Mulgrave by about 2030. We'll hold 295 across the bay. I'll call you when we make the Cape Argos buoy."

"Good," Belanger replied. He was always on the bridge when *Lakeville* made a landfall, and the buoy marked the final approach to the Strait.

Belanger returned to the open bridge and found Fergus standing in the lee of the charthouse, watching the shoreline and taking in the sun.

"Even if there is a sub up there, what chance do we have of finding it?"

"About even, I should think," Belanger replied. "I talked to the former commander of *Megantic*. He was with SQ 36 when the convoy was attacked off Cap Chat in broad daylight last summer. Claims you could see the bubble traces of the torpedoes running right up to the targets. But they never found the U-boat."

"Asdic conditions are impossible in the river, what with the mixing of sea and river currents. Better out in the Gulf, around the

Magdalens. And," Belanger added with a smile, "we don't have to worry – yet – about surface warming. That just traps the asdic echo on the surface layer and you have no chance at all."

"It'll be a few months before we can complain about heat, I suppose."

"Spring and fall are the best times for U-boat hunting in the Gulf. That said, it's a piss-poor place to try to find a sub. According to *Megantic*'s commander when *Charlottetown* was sunk off Gaspé in broad daylight last September civilians saw the sub, tried to warn the Navy, but communications were too primitive. *Charlottetown* steamed right into a two-torpedo spread – broad daylight, bodies and wreckage everywhere – and the sub got clean away."

Belanger sensed that he was becoming maudlin. "We should have good luck around the Magdalens, though. The water conditions are good. With luck we can nab him there. Especially if we can catch him on the surface."

Belanger gestured towards the new radar antenna. "If that kit is half as good as Smythe and everyone else claims, we should be able to establish an effective radar barrier. The British groups in the mid-ocean did it last fall with them. We should be able to do as well. And if all else fails, we'll catch him on the surface in the landing area."

"Do you trust Wagner to pull this off?" Fergus asked, rather directly.

Belanger weighed his answer and then said quietly, "I suppose not. You know, Fergus, Wagner is impetuous and in a hurry to impress. He'll push hard to get this sub, if there is one, before the destroyer arrives. But, in the end," Belanger said with resignation, "he has only a couple of real options and he might have enough sense to choose one of them."

"Well," Fergus observed, momentarily nonplussed by Belanger's candor, "that's encouraging. So, is this an attempt to sink a U-boat or an exercise in cutting an ambitious officer down to size?"

"I think it's both. Admiral Murray is not convinced there's a sub up here, although Prentice seems to think there is ..."

"But he thinks there's subs everywhere."

"Yes, well. Wagner is bound to screw up, and we're here to get the job done. We can only hope the admiral has enough sense to notice both."

Chapter 8

The orders came in the early hours of the morning. Fortunately most of the crews were sleeping away their first night ashore in barracks at the new Point Edward base. Another night and they would have been scattered in bars all over Sydney.

The order to return to sea so soon after arriving in Sydney was met with bitterness and anger by Commander Dickson. "Sorry, chum," the duty officer said, but Dickson had been too stupefied to answer. The orders instructed the 8th Flotilla to sail at 0800, absurd given the crews' state of exhaustion. Dickson persuaded the local staff that the dearth of stores on the launches, especially food and water, and the need to repair weather damage precluded such an early departure.

"What's the rush, anyway?" he growled at the operations officer who briefed him.

"Apparently a sub has slipped into the Gulf, or is about to. You're supposed to backstop the Brit trawlers, patrol in behind them – and the ice – just inside the Gulf."

So maybe that kid from Saskatchewan saw something after all, Dickson thought as he stumbled his way through the blacked-out base to the wardroom. Naw! Couldn't be. Too early in the season for a U-boat to enter the Gulf. But why else would they be doubling the patrols at the entrance?

To have the boats ready by 0800 would have obliged Dickson to get everyone out of their micks after only a few hours' sleep. Better to muster the crews at 0630 and get away as quickly as possible thereafter. Besides, three British trawlers already patrolled the Cabot Strait, and no-one at Sydney was informed enough to tell Dickson what all the haste was about. Just another mindless order from some faceless officer in a warm office moving a coloured pin on a map. The men could sleep.

The business of mustering the crews and preparing for sea proved to be an act of simple, blind will, for there was little other than food or duty at Point Edward to draw tired sailors from their comfortable barracks. The new naval base on the South Arm of Sydney harbour was a dreary place. Recently hacked from abandoned pasture and woodland, it was laid out in a neat grid pattern of streets: two main streets ran up from the wharfs between Crawly and Barasois creeks. Uninspired but wholly functional red-brick workshops and stores buildings lined the waterfront, while a tidy array of white, wood-frame barracks, messes and offices sprawled up the gentle slope.

Firm roadways were topped by crushed rock. Cinder pathways and duckboards ran to building entrances but these were not completely effective against the mud. On this May morning the puddles in Point Edward's main roads lay covered by a thin veneer of ice that shattered under the feet of sailors going about their tasks. Seaboots carried the ooze into every building, coating the floor of the seamen's mess, and onto the decks of the motor launches despite the best efforts of petty officers and the laying on of fire hoses. The cold, the mud, the wind, and the endless expanse of low, dark clouds reduced the morning's efforts to sullen, reluctant obedience.

By the time the launches got to sea at around 1100 the day was still chill and damp. Once clear of Sydney harbour and out into St. Ann's Bay the wind was raw, blowing directly from the cold waters of the Gulf and over the last of the winter's ice. Had it not been for that plug of ice, wedged tight against the tip of Cape Breton Island and reaching into the Cabot Strait, such a wind would have produced a long, heavy swell. But the ice dampened the wave action and the launches rode easily over the short, sharp little seas.

But it was cold. God, it was cold. They were headed into the teeth of the arctic wind, and those on the bridge were chilled to the bone. As they stood out into St. Ann's Bay Dickson put his back against the bridge bulkhead and pulled his watchcap down even with his eyebrows. Moisture from his breath glistened on his cheeks and dampened the edges of his collar. Babineau, the chief petty officer, stood beside Dickson, his face reddened by the wind, tears forming from the cold.

"You can smell de ice, Sir," Babineau observed, drawing a long breath.

"That you can, Babs."

The chief's comment seemed to rouse Dickson to speech, and there was much on Dickson's mind.

"You married Babs?"

"Yes Sir. Twenty-two years."

"Bin at sea all that time?"

"Longer, since I was thirdeen."

"Any kids?"

"Tree boys and a girl, all 'ealty. Da girl's married to a guy from 'illsborough, not far from Moncton. Two of da boys are overseas in the Army, and da youngest boy is still 'ome wit his mudder."

Dickson shuffled his feet and pulled his coat tighter around his neck. "Do you see them much? I mean, you've spent your life at sea – must be hard to do that and have a family, too?"

"Weeelll," Babineau drew a mittened hand across his nose to catch some of the dripping moisture. "I spent mos of my time in coastal work, you know: fishin' in da Nortumberland Strait, on da PEI ferries. It's only in the da tirties I started to go furdder off, on da Lady boats to da Caribbean, away from 'ome for munts at a time ..."

"Your wife never complained?"

"Oh, for sure, but what could she do, eh? What could I do?" Babineau shrugged his shoulders. "I was makin' good money when any money was 'ard to come by. 'Sides, by den all the kids had come along. She din't want no more enaway. She gut tired of me following her around when I was home on leave!" he said with an impish grin. "No, she gut her family 'round her – parents, brudder, sisters, huncles, all dat you know, and her own children – she don't need me much. And da church. It keeps 'er busy. I jist get in da way, so I'm better off 'ere."

The idea that someone would be happy at sea in a small boat far removed from loved ones had not occurred to Dickson. Babineau detected the puzzled look on Dickson's face, and shrugged. "Dis is what I know," Babineau said, "life at sea, dis coast. I'm a fish out of water at home ... Oh, I can drive a few nails here and dere, fix stuff, you know, and I've worked in da woods some in da lumber camps in New Brunswick – I did the 1934 spring drive on the Nashwaak. It's much like dis – all men, hard work. But I'm not a farmer or lumberjack, I 'ave no use for church and don't fit polite comp'ny. So I send mos of my pay home, see da wife and kids when I can – or when I want – and spend my days doing what I'm bes at ...

"So why'd you ask? You got a wife, Sir?"

"Oh, no ... no wife, Babs ... nope."

"But a girl, right?"

"Well, there's somebody in Kingston, maybe. But I don't think she'll want to marry a sailor," Dickson said, smiling at his grizzled officer.

"Not if she gut sense, Sir!" Babineau smiled, adding, "But yer not gonna be a sailor after da war – that's for sure – she gonna wait!"

Dickson did not respond.

"She didn't wait already, dat right."

Dickson remained silent.

"Some army guy?"

Dickson finally muttered, "Nope, air force. Some guy from a training base near Kingston, Australian or somethin'."

"Hurt pretty bad, eh?"

"We got engaged just before I left for Halifax. I didn't get home much in '42, and I guess she got bored, met this guy in a bar... Got the news in the mail last night ... buddy of mine wrote."

"Tough news, Mr. Dickson."

"Yup."

"So mebbe you gonna join the navy after all?" Babineau tried to ease the tension with a grin, but Dickson's face remained expressionless.

After a moment Dickson turned, pushed his head up into the wind and took a long breath. "You know, Babs, I think you're right. I think you can smell the ice."

"For sure, Sir. It's only a few miles away, nort or jist west of nort.

Dis wind'll drive it down along dis shore in big chunks and pans. Da sooner we're out of here da better."

"That's probably why they wanted us out of Sydney and gave us a patrol area off Cape Ray ..."

"Yes, Sir. The current sets west off suddern Newfoundland, dere'll be no ice along dat shore. Anyway, dis wind won't hold. It's too early in da season for steady nortwesterlies. It'll back tomorrow to da south." Then Babineau grinned. "And den we'll just have da fog to worry about – an' mebbe some ice trown in for good measure!"

The image of her shimmered in his brain: the tantalizing line of her dress curving over her hips, those marvellous breasts swelling under her blouse, the softness of her hair to his touch, the luscious pouting lips, and those huge, longing eyes. Even her scent consumed him.

It seemed to take hours. But he had finally managed to get her out of her clothes. Slowly, piece by piece. Then she took him by the hand and led him to what they had both longed for, a blur of fevered groping and frantic kisses and, at last, her legs slipping apart. The soft brush of her thighs against his hips, her moistness and the warmth of their embrace – and so the rhythmic thrusting began, steady, long and slow. Dickson could feel his whole body moving rhythmically. And he could hear his name called out with each thrust – "Dickson! Dickson! ... Dickson!" growing steadily louder.

Then his eyes opened to grey paint on the wheelhouse bulkhead.

Noiles' hands were still shaking him from the stupor into which he had fallen on the bunk.

"Andy! Shit! What the hell ..."

"Wake up Dick, we're coming up on *Ayrshire*."

Noiles swung Dickson's feet to the deck, slapped him on the shoulder and returned to the bridge. Dickson rubbed his head, trying to log away as much of the dream as he could. *No face, can't recall a face.* As he stood to stretch and tighten his dufflecoat Dickson caught a glimpse of the British anti-submarine trawler *Ayrshire* through the wheelhouse window. Noiles had left it damned late, he thought, and scrambled up to the bridge.

Like all little warships engaged in the Atlantic war, *Ayrshire*'s white and pastel blue paint was grimy and stained. It was also soot-blackened from her coal-fired boilers.

"Put us alongside, Cox'n!" Dickson ordered through the wheel-house voicepipe.

As they eased in, *Ayrshire* heaved gently on the short swell. Her open welldeck was designed to be close to the sea so that the trawl could be easily handled. Even in this sea it shipped water through the washports and spilled it out each time she rose. Her captain, identifiable by his service cap, stood by the wheelhouse railing, megaphone in hand.

Q246 was able to come alongside without much danger of collision and Dickson, on his bridge, was only a few feet lower than *Ayrshire*'s captain. Megaphones were unnecessary.

"Good evening *Ayrshire*!" Dickson called.

"And good evening to you, Canada!" her captain replied in a proper, educated British accent. No old salt here, Dickson said to himself. "And what brings you lads out this fine day, Canada?"

"The same as you, Lieutenant," Dickson answered. "Orders!"

"Ah yes. But we've been naughty, you see. We've been rusticated: banished to the colonies for our sins.

"God save thee, Ancient Mariner!
From the fiends that plague thee thus! –
Why look'st thou so? – With my crossbow
I shot the Albatross."

"Christ, Noiles!" Dickson muttered. "A hundred miles from nowhere and we find the only fuckin' rust bucket in the British navy commanded by a fuckin' Oxford Don!"

"Tennyson, I think," Noiles whispered.

"Very appropriate, Lieutenant," Dickson called, "Tennyson, I assume."

"Coleridge, actually."

Dickson threw a cold stare at Noiles. "We didn't do much Coleridge in the engineering program at Queen's."

"Quite so. And here we are, doomed to steam the edge of the ice in perpetuity 'And ice, mast high, came floating by!' But I say, we know why *we're* here. But you must have committed some heinous crime to have been ordered into the icy fastnesses, old boy?"

"Perhaps – but you must have sodomized an admiral!"

"Would that I had, old boy! By God, if I'd done the old bugger I'd be safe as houses, banished to Bermuda, eh what! So what are you up to?"

"We're passing beyond you to patrol between Cape Ray and the northern edge of the ice."

"Egad, Canada, you have been naughty. What are you supposed to find up there?"

"Apparently there's a sub inbound for the Gulf. We're supposed to backstop you – to provide an inner barrier. Haven't you heard?"

"Nothing at all."

"Well perhaps you don't need to know, you're already in position. Odd, though."

"Well, not to worry, we're hardly the Home Fleet you know. No-one tells us much. Anything we can do to speed you on your way?"

"No, not unless you know where the ice is."

"Indeed we do. It's about twenty-five miles northwest. I suspect that this wind has pushed it farther southeast today and may have broken it up a bit. I'd be bloody careful in those little boats of yours."

"Yes, well, the wind's falling a bit now. We'll try to run around the northern edge before dark."

"Well then don't linger, Canada. Can we offer you anything?"

"No thank you, Lieutenant. We left Sydney around noon and we're well provisioned."

With that Dickson bent to the wheelhouse voicepipe and ordered the cox'n to begin pulling away.

"Good day, *Ayrshire*!"

"And good day to you, Canada. Happy hunting."

Dickson smiled and waved. With a throaty roar of her engines *Q246* dug her stern in and slipped around *Ayrshire*'s stern and northward. The rest of the flotilla, which had been waiting to leeward, fell in behind. A slight brown smudge on the northwestern horizon indicated the location of another British trawler: the third would be off to the south somewhere.

By now the wind had veered to northerly and fallen to less than five knots. The flotilla had some distance to go before they could be sure they were past the ice and it now became a race against time.

They lost the race around 2100.

Dickson was peering through the gathering darkness when his worst fears were realized. "Ice, Andy," he said without lowering his glasses, "Ice as far as the eye can see."

There it was, a vast field of broken ice, beaten by the winds and waves into a broad expanse of pans and pieces. Dickson glanced skyward, back at the ice and then back at the sky, looking for the moon. The sky was clear to the south, the line of clouds sharp against the twilight.

"Think we can slip through?" Noiles asked.

"If we get some light, yes. It's clearing so we should get starlight and maybe a bit of moon later. That'll highlight the ice and we ought to be able to steer through."

"But Dick, what if it's solid? What if the whole field has shifted this way? We'll never get through."

"The mass of the ice is still west of us. This stuff has probably only broken off the leading edge by wind and wave action. I think we can winkle our way through."

Babineau listened to the whole discussion, said nothing and made no attempt to intervene. Dickson cast him an unobtrusive glance and received a discrete nod in reply.

Noiles was not so sure, but he had to admit that as they got closer the ice looked less thick, with wide avenues between the larger pieces.

"Cox'n!" Dickson barked through the voicepipe, "hold her here. Saunders, tell the flotilla to close up for orders. Andy, check the glass and see what it's doing."

As *Q246* drifted to a stop Noiles slipped into the wheelhouse to look at the barometer. When all the motor launches were assembled Dickson explained his belief that the ice field was only a scattered remnant driven downwind during the day. Since the barometric pressure was rising and the sky nearly clear, he intended to use the starlight and moonlight to pick his way through. "It's probably only a few miles anyway."

Minnifie protested that the Fairmiles could not withstand any ice and recommended that they slip a few miles east, where the ice might be even more dispersed. Dickson agreed. *Q246* led the flotilla northeast for about an hour, keeping the icefield visible to port. Finally, with the sky now sharp and clear overhead Dickson brought *Q246* to a halt.

"Saunders! Order them to close up behind us and everyone but the last to burn a taillight. Tell them to keep two cables apart so we don't have to do a lot of backing up in case we enter a false lead.

"Chief! Muster a party on the foc'sle with boathooks and oars to fend off anything we don't see. I'm going up here," and he pointed to the top of the wheelhouse. "Andy, you stay put and pass along my helm orders in case the cox'n can't hear 'em."

With that Dickson clambered over the forward edge of the bridge and up into the wheelhouse. Saunders flashed the orders astern and Babineau led a party of men armed with boat hooks and oars onto *Q246*'s bow.

"We might just make it," Noiles muttered to himself.

With that Dickson ordered "Ahead on both, dead slow," and turned the 8th Flotilla north into the ice.

The first hour or so went well. Babineau's foc'sle party had nothing to do as *Q246* and her followers slipped easily between widely spaced pans of ice. Dickson ordered an increase in speed, and everyone relaxed a bit.

After midnight, however, the wind veered to the south; a gentle easy breeze, but warm and moist. The mass of southern air arrived in the form of a fogbank, advancing like a wall across the sea.

One by one the trailing boats disappeared from sight. Dickson ordered a full stop as the fog poured in over them. Stars were still visible straight overhead but the thick fog at sea level cut visibility to a few yards.

"Shit!" Dickson muttered as he clambered back onto the top of the wheelhouse.

"What can you see, Dick?" Noiles asked, hoping that Dickson's higher perch put him above the worst of it.

"Not a damn thing. It's all I can do to see the sea!"

"Now what?"

"Fucked if I know!" Dickson growled as he jumped down. "Babineau!" he shouted over the bridge windshield, "Get some men down along the sides as well."

"Saunders, tell the flotilla to form on us, use our foghorn as a rallying point. Tell them we'll wait this out for a while, hope it blows away or burns off quickly in the morning. Got that?"

"Yes Sir. There's two simple options. I can send out a steady Morse 'CS', that's the International Code for 'You should try' – er 'endeavour' I guess – 'to come alongside' or 'KV', that means 'You should come under my stern'."

Dickson didn't want a lesson in foghorn signalling at sea, he wanted the flotilla to gather around *Q246* and stay close in the fog.

"Which one is easiest to send?"

"'CS' Sir."

"Right, well send that."

Saunders stepped to the foghorn, sent the 8th Flotilla's four-letter call sign and then began a regular series of 'CS' in Morse. The blaring of the horn was tedious, but the answers allowed Dickson to get a rough idea of range and bearing to the other boats. Soon a couple of dark shadows appeared in the fog and Dickson was able to speak to them through his megaphone – Minnifie and Jackson. Two more to go.

Everyone waited in tense anticipation on *Q246*'s bridge as Saunders repeated the order. Apart from the horn and the gentle throb of the engines little could be heard until, in an interval between one of the Morse signals, Jackson sent a signal of his own.

Dickson cast a questioning glance at Saunders.

"It's Mr. Aubrey's boat, Sir. He sent 'IW: I have been in collision'. I assume he means with the other boat."

"Ask him if they need help."

Saunders sounded the horn again: dot, dot dot dot dot – 'EH: can I assist you?'

In a moment the simple answer came: dash, dot – 'N: no'.

Dickson understood the signal and ordered Saunders to keep sending 'CS'.

After about twenty minutes Jackson reported Thoreau and Aubrey visible in the gloom astern.

"Jackson!" Dickson called through his megaphone. "Check with those two and find out if everything's all right!"

He could hear voices farther back in the fog, quite a conversation, but no-one in *Q246* could tell what was being said. Finally Jackson spoke up.

"Thoreau's fine. Aubrey's boat had minor damage. Had to avoid ramming Thoreau. Bumped a sheet of ice rather hard astern, near the fuel tanks. Aubrey says she's taking a bit of water but nothing the bilge pumps can't handle. What now?"

"Keep your running lights on, and stay in contact. We'll go to dead slow and push on."

And so they did throughout the night, pushing small sheets of ice clear or nudging themselves away from larger pieces. The steady and very slight southerly breeze helped push the launches northwards through the icefield.

What Dickson feared most was getting caught in a narrow lead; too tight to press through, tricky to back out of, and in danger of closing if the wind shifted. But what they encountered was the rotted remnant of the winter's ice beaten into large pans and fields of small pieces and slush. Occasionally they came into stretches completely free of ice.

But the night required constant vigilance to keep *Q246*'s bow clear of larger pieces and find a course through the ice. Saunders remained on the bridge, ready to transmit instantly to the flotilla. Only once did he have to send a prompt signal to stop them in their tracks, flashing a 'K' – dash dot dash – with his signal lamp and sending it by foghorn at the same time: 'You should stop your vessel instantly.' *Q246* had run up against a large sheet of ice and for a moment the way around was unclear.

This is damned stupid, Dickson thought, no place for wooden boats! But instinct told him to swing to starboard and the flotilla crept along the edge of the sheet until it began to curve northward. Then, as they resumed their northerly course, the sheet disappeared into the murk on the portside.

Even with the warm air pouring in over them it was cold work. Air temperature at sea level was around freezing and the air was saturated with moisture. Noiles organized the deckhands into relays, with one group always below sucking down vats of cocoa and warming themselves while the other waited on deck, boathooks and oars in hand.

Dickson and Noiles took turns, too, one standing in the very eyes of the boat, watching for ice and passing helm orders to the other, who took what comfort there was from the shelter of the bridge. Only cocoa and an overwhelming sense of responsibility for the safety of the flotilla kept the two officers going.

An hour or so before dawn they were clear.

Dickson kept them closed up and motoring slow ahead until the sun came up, just in case. As the day brightened Aubrey came alongside to report his damage. When his boat rose on the gentle swell a jagged gash could be seen just below the waterline.

"She handling it okay?" Dickson asked.

"Oh yeah, not much coming in. The Chief's more worried about fuel contamination, 'specially if the water rises between the fuel tank bulkheads."

"You stay right in behind me for now," Dickson ordered as the 8th shaped a northerly course through the fog, hoping to make a landfall off Cape Ray, Newfoundland.

"So far so good!" Andy sighed as *Q246*'s engines increased their tempo.

"Yeah," Dickson snapped. "If we can figure out where the hell we are. Finding a fuckin' U-boat can damn well wait ... You want some cocoa?"

"Sure Dick, I'll get it – "

"Naw, Andy. You dunno how, let me show ya ..."

Chapter 9

Monday's naval staff meeting in Ottawa had concentrated on the enduring problem of asdic sets for the fleet. Few on the naval staff had needed convincing. The new Captain of Destroyers at St. John's, a Brit officer on loan, was already complaining that his ships could not kill U-boats. "The problems of a corvette captain trying to attack a submerged U-boat with a type 123A asdic and a swinging magnetic compass," he complained to Ottawa, "are well-nigh insoluble."

"This problem admits of no quick solution, gentlemen," Nelles had told the staff. "I think we are all agreed that the best way forward is to concentrate our limited supply of modern asdic equipment in the new-construction ships, especially the frigates." Heads nodded around the table. "And all the latest is, in fact, being manufactured here in Canada, is it not?"

Again heads had nodded around the table. Then the Staff Officer, Anti-Submarine chimed in, "I believe so, Sir. The Royal Navy has extensive contracts with Research Enterprises Limited in Toronto and some other firms to manufacture the type 144 asdic and the new 'Q' attachment."

"Find out, would you Commander? Looks like we'll have to get the government involved."

"I hope our balance of payments is good, Admiral," Captain Lay, the Director of Operations, said with a smirk.

The previous December the Navy had watched the first Canadian-built frigates steam down the St. Lawrence to join the US Navy. These were ships the Canadian Navy desperately needed, but they had been built under British contract and paid for by the Americans under lend-lease. As Canada needed the contracts – and the US dollars –no politician raised a finger to stop them going. Nelles had protested to no avail. "Yours will be along soon enough," Macdonald explained.

The whole business was quite impracticable, and now Macdonald was carping openly about having built the wrong kind of fleet. Even his executive assistant, J. J. Connolly, whined about the need for more destroyers and possibly aircraft carriers.

All this weighed on Percy Nelles' mind as he headed down the corridor to his office. He had scarcely taken a step when Jones, the Vice Chief of the Naval Staff, intercepted him.

The Navy still functioned in the old way, Nelles thought, with followers clustered around a rising star. It was not surprising then that since arriving at headquarters Jones had moved many of his own people into key positions. Gangs, really. The Murray gang on the east coast, the Jones gang in Ottawa. The Hatfields and the McCoys. Nelles heard rumours that Jones was talking to Macdonald. He had given the rumours little credence until a few days ago, when he'd seen Jones lingering in Macdonald's outer office. Jones had heard their whole row, yet said nothing about it; no words of conciliation, or support – or explanation. What had he been doing in the Minister's outer office in the first place?

"Thought you might like to see this, Admiral," Jones said, handing Nelles the latest *Maclean's*. "I picked it up at the Chateau Laurier this morning. Have a look at page six."

Nelles passed his stack of folders and notes to Jones in exchange for the magazine, and flipped to the feature article. Two large photos dominated the opening page, one of an air navigator "outwitting wind and weather" to find a U-boat and the other an aerial shot of a U-boat under attack – presumably as a result of the navigator's unerring skill. The title across the top of the page read, "They Kill U-Boats".

Nelles snapped the magazine closed and thrust it towards Jones with a brusque, "So do we!" grabbed his files and turned away.

"Yes," Jones called after him, "but perhaps not often enough."

Jones had meant his comment as a plea, but for Nelles it was a red flag. He turned on his heel and strode back to point-blank range.

"Look," he said, pushing in close so the anger in his words would not carry far, "the Prime Minister had one kill to announce to the House when it opened in February, and another in March. He will have a couple more in the next few days once the final clearances are complete. We sink U-boats, too, and with some skill, I might add, despite our equipment."

"Yes, Admiral," Jones said in a conciliatory tone, "but all of these recent sinkings have been thousands of miles away – in the Mediterranean or off Portugal, for God's sake! The piece in *The Globe and Mail* on *Port Arthur*'s U-boat last Saturday was good coverage, but the air force has sunk U-boats close to home and as a result, they get better political leverage out of their kills."

"What matters most, George, is that U-boats get killed. It doesn't matter a tinker's damn where it happens. This is a global war, not some petty campaign in Canadian inshore waters." Nelles was starting to fume. He had been over this ground time and again.

"If we could get all the U-boats in the world into the Gulf of St. Lawrence and then never sink any of them," Nelles said, raising his voice a decibel or two, "we would win the war. Saint John and Halifax can handle all our shipping needs: they do it during the winter months, they can damn well do it during the summer, too."

"Surely you cannot believe that closing the nation's largest east coast port to ocean shipping is of little consequence ..." Jones retorted.

"It's a major political problem, George," Nelles barked, jabbing a finger in Jones' direction, "but that means it's Macdonald's problem, not mine. I have a war to fight. If Macdonald is so bloody concerned about the image of the naval war he should get some of his political organization onto the press. That rag you're holding," Nelles pointed contemptuously, "has consistently ignored the naval war effort. The Battle of the Atlantic is reaching its climax, and not once," he said, his face now red with anger, "not once this year has it featured an article, let alone a cover story, on the Navy. Who's fault is that? Eh? Mine? They've featured British generals – Montgomery and Alan Brooke – and Canadian generals – MacNaughton at least. They've written up

Buzz Beurling and Air Vice Marshal Edwards, but the only sailors you see in the press are Players cigarette ads! Thank God the *Globe* deigned to cover the change of command on the east coast last Saturday."

The long feature article on the front page of the *Globe* had described the athletic and energetic Admiral Murray as Canada's answer to the U-boat problem. Jones quaked at the thought.

"Headline articles," Nelles went on, "are just the tonic we need. Their reporter is right: Murray and Prentice are the men to tackle the U-boat menace. We've had to manage for almost two years with the Americans on our back. Now we can get on with the war, in our own way, managing our own resources. But it's not my job to sell the Navy to the Canadian people. That's for the politicians – for Macdonald." The admiral's finger drove home each point just short of Jones' chest, "I suggest you tell him that, and let me get on with the war!"

"So what are we supposed to tell them, the Canadian people? 'Another convoy arrived safely today!' Canadians expect their sailors to fight, not herd cattle. We need dramatic action *here*, Admiral. We need a complete restructuring of the fleet, we need new ships – destroyers, aircraft carriers, maybe cruisers, and we need them soon."

"Start by telling them the truth, as boring as it is. As for the ships, I couldn't agree more but we aren't going to pull them out of a hat. Meanwhile we work with what we have, consolidation of the fleet and the inshore offensive Murray and Prentice have planned."

Jones could not disagree more. He looked away and mumbled something that sounded like 'Laurel and Hardy'.

"What?"

"I said, hardly – hardly likely to succeed. Look, Murray and Prentice," he uttered the names with some contempt, "are not going to sink subs inshore. We tried that all last year and it doesn't work. Fiddling with training and doctrine isn't going to solve the riddle, the River and Gulf waters are just too complex and our asdics are too primitive. If the Navy wants to make the national press it has to take the war to the enemy. We need our own U-boat killers operating where the asdics work and where the U-boats are – northeast of Newfoundland. And we need big ships engaged in high-profile operations."

Jones took Nelles gently by the arm, making his final point in soft but deliberate tones. "Macdonald is under intense pressure in Cabinet. The whole naval program – now and postwar – hangs in the balance." With this clear threat to the Navy Jones pressed his case. "There are four federal bye-elections this summer and the Ontario provincial election. It looks as if they will all go Tory. Put yourself in Macdonald's place! We need to stop playing it safe. If we are to close the Gulf, put those extra forces where they will do the most good! Strip Murray's command of spare ships, re-organize our escort groups in the mid-ocean to redeploy the best ships for hunting, and get our own killer groups out where the U-boats are – now. And we need to push for Canadian escort aircraft carriers by the end of the year."

Nelles did not like being bullied and threatened by his vice chief, but he had to admit that Jones had a point. They were all in the soup if Murray's scheme for an inshore offensive against the U-boats in 1943 failed.

"Look, George," Nelles responded grimly, "if Mr. King had not let the army sit on its ass in Britain for the last three years his government wouldn't be on the ropes now. It's a bit late to ask the Navy to pull the Liberal Party's feet from the fire! We are committed to operations that cannot be turned off and on at the whim of politicians. The British will not allow us – "

"The British be damned! It's our war, too, and we have the forces to take action on our own. Good God, Admiral, half of what Roosevelt and Churchill do is because of political pressure!"

"Yes, but Mr. King is not Roosevelt or Churchill. *They* run the war. Mr. King does as he is told, and so, I am afraid, do we! And besides, we cannot manufacture U-boat kills – the German submariners actually do try to avoid us, you know! It's their job to avoid getting killed!"

Nelles was now getting steam up again, but restrained himself. He ought to save his worst for Macdonald, not squander it on Jones.

"But we can hedge our bets," Jones insisted, "by putting our best ships where the action is, and the action is now in the mid-ocean."

"George," Nelles took a softer tone. "You may be right. But for the moment the inshore offensive allows us to get the fleet close to refit yards and back on its feet. Besides, we cannot let the Cabinet dictate where the ships will go, that's our job as Navy men. Those bastards have already sold the army to the devil by packing off the 1st Infantry Division to Sicily just to slake the mob's thirst for blood. But I will be damned, George, if I am going to change course every time the political wind shifts a point or two. No, we'll trim our sails but hold our course. The U-boat kills will come."

With that, Nelles set off down the corridor.

The nascent Operational Intelligence Centre was emerging from the ongoing re-organization of naval headquarters. It was run by the marvellously eccentric Commander Jean deMarbois. Born in the Mascarene Islands of Scottish parents, he had most recently been instructor of languages – Russian, Arabic, German, French, Chinese, Turkish and Bantu – at Upper Canada College.

"Jock, what's the status in the Gulf?"

Nelles' unannounced entrance caught the Director of Naval Intelligence by surprise. "Oh! Good morning, Admiral! Yes, just a moment while I get things squared away ... Ah, yes, here it is. At the moment we have no confirmed U-boats anywhere in the Gulf, nor, for that matter, has OIC in London – at least that's what they tell me. We've got no decrypted tasking signals assigning a U-boat to the area. Our direction finding stations report no transmission in the area, either.

"The only evidence of U-boats – tenuous at best, but in the right spot – is from an observer on Miscou Island in northern New Brunswick. He reported a flashing light at sea about six miles offshore and directly opposite Chandler. Investigations by the army and RCMP along that coast last night and this morning turned up nothing. But that's about where our chap should be – perhaps a little ahead of our estimate, but not appreciably. Unfortunately, this is not the first such report this spring. Nor will it be the last. That coast still has the jitters from last year."

"Very well, Jock, but it is promising. We seem to have fallen behind in our deployments, don't you think?"

"Well, yes and no, Sir. The British trawlers and the 8th Motor Launch Flotilla are in the Cabot Strait, where they've been since last evening at least. The main force came through the Canso Strait earlier this morning and should be on station north of the Magdalens later today as planned. However, it is entirely conceivable that the U-boat was already well into the Gulf. If so, we have closed the barn door after the horse has escaped."

"Is the unknown light off Miscou enough to change the current deployment? Do we dare collapse the search into the landing area this early?"

DeMarbois was uncertain, and had been hoping Nelles would not ask him that question, even though it was the only logical one now. It was best, he thought, to work through the options.

"If the object is to prevent the agent landing, we may already be too late. A search by local army and RCMP is not conclusive. They caught Janowski at New Carlisle last year because he was stupid, or more likely he wanted to be caught. This Frenchman has a motive for staying at large and much greater likelihood of fitting in locally, especially if he has local contacts."

"Agreed, but let's assume that sinking the U-boat is the top priority. If the agent is still aboard, so much the better, but sinking the submarine is vital."

"Well, the best bet may be to call in the air force and have them localize the contact for us."

"No," Nelles cut in icily, "the air force will only make him aware that he's being tracked. They'll drive him down and we'll never find the bugger. It's our show. No, our best chance is to give the ships the first crack at him, before he gets spooked."

"All right, then I suggest we concentrate the search forces in this area," deMarbois said, scribing an arc on the map about thirty miles offshore running from Miscou Island to the entrance to Gaspé Harbour. "He has to enter this area to put someone ashore, at least where we have been told he will do so; but it's far enough to seaward not to spook him at the landing place itself. Unless you can find a few more ships, I don't see what else we can do."

Nelles was inclined to agree, but instinctively opposed moving so quickly into the landing area. He was concerned about compromising the source of the special intelligence – always a concern in these cases – and anxious that the sub be allowed to go deeply into the trap before the main force sprang it. The choices were just not very good.

"And you've managed a cover for this deployment?"

"Yes, in consultation with Admiral Murray and Captain Prentice we have labelled this another part of the working-up program for the Gulf forces."

"Good. Leave the deployments for the moment. Let me know if anything changes."

Gulf of St. Lawrence, Monday 3 May 1943

All things considered, it was an excellent afternoon for flying. The remnants of Sunday's high pressure system remained, marred only by a thin layer of alto-cumulus cloud at 10,000 feet; the mackerel sky that warned of another approaching low pressure system. The wind in the central Gulf had swung to southeasterly; this, too, evidence of advancing rain. But for the moment the sun poured down, and the southerly breeze warmed the low, sandy Magdalen Islands, cutting at the traces of snow that lingered in the shelter of evergreens, and driving swirls of dust and sand along the beaches.

Paul Gallagher and the crew of Canso J, a flying boat from 273 (Bomber Reconnaissance) Squadron of the RCAF, had lifted off from Dartmouth four hours earlier en route to Gaspé with some stores. The Gulf flying season was about to commence, and a detachment of Cansos would be based in the harbour at Gaspé. Gallagher was leading the advance party.

Even when fully loaded a Canso could fly all day and then some, and Gallagher had his CO's permission to use the transit as a familiarization flight. They had flown over the Cabot Strait to get a bird's eye view of the last vestiges of winter ice, and buzzed a few warships patrolling between the ice and the Newfoundland shore. Poor bastards, such a lonely vigil on that vast and brutally cold sea. Gallagher then swung his aircraft westward to Gaspé and had come upon Northeast Cape, two-hundred-foot sheer cliffs that tower over the sea on the Magdalen Islands.

A straggling outcrop of red sandstone cliffs, long sandy dunes and beaches, and verdant evergreens, the Magdalens lay like jewels in the brilliant blue waters of the Gulf. The sight was too much for Gallagher to resist. With an easy breeze blowing and only a few whitecaps Canso J flew with ease at sea level, steering long, lazy turns down the eastern side of the islands.

Gallagher was tempted to set her down in the lagoon in front of Cap aux Meules to see what local delicacies they could cabbage.

As the Canso swung in low over Pointe Basse light he called the flight engineer on the intercom. "Maxwell, this is the Cap'n here. Everything okay? That port magneto isn't acting up again, is it? Think we should sit her down for a few minutes to do a check?" A dour mechanical type who prided himself on his skill at keeping Canso J flying, Maxwell missed the point entirely.

"Everything's just fine Skipper. We can keep this baby in the air all day!"

Gallagher shot a glance across at Turner, the co-pilot, who simply rolled his eyes. "You're sure, Max?" Gallagher prodded.

"Yup, absolutely Skipper."

"Nothin' that wants fixing at all? Yer sure?"

"Nah, not a thing: she's purring along just fine."

So, instead of a few quiet hours at Cap Aux Meules, Canso J swept southward over Pleasant Bay, south of Grindstone Island, and crossed the sand dunes that connected Grindstone with Amherst Island, nearly low enough to brush the sedges on the dunes. Then Gallagher swung the aircraft northward, along the western dune to Grosse Isle. His crew waved to the locals while he revelled in the sheer pleasure of unrestricted flight.

As they reached the end of the main islands, Gallagher was drawn in a northerly direction by the sails of several small fishing boats, to Brion Island and Bird Rock – more stuff to buzz at low altitude. They 'attacked' Brion Island at sea level, roaring in – if one could use that term for the lumbering Canso – from the lower south side, and rising as if driven upward by the sheer force of the air compressed between the sharply rising island and the underside of the wings.

As the aircraft levelled out on a northerly heading Gallagher wondered whether to check out Bird Rocks, two barren plugs of red sandstone ten miles to the east occupied almost exclusively by gannets, puffins and gulls. Gallagher's windscreen was so caked with salt spray that he could only see clearly by glancing sideways out the open window, so he was inclined to head for Gaspé. The air gunners in their blister canopies who had an almost unobstructed view, lobbied for Bird Rocks. Burke, the bomb aimer, could not have cared less – he was sacked out on a bunk behind the wireless operator and navigator. They, too, had had enough, as had Turner, the co-pilot. Grantham, the radio operator, had no opinion: he was busy cleaning up the coffee spilled during the run over Brion Island and cursing Gallagher.

As the debate went on Canso J slipped effortlessly northward, pushed gently by the following wind. Finally, Gallagher squeezed the button on his intercom, "Nav? Give me a heading for Gaspé."

"Right Skipper, turn left onto 290. If you bring her up to 5,000 feet and hold her steady at 120 knots we should be down in about an hour and twenty minutes."

"Right, thanks Nav. Grantham? You back?" The radio operator had slipped from his post to fetch more coffee.

"Skipper, this is Nav again. Grantham's having a piss, or barffing, don't know which."

Gallagher acknowledged, and glanced down at his instrument panel to check his current status before executing the turn. Just then Turner jabbed him in the shoulder. "What's that down there? Straight ahead, d'ya see it?"

Gallagher glanced out his open window. There was definitely something there, less than half a mile ahead, low and long, its wake barely discernible amid the scattered whitecaps. They were closing very rapidly. "It's a sub!" But it didn't look like any of the U-boats in the recognition pictures. "Maybe American. Look, the conning tower seems to have guns on both ends – never seen anything like that before." Could it be a British sub? Gallagher wondered, just as the first 20mm rounds slammed into the cockpit.

Chapter 10

Dawn had not yet broken behind the dark hills of Cape Breton, as the Main Force began to win its anchors from the muddy bottom of Venus Cove. The wind had dropped early in the middle watch and by 0300 local time Wagner had the ships moving.

If the clattering of *Lakeville*'s steam winch was not enough to wake the good citizens of Mulgrave, petty officer Ryan was on the foc'sle, adding to the din. "Keep that hose on the cable, Macpherson, you fat-arsed lubber!" he bellowed, "I'll have you clean the friggin' cable locker with a toothbrush! Jaysus, Jaysus, how we gonna win this war with this friggin' bunch!"

Belanger was convinced the whole exercise was futile, so he had welcomed a few hours of uninterrupted sleep off Mulgrave; but the decision to leave as soon as the wind dropped was prudent. The sooner they were on station, the better the chances of actually intercepting the submarine in deep water – if there was a sub.

And so the main force was soon in line ahead off Macnair Point heading for the narrowest part of the Strait. The black hills of Inverness County brooded down on them from the north, and the great lump of Porcupine Mountain rose sheer from the southern shore.

"You see that hill," Macpherson said to 'Phonse as they lingered on the foc'sle clearing away lines and cables, "some day somebody's gonna dump that friggin' thing down into the strait and you'll be able to drive to Cape Breton."

122

'Phonse looked up at the sharply rising, tree-covered slopes. "Ya, fer sure. Ya know, dis place, its remind me of da Saguenay. You hever bin on da Saguenay River, Mac?"

"No, never bin up it, but I was sure past it often enough last summer. Real pretty, lotsa whales and stuff, eh?"

"Yep!"

The two men puttered on the foc'sle, trying hard to stretch out a few minutes' work. The serenity of the scene and the retreat of everyone else out of earshot gave Macpherson his chance.

"You know, 'Phonse, Kos is pretty pissed off at you 'bout last Saturday."

"Look, Mac! I was not dere by da time you guys guts in dat fight, eh! Audrey an me, we tooked a walk in Points Pleasant's Park and ..."

"Yeah, I know, I know!" Macpherson did not feel 'Phonse had let them down. "I think that may be part of what Kos is so pissed about. You nabbed a bint and Kos, well ...."

Suddenly Ryan, noticing the slackers, put an end to the conversation, if not to the issue of 'Phonse's absence from the brawl.

By the time the sun was up *Lakeville* and her consorts were clear of St. George's Bay, headed northwest. The day was fine and clear, with a gentle southeasterly breeze behind them. It was a superb day to be on the water. Although the sea was cold, the sun beat down and by afternoon it was shirtsleeve weather on deck. The highlands of Cape Breton, emerald green and strikingly beautiful, looked down upon them until mid-afternoon, fading slowly to starboard as the first dog-watch was called. For a brief stretch in late afternoon there was nothing to be seen but *Tracadie, Castlegar, Innisfail, Watson Lake* and *Lakeville*, ploughing northward, their white and pastel camouflage schemes clear against the dark blue sea. By suppertime there were sunburnt faces all around.

The routine of patrolling northeast of Bird Rocks, in the deep water of the Gulf, began in early evening.

"Signal from *Tracadie*, Sir," Maynard reported to Belanger. Fergus peered over his shoulder and read the signal aloud.

"'Main Force is to conduct endless chain patrol due north of Great Bird Rock along a line between 47.55N/61.08W and 48.20N/61.08W. In accordance with CB 4097 (43), para 379 (e), ships are to maintain a distance of 7,000 yards. Ships proceeding north will keep 5,000 yards west of the search line, those proceeding south will keep 5,000 east of the line. Zero time 2400Z: speed 12 knots: asdic range maximum: *Watson Lake, Innisfail, Tracadie, Castlegar, Lakeville*: radar and active asdic to be used.' I'll get Confidential Book 4097."

"Don't bother. Wagner briefed the captains on his intentions at Mulgrave. The plan is essentially in accordance with the Anti-Submarine Patrols manual. The only thing he hasn't got right is the size of the search. The ship spacing of 7,000 yards is supposed to include the distance on both sides of the box. That would have us doing an endless chain patrol for only about ten or twelve miles north of Bird Rocks. He's got us going nearly thirty."

"Do you think he knows?" Fergus asked.

"Oh yes. He thinks that the concept can be applied to a line."

"And you don't?"

"We'll bunch up at either end and leave a lot of water unattended astern, Fergus, but there's no point arguing with him. It's not an unreasonable or unworkable plan. As CB 4097 says, 'risks must be taken when a patrol of this kind is established'."

"Quite so," Fergus replied with mock solemnity, thrusting his right hand into the front of his duffle coat like Napoleon, "Something must be left to chance!"

Belanger looked at him with a grin, "Wrong fellow, Fergus! That's Nelson you just quoted, not Napoleon."

"Even better!"

And so in the early evening of May third *Watson Lake* led the endless chain patrol north of Great Bird Rock. *Innisfail*, Wagner in *Tracadie, Castlegar* and *Lakeville* followed in line ahead. The only change Wagner made in their night orders was to increase the distance between the ships to 7,500 yards, as specified for ships equipped with type 271 radar, based on the assumption that any submarine travelling at night would be on the surface and that 7,500 yards gave good overlap in radar coverage.

By the time night fell the wind had risen to thirty knots from the southeast and intermittent rain had begun. With the wind came a rising sea that struck *Lakeville* and her consorts just as they made their first turn at the northern end of the patrol area. As they moved down the southern leg of the search the sea met *Lakeville* on her port bow, creating an uncomfortable corkscrew motion. The men on deck were lashed by a cold rain and salt spray as *Lakeville* shouldered her way through each oncoming sea.

After a day of brilliant sun the cold, wet, impenetrable darkness encouraged everyone not on duty to curl up in their mick. The seamen's mess was darkened at 2200, and the middle watch, the midnight to 0400 shift, snored blissfully, their hammocks swaying gently as *Lakeville* rolled and pitched. The only two seamen not sleeping as the first watch drew to a close were Kozlowski and 'Phonse.

They had not spoken since the altercation at the Ajax Club on Saturday night, and 'Phonse was not about to bring the subject up. They sat, as they usually did when they had drawn the middle watch, drinking tea, eating bread and molasses, and playing cribbage.

This silent return to routine seemed to presage a rapproachment. Even the lack of talk was typical – Kozlowski and 'Phonse played crib so frequently that they had long since given up calling out the cards played, or counting points aloud. Each card was played with solemn deliberation, and the points pegged off in silence. The only sound was the shuffling of the deck, the flick of the cards as they were dealt, and the occasional snap as a particularly decisive card hit the table. There were, after all, only so many combinations one might hold, and both could assess the value of a hand at a glance.

As usual, 'Phonse was well ahead, leaving Kozlowski to struggle to the skunkline despite his habit of pegging more points than his hand allowed. Usually 'Phonse just moved Kozlowski's peg back to where it ought to be, and as long as Kozwloski was well out of the game there was never a protest. On one occasion a seaman had warned 'Phonse that Kozlowski cheated. 'Phonse brushed the snitch away with a curt "So do I!" but no-one had ever seen him do it. It was only when it looked like he might actually win that Kozlowski aggressively defended his ill-gotten gains. Tonight Kozlowski was taking his lumps without protest, consoling himself that cribbage was simply something to do with one's hands while waiting to go on duty. 'Phonse took the game no more seriously, but delighted in consistently beating Kozlowski without effort.

Not a word had been said through three games. When, as inevitably happened, 'Phonse sank his peg in the final hole Kozlowski simply threw his cards on the table, rose and went out on deck. After putting away the board and the cards 'Phonse followed him for the final pre-watch ritual, a quick smoke in the welldeck.

'Phonse found Kozlowski leaning against the door to one of the seamen's toilets on the port side, well in under the foc'sle overhang, peering out through a gap in the blackout curtain. The deck was awash. Every time *Lakeville* buried her bow the sea came in over the port railing and filled the welldeck with about a foot of water. As she rolled and rose on the wave it poured aft, down the deck towards the depth charges and out the washports. Then down she went again, and in came the water. You could set your watch by it.

Kozlowski gazed absently into the inky darkness, mesmerized by the regular roll and crash of the ship. After lighting up 'Phonse braced his feet against the motion and held onto a bracket in the deckhead. Finally, Kozlowski spoke, softly but purposefully.

"Where the hell did you get to?"

"I was busy."

"Busy my ass! I seen that skirt you was chasing all evening. Too busy to help friends when they needed you."

"Dat's bullshit, Kos, an' you know it! We din't go dare to have no fight," 'Phonse responded in measured tones, "I was doin' what I taught we were all s'posed to be doin' – 'aving a good times. You an' Macpherson, if you can't get no girls you jus get drunk and pick a fight. Me an' Audrey was 'aving a quiet walk trew Points Pleasant's Park about da time your fight start."

"Friggin' typical. Things get tough and the bloody Frog is nowhere to be found. You people piss me off, you know 'Phonse, you piss me off!" Kos gestured towards the sea. "Scuttlebutt has it we're freezin' our asses off here in the middle of nowhere to keep some friggin' spy from landing in Quebec – Quebec, 'Phonse! Can't be an accident, eh?" Kozlowski was getting loud. "Christ, nobody there wants to fight this war ..."

'Phonse replied coldly. "What de hell am I doin' here, den! And my brudders - eh? Tree of dem," 'Phonse pushed three fingers towards

Kozlowski's face, "tree of dem in La Regiment de la Chaudière, overseas right now!" 'Phonse muttered an oath or two, drew long on his cigarette.

"Ya know what da problem is, Kozlowski, eh? It's dat we French Canadien don't got to go all da way to Europe to fight stupids heads, eh?. We gots lots of dat here in Canada."

Ryan, who had been aft talking to the quarterdeck lookout moved up the starboard side of the ship until he could hear much of the conversation, especially as it grew more animated. Bickering was not good for morale, and this was bickering of the most petty kind. "You men, there," Ryan said, stepping in under the blackout curtain, "douse those cigarettes. You know better than to smoke on deck after dark."

'Phonse pinched his between his fingers and put the butt in his pocket. Kozlowski took a few steps forward and, with an exaggerated swing threw his over the side, then slipped past the two other men back into the messdeck.

"Don't let him get to you, 'Phonse. Kozlowski might be a good asdic operator but he don't know shit." There was no reply from 'Phonse so Ryan filled the silence. "If it wasn't for the war, you know, he'd still be looking up the arse end of some plough horse on a Godforsaken farm in Alberta. The whole friggin' fleet's full of these buggers, saved by the war, made into something important – for a few years at least."

"Me too, Chief," 'Phonse answered with a tinge of irony, "me too! I din't go to war to save nudding but myself. I don't give two shits for da war against 'itler or de Italians: it was dis, or work in a mill. So, here I am ..."

Ryan finished the sentence for him "... just like all the other misfits and would-be heroes, right?"

Before 'Phonse could answer the alarm buzzer sounded Action Stations. Within seconds *Lakeville* was a swarm of activity. Dark figures clad in raingear, wool caps and seaboots poured from the messdecks, scurrying in all directions as men raced to their stations. For 'Phonse it was a short sprint down the deck to the starboard depth-charge throwers, where he was joined by Macpherson and the others.

By the time Kozlowski re-emerged from the messdeck, climbed the portside bridge ladder and reached the asdic set Fergus, the asdic officer, was already there listening to the contact on the headphones. Fergus gestured for Kozlowski to take the set from the rating on watch.

Given *Lakeville*'s primitive type 123A asdic set, much depended on the ears of Kozlowski and Fergus. The core of the ship's asdic was a quartz-steel sandwich transducer housed in a dome below the keel. An electric current caused this sandwich to oscillate, producing a series of refractions and compressions, a wave train, that traveled through the water at the speed of sound. If it struck something solid a portion of this wave train was sent back to the transducer which then transmitted it to the controls in the charthouse. Kozlowski and Fergus could hear the 'ping' going out and whatever came back. The time elapsed between the transmission and the return indicated the target's range, which was also displayed on chemically treated paper etched by an electric stylus.

Kozlowski, who excelled at discriminating among the subtle tones of asdic echoes, operated the equipment. He and Fergus interpreted the information. The work was tedious, and asdic operators went stale if they never got a solid contact, even if only in training. The trick in classifying an asdic contact was patience, a discriminating ear, good luck and a healthy measure of instinct. A skilled asdic operator usually meant the difference between a successful anti-submarine ship and an ineffectual one. Kozlowski was good at his job and he was tolerated because of it.

The two men stood silently listening on headphones and watching the recorder trace. Finally Belanger could wait no longer. "What d'you think?"

Fergus raised his hand, indicating his need for more time. Both he and Kozlowski glanced furtively at the trace, but it was unclear. Belanger paced. Finally Fergus said softly, "It's a good contact, no metallic sound but good doppler – the echo's slightly low, moving away from us across the starboard bow, bearing green 035 at about 1200 yards."

"How deep?" Belanger asked.

Fergus looked at Kozlowski, who answered, "Don't know yet, but I would estimate 150-200 feet. We'll have to do a proper classification to be sure."

"I suggest we close the target slowly," said Fergus, "and find out when we lose contact, and then we can stand off and get a cut-on to determine its size."

The size of an underwater contact could be determined by playing the asdic beam across it, and measuring the angle between the point at which the contact was picked up and when it was lost. The 'cut', the angle between the two ends of the target, plus range to the target, was sufficient to estimate its size.

"Okay," Belanger replied, and stepped to the wheelhouse voicepipe to order starboard fifteen and a new heading. *Lakeville* swung away from the contact, opened the range and then settled on a new course. Kozlowski lost contact at a range of about 400 yards, so the target was about 200 feet down. Kozlowski began moving the asdic transducer from left to right and back again, transmitting every few degrees until he lost the echo on either side. It seemed to be about 300 feet long, assuming they were viewing it from the side.

Belanger decided to probe the target further with high explosives. "Captain here!" he barked down the wheelhouse voicepipe, "Revolutions for twelve knots, port fifteen, bring us around to course 240." Then, as he stepped out on the open bridge, "Yeoman, make to *Tracadie*: 'am attacking contact'," before scanning the area from the starboard side of the bridge with his glasses.

There was nothing to see.

Fergus passed depth settings and instructions for a ten-charge pattern to the quarterdeck. *Lakeville* carried about 100 depth charges. Half of them were weighted to sink faster in order to create a three-dimensional explosion around the U-boat, crushing its hull and sending it to the bottom.

The depth charge crews had already cast off the lashings on the throwers, and while 'Phonse primed the aft starboard thrower Macpherson turned the hydrostatic fuse setting on the charge to 220 feet for the heavy charges. Hands repeated the pattern at the three other throwers, two of them setting 175 feet on the fuses of light charges. Further aft, other crewmen cleared the two stern depth charge rails; heavy to port, light to starboard, and set the fuses of three charges on each rail. The quarterdeck reported itself ready to fire.

In the meantime *Lakeville* had opened the range to 1500 yards, and swung around onto heading 240. With a southeasterly wind driving the sea, the new course laid *Lakeville* broadside to the swell and she rolled her rails under. Belanger cursed his own incompetence and ordered a new course that gave *Lakeville* an upwind approach, straight into the sea. She pitched, to be sure, but the rolling eased. As the corvette worked up to twelve knots and turned back on the contact plumes of spray drenched those on the bridge, and water sloshed in through the washports along the deck, making the task of depth charge crews treacherous. Moreover, the pitching and rolling of the ship degraded the effectiveness of the asdic.

Lakeville's attack run was directed towards a darkened patch of breaking sea, below which lay her target.

According to British procedure, a corvette captain advanced towards his asdic contact at his best searching speed, seldom more than ten knots, to the 'throw off point' about 800 yards short of the target. Then he was to increase to the corvette's maximum speed of about sixteen knots and alter course to place the depth charges where the target would be by the time they sank to the sub's estimated depth.

Prentice taught Canadian corvettes to be more deliberate in their attack. So *Lakeville* maintained a steady ten knots throughout the whole attack run, even through the final stage when the charges were thrown. This slow, steady speed allowed the asdic operators to hold onto the target until the very last minute, and did not produce a tell-tale increase in ship noise that alerted the submariner to the attack. The down side was that it also put the corvette at greater risk from the shock of her own charges, a risk Prentice thought worthwhile.

In this instance the slow approach was crucial. Despite intense concentration Kozlowski lost contact at about 500 yards. "I've lost it!" he shouted. "It's deeper!" Fergus ordered a change in setting to 300 feet, which sent crewmen on the quarterdeck scurrying to reset fuses at the last second.

As the firing buzzer sounded on the quarterdeck, ratings tripped the release at the two stern depth charge rails, and the first charges fell from *Lakeville*'s stern. A few seconds later and 'Phonse pulled the lanyard on the aftermost starboard thrower, as did his opposite number on the port side. The depth charge, cradle and all, hurled itself into the murk fifty yards from the side of the ship.

The sharp crack of the throwers was heard easily on the bridge, and the charges themselves could be seen tracing a shallow arc to the sea. The crews laboured on the dark, heaving deck as quickly as possible to reload, thumping a new carrier into the thrower, rolling a new 350-pound charge into position, and hefting it up by block and tackle before lowering it onto the carrier, then loading and priming the thrower.

Another few seconds and two more depth charges rolled from the stern; then the two other throwers fired, followed again by two more from the stern, ten charges in all. By the time the last hit the water the sea astern of *Lakeville* was convulsed in foaming water. These were not the tall geysers produced by the shallow charges used for newsreel footage, but the dull, heavy grumbling of deep charges rending the sea. As each charge exploded *Lakeville* heaved, deck plates shook, dishes rattled and the whole ship was thrust forward as if by some unseen hand.

Every crewman counted them as they went: one, two, three, four and five close together, a long pause ... What happened to six? ... then a low, barely audible rumble indicating a faulty fuse and a very deep explosion ... seven, eight, and finally, the last two.

Even as the last charge exploded Belanger had the corvette turning sharply back towards the contact. Seawater poured over the starboard side as she heeled over, soaking the deck and making the already difficult task of reloading the depth-charge throwers even more dangerous. But the crews on the quarterdeck understood that there was a chance that the U-boat – if there was one – would be blown to the surface. It was imperative to get the main gun and the asdic trained back on the spot quickly.

Lakeville was still in the middle of her turn when Maynard reported to Belanger. "Signal from *Tracadie*, Sir. She wants to know the status of our contact and the results of our attack. You are asked to respond on the radio-telephone."

"Thanks, Maynard. Can we use the R/T tonight?" The VHF radio telephone was notoriously fickle in Canadian waters, not least because on clear nights it was often jammed by New York taxi drivers transmitting on the same frequency. But tonight the heavy clouds and low pressure system now lying over the central Gulf kept the cabbies at bay.

After checking the radio call signs, Belanger picked up the handset, squeezed the button and spoke:

"Antler this is Cattail!" A pause of crackling static left Belanger to reflect on how stupid the call signs were. Who made these up?

"Cattail this is Antler. What's your report, over?"

"Have made one attack, no clear result – too dark to see anything on the water. Trying to re-establish asdic contact, over."

"Very well, Cattail. I have ordered Badger" – Belanger quickly scanned the list of call signs. Badger was *Innisfail* – "to commence a square search around your position. Will leave the others to continue patrol. I'm coming in to take over the search, over."

"Antler, suggest you hold present dispositions until nature of the contact is confirmed, over." Belanger could not yet see the merit in abandoning the whole patrol line until they had established what the contact was. Wagner, however, had felt the concussion of depth charges and wanted in on the action.

"Negative, Cattail. Proceed as ordered. Antler out."

Belanger slammed the handset down and turned to Fergus, who was waiting with his earphones wrapped around his neck while Kozlowski listened for the target. "He's coming in to take over our contact!"

Fergus snorted. "So much for our endless chain! Wagner! Perhaps we should start a plot of the action. That will help us keep track of things."

"Good idea. I'll send you a warm body as a runner."

The positions of other ships and the information from the radar sets needed to be passed manually to the plotter. While Fergus turned over a chart and set up his plot on the back, Belanger wandered aft to the 271 radar hut.

Harkness was at the set with Smythe standing by. It was all Belanger could do to shoulder his way in for a glance at the screen.

"That's *Castlegar*, Sir, to the north," Smythe said, pointing to a fuzzy blob of green light on the screen, "and that's *Innisfail* closing from the south. *Tracadie's* too far north to pick her up yet."

"Right, well watch for *Tracadie*. She's on her way. Nothing else on the screen Smythe?"

"No, Sir."

"Okay. Fergus is running a plot in the charthouse. See that he gets the latest developments on a regular basis."

"Aye, aye Sir," said Smythe. "I'll send Harkness, here, with regular reports."

"No, keep Harkness here on the set. I've assigned Camberly to act as a runner. Who's at the SW2C?"

"Should be Bates, Sir. But there's little point in following the action from that set so long as we have a good picture here."

"Agreed. Keep me informed ..."

A tap on his shoulder drew Belanger's head out of the radar hut. It was Camberly.

"Lieutenant Fergus reports they have regained contact, Sir."

Again inside the charthouse, Belanger snapped, "Well?"

"It's a bit more woolly, less well defined and hard to get a cut on," Fergus replied. "Kos thinks it's fish. I'm inclined to agree."

"It's not the disturbance from the previous attack?"

"No, shows movement ..."

"Beg yer pardon, Sir." It was Maynard. "*Tracadie* has a contact, and we are ordered to assist."

"Is *Tracadie* on the R/T?"

"Yes Sir."

With some trepidation the young signalman passed the handset to his agitated captain.

"Antler, this is Cattail. Our contact is a school of fish. Suspect yours is as well. Suggest we abandon the hunt and return to patrol, over."

"Cattail, this is Antler. We have a firm contact about 200 feet down, good extent of target and it shows doppler. We will hold until you arrive and gain contact, over."

"Antler, with all due respect – "

"That's an order, Belanger!" Wagner barked, in a breech of both service etiquette and radio security.

"Antler, this is Cattail, we're on our way, out." Belanger thrust the handset into Maynard's chest, shot a glance at Fergus, and stepped to the voicepipe to pass helm and speed orders.

Lakeville came around to 360 and, leaving *Innisfail* to the south, Smythe guided her northwards by radar. In about twenty minutes *Tracadie* could be seen in the gloom, steering slowly through the rising sea and light rain. The range and bearing of her contact were passed to *Lakeville* by signal lamp. Fergus and Kozlowski quickly made contact, while Belanger brought his corvette to a virtual standstill.

"Maynard, tell *Tracadie* we have their contact, bearing red 020, 1200 yards, estimated depth 250 feet, slightly low doppler. What d'you think Fergus?"

"It's got the same characteristics as the contact we just attacked. Probably another school of fish we'll blow to catfood ..."

Waiting for Wagner to decide what he wanted to do, Belanger stuck his head into the radar hut, got a bearing on the ships around him – "We've lost *Innisfail*, Sir" – and then went to the forward edge of the bridge to pick them out.

Tracadie, 1500 yards off the port bow, could be seen with the naked eye, but without his binoculars it was hard to see which way she lay: just a black blob against a black backdrop. *Castlegar* ought to be just ahead, about two miles out, engaged in a square search around the contact, but he could see nothing in the low cloud, rain and darkness. With the air temperature hovering near freezing this was, Belanger thought, no time to be killing fish with depth charges.

While Belanger ran these thoughts through his head Maynard appeared once again. "Signal from *Tracadie*, Sir. They will attack with ten charges. We are to maintain contact and pass through the area to check for debris. We are to use illumination, Sir."

"Lights?"

"Doesn't say, Sir. Just illumination."

"Let me see that." Belanger snatched the signal pad from Maynard's hand.

Belanger was appalled by the order to use lights, but maybe with this rain and the inky darkness not too much harm would be done. He handed back the pad.

"Thanks Maynard. See that Mr. Fergus is informed."

Belanger then trained his glasses on *Tracadie*. Gradually the squat black mass lengthened and the profile of a corvette revealed itself. She had altered course to commence her attack. The wind blew *Tracadie*'s funnel smoke northward, and so *Lakeville*'s crewmen had a good view of the action. Most of the officers and some of the more experienced hands counted off the seconds as she moved forward, trying to estimate when the first charge would fall. They were too far away to see them go, but the report of the throwers – delayed and muffled by the distance and the rain – was proof that the attack had begun. Soon the dull rumble of exploding charges could also be heard, especially by those below in the engine and boiler rooms. On deck some thought they saw dark plumes of water rising astern of *Tracadie*, evidence of quite a shallow setting, maybe 150 feet.

When the final charge had blown Belanger ordered *Lakeville* to move ahead at slow speed, picking her way through the scene of the attack.

"Turn them all on, Fergus!" he ordered. "If the man wants lights, by God we'll give him lights."

The twenty-inch signal projectors on either side of the bridge and the large searchlight mounted aft groped out over the water, thin shafts of light slicing through the pall of rain and darkness. No one on *Lakeville*'s bridge was surprised by what the searchlights revealed. Hundreds of fish, floating belly up and shining silver in the glare of the lights.

"Douse those lights!" Belanger barked, as he strode for the charthouse and the radio/telephone.

"Antler, this is Cattail ..." and Belanger informed Wagner of the fish – cod, hundreds of them, crushed by the concussion of the exploding charges. As he hung up the handset Camberly was standing by. "Beg yer pardon, Sir. Cook wants to know if he can collect some of the fish. Seems such a waste to leave them."

"For the love of God, Camberly, no! Tell the cook there's a bloody war on!

"Stand down from action stations and resume the patrol." It wasn't the first time Belanger had spent nearly two hours in the middle of the night killing nothing but fish. It went with the job. But Belanger loathed keeping his cold and rain soaked crew standing needlessly by while contacts were classified. They should have been stood-down after *Lakeville*'s attack, but Wagner insisted on asserting his authority, and so everyone was up for another hour until the obvious was proven.

In a few short minutes the number of figures on deck dwindled to the duty watch. Fergus, due to go on watch in little over an hour, flaked out on the cot in the charthouse. That meant that Belanger would have to descend to his cabin; more ladders than he had a feel for at the moment. Tiredness nonetheless pulled him towards his bunk, first down the bridge ladder to the top of the galley, then along the starboard side of the wheelhouse to the ladder down to the main deck. He was only two rungs down the final ladder when a face appeared over the railing above.

"Thought you might like to see this before turning in, Sir." It was Letherby, the duty wireless operator. "I've made a copy for the officer of the watch." Belanger took the signal, stuffed it in his duffle coat pocket, and told Letherby he would read it in his cabin.

When he reached his bunk Belanger flopped – coat, cap, seaboots and all – on his bunk and felt his whole body sink into the mattress. He would have been asleep in seconds except that his right hand, still jammed in his duffle coat pocket, crushed the signal paper as he pulled on the pockets to smooth the coat under his back. Damn!

With decided lack of enthusiasm Belanger switched on the reading lamp and read the signal. It was from Admiral Murray to Action Information Group 409-055 – the whole friggin' fleet – with repeats to Naval Service Headquarters, the Admiralty, and the US Navy. RCAF Canso J was overdue at Gaspé and believed to have gone down over the central Gulf of St. Lawrence. God, Belanger thought, what a night to be stuck out here in a rubber raft. Then sleep overwhelmed him.

Chapter 11

"Damn! Damn!" A softly muttered oath was all Lieutenant Paul Vanzetti dared as his first coffee of the morning poured over the desk, oozed under a sheaf of signal traffic, and dripped onto the floor. Few nearby heard the outburst, but there was little mistaking the significance of the dripping pile of signals Vanzetti held aloft.

The frantic activity drew snickers, broad grins and thoughts of 'Vanzetti again, typical' around the plotting room. A few willing hands moved to help salvage operations, and finally a very tired "Get a rag, Vanzetti, and clean it up!" came from Lieutenant Commander Nickerson, the duty watch officer. This done, Vanzetti relieved his opposite number on the North Atlantic plot.

The plot covered one wall of a very large room on the third floor, wing seven of Main Navy, a temporary First World War structure built on Washington's Mall near the Lincoln memorial, that served as the US Navy's central headquarters. Vanzetti's plot, forty feet long and sixteen feet high, covered the area of the main trade convoys from the Gulf of Maine to the English Channel, and forty degrees north latitude to just north of Iceland.

Other plots in the Convoy and Routing Section covered other areas of ocean, many of these small, quite discrete zones. Vanzetti's was far and away the busiest, with convoy tracks criss-crossing the board. Along the main New York to UK routes – the famous HX, SC and ON series – twelve large convoys sprawled over the sea between Nova

Scotia and Britain. Here too, more than a hundred U-boats were hunting. The pins marking their estimated positions peppered the plot, with especially heavy clusters in the mid-Atlantic east and northeast of Newfoundland.

A second cup of coffee now firmly in hand, Vanzetti scanned the plot. "Not a lot of change, Arch," he said to Lieutenant Hollinger, who was about to go off watch.

"Naw," came the laconic southern drawl, "The action around ONS 5 seems tah be a dyin' down, and they ah off on a new tack."

"I see that." Vanzetti slurped his scalding coffee. "It looks like the whole friggin' U-Waffe is off Cape Farewell ..."

"Almost. Theah's about forty or fifty U-boats a'millin' just south of Greenland. They seem to have given up on convoy ONS 5, fer now at least – looks like they lost contact in heavy weathah. 'Bout thirty of them ah bein' redeployed to intercept SC 128, from the look of things." Hollinger pointed to an eastbound convoy inching its way northward of ONS 5 off the southern tip of Greenland.

"It's not cleah yet," he went on, "if they ah givin' up on ONS 5. Either convoy's a good bet: SC 128's slow and laden, ONS 5's westbound against heavy weathah in ballast. Germans got 'em both treed! Easy meat. Th'other convoys nearby ah in much less trouble, although if the Brits ain't careful they'll drive ONS 6 and ON 181 rait into a hornet's nest."

Vanzetti nodded. Convoys just heading out into the Atlantic from North America were routed well to the south, clear of danger – especially the Canadian escorted ones. But not all the U-boats could be avoided, and it seemed curious that some of the convoys were aimed directly at U-boat concentrations.

"A few days ago this big battle northeast of Newfoundland would have been ours to run, Arch. The whole damn thing's happening well inside our old zone, west of the old Change of Operational Control line at 35 degrees. It's all a British battle now. That's why they call it that. We've been 'chopped' right out of the action, if you ask me."

Both men studied the plot for a moment before Vanzetti continued.

"And look at the way the Brits are playing this one. All of the convoys in the danger area are British escorted, right?" Vanzetti ran down the brief list: SC 128, ONS 5, ON 180 – no, that one, farther north than even SC 128 and comparatively safe, was Canadian escorted – ONS 6, ON 181. "And here, the Brits are running the play down the edge of the field: right along the touch line, keeping it in their part of the Atlantic. Look ... just look ..." he said, running his hand along the 47th degree of west longitude, "they've routed SC 128 into the U-boats just east of the new CHOP line. See it? Even the new diversion assigned to ONS 5 keeps it in the Brit zone as long as possible. If the U-boats stay on ONS 5's tail virtually the whole play will be run in their slice of the ocean ... Pretty clever, those buggers."

Hollinger looked on in silence, incredulous that anyone might deliberately run merchant convoys into danger just so U-boats could be attacked. "Jesus, boy," he finally said after a lengthy pause, "you have a devious mind, you know that. The devil is at work in yer heyd! Er you bin readin' too much of that spy shit, Vanzetti, one or t'other."

"Come on Arch, fer Chrissake! Look at the plot! The U-boat concentration, the convoy battles, the routing – it all adds up. The Brits are in this one for keeps. This is it, Arch, I tell ya. They're trying to win this friggin' war. If that Cracker head of yours wasn't full of sawdust you'd see that!"

There was, in the end, little point to the discussion. To Vanzetti the significance of changes in command structures in the Atlantic war made at the end of April lay graphically before him on the plot. Hollinger couldn't see it so clearly, he took the world as it came. Vanzetti's theory escaped him.

"What else should I know?" Vanzetti said, throwing back the last of his coffee and changing the subject.

"Well as you can see," Hollinger went on with the brief, "theah's a bit of U-boat activity off northern Spain, but no convoys in any danger. They all bin routed well clear. Not much hap'nin' in the western Atlantic, eithah. Most of the air activity is concentrated around the battle north of Newfoundland – everbudy's in on that one. The Canadians ah still patrollin' the Cabot Strait, in fact they've augmented those patrols though God alone knows why since the Strait is still closed by ice and we have no U-boats plotted inbound. Commander Task Force 24 in Argentia says he thinks the RCN has also sent ships into the Gulf of St. Lawrence, but he's not sure why. The Canadians ah supposed to keep us informed of what they ah up to in theah new zone. It appears we've not yet worked out all the bugs in the relayin' and repeatin' of taskin' signals. Guess that will take a few days more ... Oh! We did get a repeat of a signal from CinC, Canadian Northwest Atlantic, earliah this mornin' ordering two ships into the Gulf: the Bangor class escort *Mabou* and the old four-stacker destroyer *Yukon*. That seems to confirm CTF-24's suspicion, I guess. It bears watchin'."

Hollinger looked at the plot to see if he had missed anything. "Oh, and apparently theah's an overdue Canadian Catalina in the central St. Lawrence Gulf. No word yet on what happened, the signal's filed. Maybe that's what the Canadian ships ah aftah."

"Okay, thanks, Arch. I guess I can handle it from here. Has the Old Guy been in?"

The Old Guy was Commander Kenneth Knowles, the geek who ran Combat Intelligence Section F-21, the Atlantic Branch. Knowles had several offices across the hall, all strictly out of bounds to everyone, at all times, and said to contain another plot of the North Atlantic in the Submarine Tracking Room. Few in the Convoy and Routing Section, and certainly not Vanzetti and Hollinger, knew what wizardry Knowles worked in his mysterious chambers. But the pins marking the locations of the U-boats on their plot were placed with information from Knowles' organization. Knowles visited the main convoy and trade plot periodically to see just how the action was shaping up.

"Yep." Hollinger yawned. "Ah guess he was in most of the night watchin' the action around ONS 5 and SC 128. No question he was in often durin' my watch. Ah'd guess that he's in the rack somewhere by now and you won't see him. Anyway, Ah'm off. Ah've got to catch some zees before 1600 and I'm beat."

"Out last night?"

"Oh, yes suh! With Lieutenant Jurgensen, that WAVE with the incredible legs who runs the Eastern Sea Frontier plot."

"Yes, I've often admired her plot," Vanzetti answered with a grin.

"Yes, Ah am sure you have. Well me and Lieutenant Jurgensen burned up Georgetown last night and then Ah came straight in for the mornin' watch."

"Third time in less than a week. Sounds serious to me."

Hollinger gave him a cold stare.

"Don't tell me it's love, Arch? Not you, not yet!"

"Vanzetti, you ah an evil man, you know that, and a powerful bad influence on a poah country boy like me.''·

Hollinger threw his jacket over his shoulder, grabbed his hat, winked at Vanzetti and turned to leave. "Oh, Ah hadn't yet got a chance to put the movements of *Mabou* and *Yukon* up on the plot. Ah s'pose you better do that before you ferget."

Gulf of St. Lawrence, Tuesday 4 May 1943

Monday's brilliant spring weather gave way by Tuesday morning to yet another of the deep low-pressure systems that characterize spring in Atlantic Canada. As Motor Launch *Q246* and the rest of the 8th Flotilla patrolled northward of the icefield in the Cabot Strait a gentle, wet snowfall coated the boats and the crewmen on deck. The cold was damp and penetrating, and it was little relieved by the sunless dawn. The daylight gloom served only to turn the snow into an icy drizzle and reveal a dense, oppressive grey cloud cover that nearly touched the masthead.

Babineau was right, you could smell the ice. Shortly after sunrise, it could be seen through the murk like a long white band on the southern horizon. The only bright spot in this otherwise bleak day was the realization that with the ice to windward, the sea would remain almost a flat calm. *Q246* and her mates could cruise westward with ease.

Noiles had long since laid off the course for Grande Entree in the Magdalens, where they were to refuel enroute to their new patrol area, about halfway between the Magdalens and Gaspé. The rest of the flotilla was tucked astern like ducks on a millpond. There was scant likelihood of anything else on the water this early in the year, and little for the crews to do. Even Babineau, seldom lost for words and given to idle chatter, stood silently on the bridge.

A few feet away Dickson loitered, passing the time by slowly making and smoking cigarettes. Unlike most of the younger men, who preferred the Sweet Caps sold duty-free to servicemen, Dickson had acquired a taste for 'makins'. The tobacco pouch and papers he kept in an inner pocket, and if he stretched the process long enough a smoke break could last nearly twenty minutes.

Shortly after he flicked a butt over the side Dickson drew out the papers and pouch and started anew. Once rolled the cigarette was stuck in the left corner of his mouth where it hung, glued firmly to his lips.

"So, Babs, I hear you lost yer shirt on the Allen Cup, betting on Victoria Army ..." It was a taunting question. Dickson knew his hockey and knew that Babineau followed it passionately.

"Naw, not so bad, a few bucks," Babineau replied. "I figured dey had a pretty good chance, so mebbe I played de odds a bit. Dey might'a done it too, you know, doz army guys."

"You ought to know better'n bet against the air force, Babs. They have the best hockey recruiting system in the country. Christ, most RCAF fellas don't do anything or go anywhere, so they can stack the teams. Besides, you should have figured on the Kraut line carrying them through."

"Mebbe yer right, fer dis year enaway. Dere's no question dat with Hurd in nets for Halifax RCAF our local team ain't goin' nowhere. Jeeze, he was sensational. We played da whole friggin' series in deir end and it was like shooting at a wall. I seen a couple games. Mebbe they gonna post Hurd overseas, eh? Next year we gonna do better, enaway, so maybe I'll put some money on da Navy. But not Halifax, no siree: I'll bet on Victoria."

"What makes you think Victoria Navy's got a chance?"

"Come on, Mr. Dickson! You know da Bentleys have joined da Navy, eh? All tree of dem!"

The three Bentley brothers had played for the Chicago Black Hawks in the 1942-43 season.

"Dey bin playing for Victoria Navy since early April. When dey played da Montreal Canadiens, dere, a coupla weeks ago dey only lost seven to five and da Bentleys scored all our goals! Elmer Lach and Toe Blake had a great game for da Habs, but dey was jis bearly beat us. Doug Bentley alone will turn tings around, he won da NHL scoring title dis year."

"So I heard."

"Max won da Lady Byng trophy, but he's no patsy, and even Reg is a good player."

"So, is it true that Gaye Stewart's gonna join the Navy, too?"

"Oh, jeeze, I tink so – I hope so! Jeeze, If we could add da rookie of da year to da Bentleys anyting's possible ... But I can't imagine da Leafs, dat likely Conn Smythe, lettin' 'im go. Smythe's a major er something in de army, you know?"

"Yup, a major."

"So, if a Leaf player joins up, dey gotta go in da army or dey won't play fer da Leafs after da war!"

"Probably right, Babs."

"Dam' right." Babineau was prepared to believe anything bad about the Leaf organization. "Bot' de army and de air force have picked up some first-class players too. We might get Stewart from da Leafs, but Syl Apps, he joined de army already ..."

Dickson drew on his cigarette and after a pause, prodded the conversation a little farther, to see how far Babineau would go before he came unstuck.

"Anybody from the Canadiens joining up? What about Drillon or that new French guy, what's his name ... Reeshore?"

"Richard!" Babineau said, putting the proper French spin on the name, "Richard! Aw, I don't know about Gordie Drillon. I ain't heard nuddin' from home. Seems he'd radder play in da NHL. It's gonna get easier, next year eh, when dere's nobody left!"

Dickson saw his chance.

"Drillon won't join up. None of those maritime players will go anywhere except for money, and he sure won't get a pay raise by joining up! All those Maritimers are just mercenaries, have been since the early thirties and the Big Four League."

"That's a cheap shot, Mr. Dickson!"

"That's why the Halifax Wolverines couldn't go to the '36 Olympics."

Babineau's face reddened. "Da Wolverines was as amateur as any team in dis country! Dey won de Allen Cup fair and square in '35 and deserved to represent da country. It's jis da CAHA which is dominated by Ontario eh, do dey decide at da lass minute dat da Wolverines was not amateur. Well, ain't dat handy. An' who do you tink gets to go to de

Olympics, eh? An Ontario team! Aw, Mr. Dickson, you don't need to be a rocket scientist to figger dat one out."

"C'mon Babs, The Big Four was semi-pro."

"Not true! Dey operated da same as all de udder leagues dat sent teams to the Allen Cup. C'mon yerself, Sir. You can't award da national amateur championship to a team one year, and den say da next dat mebbe dey was not amateurs. Dat is, unless you want some Ontario team to go to de Olympics!"

"It wasn't the CAHA's fault, the Big Four folded ..."

"Sure it did! Da CAHA declare most of the da Wolverines' key players ineligible for amateurs status, eh? And den de Ontario and Quebec teams raid de udder teams in da Big Four so da league can't play. No Mr. Dickson, you Upper Canadians, eh, you stole dat from us Maritimers and we ain't never fergot. *An'* Ontario lost in de Olympics, eh! My God, we got beat by England – dat great ice hockey powerhouse! Says a lot about the Port Art'ur team." Babineau finished with a wry grin.

Dickson conceded that round to Babineau and shifted focus. "So what about that Richard guy, he gonna make it in the NHL?"

"I don't spect much from Maurice Richard. He's too small, eh, like me! Once da fellas come back from da war dey gonna drop him like a stone for sure. Good skater, I hear, and quick, but he needs a bit of size ..."

Dickson and Babineau droned on about the relative merits of teams and players, about the decline of the NHL, more about stacked RCAF teams, about the Allen Cup champion Commmandos from Ottawa and whether they could beat the Stanley Cup champion Detroit Red Wings – until Saunders interrupted.

"Beg yer pardon, Sir. Short message from Lieutenant Aubrey's boat."

Dickson glanced down at the signal pad: contaminated fuel, again. Seawater still seeping into the boat's diesel tanks. "Right, acknowledge and tell him we'll have a look when we get alongside in the Magdalens. And tell the rest of the flotilla to slow to eight knots."

While Saunders flashed orders to the other boats, Dickson passed his own down to the wheelhouse. As the 8th Flotilla settled into its new rhythm, Dickson continued to bait Babineau into a fit, over lost wagers or the hapless Habs, and Saunders joined the debate.

"I happen to know for a fact," he said solemnly, "that the team to beat is the US Coast Guard 'Cutters'. They stacked it with every good American they could find, which ain't a lot. But they posted them to stations near rinks what have year 'round ice. So they practice all the time. The Yanks might not be able to beat the Germans at sea, but they sure as hell seem bent on beating us on ice!"

Dickson and Babineau were surprised for a moment by Saunders' remarkable, and hitherto well disguised, knowledge of hockey. Saunders' sport was baseball, and the tedium of his statistical mastery of the sport was the bane of the messdeck. Neither Dickson nor Babineau wanted to encourage Saunders, so Dickson changed the subject.

"Now, somewhere off here on the starboard bow is East Point in the Magdalens. We don't want to hit it, right? We'll get gas at Grand Entry and then be on our way. Pity we can't stay the night, eh? That RCAF Canso is missing somewhere just to the northwest of those little islands. We're to look for wreckage and survivors as we pass through. In the meantime, gentlemen, let's try to avoid becoming another statistic ourselves, shall we?"

"Aye, Sir," Saunders replied. Babineau just smiled, but all eyes turned to windward in search of the landfall.

Washington, DC, Tuesday 4 May 1943

By the time Vanzetti returned for the first dog watch on the main Atlantic plot in the Convoy and Routing section, anticipation had begun to rise. It was 4:00 pm in Washington but far to the northeast, between Newfoundland and Greenland, it was already early evening.

A quick glance at the plot revealed that the situation around ONS 5 had worsened during the day. The long passage and heavy weather had forced several key escorts to leave due to fuel shortages, and left a tail of stragglers, one of which was sunk early in the afternoon. Moreover, the Germans had re-established contact with the main body of ONS 5 and at least five, maybe six, U-boats were shadowing, waiting for nightfall to launch attacks, and another ten to fifteen U-boats en route to the scene. There were no forces available to reinforce the escort. It promised to be an interesting night.

Fortunately, Vanzetti reasoned, there was not much to do during his two hours on watch and the prospect of following a major convoy battle when he came back on duty at 2400 made the middle watch seem almost desirable. Having familiarized himself with the current plot, Vanzetti leaned back in his chair and, with a coffee in hand, started to leaf through the signals filed since he'd left at 0800. It was all routine, and explained the recent changes in the plot. Vanzetti was nearly through the stack of printed messages when a signalman arrived at his desk.

"Beg yer pardon, Sir, this has just come in from CTF-24." The signalman thrust several thin sheets of pink paper into his hand. They were repeats, much delayed, of three Canadian tasking signals from very early in the day. The first, addressed to *Castlegar*, with repeats to *Lakeville, Tracadie, Watson Lake* and *Innisfail*, ordered something called 'Main Force' to fall back to the Gaspé coast. The second ordered the 8th Motor Launch Flotilla to abandon its patrol in the Cabot Strait and assume a new patrol line between 48.10N/63.50W and 48.30N/63.10W. The third ordered *Mabou* and *Yukon* into the Gulf.

It wasn't unusual to receive signals late, especially repeats – traffic picked up by one source and rebroadcast. It was curious, however, that none of the original Canadian tasking signals were addressed to any US Navy authority, even 'for information'. Vanzetti put that down to a simple oversight resulting from the recently changed operational control arrangements.

Yet, as he passed the information to the duty plotter and watched her place the pins, something else that was odd caught Vanzetti's attention. If the Canadians were looking for an aircraft that disappeared late yesterday north of the Magdalens, why was 'Main Force' being moved from the most likely search area to one farther westward off the Gaspé coast? And why was the motor launch flotilla being assigned a linear patrol area, again farther westward, instead of an area search?

The deployments did not square with his previous assumption that the Canadians were looking for a downed aircraft. It looked more like a series of barriers intended to intercept the movement of a ship. It must be an exercise, Vanzetti concluded. There were no U-boats plotted in the Gulf, and none anticipated. Maybe the Gulf of St. Lawrence, secured by the barrier of ice and the lack of targets, was just a good place to train. Surely, if the Canadians wanted to sink U-boats the place to be was northeast of Newfoundland.

Once he had plotted the information Vanzetti filed the signals, as he did with the steady stream that came across his desk over the next hour and a half. As the first dog watch drew to a close a WAVE plotter from the Submarine Tracking Room came in to update the U-boat situation. For the younger male inmates of the plotting room this was often the high point of the day. They got to watch a well-filled skirt climb the short ladder in front of the plot. Professional interest obliged them to stare, ostensibly at the changes being made in the plot.

As expected, most of the U-boat pins stayed put or moved position only slightly. A couple of pins were removed, but in the end it all looked pretty much the same. As the WAVE stepped down from the ladder Vanzetti studied the plot more closely. The only perceptible change was the ring that seemed to be tightening around ONS 5 – one convoy, a handful of escorts, and scores of menacing U-boats.

The pert little brunette subplotter, silent and burdened by the secretive work done in her star chamber, left as quickly as she had come, steaming past Vanzetti as if he did not exist. The plot, too, was unfolding in an unsurprising fashion.

Vanzetti had no sooner gone back to reading the signal traffic when Knowles walked in. His entry was entirely unobtrusive, but everyone knew when he was there. For the most part he simply gazed at the plots, etching them in his brain, asking a few quiet questions, and then, after a few minutes, stealing silently away. Given the battle northeast of Newfoundland Vanzetti was not surprised when Knowles came directly to his plot and stared fixedly at the northwest Atlantic.

Vanzetti tried not to stare at what so interested someone who already knew more about what was going on in the Atlantic than anyone in Convoy and Routing. It seemed, however, that Knowles was not looking at the action around ONS 5. Rather he was puzzling over the markers in the Gulf of St. Lawrence. When Vanzetti next looked up Knowles' face was only inches away.

"What are those Canadian escorts doing in the Gulf of St. Lawrence? Do you have the tasking signals? Let me see them?" Knowles' voice was low, breathless but intense.

Vanzetti's immediate reaction was near panic – 'What the hell have I done?' Grabbing the file board he thumbed anxiously through the stack of signals while Knowles brooded. After what seemed an eternity Vanzetti located the pertinent ones and passed them to Knowles. The director of the submarine tracking room said nothing; he read through the signals quickly and flipped back through, checking the times of origin and times of repeats.

"When did these come in?"

"Um, shortly after I came on watch, Sir, about 1610 or so."

"I see," Knowles answered absent-mindedly, glancing at the plot and then back at the thin sheets. "They are routine traffic, Sir," Vanzetti said, attempting to deflect the criticism he felt sure was to come his way, although for what reason he could not fathom.

But Knowles' mind was elsewhere. After a brief, awkward pause, Knowles realized that Vanzetti was bracing for a dressing-down. He muttered a few soothing words then asked if he might have the signals.

"I'll have them copied and send back the originals to you right away," Knowles offered.

"Fine. Of course, Sir." What else could he say? Besides Knowles would do as he had promised, he always did. Knowles waited, impatiently, as Vanzetti removed the signals from the board. Then, without another word Knowles made off in something approaching indecent haste. Vanzetti had never seen him move so fast or with such determination.

Washington, DC, 4 May 1943

Only a small lamp illuminated the office, casting a bright glow on the papers piled and scattered over the desk. Outside this low cone of light, scarcely discernible, peered a round face adorned by half glasses and propped up by a forearm and hand that shaded the face from the glare. Somewhat disembodied by the shadow, another arm was poised to turn the top page of a stack of papers.

Despite the quiet setting, the man behind the desk was alert, and was not startled by the gentle knock on the door. "Yes! Come in!" he responded, just loudly enough to be heard through the heavy door.

It was Porter, the night duty officer at the Legation. "Er, excuse me Mr. Pearson, there's a Mr. Murphy from the State Department who wishes to talk to you."

Pearson glanced at his watch. It was 11:45, much later than even he had realized. "Very well. Show him in."

Lester Pearson, a career diplomat noted for his bow ties and sharp intellect, was the Minister-Counselor, effectively the second in command, of the Canadian Legation. Technically, Canada's interests in the US were still handled by the British Embassy, but these interests were now too large and too important to leave to the mother country. Yet, wartime was no time to press Canada's new independent status on an embattled American capital, so the Legation was, *de facto* if not *de juri*, Canada's embassy in Washington.

While Porter fetched Mr. Murphy, Pearson squared away his desk, putting sensitive material out of sight, and rummaged in his mind for information. He recalled easily enough that Murphy had served for some time as Roosevelt's personal emissary to French North Africa. Certainly Murphy had been there during the Vichy years. Pretty sordid business, all things considered. It was likely, Pearson surmised, that Murphy had come to discuss Canada's plan to sell farm equipment to the newly liberated French territories.

In theory, the Allies now occupied French North Africa. In practice, it was an American occupation, and a captive market for American goods. However, much of the modern agricultural equipment in French North Africa was Canadian in origin, and parts and replacements were desperately needed. But the Americans objected to any foreign commercial presence. Since Canada was heavily dependent on the US for many things, Pearson and his colleagues at External Affairs had little leverage. Murphy was probably coming to tell him, once and for all, that Canadian business should stay out of the liberated French colonies. At least with the Germans, Pearson chuckled, we know where we stand!

When Murphy walked through the door Pearson recalled that they had met at a Washington function. Certainly Murphy was trading on this slight earlier acquaintance as he thrust out his hand and offered a quiet, "Good evening Mr. Minister, very good of you to see me at this late hour."

Pearson grasped Murphy's hand firmly and replied with an honest, "Not at all, my pleasure. Please have a seat. May I offer you something? A little port perhaps, or some coffee?"

"Some port would be delightful, thank you." Murphy sat quietly while Pearson poured two small glasses, passed one to his guest, and took his seat behind the desk.

Murphy wasted no time.

"I have come on a matter of some delicacy," he said hesitantly, "and it is difficult to know just where to begin." Pearson sipped quietly saying nothing. "It concerns our – the State Department and, I dare say, the President's – plans for postwar Europe, actually for postwar France. We were, as you know, supportive of Admiral Darlan as the man to lead France now and in the postwar era ..."

"Darlan's assassination was very tragic."

"Very, Mr. Minister, but we feel that General Giraud is Admiral Darlan's natural successor as leader of the French resistance and ultimately as the man to lead the reconstruction of France after the war."

Murphy took a sip of port, largely to collect his thoughts. How much could he say? How much should he say? "You will appreciate the importance of these men to metropolitan France, even during the Occupation. This much, I believe was recognized by your own government until quite recently." The latter was almost a question.

"Not quite true, Mr. Murphy. We did maintain very close ties with Vichy until after the invasion of North Africa last November. We did this largely as a service to the alliance, to keep open a channel, rather than out of sympathy for Marechal Pétain's regime. Once the Germans occupied the rest of metropolitan France we were at liberty to abandon the charade that Pétain's government represented France, and severed our relations with his regime."

"Yes, quite so," Murphy replied, "I did understand that to be the case. Of course, our plans for salvaging something from the collapse of the Vichy regime died with the unfortunate Admiral Darlan. He was clearly the best hope for rebuilding a strong and pro-western France after the war. Of course, now General Giraud is Darlan's logical successor ..."

"Surely," Pearson interjected, "General de Gaulle has enough support and charisma to effect the same result ..."

Pearson's comments were as much wishful thinking as fact. De Gaulle was still, to many people and especially to the Americans, a British creation. Canada hoped that British and American policy on France would eventually line up, as it had seemed to do earlier in the year.

Murphy's reply was therefore not comforting. "We do not believe that de Gaulle has sufficient support within France itself to rally the resistance. His efforts, you see," Murphy leaned forward to emphasize the point, "are likely to split the pro-western resistance movement. Most in metropolitan France supported Admiral Darlan and see General Giraud as his natural successor. De Gaulle sided with the British, the very people, if you will excuse me, who attacked and occupied French Syria and who attacked the French fleet at Mers el Kébir in June 1940, killing hundreds of French sailors.

"No, Mr. Pearson, de Gaulle may have chosen the correct side, but he did so at the wrong time. By advancing his cause the British threaten to split pro-western support in postwar France. That would allow French leftists to take effective control. By the time we get there with an invasion force – next year, perhaps? – the Germans may already be too weak to resist a general uprising under the communists. We would then be faced with eastern Europe under Russian domination, possibly Germany as well, and a pro-Soviet France."

"Surely this is a worst-case scenario, Mr. Murphy, and one even the British would want to avoid?"

"Only some British, Mr. Pearson, if you will forgive my candour." Murphy ran a finger idly around the rim of his glass collecting his thoughts. "There is no question that Mr. Churchill and his cabinet believe that by backing de Gaulle they are backing an anti-communist force. Technically that's true. I don't believe de Gaulle is the dupe of any leftist movement. It is simply that he has no standing of consequence in metropolitan France. None! Moreover, it is widely known within Washington circles again, if you would permit me a slight indiscretion, that British policy, for example, in Yugoslavia is decidedly pro-communist. Most of their aid goes to Tito, while the monarchists get precious little. Yet, only the monarchists are actually fighting the Germans." Murphy smiled as he made the last point.

"Tito's not interested in the Germans, he's content to let them kill the Chetniks and other monarchists while waiting for us or the Russians to finish off the Germans. Then he will have a free hand. France is far too important to us – to all of us – to let that happen there."

The conversation faltered as Murphy realized that he was getting deeply into Anglo-American rivalries. Finally, Pearson broke the silence.

"I don't see how this affects Canada."

"Well, if you'll forgive me, Mr. Minister, it ought not to affect Canada at all, and in general it doesn't. We and the British are in general agreement on where we ought to be going; we just have some differences over how to get there." Murphy polished off the last of his port, and replaced the glass on the corner of the desk.

"Which brings me to the reason for my coming here tonight ... Do you mind if I smoke?"

Pearson pushed an ashtray across the desk towards Murphy, who lit a cigarette before continuing.

"The power struggle in North Africa late last fall that culminated in Admiral Darlan's assassination ripped the French resistance movement into bitter factions. Many are in favour of working with the Allies, others are fearful of the consequences of such action for metropolitan France, and still others are as committed to having nothing to do with the democratic powers. Darlan's death at the hands of a monarchist was just the most obvious example of their rivalry. There is, as I am sure you know, Mr. Pearson, a very strong fascist element in the French right. Many in the Vichy regime were not only collaborators with the Germans but identify their future – and that of France – with the new European order."

Murphy paused to draw deeply on his cigarette, as if to emphasize his point, and continued. "Many pro-fascist French businesses and banks have invested heavily in German war industry and production. In addition to such white collar collaboration, organizations such as the

Cagoule and the SOL – the Service d'Ordre Legionnaire – are part and parcel of this new European order. The right of French politics, even now, is therefore a battleground, one where the fate of France, and I daresay of western Europe, is being determined."

"Go on, Mr. Murphy," Pearson said quietly. "I am very anxious to see how Canada fits into this."

"It has been necessary," Murphy said nervously, fidgeting now with his cigarette, "in recent months to find havens for pro-western, anti-fascist elements of the French right. Places, if you like, to incubate and keep secure the appropriate pro-Allied Vichy personnel. Many of these men are powerful and influential, and are therefore targets for assassination. They are unsafe in the liberated French colonies. Since we – the United States – have little faith in General de Gaulle's ability to unite the French resistance, we have been working to preserve these pro-Allied elements in the hope that we can employ them later in the reconstruction of France."

Pearson could sense that Murphy was getting perilously close to saying much more than he ought.

"How many have you stashed away in Canada?" Pearson asked in a calm and very restrained voice.

Murphy's face remained unmoved, and for a moment he said nothing, hands clasped under his chin, a gentle wreath of smoke rising from the end of his cigarette. Both men knew that Murphy was on the spot.

Finally Murphy parried in equally measured tones.

"There is, as you know better than I, Mr. Pearson, very strong support for Vichy France in certain parts of Canada. Oh, not just for the state itself or Marechal Pétain, but for the religious, political and cultural ideals of the French race. Such support might not be so strong, even now, if your government had not given full rein to Vichy French 'diplomatic' activity for the past three years."

Murphy was right. Canada had indeed harboured a Vichy embassy until the end of 1942, allowing its staff to distribute blatantly anti-war and anti-Allied propaganda within the French Canadian community. Pearson knew his government had played a dangerous game forging this 'unique' Canadian connection to the rump of the legitimate French government. It was, he knew, hard to tell how much of the present anti-war sentiment within Quebec – and support for the Bloc Populaire in Parliament – was owed to the work of 'enemy' agents within Canada. Mackenzie King's government had played with fire by harbouring a Vichy embassy. They hadn't burned the house down, Pearson thought, but there was a lot of smoke damage.

"Canada never looked upon its ties with Vichy as anything more than a useful Allied conduit to a former ally within the German orbit," Pearson remarked, "and we have taken steps to detain the worst elements of our own pro-fascists, such as Houde and Arcand."

"Oh yes, Mr. Pearson," Murphy replied sympathetically. "I didn't wish to imply that Canada has misjudged its role in relation to France: I think it has been entirely commendable. Mr. King's government has done yeoman service to the war effort in its handling of Vichy over the years. I wanted only to suggest that Canada, especially French Canada, is a logical place for refugees of the current French political struggle to be kept safe."

"I see your point." Pearson was sufficiently astute in the wiles of international politics to know that such clandestine activity was the norm. But still, it touched a nerve to hear of such action from an agent of a foreign government.

"So how may I be of assistance?"

"Let me be direct ..."

"Please."

"A key player in our postwar plans for France, a certain Monsieur Lemaige-Bonnier, is currently en route for Canada, with some of his aides, in a submarine." Murphy paused briefly before going on. "We have learned that there is considerable Canadian naval activity in the general vicinity of the submarine's planned landing site. Frankly, Mr. Pearson, we would like it to stop. As soon as possible."

"I see. You are certain that the naval activity and the submarine's path coincide?"

"Oh yes, indeed they do. Your Navy is currently undertaking rather extensive operations in the western end of the Gulf of St. Lawrence for reasons that are entirely unknown to us. The safe route for the submarine is only known to a very small number of people, including the head of the submarine tracking room at Main Navy. He assures me that there is no evidence of any German activity in the area, and that the Canadian ships – in fact their whole search pattern – seem poised to intercept the sub."

"To intercept it?"

"This is what I have been told. The essential point is to get the searches stopped."

"When is the submarine due to land these men?"

"I'd rather not say precisely."

"Mr. Murphy. My ability to intervene is directly related to the credibility of your story and my ability to present it credibly to my government. If you want these searches stopped, then I suggest you tell me as much as you can."

In the strictest sense, Pearson was right, at least about convincing someone in Ottawa to turn the Navy off. But there was also no point in allowing such an opportunity to go to waste. Murphy needed help, and he would trade on that to get as much information as possible about clandestine US State Department dealings in Canada.

Murphy, too, knew how the game was played, but for the moment Pearson was winning. It was best, therefore, to spread the responsibility widely.

"Very well," Murphy finally said, reluctantly. "If you can take the time, there are two brief visits we should make: one to the State Department and the other to see Commander Knowles at Main Navy. What you learn during these two calls will also help determine the best course of action to take with your own government."

Pearson sat, unmoved, drawing slowly on his port, seemingly lost in thought. Murphy waited a moment before disturbing him. "We should go now Sir, if you please? Time is crucial."

"Very well," Pearson replied, reaching under the desk for the bell switch. "Porter will see you to the door. I'll just clear away a few things and get my coat."

Chapter 12

Rear Admiral George "Jetty" Jones was loyal to his friends and followers, cutting and intolerant of those who stood in his way. From September 1940 to September 1942 he held the Navy's most important operational post – Commanding Officer, Atlantic Coast. The Canadian Navy's massive wartime escort fleet was whipped into shape largely under his direction. Even Jones would claim he had created it; but the fact that the fleet was widely engaged in important tasks throughout the Atlantic owed much to his drive to get, and keep, ships at sea.

Indeed, the sheer scale of that effort was the principal reason why a new, independent Canadian theatre of war had just come into being. Rewarded for his efforts by promotion to the post of Vice Chief of the Naval Staff, Jones ought to have taken pride in his accomplishment. But it was marred by two things. First, the new command at Halifax had fallen to his main professional rival and bitter personal enemy, Leonard Murray. Their mutual dislike was so intense that Jones and Murray could not bear to be in each other's presence. In 1940, when Murray took over *Assiniboine* from Jones, the Navy had to appoint Cuth Taylor as temporary commander so the two did not have to meet.

By 1941 Jones was in command in Halifax trying to build a fleet as quickly as possible, while Murray – as Flag Officer, Newfoundland – was the fleet's main user. While Murray was battling U-boats, Jones was building up the fleet, feeding expansion off the operational ships from Murray's command. As operational ships arrived in Halifax for repairs or new equipment Jones stripped them of their trained and experienced crewmen, spread them into newly commissioned ships, and then sent Murray's ships back with a new crew, too. For Murray it was like running in sand. Escorts that he could rely on one week were floating disasters the next, many hard pressed even to find their way home. Murray dubbed Jones' manning personnel "Pirates", and it often seemed that the real enemy was the establishment at Halifax. But without Jones, Murray would have had too few ships to do his job.

Perhaps for that reason Jones gained a march on Murray in December 1941. He was raised to flag rank one day earlier, and his ultimate victory seemed to be his posting as Vice Chief of the Naval Staff in December 1942. But in early 1943 Murray got the plum, the post of Commander-in-Chief, Canadian Northwest Atlantic. When Admiral Nelles was finally pushed from the post of Chief of the Naval Staff, as he would be soon, Jones would have command of the Navy itself, while Murray commanded its ships. The RCN was a house divided.

The other thing that clouded Jones' typically grim demeanour was his boss, Percy Walker Nelles. Everyone at naval service headquarters was given to know that Nelles was tired beyond his years, that his health had collapsed in 1942 during the disastrous campaign in the Gulf of St. Lawrence, that he smoked and drank too much for his own good, that he had no power of suasion over the minister, and that – perhaps worst of all – anything the British asked him to do, he did.

Not surprisingly, the new members of the naval staff whom Jones brought with him from Halifax at the end of 1942 shared his views. The 'Jones boys' were soon whispering behind Nelles' back to Macdonald and Connolly, his assistant. Jones knew full well that Macdonald was weak and feckless – that he kept Nelles on so long was evidence of that – and Jones was deeply unimpressed by Macdonald's maladroitness in Parliament over the Navy's activities. Macdonald's only use might be ridding the Navy of Nelles.

In the meantime, Jones was re-organizing naval service headquarters, trying to draw system and order out of the chaos of three years of unbridled naval expansion. They now had a new building and a new plan, which would see him take over all important operational staff functions. Murray might have the fleet, but Jones had the whole damn

Navy and, with luck when Nelles went, as surely he must, Jones would be Chief of Naval Services.

During the past week, Murray's picture had been plastered on the front page of the Toronto *Globe*, which trumpeted his ascension to the new command. Nelles was trying to salvage something from the wreckage of 1942, both the political heat of the Gulf closure and the operational, and indeed political, defeat at sea. The Navy was now back into the battle in the mid-Atlantic, or at least would be this month and Prentice, Murray's boorish alter ego in Halifax, was making irritating noises about an offensive in Canadian waters.

Good luck to them, Jones thought, as he went down the list of candidates for the new post of Director of Warfare and Training. The reorganization of headquarters was taking up all of Jones' time, but even he admitted that he had never been much of a ship handler. But he did not deserve the nickname "Jetty" Jones, for all that. He earned it in 1940 when his destroyer, *Ottawa*, struck the Halifax to Dartmouth ferry and was forced to lie alongside while the rest of the fleet sailed for the war zone in Europe. It was an accident, of course, but the nickname followed him remorselessly. Jones took solace in the thought that having built a fleet he would now complete his task by raising a headquarters from the rubble left by Nelles and building a naval establishment that would put even Murray in his place.

The blueprints for that new empire lay strewn across Jones' desk, and he pored over them in his shirtsleeves as the warm afternoon sun brightened the room. He hadn't bothered to stop for lunch; a cold sandwich and a mug of coffee at his desk sufficed. He was nearing the end of a long, undisturbed afternoon when the soft sounds of his secretary entering the room caused him to look up.

"Beg your pardon, Sir. We've received a request from the Prime Minister's Office: they would like the chief of naval services to attend a meeting there immediately."

"What does that have to do with me?"

"Well, Sir. Admiral Nelles is in Montreal this afternoon and cannot get back in time ..."

Jones pushed his glasses down to the end of his nose, raised his eyebrows and looked sternly at his secretary. "Surely there is someone from Policy and Plans we can send, or perhaps Connolly from the minister's office ... or they can reschedule for tomorrow."

"I'm sorry, Sir," the secretary said, with some firmness, for he was used to dealing with the admiral, "but I've already suggested that. Apparently it's not a policy or planning issue, and they do not want someone from the minister's office. They say it's so urgent that the meeting cannot be rescheduled. They want the most senior officer present in lieu of the chief, and they want him now. In fact, Sir, I understand the War Cabinet is waiting for you.

"I've ordered a car, it will be out front momentarily, Sir."

Jones rose from his chair, took his coat and hat from the secretary and left the office, fuming at the machinations of politicians and their minions.

It was less than three blocks from naval service headquarters to the Prime Minister's office on the Hill, and the weather was superb. But the car's dark back seat suited his mood.

The group waiting for him in the cabinet room confirmed that this was no ordinary policy bull session. The Prime Minister, that bulbous little man, was there, sure enough, and his hulking Deputy Prime Minister and Quebec lieutenant, Louis St. Laurent. So, too, were Macdonald, the Naval Minister; Colonel Ralston the Minister of Defence; and Norman Robertson the Secretary of State for External Affairs. Also present was a small, stout man in a bow tie and crumpled suit whom he did not know. A curious character, Jones thought after shaking Pearson's hand. Rather scruffy in appearance, nervous in speech, bit of a lisp too, and dressed like an Oxford don. He had just arrived, Jones was told, after a long train trip from Washington.

It was clear that they had been waiting for Jones for some time, so the Prime Minister wasted no time calling the meeting to order and passing the proceedings along to Colonel Ralston.

"I think, gentlemen," Ralston muttered, "it is best to cut straight to the chase. Mr. Pearson would you please repeat for Admiral Jones what you have just confided to us."

Pearson simply recounted the basics, the Vichy French agent, the American state department sponsorship, the bare bones of the international and postwar politics of the case, his own briefing at Main Navy by Commander Knowles, his train trip and the problem of Canadian warships in the sub's landing area. Pearson ended by saying that the Americans wanted the Canadian search abandoned as soon as possible.

Jones was dumbfounded. Why hadn't he been told? He kept his face expressionless, but it was painfully clear that the men in the room wanted some explanation of why Canadian warships were concentrated in an area where only a few people – and until quite recently none of them Canadians – knew there was a submarine.

"Surely," Jones observed, looking alternately at King and Pearson, "the notion of a U-boat landing a senior French politician in Canada is preposterous."

"Perhaps not," Pearson said, placing his elbows on the table and working his hands nervously. "There are many – many – connections between the French right and the Nazis. We have no particular knowledge of what pretexts M. Bonnier may have invoked to arrange his transit. We do know, however, that Canada's domestic tensions have been widely reported, and are certainly well known within Vichy circles. The windfall from stirring up instability in Canada – the impact on industrial production, shipment of goods and raw materials and, potentially, on Canada's military effort – is considerable for so small an effort as landing an *agent provocateur*. Moreover, it would not be the first time that the Nazis have landed an agent on the Gaspé shore. I can assure you that the information I received in Washington yesterday was entirely credible, and the presence of Canadian ships in position to intercept the submarine suggests that others are aware of the operation as well."

"Point well taken, Mr. Pearson," the Prime Minister said. "The issue of the moment, Admiral, is can you recall those forces promptly?"

"Well, yes Sir, that's easily done," Jones replied, adding, in a moment of inspiration, "if that's what you want to do."

The idea that the Navy should be allowed to go ahead and sink the submarine, if it could, had already been discussed among the senior Cabinet members, and had entered a few other heads in the room, too. But for Jones it was a tactical move. By raising the option he might deflect attention away from his own ignorance of the whole affair long enough to find out what was going on.

"I take your point, Admiral," Mackenzie King said. "I don't need to remind those around this table of the great value our government, not to mention the Navy, would derive from the sinking of a U-boat in the Gulf of St. Lawrence. I am, moreover, deeply offended that we should be asked to allow an enemy submarine to enter our waters and land an agent of an openly hostile and anti-democratic regime, whom we should then harbour against some long-term scheme of a foreign government. It is simply preposterous! Absolutely unacceptable!

"Indeed, when Colonel Ralston, Mr. Robertson and I discussed this earlier this morning, we agreed to delay our decision until Mr. Pearson arrived and the whole War Cabinet could be assembled. We are, you see, not entirely convinced we should act so precipitously when the US state department demands it."

"I agree wholeheartedly, Mr. Prime Minister," Ralston chimed in. "As I argued this morning we could allow the present scene to play itself out, do nothing, let the ships continue their patrol and see what happens. At the very least, we could delay the recall notice sufficiently to give our ships a chance. With all due respect, Angus," he continued, with a gesture towards the naval minister, "our ships have had no luck actually sinking a submarine in those waters and – "

Macdonald, his nerves worn raw by the disasters of 1942, took the bait. "Mr. Prime Minister! As I have informed the Cabinet on a number of occasions, the Navy has taken considerable measures to ensure that any penetration of the Gulf or River this year by U-boats will be dealt with effectively. These plans, devised by Admiral Murray and his staff are, I am told, " and he looked to Jones for assurance, "foolproof."

An uneasy stillness hung over the room. Jones, pleased that he had set the politicians among themselves, said nothing.

"Indeed," Macdonald droned on, "I would not have recommended to Cabinet that we close the Gulf to ocean shipping this summer had I thought that the Navy was incapable of switching its escort forces to an offensive designed to sink U-boats! If the government wants this U-boat killed, we will do it."

Macdonald was growing animated. He had promised much from the vastly expanded wartime fleet, but so far the Navy had been unable to deliver the government from its critics.

"Admiral Jones is fully versed in the Navy's new offensive strategy for 1943," Macdonald continued, "and I am sure he would be happy to review them for – "

Mackenzie King cut him short. "For Heaven's sakes, Angus, you are not on trial here! The question to hand is whether or not certain naval operations ought to be allowed to proceed. I, for one, am most anxious to hear what Admiral Jones has to say. Admiral?"

No-one was more anxious to hear what Jones would say than Jones himself. It was clear that Macdonald, typically, didn't have the foggiest idea what the hell was actually going on in the Gulf, but how could Jones disguise the fact that he didn't, either?

Jones watched the main plots at naval service headquarters routinely, often several times a day. He had been told that the vessels in the Gulf were simply Prentice playing at war. "Advanced training for the Gulf," a plotter told him. He hadn't taken much notice as, like everyone else, he was taken up by the convoy battles northeast of Newfoundland. Today he had assumed that the ships were being redeployed to search for the lost Canso.

"A number of small escorts, a couple of corvettes and minesweepers are in the central Gulf. They are engaged, for the most part," he said with some hesitancy, "in a training exercise and, lately, in a search for a lost aircraft. It's all routine, gentlemen."

This much was likely to be nearly right regardless of what the truth turned out to be. Everyone in the room seemed content, except for Pearson, who seemed puzzled by what Jones had said and shot him a knowing, almost accusatory, glance that left Jones uneasy.

"You see," Macdonald interjected quickly, "we have been preparing our hunting forces under all conditions in which they might be expected to operate. The fact that we would blend the search for an aircraft with training is simply an indication of how committed we really are."

The Prime Minister cast a weary glance at Macdonald. "Oh for goodness' sake Angus, relax. The question is not how committed you are to training, but whether these ships ought to be called out of the area and the U-boat allowed to land an agent!"

"Mr. Prime Minister," Ralston blurted, "Forgive my speaking out of turn, but I am appalled that we would willingly allow the intrusion of an enemy warship into this country's waters, allow it to land an agent, and then allow it to escape. Surely, as a sovereign state we have the right to act in our own interest and I, for one, feel we should let events in the Gulf play themselves out. There is, after all, no certainty – forgive me, Angus," he said with a nod towards Macdonald, "that the Navy can or will sink it. But surely to God," he concluded, thumping his fist on the table, "we should try!"

At Ralston's suggestion that the international ramifications of sinking the submarine be brushed aside Norman Robertson, the secretary of state for external affairs, shifted anxiously in his seat.

"Mr. Robertson?"

"Thank you Mr. Prime Minister. I share Colonel Ralston's frustration regarding the Americans' high-handedness. But surely there is more at stake here than national pride. We do have foreign interests, particularly in the future of Europe and the ultimate fate of France, not to mention that of our continental friends. We would be foolhardy to prejudice the long-term stability of postwar Europe – or our good relations with the US – by responding to short-term, and dare I say rash, domestic political pressures."

Robertson's words acted like oil on troubled waters. Ever the politician, Mackenzie King took his point. "I am afraid, gentlemen," he said, addressing Ralston and Macdonald in solemn tones, "that the interests of the government do not warrant active pursuit of the submarine at this moment. I do not take this position lightly, I assure you. National unity, not to mention four looming federal bye-elections, demand hard decisions and forthright action. Unquestionably, a sub sinking in the Gulf would buoy the fortunes of this government and deflate much of the anti-government and anti-war sentiment present in the land. But, we shall have to find other means of accomplishing that aim."

"I would like to echo the sentiment expressed by Mr. King," Louis St. Laurent added. "We have come through four very difficult war years trying to hold this country together. There are those in my own province who feel very strongly that this is not their war, or, if it is, that it should be fought here, in defence of *la patrie*. I have, for all those years, shared Mr. King's belief that the war to defend Canadian democracy cannot be fought solely on our own doorstep. Most of my fellow Quebeckers feel the same, and many have enlisted for active service. I must add, Mr. Prime Minister, that I, too, am deeply offended by this manipulation of Canada, and by the cynical exploitation of its cultural duality."

St. Laurent was a gifted speaker and a man of eminent good sense. He spoke with passion of his commitment to Canada and the justice of the war. Finally, he raised a point that had escaped everyone's attention. "I should think, Mr. Prime Minister, that the Solicitor General ought to be informed, and that once this particular agent is ashore, he should be held in protective custody by the RCMP. If the Americans want him safe, we have some prisons that will do the job very nicely. The details could be worked out with the US state department and we could, if we saw fit, pass him along to the Americans at a later date."

"I should think," Roberts responded, taking up St. Laurent's suggestion, "that such an arrangement is possible. However, given our general support for British policy on postwar Europe and our sympathies for General de Gaulle, the sooner M. Bonnier is passed on to the Americans the better. It is clearly in the British interest to have M. Bonnier removed indefinitely from the current power struggle in the French resistance. By incarcerating him, we would be de facto supporting British policy. By detaining or harbouring him in Canada we would be caught between British and American interests. Mr. Prime Minister, I would support Mr. St. Laurent's suggestion that he be taken into custody immediately, but he should be transferred as quickly as possible to American hands."

The quiet nodding of heads indicated general approval. King was about to say as much, when Macdonald broke the silence. "But the issue of the submarine remains. Surely we cannot allow an enemy submarine into our waters in time of war, allow it to complete its mission, and then let it simply sail away!"

Ralston turned sharply to Macdonald and observed with dark humour, "Why not, Angus? We've done it before!"

Stunned silence and incredulity filled the room. Pearson's chin nearly dropped to the floor and Robertson stared blankly out the window trying to maintain his composure.

"If you will permit me, Mr. Prime Minister?" Jones intervened. "Submarines on clandestine missions never engage in other activities until after their primary task has been completed. Typically, they would clear well away from the landing site before they'd start to attack shipping, for example."

"What's your point, Admiral?"

"Simply this. The U-boat is unlikely to attack shipping in the Gulf before it has landed the agent and, likely, not even after. However, it will probably end up off Halifax or St. John's for a few weeks of hunting before going home. We could call off the present operations, allow the agent to land, and then sink the bastard on his way home!"

Jones had hit on the solution to a previously intractable problem.

"Is this possible?" Mackenzie King asked.

"It will be harder to do, no question, Sir," Jones replied. "The sub has at least two possible routes out of the Gulf, and we would give up our easiest chance by not laying a trap in the landing area. But if the fleet is as ready as Murray and Prentice contend, they should be able to catch the sub on its way out."

This plan, too, gained general approval. St. Laurent was instructed to contact the solicitor general to ensure that M. Bonnier was taken into custody immediately. Robertson and Pearson were to work on the Americans, to facilitate Bonnier's transfer as soon as possible.

"Admiral Jones," Mackenzie King said turning finally to the vice-chief of naval services, "you will recall your ships from the central Gulf of St. Lawrence for the time being. Understood?"

"Perfectly, Sir."

His orders clear, Jones promptly left the meeting on the excuse that the orders should be conveyed immediately, relieved that he managed to slip away before someone asked him a pointed question.

Returning a quick salute to the guard at the entrance to naval headquarters, Jones headed straight for the plotting room to find out what the hell was going on.

The plots occupied a long, narrow wing of the main floor. A row of windows, filing cabinets, desks, telephones, teleprinters, tables and stools stood down one side, a series of large maps down the other. The maps were tended by WRENS, who climbed the short ladders and moved the pins and flags according to information provided by the duty officer for each plot.

Jones hauled up in front of the plot for the new Canadian Northwest Atlantic. A quick glance revealed four corvettes and one Bangor just east of Gaspé, a flotilla of motor launches east of them, two other ships enroute to the central Gulf, and three British trawlers on patrol in the Cabot Strait. Pearson was right – it looked like a plan to intercept the submarine.

"So that's why that little bow-tied creep gave me such an evil look when I said the ships were training," Jones muttered. "Someone in Washington briefed him well."

He also glanced at the battles developing east of Newfoundland, in the area now under British operational control. The swarm of U-boats that had dogged ONS 5, the slow westbound Royal Navy-escorted convoy, had caught up, and it looked like the convoy had steamed right into the path of another waiting pack. A quick glance revealed that none of the Canadian-escorted convoys was anywhere near the massive U-boat concentration. "Fine by me."

"Where's deMarbois?" Jones demanded of no-one in particular. A WREN plotter suggested that he might be in the Operational Intelligence Centre, since battle had been joined off Newfoundland and the OIC was deeply involved.

Jones steamed down the hall, bursting into the OIC plotting room like a runaway freight train. When he met deMarbois' eye Jones barked, "A word with you, Commander. Now!" Jones never visited for casual reasons or out of simple human interest, and the abruptness of his entry indicated that this was not going to be pleasant.

"Perhaps we should slip into my office, Sir?" deMarbois said as he stepped past Jones and across the hall. DeMarbois closed the door and moved behind his own desk. He was about to invite the admiral to sit when Jones cut him off.

"What's going on in the Gulf?" he demanded sharply.

"Sir? ... I ..." deMarbois mumbled.

Jones drove a fist hard into the desktop, "What the bloody hell is going on in the Gulf of St. Lawrence? What are all those ships at?"

"Oh, I see, Sir. The ships in the Gulf ... Yes, well, there has been an aircraft mis – ”

"Don't give me that bullshit, deMarbois!" Jones snapped. "They're not deployed to search for some bloody aircraft, they're after a damned submarine! I want to know why, and I want to know why I was not apprised of it!"

DeMarbois was damned if he was going to take all the heat for this one, but how much should he say?

"The operation has been conducted in utmost secrecy under the direct orders of the Chief of Naval Services himself. I am not sure I am at liberty to say more."

Naval intelligence was not Jones' strong suit, nor indeed, given the restriction on 'need to know', could he easily pull rank and press deMarbois for his sources. But it was worth a try.

"When did this operation commence?"

"Last Saturday."

"I see. And upon what information was it based?"

"I am not at liberty to say, Sir."

True enough; but all good interrogators can winkle information from a witness with a mixture of bluff, bits of information and thinly veiled threat.

Jones lowered his voice and said coldly, "Do you know who is in that submarine?"

"I cannot say ..."

"Damn you deMarbois!" Jones shouted, slamming his fist repeatedly into the desk. "I'll tell you who. A Frenchman! A senior bloody Vichy Frenchman, that's who!"

"Well yes, Sir," deMarbois said hesitantly. "It was a senior Vichy agent – ”

"Agent!" Jones threw his hands aloft in mock surprise. "DeMarbois, this man is a senior French politician whom, it turns out, the Americans," he said with particular emphasis, "are sending here for safekeeping – if we don't kill him first!"

Jones leaned over the desk, pressing his face close to deMarbois' and asked icily, "We *are* trying to kill him, aren't we deMarbois?"

"We're trying to sink the U-boat, Sir, if that's what you mean – ”

"That's exactly what I mean! You know there is an agent of some type on that sub, and the fleet has been deployed to sink it. Plain and simple, right?"

"Yes, Sir, I suppose so ..."

"And," Jones went on, "if this was just your ordinary garden variety U-boat entering the Gulf to begin the 1943 offensive against shipping in Canadian waters, then the whole of bloody naval headquarters would know about it! Wouldn't they?"

No response.

"Damn it! Wouldn't they!"

"Yes Sir, I suppose they would."

"Yes." Jones sighed, having won his point. "I suppose they would."

"I also suppose," Jones said with more restraint, "that since the Americans want this thing stopped, the only plausible source of intelligence for this operation is British. Am I right?" Jones looked deMarbois straight in the eyes.

DeMarbois would not – could not – answer, but he also could not hold Jones' glassy stare.

Jones muttered softly to himself, "I thought so, I thought so ... Played for fools again. My God we are babes in the manger when it comes to dealing with the mother country."

Without another word Jones set off down the hall for Nelles' office.

The Chief's secretary could manage only a "Good evening, Admiral, the CNS is – " before Jones burst past him through the partially open door to Nelles' inner office.

"Hello George!" Nelles offered, taken aback by the sudden intrusion.

"We have to talk."

"By all means, have a seat."

Jones ignored the invitation. "Admiral, what the hell is going on in the Gulf?"

"Training, you know that."

"No Sir, not training ... we're trying to kill someone."

"What do you mean, George?" Nelles asked innocently.

"Look. This afternoon, while you were on your way back from

Montreal, I was called to a meeting of the War Cabinet, where I was informed that our ships in the Gulf were deployed to destroy a U-boat that the Americans believe is carrying a high-level Vichy French politician."

"I see," Nelles said coolly, tossing back the last half of his first drink of the evening. "And how do we know that?"

"The US state department, their office of strategic services, and apparently the US Navy have contrived to get this guy to Quebec. They want to incubate him in Canada, keep him safe from radicals until he can lead the French resistance. Anyway, it appears that we are trying to kill this man, and the Cabinet wants it stopped. You know all about this, don't you? It is your operation."

"I know about the U-boat, yes," Nelles admitted coyly.

"And you initiated the operation to sink it?"

"Yes, I did." Nelles lit a cigarette and leaned back in his chair.

"And you did not feel you could take me into your confidence?" Jones demanded.

"The intelligence we had was of a very secret nature. There was no point in drawing more people into it than was absolutely necessary."

"Murray and Prentice know, no doubt?"

"Of course, strict need to know. They had to plan and execute the operation."

"And how did you find out about the sub? DeMarbois? Radio intelligence decrypt? How?"

"I don't think that matters, George."

Jones looked down at him, trying to keep himself from exploding.

"I think it does, Sir. Clearly you did not get this information from the Americans, so it must have come from the British."

No response.

"Am I right, Admiral?"

Nelles rose slowly, moved over to the file cabinet, pulled out the whisky bottle and poured himself half a tumbler. He waved the bottle at Jones, who shook his head. Nelles took a long swig.

"What difference does it make if the intelligence came from the British, eh? We get the sub and this Vichy bastard is dead. Suits everyone."

Jones turned back and stared coldly. "It suits the British! The Americans want this... this...Bonnier guy alive!"

"And why should we do them any favours?" Nelles' tone sharpened. "Don't you think it's a bit much for a foreign government to use Canada as some kind of hothouse for its own puppets? And besides, we have only their word that M. Bonnier is to be incubated. He is a nasty piece of work George, a fascist, a Nazi sympathizer, and a Vichy *agent provocateur*. What difference does it make if he dies in the sub?"

"None," Jones had to admit. "None. Except that we will have acted as assassins for the British."

"You're being a bit harsh. If sinking a U-boat is assassination then I'm afraid we've assassinated a great many men in this war."

"But don't you see, Admiral! We're being used by the British. Duped into doing their dirty work."

"And if we don't sink this U-boat we will have been manipulated into compromising Canadian sovereignty by the Americans."

Nelles let Jones reflect on the dilemma for a few moments before breaking the uneasy silence.

"You know as well as I do, George, that if we sink this U-boat in the Gulf the whole complexion of the war here at home will change. My God, there will be a ticker-tape parade down St. Catherine's Street!"

"Yes, Sir. And you know equally well that we must call the ships off."

"I do?"

"Yes, Sir. It's a direct order from the Prime Minister and the War Cabinet."

"I see," Nelles said softly. "And what do *you* think we should do?"

Jones watched Nelles slowly swirling the rye around the sides of the tumbler. What was he thinking of? Deliberately disobeying an order from the government?

"I think we must turn it off, Sir. Immediately."

Nelles said nothing for a moment, then spoke in a low voice. "So you think we've been had again, eh? Suckered by perfidious Albion."

"Perhaps."

"Is that what you'll tell Macdonald?"

Jones refused to be baited. "More to the point, it's time we began to look after ourselves."

"And how would not sinking a U-boat in Canadian waters be seen as looking after ourselves?"

Jones looked absently out the window. Nelles came around his desk, stopping several feet behind Jones.

"Have you seen the plot lately, the North Atlantic plot?"

"Yes," Jones answered, without turning around.

"So you've seen the U-boat concentration south of Greenland, and the routing of the convoys?"

"Yes."

"And did you notice where our convoys were routed?"

"Yes."

"Uh huh." Nelles slumped against the desk and crossed his arms.

"We'll get our share of action, Admiral. We're bound to run into something sooner or later."

"I suppose," Nelles answered idly, "but not if they constantly route us clear of the enemy."

"When our own support group is operational we can be in the thick of it. We should forget about Murray's hare-brained scheme for an offensive inshore and concentrate our forces where the U-boats are."

"And give up on killing U-boats inshore, in the Gulf?"

"We should kill U-boats where we can."

"I agree. That's what I've been telling the minister. So what about the one we're after now in the Gulf, eh? My God George, a U-boat kill in the Gulf is a dream come true for both us and the government. Can we just give up on it?"

"I – we – have been ordered, Admiral, by the Prime Minister and his Cabinet to cease submarine-hunting operations in the Gulf of St. Lawrence."

"Then you had better issue the re-call order, George," Nelles said, and threw back the rest of the rye.

Chapter 13

"Watch out, Fergus! You'll get that all over the plot!"

Belanger seldom spoke sharply to his officers in front of the crew, but Fergus was notorious for wandering around with food in his hands. Belanger tolerated the habit only because, like most of the crew, Fergus was a young man and his days were one long meal, punctuated by formal sittings three times a day. The front of his dufflecoat, stained by cocoa and molasses, bore mute testimony to Fergus' eating habits.

Pulling back from the plotting table, Fergus licked the sticky molasses that had dripped from the corner of the bread down onto the palm of his hand.

"Sorry Uncle," he quipped casually, "What's the gen?"

Belanger glanced back at the chart, getting his bearings before responding. "*Tracadie* has issued his night orders. We are to switch places with *Innisfail* and take position in the centre of the sweep, and try to hold *Innisfail* and *Tracadie* at maximum radar range on either side – in this sea about 5,000 yards. Smythe tells me the 271's working fine, but make sure that the SW2C is warmed up and running, too."

"Aye, Sir," Fergus replied, stuffing the last of the bread into his mouth.

"Once we have assumed night stations I want the asdic alternating passive and active modes. If there is a submarine moving here-

172

abouts we are more likely to pick up the sound of its diesels than find it by active pinging."

"I agree, Sir, but may I suggest that we maintain only a listening watch on asdic. The sea's fairly calm, but the visibility's the shits in this drizzle – can't be much more than a mile. There's patchy fog, and the cloud cover's right down on the masthead. If I was a submariner I'd be making time on the surface, navigating by echo sounder, or maybe even by lead line. As long as this wind holds from the east," Fergus concluded, as he squinted out through the sea-smeared window, "things won't change much. Maybe we can pick up his diesels."

Belanger weighed the recommendation briefly and then concurred. "All right, Fergus, keep the asdic on a listening watch. No point in giving our position away by pinging all over the ocean."

"No, Sir, the rest of the main force can do that!"

Belanger then took a moment to ponder the effect of this concession. Wagner had specifically asked for the alternating passive and active asdic watches, and no doubt the other ships would conform. But Fergus was clearly right. Any sub moving in towards the coast tonight would likely be on the surface running on diesel engines. If they were submerged they would probably be edging inshore using their echo sounder to get a bottom profile. Either way, it was better to listen for the sub than to fill the water with noise. In any event, Wagner probably would never know that *Lakeville* had gone totally passive.

"Now," Belanger continued, "the larger plan is to sweep towards the coast at midnight, along a heading of 285 and then at 0030 to split into two divisions and patrol along the shoreline at the two most likely landing places. Here," Belanger pointed with the end of his pencil, "just south of Cap d'Espoir, and here just south of Cap Blanc. The motor launches will come up astern to provide something of an offshore barrier."

Fergus was perplexed. It was the first time that the force had anticipated a landing and moved inshore to patrol the sites. Belanger had delivered the plan with equanimity, but Fergus was not sure that his captain liked it much. "Is this wise, Sir? I mean splitting the force and tipping our hand by moving right inshore? How do we know when the U-boat will attempt to put people ashore? What if we spook it?"

"All good points, Fergus. I have discussed this with Wagner on the R/T. I don't think it's the best plan, although with a small force to watch a large piece of coastline it is not an unreasonable one. You know, of course, that the old destroyer *Yukon* is on the way – she'll likely join sometime in the early morning. When that happens Commander Collishaw takes over. Perhaps Wagner is trying to win the game while he is still in charge."

"No doubt," Fergus sighed.

"At the very least, Fergus, this is a very useful training exercise, and once we break into two divisions we will be rid of Wagner for the night! We and *Innisfail* have been tasked to search what Wagner deems to be the secondary landing site, just south of Cap Blanc, where the road from Percé to l'Anse au Beaufils runs close to the sea. As you see, deep water runs well inshore along that part of the coast, so it's an excellent place for a nervous submariner to put someone ashore."

The chart showed a rugged shoreline, with rocky promontories between shallow bays. The cape to which *Lakeville* was assigned lay just south of Percé, with Bonaventure Island offshore. From Cap Blanc the coastline ran west-south-west for a few miles before curving due south to Cap d'Espoir, where Wagner would be searching. The chart showed depths of sixteen fathoms within a few hundred yards of the beach at Cap Blanc, dropping quickly to a wide seabed plain of thirty-five to forty fathoms.

"The water off Cap d'Espoir is deeper, closer inshore," Belanger explained. "You see, it drops off to nearly 100 fathoms within a few miles. That's why Wagner thinks the sub will go there first.

"And why he's taking three ships with him."

"Precisely."

"So how do you plan to catch 'im, Skipper, with just this ol' girl and a Bangor?" Fergus asked, the last traces of molasses now licked from his hands, and his face eagerly poised over the chart.

"Well, I've worked through several scenarios, but the most likely one is to use Cap Blanc and Bonaventure Island for cover and watch the shoreline on radar. If we slide in along the south side of Bonaventure Island and round up along the coast just below Percé Rock, here ..." Belanger traced his intended track, "we have enough water even at low tide to lay close inshore right up under Cap Blanc." Belanger pointed to the chart, which showed more than nine fathoms right off the cape. "We can poke our nose out from the point just far enough for the 271 to watch the area below the cape, and we'll have the darkness of Bonaventure Island behind us to prevent our being visible on the horizon. Something, I admit, that's not likely in this weather, but a useful caution in any event."

"And what about *Innisfail*? Do we keep her with us, or what?"

"Good question, Fergus, good question. There are a number of plausible options. *Innisfail*'s main value lies in her asdic set and depth charges, although we cannot count out her twelve-pounder if it comes to a surface action. I had thought of holding her in an ambush position roughly here," he pointed to a spot about three miles south of Bonaventure Island, "or perhaps even tucked under the shadow of the island itself. But if the 'sweeper gets too far away we can't control her on our radar; her SW1C is all but useless and she might well miss any sub we spook southwards. If we had another corvette with 271 an ambush would be possible, but we'll have to keep *Innisfail* close astern. Then if we drive the U-boat down with gunfire she will be right there to start the asdic search."

"But what if the U-boat runs?" Fergus replied. "I mean, jeeze, we couldn't catch a sub on the surface if our life depended on it. They all have a knot or two on us at the best of times."

"Yes, but look. If they run south, or even southeast, we can call up Wagner's group and catch her in a rather larger ambush." Fergus raised his eyebrows – the old guy really had thought this through. "If the U-boat tries to land people along this coast," Belanger went on, pointing to the shoreline that ran almost due west from Cap Blanc, "we have the weather gauge; our mere presence ought to drive them south, at least initially."

Fergus nodded approval.

"Right," Belanger said, "Any other questions? ... Okay! We'll shift to night stations at 2045 for the run-in to the coast. Assuming nothing else happens, we will close up to action stations at 2130. We should be off Cap Blanc by 2200. I suggest you get some rest after dinner – it promises to be a long night."

Belanger came on deck shortly after 2100 to find that the wind, which had backed and veered all day between northeast and southeast, now drove straight from the east at a steady twenty-five or thirty knots. The moist air pouring in over the cold sea produced great grey banks of fog, a steady soaking drizzle and a rising swell. *Lakeville* was yawing and pitching as she took the following seas under her starboard quarter, and the wind whined through the corvette's rigging and signal halyards. It was just as well they had the wind astern, Belanger thought. Driving into this wind and sea would create quite a din on the open bridge, and one would have to shout to be heard.

Belanger lingered in the open long enough to determine that little could be seen through the murk, and with the sea running before that wind it would be dicey for any submariner to try landing people either at Cap Blanc or Cap d'Espoir. Maybe Wagner would call off the search.

Belanger left the bridge to the sodden and shivering lookouts. In the charthouse Samuels shared Belanger's estimation of the situation. "Bit tricky to make a landing anywhere along the Gaspé shore tonight," Samuels mused. "There'll be a good surf running along the shoreline. Probably impossible to put someone ashore from a sub."

"But we shall have to wait and see what our leader thinks."

Lakeville's captain had no sooner uttered those words than a signalman arrived from the wireless room, a deck below, with a pencilled note and a signal in hand.

"Beg yer pardon, Sir, I have a signal direct from naval headquarters, addressed to *Tracadie* with repeats to the other ships, which we have just decoded. And an order received over R/T from *Tracadie* himself." He passed both to Belanger, and waited for any replies.

The scribbled note from Wagner said simply, "Search has been suspended. Await further orders."

As it turned out, Wagner's message was basically a repeat of the signal from NSHQ:

MOST SECRET
NAVAL MESSAGE

TO: *Tracadie*   *FROM:* NSHQ
   (R) CinC, CNA
Castlegar
Lakeville
Watson Lake   HUSH MOST SECRET
Innisfail   Main Force, 8th ML Flotilla to suspend
Mabou   operations immediately (R) immediately.
Yukon,
8ML Flot   2. *Yukon,* Main Force and MLs to proceed to *Fort*
               Ramsay: *Mabou* to proceed to Pictou for further
               training.

TOO 060014Z

T/T   CYPHER   TOR 060020Z/5/43   MHR 6734

Belanger passed the messages to Samuels, who also read them silently. It was a few moments before Belanger spoke. "So, I guess that settles it. No landing tonight, or any night probably."

Samuels was not so sure, "Or the landing has taken place, Sir – they've caught the buggers, and we've missed the chance we've hoped for."

"No," Belanger replied, "these orders suspend the entire operation, period. If there had been a landing they would have sent us packing back to the Cabot Strait or the Strait of Belle Isle to try to catch the sub on her way out. No, Sam, the search is over – abandoned. Anyway, if there was a sub out there, the way Wagner had us chasing phantoms day and night the whole Grand Fleet could have steamed through our so-called 'barrier', and we'd never know! I'd better talk to Wagner."

"Get *Tracadie* on the R/T," Belanger barked to the signalman. In a few moments he passed the handset to Belanger. "Antler this is Cattail. What gives?"

"I don't know much more than you." Wagner's voice rose and fell like pounding surf through the soaking ether. "I've raised Halifax, but they aren't saying much. I don't think they know anything yet: it appears the orders came straight from Ottawa."

Belanger lost the last part, which faded badly just as a rating opened the wheelhouse door. "I'm sorry, Wagner," Belanger shouted into the phone, "what was that last bit about Ottawa?"

"I said, it appears that Ottawa ordered the abandonment of the search! But damned if I know why."

"I see. I understand that we are to proceed into Gaspé. Over." Belanger found himself compensating for the oscillating strength of the signal by shouting.

"Yes," was the garbled reply. "But they have asked me to send a 271-equipped ship to bring in the motor launches – a task I pass to you, Clive. Over."

"Surely *Yukon* can pick them up as she passes? Over."

"Not a chance. She's already turned back – she's turned back! already – for Pictou with condenser trouble. You're it. Over."

"Very well. Where are they?"

"About forty miles southeast by east of your present position. They've been out from the Magdalens for over a day now, and Halifax thinks this weather will last for a few more. It would be hard for them to get in safely on their own. Over."

Belanger couldn't but think that the motor launches were a nuisance at the best of times.

"All right, I'll leave now, if you agree. Over."

"Yes, at your convenience. Over."

"Right, then you will have to close *Innisfail*. She'll not likely find you in this chop with her SW1C. Over."

"Yes, I'll see to *Innisfail*. Good luck to you. Over and out."

Belanger put the handset back into its cradle, then stepped to the wheelhouse voicepipe. "Wheelhouse, this is the Cap'n. Revolutions for fifteen knots," Belanger ordered. "Bring her around and steady her on 125, then reduce speed to twelve knots." Belanger listened while the orders were repeated, and then caught Samuels' eye to ensure that he had heard them, too.

Lakeville was soon wallowing as she commenced her turn. It was now up to the men on watch to try to find four small wooden ships in a fog-shrouded, tossing sea. Fergus worked out the course and a simple search pattern, confirmed Belanger's course and speed orders, alerted Harkness on the 271 set and the lookouts, and tried to raise the launches on the wireless.

The corvette's motion on the new course was easier to take. The yawing stopped, she just pitched and rolled, but she was now driving straight into the sea and wind. About every third or fourth wave she buried her bows a little, sending great plumes of spray high over the ship, adding to the misery of those topside and dumping tons of water onto the foc'sle. The change in motion was readily evident to those forward in the messdecks, which now rose and fell sharply, while the pounding of the oncoming waves on the bow echoed throughout the ship. Overflowing the scuppers and trapped in the open welldeck, water poured into the crews' quarters. It was not a particularly ugly night to be at sea but, as Ryan said, a corvette would roll on wet grass, and *Lakeville* was shouldering more than dew.

Belanger left things in Fergus' capable hands and went below to catch a few winks. There was little enough for the first watch to do once they had settled onto the new course. To ward off the cold and damp, they had steaming mugs of thick cocoa. Fergus dipped slabs of bread into his cocoa and had just finished mopping the sides of his mug with a crust when word came that Harkness had a radar contact.

By Fergus' reckoning it was too early, much too early, to have made contact with the motor launches, unless they stood farther westward than anyone estimated. Fergus opened the charthouse door, waited for *Lakeville* to struggle up onto the next wave, then took a few short steps to the 271 radar hut, arriving just as her bows went down again. He met her forward pitch, swung the radar room door open and wedged his shoulder against the casing.

"What d'ya got?"

"Come in, Sir, please. The water's not good for the set."

Inside the tiny hut Harkness explained.

"Just a single contact Sir, bearing green 015 at a range of about 4000 yards – there, see it?" Fergus squinted, but there was so much clutter on the screen he could not be sure of anything.

"Wait a minute, Sir. I'll try to sharpen it up and reduce some of the wave clutter." Harkness wiggled some knobs, which changed the brightness and contrast until finally, in the top right hand corner of the screen, one blip was sharper than all the rest.

"There, Sir."

"I see," Fergus said, not quite convinced there was anything to see. "Is it a motor launch?"

"Oh, not likely, they're small and wooden. They won't give such a good return echo at that range in this weather."

"So, it must be *Yukon*. She was due to join early this morning. Does it look like a four-stacker?"

"Hard to say, Sir. It's still much too far away. All I can say is that its a good, strong contact; could easily be from a destroyer."

"What's our rate of closing – the contact's estimated course and speed?"

"We're closing quickly, Sir, maybe a total of twenty-five knots. Its course appears to be crossing ours slightly; roughly 335."

"Well, if it is *Yukon* she's on a good course for Gaspé. A little slow though, maybe her radar's down. Thanks, Harkness. Keep me posted."

Fergus beat his way windward, back into the charthouse, and reported the contact to Belanger by voicepipe, adding his suspicion that it must be *Yukon*. Fergus did not know what to make of the reply. Belanger muttered something about "apology ... didn't inform you ... very sorry, Number One ... I'm on my way to the bridge ... start a plot" and the voicepipe went silent. He had barely begun to lay out the plot when Belanger burst through the charthouse door.

"What's the latest?"

"Ah, according to Harkness, we have a contact on the 271, about 4000 yards ahead just off our starboard bow, green 015. It's on a slightly closing course, but seems to be en route for Gaspé. The contact is still too far distant to get a sense for its size. I've not spoken to Harkness since I called you.

"I'm sorry to alarm you, Skipper, but its probably just *Yukon* ..."

"Can't be. I forgot to tell you, she's been re-routed to Pictou with defects. Whatever is out there is not *Yukon*." With that Belanger slipped through the door.

He was back in a just a few moments, bursting into the charthouse at a great rate of knots.

"Fergus! Sound action stations! And lay on a course to intercept the contact!"

The sound of ringing bells shattered the quiet of the messdecks, sending seabooted sailors, already dressed, from their slumber. Like countless times before, dark figures poured forth from the welldeck up ladders and down passageways until *Lakeville*'s weapons and sensors were fully manned. As each was ready in turn, its status was reported to the bridge: the cox'n at the wheel; Kozlowski and Fergus on the asdic; Samuels, the gunnery officer, in command of the four-inch gun; Smythe and Harkness at the 271; and Chartrand, another junior radar rating, manning the SW2C. 'Phonse, Macpherson and a host of others were shifting gear and depth charges on the quarterdeck.

The crew quickly rigged a block and tackle down through the hatch in the welldeck, through the lower messdeck, and down into the magazine to the powder charges that lay in the bowels of the ship – thereby opening a conduit for water to enter the deeper recesses of the crew's spaces. Soon the lower decks were awash. Meanwhile, the chief engineer and his blackgang stood silently to their tasks in the boiler and engine rooms. On the bridge the secondary armament was manned and ready, and the yeoman and another signal rating stood ready to send whatever signals Belanger saw fit. And Elliott, the youngest of the corvette's seamen, scampered aloft to the crowsnest.

Amid all this organized chaos the closest point of approach – where and when the two ships would come into contact – was worked out. New helm and revolution orders were passed, and soon *Lakeville* was corkscrewing her way through the sea on a very unpleasant northeast heading.

Leaving the development of a proper plot to Fergus, Belanger went out to 'fight' his ship from the forward edge of the windswept bridge. Given the corvette's primitive sensors and communications systems Belanger preferred to be where he could see the action unfold, running his own plot in his head. A system of runners and voicepipes kept him informed of the latest sensor information, the guns on the bridge and the main gun forward were within hailing distance, and by lowering one of the charthouse windows he could talk directly to Fergus on the asdic, who could provide compass headings and asdic information.

"Aloft there! Elliot!" Belanger called through the wind and spray. When a dark shape loomed over the crowsnest Belanger shouted, "Keep you eyes on the starboard bow!"

As Belanger peered out into the gloom, Samuels, the gunnery officer, caught his attention. "'Scuse me, Sir. Do you want a starshell up the spout for this one? Might help the visibility a bit, could cast a shadow behind the target, you know, if we don't loft it too far."

"Good idea, Samuels. Can't hurt. But make your second one high explosive."

"Very good, Sir," said Samuels, who retreated to pass his orders along to the four-inch gun crew.

Another figure slipped immediately into Samuels' place. "Lieutenant Smythe reports that the contact is now 2500 yards off, bearing green 030, still closing."

Neither binoculars nor the ship's telescope could pierce the murk, and *Lakeville* was closing quickly on a contact they still knew nothing about. Belanger, of course, was constantly working out the relative velocity of the two closing ships while calculating the dangers of closing an unknown contact at near right angles and high speed. Finally, he gave helm and revolution orders that brought *Lakeville* onto a nearly parallel course and at the estimated speed of the contact. Stepping to the charthouse window, he told Fergus, "I'm bringing her around onto 340 at ten knots. That'll ease us down on the target from off its port quarter."

Lakeville's new course was a yawing, uncomfortable track with the sea pushing her stern to port as each wave surged under her quarter. With nothing but a simple magnetic compass, it was a very hard course to steer. It was not long before Fergus was growling down the voicepipe, "Give her a few spokes at a time, Cox'n! We're all over the friggin' ocean. Don't oversteer, fer Chrissake!" All the cox'n could do was answer "Aye, aye, Sir," although he felt like telling the young fool of a first officer that if he could do any better he was welcome to take over.

Apart from the cox'n only Fergus and Kozlowski had direct and continuous access to a compass and it, too, swung wildly from 310 around to 010 and back again. Yet, they knew the cox'n was the best they had, and everyone else who normally took the helm couldn't steer a straight course in a millpond. It was hard to anticipate the sea and hard to hold the heading of 340 degrees, five degrees of closing on the contact which was still making 335.

Belanger was happy with the cox'n's efforts and, as *Lakeville* settled onto her new, slightly closing course, he went straight to the 271 hut and told Smythe he needed some indication of just what was out there – shape, length, anything. Smythe muttered acknowledgement, said something about clutter, then Belanger made his way back to the forward edge of the bridge.

He was just back at his post on the starboard bridge wing when Smythe himself appeared. "I think it's a sub, Sir! I mean, Chartrand's "A" scan on the SW2C suggests it's low and flat, except for a bulge in the middle where a conning tower would be."

"How long is it?"

"Big – long. It doesn't fit well with the notion that it's a sub. I make it out to be about 300 feet. A bit long for a Jerry U-boat, even a type IX, and about 100 feet longer than a type VII."

"In other words, about the length of a four-stack destroyer, which is low, flat, with a bulge where the bridge is?"

Smythe looked suddenly deflated. "Well ... yes Sir, I suppose."

"Thanks Smythe, keep me posted."

Belanger stepped into the charthouse to pass the information on to Fergus and get his opinion on what they were up against. "Well, what d'you think?"

"I hesitate to say. If it is a destroyer they ought to have us by now on their own radar. Maybe *Yukon* decided to head for Gaspé after all. If we are playing cat and mouse in the fog we may collide with or engage a friendly."

"Well, there's one last thing to try. We'll give a listen." With that Belanger tapped Kozlowski on the shoulder: "Anything yet?"

Kos slipped one earphone from his head, "Say again, Sir?"

"Anything yet?"

"Oh, no Sir. Too much quenching in this sea. The asdic transducer is making so much friggin' noise with the ship slapping her way through the seas like she is."

"Right." Belanger stepped to the wheelhouse voicepipes, ordering slow ahead and turning *Lakeville's* head so she pointed straight downwind to give her the easiest motion possible. "Once she steadies, have another go."

Fergus and Kozlowski bent to their task, while Belanger admonished the cox'n to hold her steady. In the dim red light of the charthouse it was hard to see the expressions on the operators' faces, but after a few moments Fergus raised one hand and beckoned to Belanger. Nothing was said. He simply passed the headphones to the captain, while Kozlowski maintained the listening watch.

Belanger's ears were greeted by a steady crackle and hiss, an annoying sound like a badly tuned radio. An immediate look of bewilderment came over Belanger's face, but Fergus raised one hand to advise patience. *Lakeville's* asdic made a distinct swishing sound as the transducer rose and fell, but there was another faint – mechanical? – sound, rhythmic and regular. It took Belanger a moment to distinguish it from the background noise, but he advertised his moment of discovery by looking directly at Fergus, and then at Kozlowski. There was something there but he could not identify it.

Belanger's expression said as much to Kozlowski, who fiddled with the controls to filter out more of the sea noises; but Belanger could scarcely tell the difference. Finally he ripped off the headphones. "What is it?"

Kozlowski, who had already shifted one phone from his left ear so he could both hear the officers and listen on the set, said simply, "Diesels."

"You're sure, Kozlowski?" Belanger demanded.

Kozlowski looked his captain straight in the eye and then without any hesitation said, "Positively." Fergus simply nodded at Belanger as he pulled on his headphones.

Belanger stepped immediately to the voicepipes, ordered *Lakeville* back on her converging course, threw a quick "Here we go" towards Fergus and headed back onto the starboard bridge wing.

In a few minutes Fergus joined Belanger by the rail. "No question about it, Uncle, it's diesel engines."

"Yes," Belanger replied, "and Smythe confirms it's low, flat and about 300 feet long." Both put their binoculars to their eyes, but the darkness and fog remained impenetrable.

"Estabrooks," Belanger finally said to the starboard bridge lookout, "tell Mr. Smythe I want continuous ranges as we slide down on that contact, every hundred yards. Fergus ..."

"Aye, Sir?"

"Make sure that all charges are set shallow."

Estabrooks soon reported. "Lieutenant Smythe says the contact is now at 1800 yards, and we're a little astern of her, Sir."

"That's not bad," Fergus observed. "If we put on a few extra revolutions we can surge up on her port quarter for the final ID." Belanger agreed and ordered revolutions for fourteen knots.

Lakeville was approaching her maximum speed, which made her asdic useless so Fergus remained on the bridge at Belanger's side. The slightly following wind pushed her funnel smoke ahead, adding to the gloom forward, but the ship now outpaced the waves. The dreadful yawing had stopped, although she still pitched badly, burying her bows in the backside of slower swells.

Inexorably the range closed – 1600, 1500, 1400 – as *Lakeville* edged her way up on the contact. Belanger ordered small changes in helm to ease her down on the target, until they ought to be close enough to hit it with a beer bottle. But still no break in the fog and darkness.

As they edged past and directly downwind from the contact, a possibility suggested itself. "Fergus, do you think there's a chance of a fog shadow?" In wind-driven fog there was often a gap caused by a ship upwind, through which they might just see it at rather long range.

"No," Fergus replied. "Whatever is out there is too low to deflect much of the fog. We'll have to close to determine what it is."

Samuels was following events closely, as it was probably his main gun that would open the action. As the range came down he was compelled to ask, "Given the range now, Sir, do you want me to draw the starshell and reload with high explosive?" At short range and limited visibility the illumination round in the four-inch gun was already useless. The gun could not elevate much and the starshell would simply bang out thousands of yards beyond and be lost in the gloom.

"Yes, quickly, Sam. We may be on the target at any moment. I don't want to be caught with nothing up the spout."

If Belanger needed illumination he would now have to use his searchlights, not a great solution since it gave the enemy an aiming point.

"Range 300 yards now, Sir, and just forward of the beam," reported Smythe from the radar hut. Just then Elliott howled excitedly from the crowsnest, "Bridge, lookout! On deck there! Green seven zero, just forward of the starboard beam! It's a U-boat! It's a U-boat!!"

Elliott had glimpsed it through a gap in the fog, although nothing could be seen from the bridge. Belanger just had time to order full speed ahead and standby searchlights before *Lakeville* entered the gap and the contact was finally visible. Its long, low silhouette with the distinctive conning tower amidships left no doubt.

"Now Samuels! NOW!" Belanger shouted, "Fire! Fire! Fire!"

The concussion of the four-inch gun almost broadside on shook the bridge and pummelled the faces of the men there. But they paid no attention to it, or to the billowing cloud of acrid smoke and bits of paper that drifted back over the ship. Steadier pounding bursts came from the twin .50" machine guns next to them on the starboard bridge wing, its gaps in firing filled by the bark of another twin .50 further aft. It wasn't much, but it ought to keep the sub from manning her guns.

In fact, *Lakeville*'s initial threat to the sub was rather small. Samuels had not had time to draw the starshell from the breech, so he fired it off. Thus *Lakeville*'s first round sailed well clear of the target and burst in the distance, hanging in the sky like a tiny distant streetlamp.

As the four-inch crew reloaded, Belanger worked to estimate how wide this gap in the fog was, how long he could pound the U-boat with gunfire, how long his puny secondary armament would keep the sub from manning her own guns, and how long it would take her to crash dive. In an instant he lifted the flap on the voicepipe to order a ramming course. "Full speed ahead, starboard fifteen!"

By the time Belanger looked up again the four-inch gun barked for the second time, now at point blank range. An almost instantaneous yellow flash from the submarine indicated a direct hit, somewhere just forward of the conning tower near the sub's main gun.

Samuels was elated. "We hit it! We hit it!" he was shouting. But he would not get another chance for a while. Already *Lakeville*, the sea boiling away from her bows, was turning onto her ramming course, heeling to port, shipping tons of water along the maindeck, and raising the muzzle of the main gun high into the air. Her third shot, fired on instinct, disappeared into the night sky. Then, as *Lakeville*'s bows turned onto the submarine, the main gun would not depress sufficiently to hit.

Belanger now cursed his order to ram. Maybe it would have been better to stand off and pound the sub at this range. But it was too late. *Lakeville* had turned and she was closing quickly on the sub. Only the machine guns on the bridge wings poured their thin stream of fire – small balls of bright light arching towards the target and bouncing at wild angles into the night sky – down on the submarine.

What Belanger needed now was speed. At sixteen knots *Lakeville* would close the distance to the sub in about a minute – a long time. "Faster! Faster!" he muttered amid the din of the machine guns, urging *Lakeville* on by force of will, pushing the forward bridge rail to help her along. "Faster! Faster!"

"She's turning!" Fergus shouted, "She's turning!"

Belanger saw it, too. The sub's stern was beginning to swing towards *Lakeville*: she was starting to turn away.

"Shit! Come on! Damn you, faster!" Belanger shouted as he pounded his hands on the rail.

The submarine was halfway through her turn when *Lakeville*'s bow struck her just aft of the conning tower. The sub's hard outer hull shed *Lakeville*'s rounded stem with ease, and what followed was Belanger's worst fear. The corvette heeled heavily, scraping down the sub's port side. The screeching and grinding of steel was not enough to drown out the cheers of the depth charge crews on *Lakeville*'s quarterdeck, who could literally touch the enemy vessel. Nor did it drown out the sound of breaking glass as they pelted the conning tower with empty coke bottles.

Bursts from the after gun position, the only guns that would depress enough to hit the enemy's conning tower, ripped through the air, but flew harmlessly over the top. Apart from ramming, oaths and coke bottles were the only short-range weapons a corvette had.

Belanger had a good look at the enemy as *Lakeville* swept past. A few figures cowered behind bulwarks and periscope housings on the conning tower, while bodies on the deck indicated that the corvette's machine gunners had done their work: the sub's secondary armament was not yet fully manned. Belanger was struck by the sheer size of the sub, and by the quadruple 20mm or 30mm guns on platforms astern and, in an arrangement he had never heard of, forward as well. Then, just as the corvette began to sheer off and right herself, came a distinct thud as *Lakeville*'s bow struck the sub's port hydroplane.

Fergus had the presence of mind to order the depth charges fired as *Lakeville* drew away, and the sea around the submarine erupted in pillars of water. Even the shallowest setting, fifty feet, was too deep to do more than shake the sub, blow some circuits, and scare the crew, but one never knew.

"Fergus! Check for damage!" Belanger shouted as the ships drew apart. "We've got to keep up speed." He then bellowed into the wheelhouse voicepipe, "Starboard fifteen!", and to Samuels, "Keep firing, even if you can't hit her!" And finally to the chief engineer in the bowels of the ship, "Chief! Gimme everything you've got, everything!"

And so the four-inch gun pounded away, sending shot after shot hurtling over the submarine as it ran. "If you can't hit her," Belanger barked, "keep her from steadying long enough to dive, Samuels." *Lakeville* pursued at close – but clearly opening – range. Belanger tried to keep the corvette on one quarter or the other of the sub as it snaked and twisted its way through the sea, to reduce the risk of stern launched torpedoes, and to reduce her speed.

The speed of the chase, the moderate sea and frequent course alterations made it difficult, and sometimes impossible, for the corvette's bridge-mounted machine-guns to keep a steady fire on the U-boat's conning tower. The flying spray was now mixed with muzzle flashes, traces of cordite, bits of burnt paper from the gun wadding, and the crackling bursts of .50" machine-gun fire sending lines of tracer ammunition into the fog ahead.

As the range opened the accuracy of the four-inch gun improved, especially when *Lakeville* pitched forward and cleared the field of fire for the gun. Geysers of water spouted near the sub as the thirty-two-pound shells ploughed in with near-misses.

The chase was minutes old when Fergus reported the damage suffered in the failed ramming. "The sub's hydroplane ripped us from the chain locker aft to the reserve feed water tank. That whole bilge is filling up, including the asdic compartment. The damage control party has pumps going, but I don't think they can stem it. Flooding will stop at the asdic compartment, but we've shipped a lot of water."

"Damn," Belanger replied, "she's already getting away from us."

Despite the desultory but steady fire from *Lakeville* the submarine finally manned her secondary armament, and the first rounds rushed silently at *Lakeville* like speeding balls of light. Some fell into the sea, others soared over the bridge. Some bridge personnel crouched instinctively below the canvas dodger and splinter mats that covered the railing for psychological if not physical protection. The main gun crew down on the foc'sle had a shield to shelter behind, but even it could not withstand the heavy fire from the sub. Belanger's desire to keep on the sub's quarter allowed the submarine on occasion to get both of her secondary guns firing on their target.

The volume and weight of the submarine's fire was devastating. Tracers crept up and over *Lakeville* until, having got the range, the sub's gunners poured concentrated fire onto the bridge and midships section. Even Belanger ducked behind the bridge railing as 20mm rounds ripped the air around his head and shattered the flimsy charthouse. Shards of glass and wood added to the shrapnel effect of the bursting shells.

Samuels sprawled bleeding on the deck, clutching his leg in agony. The starboard twin .50" guns received a direct hit on the mounting, decapitating the gunner, dismounting the gun, and leaving the loader slumped up against the charthouse. The bridge itself was soon a shambles of shattered glass, splintered wood, wounded and dead men, and small fires which served as an aiming point, drawing yet more fire from the sub.

Further aft the story was the same. Two rounds destroyed the 271 antenna, throwing Harkness to the deck unconscious, while a small shell splinter drove into the top of Smythe's head, killing him instantly. Much of the fire poured onto the starboard side depth charge crews.

The burst that hit the gunwale in front of 'Phonse and Macpherson riddled the engine room casing with shell fragments. One drove deep into 'Phonse's left arm, another skimmed off the front of his helmet, knocking him to the deck. Two other members of the depth charge crew were killed outright.

Only those below were spared the full fury of the enemy's fire, at least until a shell ripped through the mild steel of the boiler room casing and splattered on the face of number two boiler, wounding the men there and severing a steam line.

On deck the arching tracer rounds poured liquid flame onto the corvette, exploding on impact. The four-inch still barked its occasional, almost solitary, reply, but the gunners were put off their aim by the bursts of tracers that smacked all around them.

It did not take Belanger long to bend to the wheelhouse voicepipe and order "Port fifteen!" There was no point in ordering a cease fire or "Make smoke!" The corvette's fire was already sporadic and ineffectual, and the fog would soon envelop them. As the corvette heeled over on her turn to port the four-inch gun barked one last time, and then it would no longer bear. In a few seconds they were in the fog. The firing stopped.

Belanger surveyed the damage. Despite the ferocity of the enemy's fire, damage control parties were already dragging hoses up towards the bridge from the portside, working on the little fires, and tending the wounded. On the starboard side of the bridge he found Fergus wrapping a shell dressing around Samuels' leg. The young officer was nearly comatose from loss of blood. "We'll get you down to the Tiffy's right away, Sam," Belanger said softly. "You'll be just fine."

When Fergus finally stood up to survey the scene the two officers moved instinctively to the centre of the bridge. "Let's get this cleared up as best we can, and in the meantime turn back and give the four-inch another try," Belanger spoke quietly. "Leland, the quarters rating on the four-inch, claims their last shot struck the U-boat's conning tower, right aft he thinks. That may have taken out their secondary armament. With luck we can beat the sub into submission, or maybe force it down so we can attack with depth charges."

Fergus gazed distractedly at the wreckage around him.

"If we can find him," Belanger insisted, "we can finish him off, Fergus!"

"We'll never catch 'im, Sir," Fergus offered drily. "We're down by the bows and still taking on water. We'll never catch him ... and if we did, what then? They outgun us by a wide margin, and if we drive him down ..."

"We still have the four-inch, and almost a hundred depth charges," Belanger said coldly, "and they'll not be so lucky in a second ramming attempt."

"But how the hell do you expect to find her again?" He pointed to the shattered 271 lantern. "That's all shot to shit ... Smythe is dead," the first Belanger had heard of that, "Harkness' unconscious ... and we've got God knows how many tons of water forward! And besides, the asdic compartment's flooded, so that's useless. If he dives we'll never find him."

Fergus' insistence that they could not find the sub without the 271 prompted Belanger to look straight up at the old SW2C radar atop the mast. What he saw eliminated that possibility, too. The top six feet of the mast hung down at a crazy angle. The SW2C antenna was simply gone, slipped from its mounting when the mast fell.

Thank God it's dark, Belanger thought, as tears of rage and frustration welled into his eyes. He drew the back of his hand across his face to wipe them away when a large drop of moisture fell onto his cheek. The rigging always dripped moisture from the fog and sent it pelting down on the deck. But the drop that now ran into the corner of Belanger's mouth had a strong salty taste.

Belanger shot a glance up at the shattered crowsnest. "For the love of God, Fergus!" he cried, "Get Elliott down!"

Chapter 14

Slate grey cloud pressed down on the low hills and a steady drizzle fell as *Lakeville* entered Gaspé harbour around mid-morning. Remnants of winter ice still littered the shore. *Castlegar* stood off to let the crippled corvette pass through the gate first, then she followed, swinging to port and coming alongside the wharf at HMCS *Fort Ramsay*, the Navy's base at Gaspé.

Like the new base at Sydney, *Fort Ramsay* was still under construction at Sandy Cove, just inside the sandspit that formed the natural basin of Gaspé harbour. Beyond the single, L-shaped wharf lay an orderly collection of wood frame buildings in a sea of mud.

Men, ambulances, trucks and staff cars cluttered the narrow wharf as *Lakeville*'s lines were cast and made fast. A few idlers surveyed the corvette's blackened bridge and the wooden plugs driven into the shell holes in the hull. Sick berth attendants, the Tiffys, went quietly about their duty. Pumps, tools, hoses, and shoring timbers were shifted from the wharf down to the corvette's decks, as the shore patrol hustled onlookers away.

'Phonse stood patiently amid a small group of walking wounded, waiting for the stretcher cases to be carried ashore. Kozlowski saw him from the foc'sle deck and hurried down the ladder, elbowing his way through the men on deck. "How ya doin' 'Phonse?" he asked tentatively. "Ya look pretty grim."

"Naw, I'm okay. Da Tiffy says I gonna get some long leave wit dis,"

'Phonse answered, pointing to his left arm in a sling. "Some bullit broked da bone, and kinda maked shit from my arm, eh, but he says da muscle's all der and wit some luck it's gonna mend okay. You doan look so 'ot yerself der, Kos!"

Kozlowski's face was freckled with red splotches and scratches, which, apart from a few bandages, gave the appearance of a bad case of acne. "It's all just splinter scratches, not enough to git me ashore ... Jeeze, 'Phonse, yer likely to get some time in a hospital somewhere," Kozlowski said with a wry grin. "All those friggin' bored nurses. Christ, you won't need yer left arm, they'll do it all for ya!"

"You know what's even bedder dan dat, Kos? I gonna go to a hospital in Quebec, eh! I tink I like doz Quebec girls da bes enaway."

Kozlowski's face dropped.

"'Phonse! The nurses in Quebec – they're all nuns er somethin'!"

A broad grin broke out on 'Phonse's face. "Yess, of course! Dat's da bes. Dey gots no 'usband, no boyfriend, eh, nobody what dey gonna cheat on – dey all married to da church. And der's some tings dat even da church can't do for dem!"

Kozlowski punched him on his good arm. "Jeeze," he said shaking his head, "you got it figured 'Phonse."

The group of walking wounded moved towards the gangway and Kozlowski followed, carrying 'Phonse's kitbag. "You got enough smokes?" Kozlowski asked. Before 'Phonse could answer Kos stuffed three packs of Sweet Caps in the top of the bag. While the top was still open Macpherson sauntered up, drew a quart bottle – corked and without any label – from inside his duffle coat and stuffed it in the bag.

"A few drams the petty officers won't miss!" he said, throwing a wink 'Phonse's way as he and the kitbag were then passed gently into the back of the truck.

While the human wreckage of the night's encounter was being attended to, the first officer to cross the bow onto *Lakeville*'s deck was Commander George Bernard, the Naval Officer in Charge in Gaspé.

"Hello, Clive. It's good to see you."

"Thank you, Sir," Belanger said softly, pumping Bernard's hand heartily.

"Seems you've drawn some fire!"

Belanger merely smiled as Bernard eyed the bridge and with a gesture said, "Do you mind?"

"Not at all, Sir. Please come this way."

Belanger led Bernard on a tour of the shell-torn and blackened bridge. The splinters and broken glass had long since been swept away, but the perforated canvas and splinter mats, the blasted gun mount, the shattered wooden face of the charthouse, the empty windows and blood-soaked deck boards told their story. Belanger explained quietly where men had fallen, where fires had been doused, and the gist of the battle. Bernard listened intently, nodding and asking pointed questions. Finally, as they surveyed the riddled gunshield around the four-inch gun Bernard asked if they might speak in Belanger's cabin.

The captain's cabin was tiny but comfortable enough. Belanger offered Bernard the chair, and opened his liquor cabinet.

"A drink, Commander?"

"Yes, I think that would be in order."

Belanger poured a stout shot into two tumblers and passed one to Bernard before sitting on the bed. Bernard raised his glass slightly and offered a heartfelt toast: "To *Lakeville*!" Belanger smiled slightly, raised his glass wearily and they both drank deeply.

"You had no problems getting in?" Bernard asked, sucking in a good gulp of air to chase the drink.

"No. Main Force found us a few hours afterwards and *Castlegar* stood by and brought us in ... would have been a bit harder to make landfall without her radar, but we would have managed."

"I'm sure you would. She seems pretty sound all things considered ... Five dead?"

"Six. Elliott, the lad who was in the crowsnest, died about halfway up the bay, just a little while ago, actually ... and eleven wounded, three seriously. Sub-Lieutenant Smythe was killed outright when the radar was hit, and Lieutenant Samuels is in critical condition. The rest of the officers have scratches and cuts, but nothing serious. Most of the dead were on the bridge. The others were in the starboard thrower crews and number two boiler room."

"Yes," Bernard conceded, "the damage is evidence of that. What about underwater?"

"I'd be happy to show you, but there's not much to see. She's ripped, we think, between frames six and twenty, below the water line where the sub's port hydroplane struck. The stem is twisted a little too, from the impact. The bilges are flooded aft – asdic compartment, spare feedwater tank and the cable locker – to the magazine bulkhead but it's contained and didn't give us much trouble, except we had to pump the magazine continuously to keep it dry. Apart from that, a few holes from 20mm fire, and the shattered sections of the charthouse, there's no structural damage."

"Good ... well there's not a lot we can do for you here," Bernard offered, sipping on his rum. "Tomorrow we'll move you inside the wharf and try shifting some ballast to get the bow out of the water. If the gash is too low, well, we'll see that she's well shored up before you leave. It'll take a day or two for the engineers to figure where they should send you. In the meantime we'll do what we can ..."

"Yes, thank you, Sir. About the men ..."

"Yes," Bernard shifted nervously and straightened his tunic, "about the men. I have arranged, of course, to have your wounded sent immediately to hospital. As for the rest, I'm afraid they will have to remain on board for the time being ..."

Belanger was astonished. "On board?"

"Yes, quite." Bernard was clearly uneasy. "And for the time being there'll be a shore patrol maintained at the foot of the wharf to keep the curious away."

"For the love of God, why?" Belanger could think of only one reason for such restrictions on the normal movement of personnel. "If there are to be charges laid for cowardice in the face of the enemy, they should be directed at me, not the crew of *Lakeville*. These fellows were magnificent. We broke off the action only after it was clear that nothing more could be done – Fergus will attest to that! If there is to be a courtmartial then it's me, not the crew, who – "

"No Clive, no. There's nothing in your action that any sensible officer would question. Neither you nor your crew is under any suspicion or threat of charges. Please be assured of that."

Belanger slumped on the edge of his bed, took a long pull on his rum. "So why imprison the crew?"

"Actually ... I can't tell you exactly why the precaution is necessary," Bernard said, looking absently at the glass in his hand, avoiding Belanger's stare. "Except that I have orders direct from Ottawa to do so."

"Can't or won't, George?" Belanger demanded.

"Damn it, Clive, I don't know why ... honestly! If I knew, I'd tell you. The best I can do is show you this." With that Bernard pulled a signal from his tunic pocket and passed it forward. Belanger put down his drink, unfolded the paper and read the signal silently. When he was done he ran a hand through his hair, glanced briefly again at the signal, and handed it back.

"Bury them at sea?" Belanger muttered, half as a question half as a statement of fact. "That's odd. I mean, we have the bodies here, they're being landed now. Surely it's customary to bury sailors once landed in graves ashore – there are some from 1942 laid out up there now."

"Yes," Bernard conceded quietly. "The order to bury the dead at sea, now, is very unusual – totally exceptional, I'd venture," he offered, taking another stiff pull on his rum. "But, Clive, I think it's best if we get it over with. I'd like *Castlegar* to do the job this afternoon ..."

"Indecent haste, don't you think?" Belanger shot back.

"Perhaps, but not for burial at sea. You can send a party to do the honours; I'll square that with *Castlegar*."

"The whole thing smells," Belanger concluded. "The search for the U-boat was called off, for no reason – not that anyone tells us anything, anyway – and then a few hours later we're in a fight for our lives with a gigantic submarine, people get killed, we're effectively quarantined, and now the remains of the dead are to be carried out to sea again for burial. What gives George?"

There was nothing Bernard could offer to ease Belanger's mind. "Look old man, I'm just a three-striper on the end of a very long telegraph line. They don't tell me much either, although they sure enough tell me what to do." He tossed back the last of his drink. "No, we all have our orders and I suppose," he said, putting down the glass, "the best we can do is carry them out.

"Thanks for the drink. If there's anything more I can do just let me know." Bernard placed a hand lightly on Belanger's shoulder, "I'm sorry Clive ... I'll make my way out." He turned to leave the cabin, then stopped abruptly. "Ah, I almost forgot. Captain Prentice wants you to put a call through to him this morning. He wants a first-hand account."

Belanger looked somewhat puzzled but Bernard explained. "Yes, it's possible. We've had major improvements in communications along this coast since last summer, and it's a secure line. My signals people will set you up." And with that he was gone, leaving Belanger staring at the rum swirling in his glass.

Halifax, Thursday 6 May 1943

"Look, I'm sorry, Chummy. I've spoken directly to Admiral Nelles. I've offered to play our hand lightly, but it's still no go!" Admiral Murray was imploring an irate Prentice. "We've been given specific instructions – in writing and by phone – to call off the hunt. My hands are tied! We don't even have any routine traffic that we could route 'accidentally' into good hunting areas."

Prentice was pacing, hands thrust in his tunic pockets, chewing grimly on an unlit cigar. It was clear that he wasn't listening, or at least did not care to hear what Murray said.

"If Belanger is right," Prentice said, ignoring Murray's latest rejection, "and they hit her at least twice with their four-inch, there's every likelihood that she's unable to submerge. Christ, she's a sitting duck. All we have to do is block the exits to the Gulf and we've got the bastard."

Murray slumped with exasperation as Prentice rambled on. "We've still got those three Brit trawlers in Cabot Strait ... It would be better if they were 271 equipped, but we can find a couple of corvettes with good radar ..."

"Chummy!" Murray interrupted loudly, "It's off!"

This latest outburst brought Prentice back to reality. He stopped directly in front of the desk, pulled the cigar from his mouth, and said coldly, "The hell it is! What in God's name do Jones and his crowd in Ottawa know about finding U-boats? Nothing! Not a Gawd damned thing. They spent the whole of last bloody year chasing their tails in the Gulf – no concept of operations or tactics! And now these buggers run the Navy!"

"Chummy, you miss the point! Can't you see – they don't *want* to find the sub. They want it to get away – I don't know why! But the orders come from the Cabinet, not from Jones."

"I'll tell you why. No-one among that gang of thieves and pirates that moved to Ottawa with Jones wants us to sink a U-boat, that's why!"

"Oh for crying out loud, Chummy ..."

"No, I tell you, Len, it's true. None of those bastards could stomach us killing a U-boat in a place where they systematically failed. So they killed the operation instead."

"No Chummy, you're wrong. It's politics, inter-Allied politics. We can't kill the sub because the British want the man in it dead and the Yanks want him alive."

"I thought we were done with kissing American ass!"

Murray rolled his eyes, "So would you rather do the Brits' dirty work?"

"That's entirely different, we're family – the empire, the Commonwealth. If the Brits want him dead that's fine by me. Besides, if we sink the bastard, we get a U-boat kill and they get what they want – the whole family's happy."

"Not everybody, Chummy. The Canadian government wants good relations with the Yanks." Seeing Prentice bristle Murray set it out in terms closer to home. "The brass we need to modernize the corvettes, the frames we need to build the frigates, electrical fittings for all our ships, the gyro compasses, and God knows what else comes from the States."

Prentice yanked the cigar from his teeth and growled. "Yes, and as much else comes from the UK. What's your point?"

"Chummy! For God's sake, we have orders from our government to stop the operation. And so we will. It's over. Is that clear?"

"Look," Prentice was now virtually nose to nose with the Admiral. "They didn't say anything about aircraft, did they? As CinC you now control the operations of Eastern Air Command! You could order an intensified search for the Canso that went missing on Monday. If that sub is as damaged as Belanger claims, it will be on the surface and ..."

"No Chummy, no, no, NO! Now, if you'll excuse me I have a luncheon appointment." And grabbing his hat Murray headed for the door.

"I suppose," Prentice said in a conciliatory tone, "if that's the case, then we should get those ships back from Gaspé as soon as possible."

"Yes, I suppose that's wise," Murray conceded. "But, Chummy," he added, softening his tone, "in the most direct and expeditious manner possible; do I make myself clear?"

"Yes, quite. Direct and expeditious, absolutely." Whereupon Murray shot out of his office leaving Prentice still standing by the desk chewing on the unlit cigar.

Gaspé, Thursday 6 May 1943

By noon all the other vessels that had been part of the hunt were berthed at *Fort Ramsay,* the corvettes and minesweepers along the outside of the wharf, the launches nestled inside. There was, of course, much to-ing and fro-ing, but shore leave was suspended, and all were under strict orders not to say a word about the incident. It was all very strange.

At 1335 *Castlegar* slipped her lines and passed out through the gate. Six bodies, sewn into their own hammocks with the last stitch through the nostril to confirm death and two thirty-two-pound shells sown into the foot of each shroud, lay on her quarterdeck. Belanger, Fergus, the two remaining junior officers, and a party of ratings accompanied their dead. *Castlegar* steamed into a dropping southeasterly breeze and a lumpy sea for about an hour-and-a-half across the seventeen miles of Gaspé Bay.

Lakeville's officers huddled on the leeward side of the open bridge, smoking cigarette after cigarette, pouring down vats of steaming coffee, and talking quietly. It was still drizzling slightly but, as they all admitted, it was better to have your nose in the wind and have a horizon than to sit cheek-by-jowl in the corvette's tiny wardroom. Anderson, *Castlegar*'s captain, did his best to make them comfortable, but stayed well clear on the outward leg. *Lakeville*'s seamen, too, remained somewhat aloof, congregating in the open welldeck, smoking and jawing about officers, orders, and other general bullshit.

Just past the tip of Cap de Gaspé *Castlegar* swung northeast into deep water. As *Castlegar* passed into the out-flowing river current pushing against the southeasterly breeze, the seas grew suddenly sharper and the corvette pitched and rolled in the short swell. Belanger was beginning to think this spot was a poor idea, but he wanted his dead to lie in deep water. *Castlegar* had to go only about five miles into the Gulf before there was ninety fathoms under her keel.

When Belanger was satisfied with their position *Castlegar* slowed to nearly a full stop and turned her bows into the oncoming sea to minize her motion. Her ensign was lowered to halfmast and the bosun piped 'still'. Bared-headed men in weathered and worn duffle coats, woollen sweaters and foulweather gear crowded *Castlegar*'s quarterdeck and the after end of the engineroom casing. The honour guard from *Lakeville*, formed in two ranks with Petty Officer Ryan in charge, stood mustered between the depth charge rails, their rifles at 'order arms.'

In matters of religion the Canadian Navy, like the RN, was still strictly Church of England; Belanger read the funeral service from the Anglican *Book of Common Prayer*. The carefully crafted cadences and slightly archaic language seemed, even to Belanger's Catholic sensibilities, singularly appropriate to the occasion. Only the sound of the ship pitching and the wash of each wave down her side, a mournful reminder of the powers of the deep, competed with Belanger's voice. After the prayers the first flag-draped body was lifted to the gunwales on its wooden stretcher, a task made much harder by *Castlegar*'s motion and the wet deck.

"We therefore commit his body to the deep," Belanger read, as the first stretcher was raised and the body, drawn by the weighted shroud, slipped from under the flag and plunged "to the deep to be turned into corruption, looking for the resurrection of the body when the sea shall give up her dead and the life of the world to come, Amen."

An echo of Amens and a volley of musketry followed. This scene was repeated five times as each body was cast into the sea. Then caps were replaced, the ensign raised, and *Castlegar* got underway.

"Very nicely done," Anderson muttered to Belanger, who had stood next to him during the service.

"Thank you. Smythe would have been very pleased with the *Book of Common Prayer* and all."

"Smythe was a religious man, I take it?"

"Religious? Oh no, Smythe wasn't religious," Belanger replied laconically. "He was Anglican."

The subtlety escaped Anderson, who merely shook Belanger's hand in condolence.

"I would be honoured, Clive, if you and your officers would join us in the wardroom for a drink. My XO has laid it on, at the invitation of *Castlegar*'s officers."

Belanger looked at the others and ascertaining no objection, said simply, "Yes, please, we'd rather like that."

Over drinks Anderson gave full vent to his frustration at not being allowed to pursue the contact. "You could have made it into Gaspé without me." Belanger heartily agreed. "Then why the hell didn't we go after him? When we received your contact report all of Main Force turned to help, and your signal was repeated to both Halifax and NSHQ. We couldn't believe it when we got the orders –" Anderson pulled a folded sheet of signal paper from his tunic and passed it to Belanger, "– specific orders, as you can see, not to pursue the contact, but to bring you in. There's a damaged U-boat out there and every warship in the whole fuckin' Gulf is alongside at Gaspé."

"Do we know for sure that the Gulf is empty?" Belanger suggested. "I mean, it's possible – it's likely – that the air force is onto this – "

"But they don't have the radar yet, Clive: I've been told that only a few of the Cansos have 10cm sets, and the rest of that crap is useless in this kind of weather except maybe for navigation. Anyway, d'you ever see even one airplane the whole time we were on patrol? Not one. Now that's strange. I knew it was strange at the briefing last weekend when they said they weren't going to let the air force in on this one. Then *Lakeville* gets clobbered by some monster U-boat and we give up the search. I would sure like to know why."

Camberly, the youngest of *Lakeville*'s officers offered one suggestion. "I hear that *Tracadie* and *Innisfail* need boiler cleaning ..."

"That's bullshit, Camberly," Fergus interjected. "Both ships could easily steam today if they had to. They'll boiler clean to keep people busy and because it has to be done, but it's not enough to keep ships alongside in a crisis. 'Sides, a U-boat is worth a blown boiler.

"But it's still possible that the sub will be intercepted in the Cabot

Strait – I mean, that's where it'll likely go. The passage north of the ice is very narrow and easily covered by radar. If the U-boat is as damaged as we think it is, it won't be able to submerge under the ice. It'll have to clear the strait northabout on the surface. It should be easy to catch."

"You may be right, Fergus, you may be right," Belanger agreed. "I spoke to Prentice this morning. He was so excited I thought he was going to piss himself. Given a chance he'd have the whole bloody fleet mobilized by now."

"But he hasn't, Clive," Anderson added tersely. "We're the closest ships and we're sitting on our asses."

"Yes, but the U-boat almost certainly is heading in the other direction. You might have got him on radar last night, but he would have just run away from you."

"That big, huh?"

"Oh yes!" Fergus replied, "Huge!"

"Type IX?"

"Perhaps," Belanger offered. "I checked the intelligence pubs this morning. The length is right – about 300 feet – she was easily a hundred feet longer than us. But none of the illustrations of the conning towers matched. If anything, she looked like that one-off, *UA*, the one taken over by the Germans from the Turks at the start of the war. There's a picture in the USN's *ONI 220*, if you've got one aboard. But *UA* weighs in at only 1,000 tons. The U-boat last night was heavier, a good 1500 tons or more."

Fergus chimed in. "And the conning tower was different from any U-boat photo I've seen. She had a deck gun forward, plus a 20mm on the forward end of the conning tower, and another mounting aft."

"Could be *UA*," Anderson said.

"Whatever it was, it does not explain why we were ordered to abandon hot pursuit, does it?"

No-one had an answer.

Washington, Thursday 6 May 1943

At 1350 Vanzetti and Hollinger were relieving the watch at the North Atlantic plot in the convoy and routing section of Washington's Main Navy. Although convoy ONS 5 remained on the map, the battle around it, perhaps the most decisive of the Atlantic war, had ended the day before.

Forty U-boats had pursued ONS 5 between the fourth and fifth of May, making roughly forty separate attacks. The British escort counterattacked and an unprecedented six U-boats were sunk. Five other U-boats were severely damaged and twelve others at least slightly damaged. Thirteen Allied merchant ships went down.

The ships and their cargoes could be replaced, and losses of merchant seamen, although tragic, were sustainable. German losses, on the other hand, were unsustainable. As Vanzetti had theorized a few days earlier, the British, now in control of the campaign in the mid-ocean, were taking on the Wolf Packs directly. The battle of the Atlantic had reached its climax.

"ONS 6's moving into danger," Vanzetti observed, pointing up to the plot south of Greenland. "But HMS *Archer*, a 'jeep' carrier, is enroute with three destroyers, and the First Escort Group made up of Brit frigates is also on its way. Those U-boats'll get the shit kicked out of them again."

Even Hollinger, who had been sceptical of Vanzetti's pronouncements, now had to agree. He nodded as Vanzetti went on with the briefing "ON 181'll probably clear. It's HX 237 you've got to watch though. They're a little beset by fog. The mid-ocean escort; ah, let me see," he said, fumbling through some papers, "Yeah, the Canadian escort group C.2 didn't find them until late this morning. EG 5, their supporting group, is still not in contact. As you can see, Arch, some of these subs have already begun their move to intercept the Canadian convoy. The Brits have been pretty careful about this one. They shifted the routing south to get around the U-boat concentration, and EG 5 is scheduled to arrive about a day before they get into trouble."

"Canadians!" Hollinger's eye traced the routing of the convoy.

"The Brits seem to lack confidence in the RCN. But maybe they just feel really confident about their own groups. Hard to blame them after ONS 5. Either way, any convoys routed really close to the U-boats," Vanzetti pointed them out, "are Brit escorted."

When the briefing on the mid-Atlantic was complete, Hollinger asked, "So what's happened in the Gulf of St. Lawrence after that incident last night?"

Between Main Navy and Task Force 24 at Argentia, Newfoundland, the US Navy had prodded the RCN to honour its commitment to include US naval authorities – still in overall strategic direction of the western Atlantic – as a repeat in its signal traffic. This helped them to piece together a bit of what happened in the Gulf, but the Americans remained unclear as to what was afoot.

"Surprisingly, nothing, at least as far as we know. The forces that were in the Gulf are now at Gaspé, showing no signs of movement. I guess they've called off their search. Commander Knowles was in periodically during my watch, but said nothing to me. It seems that the Canadians had quite a little battle with a U-boat east of Gaspé last night – and today nothing. Strange if you ask me."

Gaspé, Thursday 6 May 1943

The spring twilight was fading slowly as Dickson and his fellow officers of the 8th Flotilla sauntered down the wharf. The wind had dropped completely and the sea inside the harbour was a dead calm: a marvellous evening despite the damp chill.

The 8th Flotilla had arrived in Gaspé tired and haggard. The trip from Sydney was not arduous in the summer months, but this spring patrol was more than Dickson cared to repeat. The passage through the icefield north of Cape Breton had been foolhardy. Had they been trapped in the ice and the wind and sea gotten up they might have lost the boats. War put all sailors' lives at risk, but Dickson was not sure his determination to push through was worth it. Aubrey's boat, now lying in the Magdalens with seawater in her fuel lines, was a reminder of the danger. And last night, low on fuel off a lee shore, in a pea-soup fog and a rising sea had tested everyone's stamina. The Gulf of St. Lawrence warmed just enough to swim in by late July and August; in the spring it was still barely above freezing. Immersion meant death.

Thoughts of the previous week crowded into Dickson's mind as he shuffled back from dinner. What was that line from Samuel Pepys his navigating instructor kept repeating? he wondered to himself. "The landman's troubles and hazards are only during a short fight ... whereas the work and labour and hazards are most of them constant to a seaman, besides what he meets in a fight." That was it!

Remembering the quote from Pepys brought a slight grin to Dickson's face. But his contentment derived more from the excellent roast pork dinner at the base wardroom, the remnants of which he was still trying to suck from between his teeth. In fact, he would would have liked to dislodge the last bits of meat with a fingernail, but he could not bring himself to do so in public.

Dickson had dined with some of the senior officers, including Belanger, the captain of *Lakeville*. As they sauntered back to the boats the flotilla's officers began to prod Dickson for information: the size and armament of the sub, how Belanger managed to screw up the ramming, whether they had hit her with the four-inch or not, and how many times.

Soon the little knot of young officers stood silently looking over *Lakeville*'s damage. "Pretty badly shot up," Jackson muttered.

"That's not the worst of it," Dickson said. "She's badly ripped forward, where the U-boat's hydroplane cut her."

"I wouldn't want to go up against that kind of firepower in a Fairmile. Look at what those cannon shells did to her charthouse."

"Our boats're stouter stuff," Minnifie grumbled.

"Wood is wood, Minnifie!" countered Jackson. "If that sub's guns ever get a chance to concentrate on your boat it'll be woodchips in minutes."

"Naw," Minnifie boasted ironically. "That charthouse's just two-by-fours and a bit of planking. MLs are made out of serious wood, couple of layers, and all that glue. 'Sides, we're lower, faster and harder to hit."

"Right, Minnifie," Dickson added gravely. "You hold him by the nose and we'll sneak up from behind and kick him in the ass."

No-one laughed. The blackened bridge, the shell-torn bulwarks and perforated four-inch gunshield, and the fact that *Lakeville* was well down by the bow was little cause for humour. If the U-boat could do that to a steel ship, what would it do to a motor launch?

That thought was on everyone's mind when Noiles, *Q246*'s first lieutenant and the duty officer for the flotilla, joined the group.

"You guys look fat and happy," he said softly to Dickson. "This'll ruin your evening!"

Dickson unfolded the pink signal paper. It was from Captain Prentice. After a quick glance he passed it to Jackson, who read it quickly and let the paper dangle from his fingers. After a few moments Dickson dropped his cigarette butt and crushed it out with his boot.

"We're ordered to sail for Pictou first thing in the morning."

"Shit! Tomorrow morning?" Minnifie muttered, "Christ, they can't fight the friggin' war without us."

"Seems like," Noiles said. Most eyes were still fixed on *Lakeville*. No-one said a word. Jackson passed the signal to Minnifie who scanned it before sending it along to Thoreau, who just shook his head silently. Meanwhile Jackson simply walked away. Thoreau passed the signal back to Noiles, who crammed it into his pocket. "Our fuel was topped up this afternoon, and we're loading the last of the stores now. Should be no problem getting away first thing, Dick."

"Thanks, Andy. Thank God this little piece of mindless excitement is over."

With that the officers drifted away to see to their men and their boats.

Chapter 15

Friday dawned cool and calm, with the temperature hovering near freezing. The low, solid cloud still crushed any hint of wind. The sound of the motor launches getting ready for sea echoed throughout the harbour. Before the first throaty roar of engines broke the morning silence the men spoke in whispered voices on deck, challenged only by the faint and incongruous beat of Glenn Miller's 1942 hit "I've Got a Gal in Kalamazoo" rising from Minnifie's phonograph.

Dickson surveyed the scene from the bridge of *Q246*, coffee mug in hand, collar pulled up against the morning damp. As each captain made his rounds and puttered on deck it was possible for Dickson, without raising his voice much, to talk to them from his bridge.

Soon, however, the diesels came to life and the space inside the wharf was filled with a steady drone and the smell of fumes. Heavily clad figures squared away lines, stood by fenders and waited for the signal to cast off. When all was ready Dickson turned to Noiles on the foc'sle, gave him the thumbs-up, then turned to make eye contact with Babineau on the quarterdeck before making the same gesture. While the lines were recovered Dickson stooped to the wheelhouse voicepipe and passed engine and helm orders to ease *Q246* away.

One by one the launches slipped their lines and followed Dickson out into the harbour; Jackson, Minnifie and finally Thoreau, the most junior. As Dickson stared back at the battle-scarred *Lakeville* he repeated, over and over in his head, his personal mantra: "Never underestimate the power of the sea ...." But *Lakeville* was a silent reminder that it was not just the sea he had to worry about.

Their course took them down the south side of Gaspé Bay, past the anchorage at Douglastown, the army's coastal guns at Fort Prevel and on to Pointe St-Pierre, a low sandstone headland thickly covered with white houses. There they headed due south across La Malbaie towards Bonaventure Island. By the time the flotilla arrived off Percé the day was beginning to brighten. Visibility increased to six or seven miles, and the sky widened under high thin clouds. A few goelettes lay at anchor off the village and several, their sails lying limp in the still air, drifted seaward on the tide, hoping for a lift as the air warmed.

Once clear of Bonaventure Island the 8th Flotilla held its southerly course direct for Northumberland Strait which separates the mainland from Prince Edward Island. Dickson had already laid the course on the chart, briefed Noiles and also Minnifie, whose boat led the flotilla today and who commanded its Second Division. The course kept them well clear of the Miscou Banks off northeastern New Brunswick, where the irregular currents and tidal streams could easily offset his dead reckoning. Besides, Miscou Island was merely a low outcrop of sandstone surrounded by extensive dunes, hard to pick out in bad weather, and its approaches were shallow. It was better to keep to seaward.

The stark red bluffs of the Prince Edward Island coast, about ten miles south of North Point, made an easier and safer landfall. From there they could run along the island coastline and down Northumberland Strait to Pictou. Except for the final leg across to the Nova Scotia shore it would all be coastal pilotage.

Although his orders had not said so, clearly they were enroute to Pictou to act as 'training aids', playing the convoy for new warships to screen, or posing as surfaced U-Boats in night training exercises. Mock battles raged, sometimes supported by aircraft, the length and breadth of Northumberland Strait. MLs dashed in and out of the convoy, the night sky was ripped by tracers, and depth charges boiled the ocean. The war games weren't arduous, just terrifying for the locals and tedious for the ML crews.

But things could have been worse and the morning passed quietly, as the steady and comforting hum of the engines carried the flotilla south without incident. After dinner crews were piped to 'make and mend', a time of leisure. Most caught up on much needed sleep. Babineau, the bosun, sat in the lee of the funnel where there was some warmth on deck, teaching one of the younger seamen how to splice and serve rope. Noiles had the watch and Dickson was soon laid out on the wheelhouse cot, seaboots, duffle coat, watchcap and all.

Try as he might, Dickson had not been able to revive his dream of the woman. He was not so much frustrated as disappointed. The dream had been so vivid, so real. Andy had woken him just before the critical moment and he felt cheated. How long had it been? Seemed like ages.

When he did dream, which was not very often, it was the other dream, the one that had started nearly a year ago. The scene was always the same. Familiar faces framed by lifejackets, splashing amid the flotsam, arms extended, fingers grasping, voices calling "Dickson! Over here, over here!" And nothing could get him close enough.

Once out to sea the flotilla had shaken out into a loose line abreast, like a line of rugby backs waiting to take the ball from the scrum. Each ML trailed a few lengths astern of the boat to port so the funnel smoke would drift clear. Minnifie was ahead on the far left. On his starboard side, about a cable distant was Jackson. Dickson, who led the flotilla's first division, followed slightly behind, and Thoreau trailed a cable off *Q246*'s starboard quarter.

Dickson held that formation into the afternoon despite a gentle westerly wind pushing up a little sea from starboard, causing them to wallow uncomfortably. The wind direction and the noticeable rise in temperature presaged an approaching warm front, likely to produce heavy rain and more fog as it poured across the cold sea. The certain deterioration in the weather urged Dickson on to an early landfall, and he pushed his flotilla across the hundred or so miles from Bonaventure Island to Prince Edward Island at a steady fifteen knots, a little better than their best cruising speed.

By the time he came on deck to relieve Noiles for the first dog watch Dickson expected that the red headlands of the island would soon appear. But Noiles anticipated the question.

"Nothing yet, Skipper."

Dickson uttered a scarcely audible grunt while sucking on scalding coffee and surveying the flotilla gliding along on a slate grey sea. "Nothing from Minnifie?" As the lead boat Minnifie would likely be the first to make a landfall.

"Nope."

"We on course and all that, Noiles? You haven't screwed up seriously over the last three hours, have you?"

"Not mine to screw up. We've just been dogging Jackson, who's dogging Minnifie. But, yes, we're on course," Noiles offered in the same cynical spirit. His voice changed as he made his proper report. "I reckon we're about fifteen miles due north of Miminegash Pond."

"Yer sure? This westerly might have set us a little farther north along the coast."

"I've calculated for that."

"Well I hope so, Andy," Dickson said, looking over his right shoulder at the sea and sky. "When this weather turns to shit I don't want to be horsing around on the reefs off North Point."

"No, I think we're okay. I checked our estimates with Minnifie's at 1500 and we agreed."

About then Saunders arrived on the bridge, coffeepot in hand and a questioning look on his face.

"Yes, Saunders, pour it on," Dickson pleaded. "Have you given up signals for the steward's branch? This isn't your week in the galley is it?"

"No Sir," Saunders offered with a smile, "but the Lord helps them that helps themselves. Mr. Noiles, Sir?"

"No thanks, Saunders, I need to get my head down, but I'll take it back for you," Noiles offered, reaching for the coffeepot. "She's all yours Skipper."

"Pictou early tomorrow, Sir?" Saunders enquired, sipping on his steaming brew.

Dickson was content to use his coffee as a source of warmth, and had his cup buried in both hands. "No, I think we'll lay over in Summerside tonight. I expect this warm front'll give us very heavy rain, and fog, and I don't fancy poking around along the coast in that."

Their attention was caught by the portside lookout, pointing to a fast approaching aircraft flying close to the sea. The sharp roar of its engines drowned out all other sounds as it skimmed in just over mast-head height. It then swung into a steady circuit around the flotilla about a half mile distant.

"It's a Hudson," Dickson observed casually, reaching for his binoc-ulars. "With that new all-white paint she's kinda hard to pick out against the clouds. You can sure see it easily against that dark stuff to the west, though."

"Yes," Saunders agreed, "so it's not one of those training machines from Summerside or somewhere. It's from an operational squadron. We saw a lot of them last summer in these waters; apparently they fly out of Chatham in New Brunswick. This guy's probably just enjoying a wee 'buzz the Navy and scare the shit out of them' on his way home. I say we shoot the bugger down, Sir!"

Dickson, his glasses now fixed firmly on the aircraft, returned the humour and brought Saunders back to his task in the same tone. "I agree, we'll splash the bastard, but let's hear what he has to say first. He's flashing, Saunders, what's he want?"

Saunders concentrated his gaze on the aircraft. "I just caught the tail end of the signal, Sir," Saunders mumbled sheepishly. "Beg yer pardon. I think he'll repeat, anyway."

"Fortunately for you! But, no doubt some sharp young signalman in the flotilla will have picked it up. Otherwise, Saunders ..." Dickson paused for effect, "after we shoot the plane down we'll flog you for dereliction of duty."

The Hudson continued its circuit around the flotilla and soon the signal began again. Saunders called out each word as it was flashed, "'U-boat ... ten ... miles ... east .. of ... you' and then 'Follow me!'"

"Acknowledge!" Dickson shouted, but Saunders already had the aldis lamp in his hand and the signal was on its way. At the same time the portside lookout sang out: "Minnifie and Jackson signalling, Sir!"

"Right," Dickson replied, knowing what the message would say. "Saunders, tell Minnifie to take the second division to twenty knots and steer north of the estimated position of the contact, but to stay in sight. Tell him I'll come up from the south."

Saunders nodded and began clicking away on his signal lamp.

The alarm for action stations and the surge of the launch to near maximum speed brought a flurry of activity on deck. Crewmen wearing life jackets and helmets scurried to the guns, the cox'n took the wheel, the depth charge crew mustered aft and Noiles arrived on the bridge with Dickson's tin hat in hand.

"What's up?" he asked breathlessly.

"Aircraft reported a U-boat about ten miles east of here. I've sent Minnifie and Jackson off to the north," Dickson replied, gesturing to the port bow, where the two MLs had already turned and were showing their tails. "We'll come up on the contact from the south. I gather the sub is on the surface, so we'll have to divide his fire if we hope to get close enough to hit. We may be able to trap him against the shore of the island and confine him to water so he can't dive. That's our only real chance of killing him."

"*Lakeville*'s sub?"

"Who knows. If so, we've got a tiger by the tail here! I hope to Jesus she's wounded, like we heard, possibly unable to dive. Let's hope *Lakeville* drew some of her teeth."

Noiles needed no reminding of the shattered superstructure and riddled hull of the corvette, let alone what such firepower might do to the wooden hulls of the launches.

The two divisions raced eastward on diverging tracks, closing the distance to the island at nearly their best speed. Soon the second division was little more than two grey dots, the white bow wave betraying their presence on the horizon.

"Tell Minnifie that's far enough!" Dickson said to Saunders, who flashed the signal across the intervening four or five miles. Minnifie had no sooner acknowledged the order than his boat was flashing again.

"Minnifie reports the contact, a U-boat, south by southeast, on the surface running north, Sir."

Every eye on *Q246*'s bridge strained to see but the sub was still over the horizon.

"Starboard ten," Dickson ordered through the wheelhouse voice-pipe, "steady on 110." The cox'n repeated the orders and *Q246* eased her course to just south of east, with Thoreau in tow.

"Opening the gap between us and Minnifie?" Noiles asked, puzzled.

"For the moment. Once she sees Minnifie's boats she'll likely turn south and try to run around North Point into the open Gulf. We've got to get a little nearer the point if we hope to intercept her."

Having explained his intentions to Noiles, Dickson ordered Saunders to pass them along to Minnifie. "Saunders! ... Tell Minnifie to drive her south, onto us, if he can, and then come down hard from behind."

"Aye, Sir," the yeoman replied, and the signal was sent and acknowledged.

By the time Dickson and the first division had visual contact the bluffs of Prince Edward Island dominated the eastern horizon, against which the hard, dark lines of the sub stood out clearly. "She's running out of searoom." Dickson's eyes were fixed to his binoculars. "Minnifie and Jackson are almost at the point. She will have to fight them if she wants to get into the Gulf."

"What do you make of her?" Noiles asked anxiously.

"Lots of tracer coming from forward of the conning tower. Looks like twin 20mm fire. Definitely not from her main gun. Don't think she's manned it. Damn, just too hard to tell yet."

"*Lakeville*'s commander said something about a lucky shot that might have taken out her main gun. Let's hope he was right!" Noiles added. "Looks as though she's got secondary armament aft as well. Jesus, quite a barrage."

"Yes, but split between the second division and that aircraft. Let's hope our air force friend has lots of bullets left."

Dickson paused briefly before barking his next order. "Saunders! Tell Thoreau to throttle back, open up about a half mile between us, and ease back to cover the seaward escape route."

"Minnifie's opened fire now," Dickson observed, "and there goes Jackson."

It was almost surreal. Men were trying to kill one another just a few miles away and they could watch it in complete safety. Yet all sound of the battle was drowned out by their own engine noise or swept away by the wind.

Jets of tracer rounds ripped through the air, arching streams of fire. The splash of near misses threw up fountains of water around the boats and the submarine. Those that went into the wooden hulls of the launches, and there must have been many, could not be seen at this distance. The submarine's steel plates, however, sent tracers spiralling into the sky. "They're hitting her," Noiles exclaimed excitedly. "Christ, look at the shit fly." Minnifie handled his boats well. The two launches remained close enough to force the submarine to split her fire, but never close enough to allow the sub an advantage. It was a tricky balancing act. And it wasn't easy to hit the submarine, even at a half-mile, with a 20mm gun from a fast moving ML. Their saving grace was that at top speed the Fairmiles had a four – maybe five or six – knot advantage over the submarine, and much greater manouverability.

"She's swinging south," Dickson announced, "probably hoping to slip between us and the shoreline."

As Dickson turned to pass helm and engine orders Noiles continued to watch the action. "Jackson's making smoke, Dick, must be hit ... Looks like Minnifie's coming on, though. He'll have to ease off, or the sub'll pound him into splinters ..."

Dickson's glasses were once again fixed on the drama. "Let's hope the bugger doesn't turn on them before we can get into action."

The sub swung briefly towards Minnifie's boat, pouring in a hail of rounds that obscured the launch in plumes of spray. Minnifie hauled off northward, covering his own retreat with smoke while the sub turned south and headed for a gap between Dickson and the shore.

The first division now raced into battle, with Thoreau astern – maybe too far astern – denying the sub an opening to the west, as Dickson moved inshore to cut off the escape route into the Northumberland Strait.

"Give her all you've got, Chief!" Dickson bellowed down the engineroom voicepipe. Q246's stern was deep in the water and her wake piled up behind as she surged forward at something better than her designed maximum of twenty-two knots. Thoreau followed, but the gap between them opened.

Q246's course and speed placed her directly in the path of the sub, which now was forced to swing eastward to run the gap between Dickson and the shore. Dickson altered course to stay between his foe and open water. The jockeying eventually brought them onto roughly parallel courses, with *Q246* closing from behind. For a few minutes their courses and relative positions were steady.

Dickson edged in cautiously to about a half-mile range. Only then did he finally order "Fire! Fire! Fire!"

At the outset only *Q246*'s single forward 20mm would bear on the target. The gunner fired bursts trying to keep the sub's men from their guns, and hoping that some of the armour-piercing rounds would penetrate the pressure hull. A few tracers went home, others rattled off the U-boat into the sky. Most missed completely as the gunner wrestled with his aim. In the end, he had to 'walk' each burst up and over the submarine; a steady progression of splashes, followed by bursts on metal, before the last few rounds passed harmlessly over the target. Then the process began again, pointing the muzzle down and stitching his way back up and across the sub.

The submarine responded with her own twin 20mm guns on the after gun platform. Being larger and heavier, the submarine was a better gun platform, and it showed immediately in the telling effect of its fire. Great gouts of water exploded around Dickson's boat, while other rounds slammed home. Glass shattered in the wheelhouse and holes appeared in the hull.

"Steady Cox'n!" Dickson yelled through the open wheelhouse door as the cox'n wrestled with the wheel amid flying splinters and glass. "Where the hell is Thoreau!" Dickson muttered to himself, his thoughts punctuated by the "clang, clang, clang" of his own gun and the shattering impact of the enemy's shells.

Q246's greater speed drew her nearer the sub and Dickson brought his after 20mm gun into action as soon as it would bear. That evened the fight slightly, although the sub still fired a heavier concentration with greater accuracy. As the two ships drew more even, about 700 yards apart running hard for the island's shore, the sub's forward guns came into action.

While Dickson contemplated how much longer he could trade fire Thoreau finally came into action. *Q272* had crept up from astern, and run up on the sub's other side. Now Thoreau was popping away with his forward gun. In an instant the sub switched the fire of her after guns to Thoreau's boat, easing the pressure on Q246. More important, a two-sided attack forced one of the sub's gun mountings to turn its exposed back to Dickson's guns. Without their protective gunshield the sub's guncrews were fatally exposed.

"Concentrate fire on the after gun!" Dickson barked through his megaphone. He hoped that Thoreau would oblige by firing on the forward gun, which was still hammering away at *Q246*. Dickson watched man after man crumple into a ragged heap or be hurled into the sea by the impact of his shells.

Relays of men kept *Q246*'s 20mm guns firing, a hazardous duty on the shell-swept deck. The after gunner had already gone down, replaced by Babineau, and two ammunition carriers lay in pools of blood in the shelter of the funnel. Most of those on deck had wounds from splinters and flying debris.

The Fairmile herself was slowly being whittled away. The wheelhouse was a shattered wreck, and the funnel looked like a colander. The wooden hull and deck were riddled with jagged ruptures. Thank God Thoreau had come into action.

Then just as Dickson felt the battle swing his way the forward momentum of *Q246* suddenly died.

"Andy! See what's happened!" Dickson shouted at Noiles, followed immediately by, "Keep firing!" to both guns.

Noiles soon returned with Stoker Peters in tow. "Chief reports that he's shut down number two, Sir," the lad said, gripping his hat against the bullets much as he would have against the wind. "It's shot through and lost oil pressure, she'd seize up in a minute anyway. T'other's taken a few hits. It'll run awright fer now, but – " he cringed as the latest burst smashed into *Q246*, "– we're down to one engine. Sorry."

"All right, Peters," Dickson shouted through the gunfire, touching him on the shoulder. "Do what you can to get it fixed, we may need it yet." Peters nodded and left the bridge, still bent against the hail of fire. *Q246*'s loss of speed was noticed by the sub and by Thoreau, who pressed home his attack to keep the sub from escaping or closing to finish Dickson off.

As Thoreau's boat edged in the sub swung to the north to clear a field of fire for its forward gun to disable the second terrier at its heels. Once again the stream of tracer rounds pouring from the sub towards

Q272 looked like a jet of flame. "Jesus!" Noiles muttered as he and the others on *Q246* watched in fascination, through the smoke and the "clang, clang," of their own guns. *Q272* could not survive such a powerful barrage.

"Take a look at her after end! There!" Noiles excitedly pointed to the sub. "Something's turned ... on her quarterdeck, there, see it?"

A portion of the sub's after casing had swung around and was pointed at Thoreau's boat. An instant later a puff of compressed air escaped, followed by a torpedo. "Christ, she's got trainable stern tubes!" Dickson exclaimed, as a second torpedo hit the water.

A motor launch is a hard thing to hit with a torpedo at the best of times; it's too shallow, too manoeuverable, and too short. But, Dickson mused, a hit by 700 pounds of high explosives would leave little of Thoreau and *Q272* but woodchips and fish food. They'd find even less of *Q272* and its crew than they had of *Raccoon* the previous summer.

Thoreau had two choices. He could 'comb' the torpedoes by turning directly at them, reducing the target to the narrow bow of his boat. Or he could turn away, offering a narrow stern and hoping to out distance them, which would also give him more time to react to the oncoming torpedoes.

"Saunders," Dickson barked, "tell Thoreau to clear off. Tell him to get away!"

But before the signal could be made Thoreau was swinging away, covering his retreat with smoke. The sub's new course carried her back into the waiting guns of the second division.

For the next few minutes the battle drew off to the north, as the sub tried to find her way around Minnifie and Jackson. *Q246* trailed badly behind the action, but Dickson held her in position to deny the sub easy escape to the south. His diligence soon paid off. The concentrated fire from the two boats of the second division soon forced the sub around yet again, driving it southward. As it ran Minnifie and Jackson ranged up on either quarter, dividing their fire and stripping the last of her gunners from their posts.

Suddenly *Q246* was back in the battle.

"Cox'n! Lay us across her bows!" Dickson ordered, leaving it to the cox'n to work out his angle of approach. Then bending to the engineroom voicepipe he added, "Chief, I'll need that other engine in a minute, fuck the oil pressure! I'll buy ya a new one when we get home!" If we get home, Dickson thought grimly.

With *Q246* and the sub on converging courses, the ML's lack of speed was immaterial, and it retained its advantage of manoeuvrability. But Dickson wanted a burst of speed for a last desperate act.

"Andy, get as many men as we can spare aft, set all the charges to fifty feet. Push 'em in as fast as you can on my signal. ... Go! Go!"

Noiles needed no urging. It was clear that they would soon intersect the sub's course. As the range closed their forward gun went into action again, but there was no return fire. The two boats of the second division poured a steady barrage onto the sub's superstructure and it was doubtful that anyone was left alive on the conning tower. The sub was trailing smoke and running blind as the cox'n brought *Q246* across her path.

Everyone expected Dickson to cross at right angles in front of the sub, but he had a more deadly plan. "Cox'n! Hard to port! Point her straight at the sub – now! Straight at her, run down her side as close as you dare!"

Q246 swung immediately, burying her starboard rail in the turn. Dickson barked another order down the engineroom voicepipe. "Give her all you got, Chief. Both engines! I need speed – speed!"

When *Q246* straightened up she was pointed directly at the sub a bare hundred yards away. Dickson thought – hoped – he felt a surge in speed, certainly there was a change in the tone and motion of the boat.

It took only a few seconds for the two ships to close; when the range was little more than forty yards Dickson shouted from the bridge, "Now Andy! Now!"

The crew had cast off the lashing of every depth charge in the fourteen cradles that lined the stern, and off the two charges in small throwers behind the funnel. On Dickson's order they sowed the sea with high explosives; sixteen depth charges closely packed ahead of the submarine and all set for fifty feet. It was a devastating concentration and the drop had to be perfectly timed. It took only five seconds for a charge set to fifty feet to detonate. Noiles had to get them away as quickly as possible and hope that *Q246* herself ran clear before they all went off.

The last charges were just falling over the side as the submarine swept past, buffeting *Q246* with her wake and threatening to spill men into the sea. By then, too, the first charges were going off just ahead of the sub, which soon disappeared in a series of towering explosions.

Q246 was making nearly twenty knots when she dropped her lethal cargo but the blasts punched her as if she had been struck by a giant hand, lifting the stern, pushing it around and rolling her on her starboard side. Everyone had grabbed a handhold in anticipation of the shock, but still they were thrown to the deck, slammed against bulwarks and fittings, or thrown into the sea, before the launch was deluged in a collapsing column of water. When it was all over *Q246* was a wallowing wreck.

Minnifie's boats were on the helpless submarine quickly, guns poised, but she drifted slowly forward, carried by the last of her momentum, and was soon settling by the stern. Grotesquely distorted bodies littered the riddled conning tower and the bent railings around the guns.

As Minnifie and Jackson watched, survivors scampered through the conning tower hatch and dove into the sea – pitifully few in number. She settled so fast that Minnifie did not even try to put someone aboard. Just as well. The submarine's black bow suddenly heaved skyward and hung vertically. Then she plunged down in a swirl of darkened water to her final rest.

The men of the 8th Flotilla looked on in stunned silence. Then gradually, hesitant at first, cheers were heard, tin hats flew into the air, and backs were slapped. But many, like Babineau, reflected on the men entombed in the sub or wounded and drowning silently in the bitterly cold sea.

"She's gone, Andy!" Dickson said in disbelief. "We sunk her! We sunk the U-boat! ... Who'd a believed it?"

As the realization of their accomplishment set in, Noiles turned to more pressing problems. "You'd better ask for help, Dick. I'll see to the casualties."

"Right, thanks, Andy, thanks. Minnifie's on his way."

While the crew of *Q246* tended their wounded and prepared to abandon ship, the rest of the flotilla searched for survivors. Minnifie's *Q287* was the first to draw alongside the wallowing flotilla leader.

"Well done, Minnifie!" Dickson shouted through the megaphone, "everyone okay?"

"Yeah. We've got a few wounded, Jackson has one dead but Thoreau's pretty badly shot up. I haven't got details from him yet. How 'bout you?"

"We need a lift home, we're a shambles. You'd better get us off. We have six wounded, some seriously. No-one dead, so far. Any survivors?"

"Yes," Minnifie replied, somewhat hesitantly as his boat drifted alongside, "Jackson has them."

"Many?" Dickson queried.

"No – a half dozen or so, she went pretty fast in the end."

"But," Minnifie proffered in a low, testy whisper, "the survivors, they're all Frenchmen ..."

The megaphone fell from Dickson's mouth – that couldn't be what he had heard. Raising his voice so it would carry the closing distance easily, he inquired, "What the hell did you say Minnifie?"

Minnifie shouted this time, his voice tinged with frustration, "I said, they're all Frenchmen – frog sailors, Dick – not a Kraut among them. It wasn't a U-boat at all," Minnifie snorted. "The submarine was French!"

Chapter 16

It was well after midnight by the time the staff car threaded its way through the lobster traps and abandoned fishing gear, crunching through the cinders on the landing road, and down onto the government wharf. Prentice was weary and anxious.

The train ride from Halifax to Moncton, New Brunswick had gone well enough. There was plenty of time for a leisurely dinner and for lengthy discussion with the naval intelligence people who travelled with him. But there was also time for Prentice to reflect on what had to be done next, and that burden weighed heavily on him during the hour and a half long trip over deeply frost-heaved roads to Richibucto.

And now the military police were refusing to allow the car onto the wharf.

"The hell with it, driver," Prentice growled, as he jumped out. "Wait for me up the road!"

The MP was right, of course, Prentice thought as he looked at the line of army trucks and air force ambulances. Too much on this wharf already, no place for a bloody staff car! In the dim light of torches and blacked-out headlights Prentice quickly discerned an orderly procession of men coming his way from the clutch of figures about halfway along the wharf. He stood watching as the men ambled forward and climbed into the back of the nearest truck.

Soldiers with rifles and fixed bayonets clustered around the vehicles on the landward end of the wharf. Officers and a few NCOs wearing sidearms milled about.

"Prisoners ... poor bastards!" Prentice said quietly, before reflecting that they were the lucky ones. The rest of the sub's crew was either floating corpses or entombed on the bottom of the Gulf. Even so, in the cold damp of a May night they were a sad sight, off to Moncton, to the waiting intelligence officers and segregation cells in Dorchester pen.

As the trucks ground their way up the landing road, Prentice ambled along the wharf closer to the launches. Sailors and medical personnel from the air force hospital at the Chatham airfield, forty miles up the coast, heaved the stretcher cases up onto the wharf. It had been built for larger vessels, and the MLs lay low alongside.

Four stretchers already lay on the wharf. The moving arms, shifting torsos and glowing cigarettes boded well. The body on the next stretcher up was completely shrouded, placed well away from the living, and left unattended. One final stretcher case was heaved onto the wharf, placed amid the living, and closely attended.

The wounded were soon moved to waiting ambulances, which pulled off the wharf one by one.

As the last of the wounded was driven off and his eyes adjusted to the dark once more, Prentice edged towards the knot of men who remained hovering over the motor launches. Even in this dark, overcast night there was no mistaking small-boat officers. Woollen sweaters, rolled-down rubber boots, stocking caps and service hats pushed to the back of the head all spoke of men who lived in intimate contact with the sea. Prentice could hear hushed voices as he approached, but the words were swallowed by the night, the gentle lap of small waves against the wharf, and the unseen wind.

"Gentlemen!" Prentice said softly as he got within arm's length of the group. The muttering stopped and a space opened. It took a moment and then Thoreau, the closest, responded, "Cap'n Prentice, Sir!"

"As you were, as you were," he replied, putting them at ease. "You got any more of those?" pointing to Thoreau's cigarette, "I seem to have left my cigars in Halifax."

A dark figure offered a quick, "Yes, Sir, here you are," and a pack of Sweet Caps was thrust forward. Prentice took one, pounded both ends on the back of the pack, then passed the package back.

"Thanks."

As Prentice put the fag to his mouth, the click and flash of a lighter illuminated the faces around him.

"Thanks, Dickson," Prentice said, catching a glimpse of the face behind the lighter before the group was once again in the dark. After what seemed an eternity Prentice asked the most important question. "Many hurt?"

Dickson answered, "Most everybody, but 'bout a dozen serious cases all told. One dead on Jackson's boat, two missing from mine. Two of my gunners're in pretty bad shape, two seriously wounded from Minnifie's and a stoker from Thoreau's boat's got a head wound that doesn't look too good. Eleven others got ashore under their own steam, but need hospitalization ... An' we've got another dozen, including Jackson here, who were treated by the air force Tiffys and will stay on ..."

Prentice muttered a subdued, "Heavy casualty list from four boats."

The second most important question followed. "And the boats?"

"*Q246* sank shortly after the sub went down. Thoreau's and Jackson's took quite a beating. *Q272* lost all power on the way in. Her stokers, God bless 'em, got some spares from Minnifie, here, and patched her up, so she came in on one engine."

"All the boats are shot to shit; hulls punctured, broken glass in the wheelhouse, and busted-up equipment on deck."

"Flooding?"

"Plenty, but manageable."

Conversation then drifted into a recounting of the action, encouraged by Prentice. The men were proud of their victory and more than willing to recall the high points of the battle. He would learn much more in this impromptu debriefing on the wharf at Richibucto than he could ever hope to glean from the formal reports that would eventually arrive on his desk. So he let the banter flow, shaping it from time to time with a short, well-directed question.

There was little need to encourage the discussion. Each of the flotilla captains – Dickson, Thoreau, Minnifie and Jackson – had a story to tell. Prentice was fascinated to learn how each saw the battle, and the events were reconciled until they arrived at a consensus on just what had happened.

"It was all quite well done, if you ask me Cap'n," Minnifie offered. "Straight from the textbook, and a sub killed. Couldn't ask for more."

Prentice agreed, adding, "Yes, by all accounts a commendable action. You are all to be congratulated. It seems, though, that the two divisions might have gotten too far out of support range, don't you think?"

There was general agreement that this was so, but in the circumstances unavoidable. The object had been to trap the sub against the Prince Edward Island shore, and they'd done that. Prentice was not so sure, but now was not the time for a detailed critique.

A short silence followed, after which Prentice said what was on all their minds. "Unfortunately, it wasn't a German sub."

Minnifie gave voice to everyone's frustrations. "It's not right, Cap'n, just not right. Here were are fighting to drive the fuckin' Nazis outta Europe, and just when we think we've nailed one of the bastards, turns out that the sub belongs to one of the bloody countries we're trying to liberate!"

"War's seldom as tidy as we would like, Minnifie," Prentice said. "There are people in all those occupied countries who have hitched their wagon to The New World Order. Go aboard *St. Albans* the next time you're in Halifax and ask the Norwegians about Quisling.

"It may be even worse for the French, if you're one of them who believes that communists and leftists sold your country down the river, eh?" Prentice paused to crush out his cigarette on the wharf. "And maybe, if you're a frog sailor you're still pissed off over our attack on your fleet at Oran in July 1940."

"We really did that, eh?" Minnifie asked with a disbelieving note.

"Oh, yes, I'm afraid so," Prentice answered sombrely. "Quite a fiasco, 1200 French sailors dead. So what would you do, eh? Wait for the bloody British Army? Or the Russians? Christ, I wouldn't want to have to make those choices."

Prentice let the cruelty of the dilemma sink in. "And we've had a bit of a run at them recently, too. Layard, the new senior officer of the Brit destroyers at Halifax, was part of the North African landings. Took his destroyer *Broke* through the boom at Mers el Kébir so he could land troops to capture French warships in the harbour. Layard got *Broke* back out to sea, but she was so full of holes she sank.

"And then, the main French fleet in Toulon did the honourable thing when the Germans appeared. They said they would scuttle the lot, and they did. Can't say I'd like to wrestle with those choices."

Then Prentice got to the point. "In the meantime, gentlemen, until we get this whole affair resolved, nothing is to be said about it. Nothing. Do I make myself understood?" The ML captains understood only too well. And so, after a short pause, Prentice asked Dickson if he could speak to him for a few moments.

As Prentice moved off down the wharf, Dickson stamped out his cigarette, stuffed his hands in his pockets and followed along.

"You did a fine job, Dick," Prentice re-affirmed softly as they ambled down the wharf, "you and your men. That was a powerful and determined adversary."

"Yes, Sir, she certainly was that. The secondary armament on that sub was incredible ... twin 20mm at least, fore and aft, maybe more."

"She didn't man her deck gun?"

"No, we never saw her even try, so I guess *Lakeville* was right. They must have hit her gun or damaged it in some way."

"And I suspect Belanger's gunners holed her pressure hull, too, otherwise why would she be on the surface?"

"True enough, Sir, that's what we all suspect." With that Dickson stopped and looked directly at Prentice. "What no-one can figure out is what the hell was she doing off North Point? Why wasn't she making for the Cabot Strait or the Strait of Belle Isle?"

"We may never know for sure. You did know that her mission was to land an agent?"

"Yes, Sir. We had some vague indication of that when we left Sydney, and heard more at Gaspé yesterday – er, I guess two days ago now."

"Yes, well." Prentice cleared his throat. "I suspect they were still trying to land the fellow, somewhere. They probably knew that there are French communities all along this part of the Gulf coast, including some in Prince Edward Island."

"But Vichy sympathizers?" Dickson asked, incredulously.

"Highly unlikely, I should think, among the Acadiens. I suspect that the French were simply looking for a French-speaking population through which their agent could 'swim' until his friends took him in charge. Where could they turn? They'd already tried the Gaspé area and run into our patrols. They probably knew that the Germans had landed someone in the Chaleur area last year, so we might be watching there again. So what's left?"

"Is that why you ordered us in here, not to Alberton or Summerside?"

"No, not really. It was just easier for me and for the naval int people to get here, and it's as close as Summerside. No. Maybe the sub headed for Prince Edward Island out of simple desperation. Our only hope of finding that out is those survivors you pulled from the sea. Did they say anything coming in?"

"No," Dickson, responded, "apart from *oui* and *non*, or thanks for the water. We didn't prod them, I must admit, we all felt rather sorry for the buggers. And we were at something of a loss to explain what was going on."

"That's all right. The naval int people will speak to them later tonight and for the next few days, I suspect. We'll get some answers."

"What will happen to them?" Dickson interrupted, "Are they POWs?"

"I suppose now that the Vichy regime has collapsed they are. Most likely we'll pass them off to the Free French, stick them ashore in St-Pierre and let them deal with it."

They had reached the end of the wharf now and stood, looking upriver at the dark shadows of the woods and angular shapes of a few barely discernible houses. "I want to have this whole business wrapped up before the people of Richibucto wake up."

"But we're in no condition to sail, and how do we explain the shot-up boats and the casualties?"

"Oh, no, you're okay here for a few days, and the boats are easily explained," Prentice said, almost light-heartedly. "The naval int people are already spreading the rumour that you got shot up in the fog by an overzealous Hudson; that the air force 'attacked' an unfortunate motor launch in poor visibility. The story is plausible enough. Certainly every sailor will believe it, eh? Not the first time the air force has shot the shit out of its own ships! The MLs here, under guard, where everyone can see you – but are not supposed to – will simply fuel the rumour.

"No, you can stay alongside here, get your motors back into shape, plug some holes, and then come along to Pictou. But as for the submarine, Dick, it never happened."

Dickson glared at Prentice. "What do you mean, 'It never happened!' We've got at least three dead, badly wounded men enroute to hospital, most everybody hurt, my boat's sunk, and the rest are shot to shit. And you say it never happened!"

"As I said," Prentice added in measured tones, "all of that can be explained away by the unfortunate strafing incident – "

"The hell it can! Jesus, Cap'n, we've trained and trained to meet an enemy submarine at sea, we've trained to sink him with depth charges, with gunfire, how to do it as individuals, how to do it as a flotilla ... Christ, we've all had friends killed by those bastards. And now – "

"The bastards who killed your friends on *Raccoon* were Germans. Your revenge has been taken on a French submarine," Prentice observed calmly.

"I don't give a shit if it was British!" Dickson snapped. "Submariners are a pack of pirates. Anyway, the shells that cut through my boats and hurt my men were real, whether they came from some fuckin' French sub or some Nazi U-boat.

"Don't you see? We did what no-one in the whole damn RCN has been able to do! We sank a fuckin' sub – and you want me to just pretend we never did. I can't. I owe it to the men of this flotilla, and the other small boats that chase phantoms in this bloody Gulf."

Dickson was now in a lather, arms waving as he made his case. It was just as well, Prentice thought, that they were having this out in the middle of the night at the end of the wharf. Dickson had the right to blow off steam.

"I'm sorry Dick, this one's an order. I want no mention of it in your report. I do not want to see anything about it in the reports from the rest of your boats. Nor are you or your men to discuss it with anyone else.

"You are to instruct your officers and men never to mention the incident. They may say what they want about being mistaken by the RCAF for a U-boat in the fog – God knows that's happened often enough. But, Dick, not a word about the French submarine – ever."

Dickson stood at the corner of the wharf gazing absently across at the sleeping village of Rexton on the other side of the river. Prentice gave him time to clear his mind and settle his emotions.

After a few moments he continued. "This sub kill can never be made public. What would the government release to the press, 'RCN Destroys French Sub in the Gulf: Vichy Agent Killed'? How would any politician explain that a Vichy French submarine was sunk in a raging gun battle in the Gulf of St. Lawrence? The fabric of the nation would be split and the whole rancorous debate over the war effort might lead to conflict here. Think about it, Dick. This incident is like a bomb: French Canada cannot confront its fascist sentiments openly, and English Canada must not. No, this whole affair needs to be buried, as deep as that submarine."

"What the hell was this agent supposed to do here anyway?" Dickson asked, not really expecting Prentice to answer.

"It seems," Prentice offered, needing to give Dickson enough information to ensure that he would enforce the ban, "that the Americans were trying to incubate him in French Canada as part of their scheme for postwar France."

"So why the hell were we looking for him: why didn't we just let him get ashore and pass him along to the Yanks?"

"Because," Prentice shifted uncomfortably, "it appears that our intelligence on the sub came from the British. They didn't tell us the Americans were involved, nor that the sub was French. We just had some int about a sub. We assumed it was a U-boat, and no-one said otherwise. Anyway, the British wanted this guy, the agent, dead."

"So we did the deed?" Dickson laughed cynically.

"Yes."

"We – us, my flotilla – we assassinated this guy for the British. Just fuckin' great. I go to war to fight the Germans and end up as a hired gun in some international plot. Jesus, Cap'n, didn't the people in Ottawa know what the hell was going on?"

"Only belatedly. That's why you were ordered into Gaspé two days ago. That's why there was no search for the sub after *Lakeville*'s action – "

A light had come on in Dickson's head. "That's why *Lakeville*'s people were buried at sea, isn't it!"

"Yes."

"Son of a bitch!" Dickson muttered. "No bodies, no evidence, just more poor bastards lost at sea."

"As soon as the government realized how we were being used, by both the Brits and the Americans, we were authorized to pursue the sub after it had landed the agent."

"After!"

"Yes, after. That way we could pass along the agent to the Americans – he was theirs, anyway – and we could save face with the Brits by sinking the sub. Everyone assumed that the submarine was German. I know it sounds stupid," Prentice said apologetically, "but no-one suspected that there were any large French subs left after the scuttling last year at Toulon.

"Obviously, they had one runner. I am told the plan was to nab this guy once he was ashore and then try to kill the 'U-boat'. Not a bad plan, given the diplomatic problems; we don't do the Brits' dirty work, we do pass the agent along to the Americans – who want him anyway – and then, on our own hook, we try like hell to get the sub on its way out. Would have worked, too, given the damage it suffered from *Lakeville*. But we never did get authorization to redeploy ships to catch the sub on the way out. Maybe the politicos got cold feet.

"In any event, that's all irrelevant now. The government can hardly build popular support for its war effort by announcing that its Navy has sunk a French submarine in the Gulf of St. Lawrence, can it?"

Dickson did not bother to answer. His mind was spinning, trying to understand the politics, but even more, wondering how Prentice, whose whole being was consumed with the urge to kill submarines, could now be telling him that this success would never see the light of day.

"Tell me, Sir," Dickson finally asked, "Did you know that the sub was in the northern entrance to Northumberland Strait when you ordered us to sail for Pictou – and within hours of our arrival in Gaspé?"

Prentice answered uneasily. "No. I had no specific knowledge of its whereabouts. Admiral Murray authorized the re-assignment of your boats to Pictou. I just ordered you out as soon as possible. There was always a chance that you might stumble on the bastard."

Stumble on the bastard, indeed, Dickson thought.

Finally Prentice moved back down the wharf towards the other men. "You did your part, Dick, you and your flotilla. I'm sorry to be losing you."

"It's true then?" Dickson asked in mild surprise, "Captain Heenan is taking over as Captain of Motor Launches?"

"Later this month," Prentice sighed. "More's the pity then, Dick, but I am afraid this submarine kill just never happened. Nothing will appear in any official records. You don't get your DSO," bringing a slight chuckle from Dickson, "and the Navy gets no credit for a job well done. We'll just have to bag the next bastard who comes in, right?"

Dickson flicked the glowing butt of his cigarette out into the river. "It never happened, eh?" he said quietly.

"No, Dick, it never happened."

Author's Note

The Diver's Guide to Prince Edward Island contains an entry for a "U-boat off North Point." The one-page entry describes an underwater feature to the west of the Point as a German submarine sunk by Canadian forces in May 1943. The *Guide* also contains loran fixes and notices to local fishermen to avoid setting nets in the area.

The action which sank the U-boat was witnessed by the North Point lighthouse keeper, who scribbled "U-boat sunk by corvette 7 May 1943" across the top of his log. Confirming evidence in the form of ammunition cases of German origin, now long gone, were said to have washed ashore. Locals still recall the battle. Their reminiscences were recounted in a feature article in the May 13, 1995 edition of the *Charlottetown Weekend Guardian-Patriot.*

The depth of the wreck at some ninety feet, the bitterly cold arctic waters at that depth and the difficult tidal conditions around North Point have kept all but a few from diving to it. Thus, despite the local legends and the indisputable fact that *something* lies on the bottom at that spot, the nature of the wreck has never been conclusively determined. The anomaly in the water and local legends are the only evidence of a U-boat being sunk off North Point, Prince Edward Island.

In fact, there is absolutely nothing in either Allied or German records to indicate that the action off North Point ever took place. Canadian records contain not even a hint of anything untoward in the Gulf of St. Lawrence in May 1943.

Nonetheless, there was a U-boat there at the time of the alleged incident. *U262* waited off the *eastern* side of North Point for many days in early May 1943 hoping to rendezvous with escaped prisoners of war. The escape was foiled and the U-boat waited in vain. At the time the Allies were completely unaware of *U262*'s presence – there wasn't even a hint in the Ultra signals. It was not until after the war that it was learned the sub had spent several days loitering east of the Point.

There were, it is true, numerous "sightings" of U-boats in the area at the time by aircraft, and by people along the coast (especially the Gaspé), including mysterious lights off Miscou Island. These "sightings" are on record, and they have been built into this story. None of them correspond to the known positions of *U262*. In the absence of other confirming intelligence, such as radio fixes or Ultra decrypts, they were dismissed at the time as false reports: whales, human error, imagination or devilment.

German records are no more forthcoming. Apart from the log of *U262*, which survives, there are no other records of U-boats in the Gulf of St. Lawrence in May 1943. Moreover, the ultimate fate of all but two of Germany's U-boats has now been determined. Those whose loss remains a mystery went missing at times that do not correspond even remotely with the apparent incident off North Point. This has been confirmed both by Canadian historians familiar with German records and by the Germans themselves.

So what is this mysterious "U-boat" off North Point? If there was a battle in early May 1943, witnessed from the shore and subsequently confirmed by local lore and artifacts from the wreck, why is there no documentary record of the incident? Why, given Canada's war weariness and the bitter legacy of the U-boat campaign of 1942 in the Gulf, was the sinking of an enemy submarine there not trumpeted from the highest hills and rung from the church steeples of the land? Why is there no German submarine unaccounted for that might explain the mystery? And if, as the lighthouse keeper claimed, there *was* a battle, why was the story never told?

Although no U-boat kill in Canadian waters has ever been confirmed, at least one senior officer maintained to his dying days that there was one. Captain Joe Heenan, who became Captain (Motor Launches) in May 1943, remained unrepentant in his belief that his Motor Launches sank a submarine in the Gulf of St. Lawrence. I vividly remember attending a presentation by a distinguished German naval historian in Ottawa around 1979, at which Captain Heenan, by then frail with age, demanded to know what submarine his forces had sunk. Captain Heenan was reminded that such an event had never happened, and then someone pulled him down into his chair.

Was Captain Heenan right after all? We may never know.

That the mystery on the bottom off North Point must be a Vichy French submarine is simply an educated guess. It is certain that the sub was not German (or Italian either, we were still at war with them, too). It is not simply the lack of evidence in German records that suggests this. Had the Navy or the RCAF sunk an Axis submarine in the Gulf in 1943, there would have been a ticker-tape parade down Wellington Street in Ottawa. Accidental sinking of an Allied submarine by friendly warships can be ruled out, as these are in the public record (e.g., the RCN's accidental sinking of HMS/M *P514* in August 1942).

So, if something was sunk off North Point it had to be something that could not then, and perhaps not even now, be revealed. In that sense, the possibility that it might be Vichy French, although not the famous *Surcouf*, is the best bet. It seems that several of the large 1600-tonne type submarines were salvaged from Toulon harbour after the scuttling of November 1942, and put back into service by the Axis. These were powerful vessels with heavy secondary armament fore and aft of the conning tower, and trainable torpedo tubes mounted astern. They also had the range to reach Canadian waters. That said, the head of the French naval history section assured me in casual conversation (not related to this incident) that all wartime French submarines were accounted for.

And so, the mystery remains.

But that mystery does provide a wonderful opportunity for an historian to dabble in historical fiction, not least because the wider historical context of the first week of May 1943 lends itself to intrigue. The inter-service rivalries, the change of command in the Atlantic, the state of the Atlantic war, the Canadian political situation and the Anglo-American battle over the future of France are all described here essentially as historians understand them. So, too, is the portrayal of Nelles, Jones, Murray, Prentice, Mackenzie King, Pearson, deMarbois, Knowles, Bernard, Macdonald, Robertson, Ralston and Murphy.

The characters, ships and aircraft involved in the actions at sea are pure fiction, with one exception. The Canadian vessels mentioned – *Lakeville, Castlegar,* HCML *Q246* and the others, and the characters who manned them, Belanger, Fergus, Dickson, Noiles, Babineau, etc –

never existed. There was, of course, an 8th Motor Launch Flotilla, but not in the Canadian Navy. No RCAF aircraft went missing over the Gulf in early May 1943. The exception to this is the three British trawlers, all as named. They were indeed in the Cabot Strait in the first week of May 1943, and they did attack a number of contacts: none were confirmed submarines.

The operations of the RCN during this period are drawn from three main works: my own *North Atlantic Run* (1985) and *The U-Boat Hunters* (1994), and Michael Hadley's *U-Boats Against Canada* (1985). Hadley's work contains a detailed account of the exploits of *U262*, which was off North Point in early May 1943. Details of the sordid Anglo-American rivalry over France are drawn from Anthony Verrier's *Assassination in Algiers* (1990). I am grateful to Derek McClellan's 1992 MA thesis at the University of New Brunswick on Canada-Vichy relations for providing the Canadian perspective, and to Mark Savoy's MA report on the 1936 Olympic hockey team.

I would like to thank Bill Richard and Lloyd Veinot of the Fredericton Weather Office for the weather and ice information of the Gulf. Mike Whitby of the Directorate of History, NDHQ, helped fill the gaps in my chart collection. Peter Haydon generously offered his insights into how a submarine might act when engaged in a clandestine mission. If I have taken liberties with the submarine's behaviour he is not to blame!

I am grateful to Steve Turner, Michael Hadley and my wife Bobbi for reading the manuscript and providing encouragement, to Hector Mackenzie for the bull session that plucked my courage to actually write it, and to Roger Sarty for finding maps and information at a moment's notice. Special thanks go to Charis Wahl and Angela Dobler for their encouragement and enthusiastic editing, and to Ben Kooter for taking the chance.

Finally, I need to thank the divers, especially Kevin Mills, for bringing the mysterious "sub" to my attention many years ago. This book does not solve the riddle, but it might push the debate toward a resolution.